Praise for LESLEY CREWE

DEATH & OTHER INCONVENIENCES

National bestseller

APMA Best Atlantic Published Book Award shortlist (2025)

"Lesley Crewe balances humour and fury in the twisty *Death & Other Inconveniences*. Turns out, the undercurrent, the true connecting thread, in Crewe's book is not loss and certainly not grief, but life's greatest challenge: growing up. Good-looking, perfectly groomed, Margo has long hidden behind a carapace of femininity, one that unfortunately attracts creeps... Nothing stays the same, seems to be Crewe's message, for change is exactly what people need, even change that arrives with a dead man watching the Stanley Cup playoffs."

–Toronto Star

"Crewe has a brand of humour that gets to the heart of the issue, with snappy dialogue throughout, well-formed characters, and plenty of cringe-worthy scenes that could only be garnered from real-life scenarios. All this makes *Death & Other Inconveniences* a highly relatable, entertaining page-turner."

–The Miramichi Reader

RECIPE FOR A GOOD LIFE

National bestseller

Indigo's Best of the Year 2023 List

APMA Best Atlantic Published Book Award shortlist (2023)

"Reading *Recipe For a Good Life* was like being on the receiving end of an enormous hug just when you need it most. Bursting at the seams with heart and humour, this book is a most glorious love letter to the amazing women of rural Cape Breton. I now want to get a time machine and move to South Head Road!"

–Bianca Marais, bestselling author of *The Witches of Moonshyne Manor*

"Lesley Crewe has done it again! *Recipe for a Good Life* absolutely delivers, with vivid characters, and plenty of moments both hilarious and touching. Lesley's writing with lots of love, here, and it shows."

–**Stephanie Domet**, award-winning author of *Fallsy Downsies*

"I fell arse over tea kettle in love with the characters in this book, and now find myself missing them on a daily basis. That's the sign of a good story!"

–**Nancy Regan,** bestselling author of *From Showing Off to Showing UP*

THE SPOON STEALER

National bestseller
Canada Reads 2022, longlist

"I loved *The Spoon Stealer* so much, for so many reasons. Emmeline and Vera were the most delightful lead characters I have read in a long time. I laughed, I cried through scenes both charming and horrifying, and I was emotionally attached to every character. Like with every one of Ms. Crewe's books, each scene and character was expertly crafted, and though the ending was perfect in every sense, I was left wishing the story would never end. An absolutely wonderful, heartfelt story of family and redemption, forgiveness and love. *The Spoon Stealer* will leave you longing for more."

–**Genevieve Graham,** bestselling author of *The Forgotten Home Child*

"Lesley Crewe artfully threads history and humour through this touching story of family, friendship, and the preciousness of memories. With its indomitable spirit, down-to-earth wisdom, and a dash of gutsy sass, *The Spoon Stealer* might just steal your heart."

–**Amy Spurway**, award-winning author of *Crow*

"Reading a novel by Lesley Cynthia Crewe is like covering yourself in an old quilt. You know you can settle in and get cozy, wrap yourself in the words and let the characters and their memories keep you company as you read."

–**The Miramichi Reader**

THE SPIRIT OF SCATARIE

THE SPIRIT OF SCATARIE

LESLEY CREWE

Vagrant PRESS

Vagrant Press is an imprint of
Nimbus Publishing Limited
3660 Strawberry Hill Street, Halifax, NS, B3K 5A9
(902) 455-4286 nimbus.ca

Nimbus Publishing is based in Kjipuktuk, Mi'kma'ki, the traditional territory of the Mi'kmaq People.

Printed and bound in Canada
NB1821

Editor: Penelope Jackson
Design & interior map: Bee Stanton
Cover image: "Scatarie West, Tower with fog alarm," 1937. Clara Dennis Nova Scotia Archives 1981-541 447 Cape Breton.

Library and Archives Canada Cataloguing in Publication

Title: The spirit of Scatarie / Lesley Crewe.
Names: Crewe, Lesley, 1955- author
Identifiers: Canadiana (print) 20250191997 | Canadiana (ebook) 20250192012 | ISBN 9781774714560
(softcover) | ISBN 9781774714577 (EPUB)
Subjects: LCGFT: Historical fiction. | LCGFT: Novels.
Classification: LCC PS8605.R48 S64 2025 | DDC C813/.6—dc23

Canada | Canada Council for the Arts | Conseil des arts du Canada | NOVA SCOTIA

Nimbus Publishing acknowledges the financial support for its publishing activities from the Government of Canada, the Canada Council for the Arts, and from the Province of Nova Scotia. We are pleased to work in partnership with the Province of Nova Scotia to develop and promote our creative industries for the benefit of all Nova Scotians.

For Rev. Dr. Deborah Lindsay

Sharing a lifetime of Cape Breton summers
in our little piece of heaven.

Publisher's Note:
Scatarie is pronounced *Sca-tah-ree*.

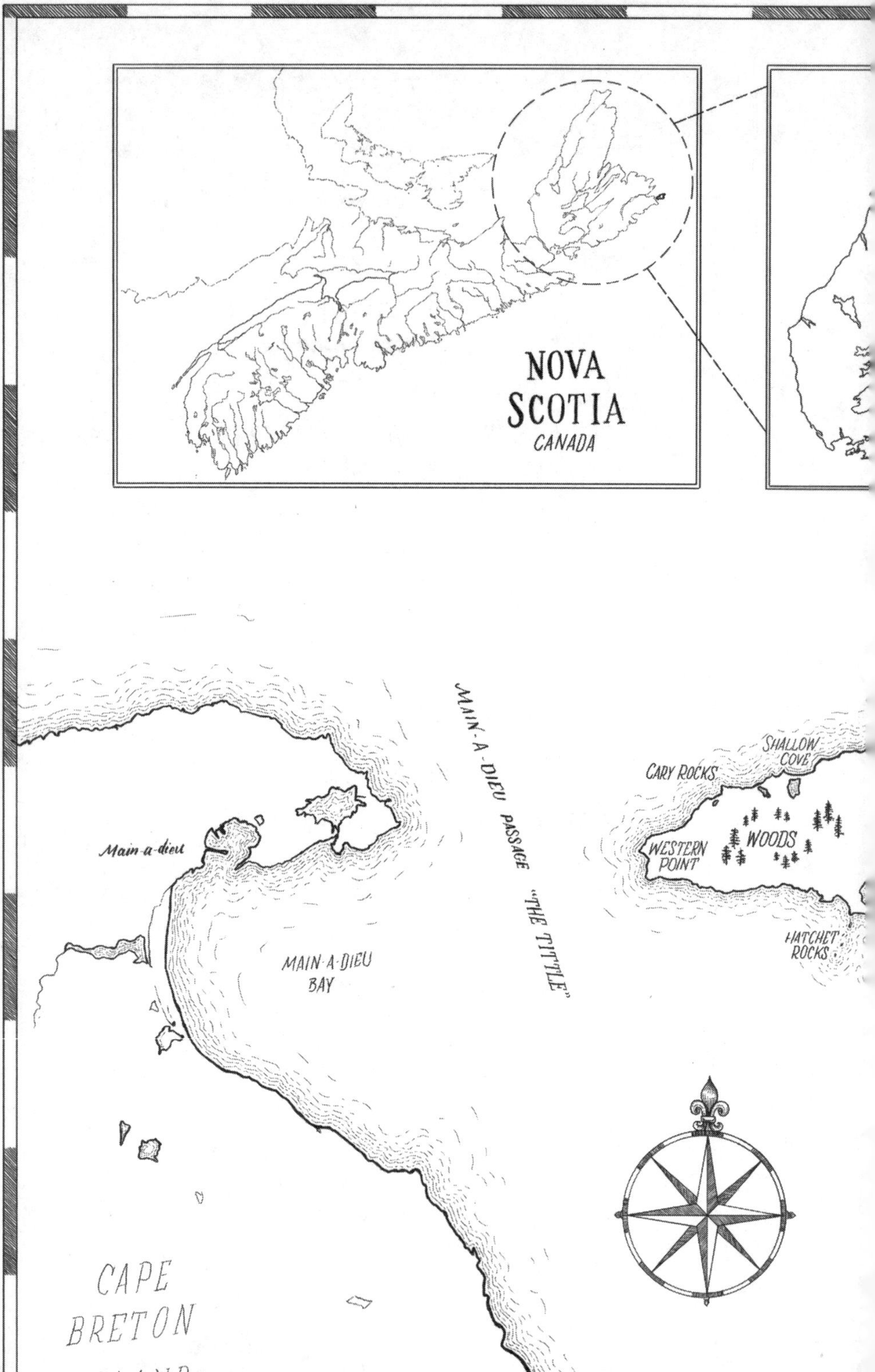
NOVA
SCOTIA
CANADA
MAIN-A-DIEU PASSAGE
"THE TITTLE"
SHALLOW COVE
CARY ROCKS
WOODS
WESTERN POINT
HATCHET ROCKS
Main-a-dieu
MAIN-A-DIEU BAY
CAPE BRETON ISLAND

CABOT STRAIT
CAPE BRETON
Scale of Kilometres
0 1 2 3 4
EASTERN LIGHT
SECRET COVE
WINGING POINT
CRANBERRY HEATH
EASTERN HARBOUR
NORTHWEST POINT
HAY ISLAND
NORTHWEST COVE
SOUTHEAST HARBOUR
SAVAGE COVE
RED ISLE
SCATARIE ISLAND
GULL ROCKS
TIN COVE
BAKEAPPLE BARREN
FLUKE COVE
TIN COVE HEAD
HOWE POINT
ATLANTIC OCEAN
SCATARIE ISLAND
CAPE BRETON, NOVA SCOTIA

AUTHOR'S NOTE

Please know that while this story is fictional, I did include a few actual events, to bring this world to life.

And Scatarie itself is real, an island off the northeastern tip of Cape Breton, stretching seven miles from Western Point to Eastern Head, three miles wide and one mile off the mainland from Main-à-Dieu. It is one of Nova Scotia's largest islands and it lives in the collective hearts of the people in this part of the world. Most locals have a story of their kinfolk who were born, lived, or died there. And when they left the island for good, through the late 1950s, their memories remained, and their stories live on.

Some believe the name *Scatori* is of Portuguese origins, a transformation of the name *Saint Catherine*. In 1734 there was a mission church on the island called St. Catherine, but it was destroyed when the French left.

In many cases, French explorers and settlers adapted Mi'kmaw terms for a given place into their own language, changing the spelling but retaining the general sound of the original word. *Main-à-Dieu*, so close to Scatarie, means "hand of God" in French. The original meaning of the Mi'kmaw word *menadou* is "great spirit" but was distorted over time to mean "evil spirit" or "the devil."

And this part of the coast must have seemed cursed. This island has seen endless grief. Untold numbers of sailors and passengers on transport vessels, brigs, barques, and schooners were drowned or injured over the past four centuries around her shores, a thousand people in three wrecks alone, their ships driven into the rocks during wild storms, smashed to pieces in the surf thanks to thick fog, or floundering helplessly in the massive ice. Some were stranded to die a lonely death before people lived there and the lighthouse was built in 1839.

There is still treasure under the sand of Scatarie, as there is around all the islands off the coast of Nova Scotia, since this province has the highest density of shipwrecks in North or South America, and some say the world. Ships loaded with gold to pay British or French soldiers, only to have those coins sink to the bottom of the ocean, along with their hapless crew. Immigrants coming to a new land, but not making it.

When you read the history of Scatarie it comes as a shock to learn of such loss, especially when you look out over the island on a glorious summer day as it shines in the sun, the tranquil blue water lapping the shore, a seemingly peaceful haven of undersized black spruce, rocky cliffs, soft amber grasses, green bushes, and bright wildflowers. Colourful berries are scattered around bogs, barrens, shallows, and fields. How can such a beautiful piece of land have such a history?

Because it is surrounded by the waters of the Atlantic Ocean and at the mercy of the turbulent tides, currents, and winds. The cruel weather that never notices the comings and goings of human beings. For millennia the world has turned and the elements beyond our control live out their wild dance. Fate? Pure luck? Who knows why some ships set sail, never to arrive at their destination?

But as heartless as that was, Scatarie was also a beacon for those who made their living on the sea for much of the eighteenth, nineteenth, and twentieth centuries. Fishers from many lands scooped up bountiful catches off her shores that kept their families going: Spain, France, America, Portugal, the West Indies. Some from Newfoundland stayed and their descendants were among the last to leave. Sea captains from Main-à-Dieu, Louisbourg, and scattered communities would trade their salt cod, salt mackerel, and salt herring for goods like cotton, tea, sugar, rum, and molasses. Rum-running was at one point big business. Pirates lurked off Scatarie, the Mira River a safe haven for more than a century. Pirate's Cove was obviously named after them.

A hardscrabble life it was on the island. Literally everything, including coal, had to be brought over by boat, enough to last the winter as the island was often inaccessible for months because of ice that blocked the way for boats but wasn't safe to walk on. Fishermen worked endless days on the water or salting their catch, while their women kept the home fires burning and raised up to twenty children in small wooden houses or huts. Most everyone shared a bed with someone else. (I'm hoping the man who claimed they kept sleeping babies in flour bags hanging from nails on the wall was kidding.)

While I gathered information from the families who remain in this area, the same surnames cropped up over and over again: Barnstable, Bourinot, Buckley, Campbell, Hall, Harris, Lahey, Locke, MacCuish, O'Neill, Parsons, Philips, Spencer, Steele, Timmons, Trimm, Wadden.

The depth of affection for this remote island is inspiring. Their families' spirits still linger there. This was and is still home.

"This island (Scatarie) being usually the first land made by vessels from Europe to any of the colonies eastward of the Bay of Fundy, and from the common occurrence of vessels being ahead of their reckoning, when steering to the westward, the first news of its propinquity being often given by the roar of its breakers or the concussion of its rocks, shipwrecks are of frequent occurrence, and few places on the coast of Northern America more obviously call for the precaution of a light house."

—Thomas Chandler Haliburton,
An Historical and Statistical Account of Nova Scotia 1829

"I'll miss the lonely cliffs and the pounding surf."

—Eliza Campbell, Scatarie's sole Western lighthouse keeper for twenty years

"Everyone was one person on Scatarie."

—Abbie Spencer, former resident

CHAPTER ONE

My favourite thing in all the world is when the coastal wind blows the grass on the barrens close to the shore of Northwest Cove on Scatarie. It's like a mother's caress on her baby's head. The gusts create velvet ripples that run wild towards the stunted forests of spruce, mirroring the ocean's waves.

If you stand on the sandy lip of the beach looking out over those barrens towards the pond, the wind will play with you, knock you over, hug you, sting you, and generally be a terrible nuisance, but never on purpose, and when you are completely winded, it will stop. Where does it go?

It follows me, so it does.

It is me.

I am remembered as Cara Murphy from Kerry Pike, near Cork, Ireland, but there is no one there left to call me to mind. I've belonged to this place for almost two hundred years now, but spirits tell me what happened here four hundred years ago, four thousand years ago.

It's all about listening to the wind. If you pay attention, the whispers of your ancestors will make themselves known, but often people are too busy trying to stay alive to worry about the stories of the past. Mind, people love to listen to yarns over a fire on the beach, but the everyday helpful murmurs are lost, running after children or breaking your back hauling up fish from the depths.

Mam told me my Irish name, Cara, means "friend." I took that to heart and have tried to be a friend to the souls I run into here on my island, but not everyone wants to listen to me. My sister for one. Aisling was six and I was fifteen, holding her in my arms when we sank beneath the heaving waves, our mother screaming for us against the fury of the storm the night our ship floundered on the rocks of Scatarie.

Da and Mam lived, and my brothers, one with terrible injuries. His broken leg never healed properly and he limped all his life. They eventually travelled to Quebec, our original destination, and while my mother lived for many years, she was never the same. She told me that. The heartbreak of losing me and her youngest aged her. Da never forgave himself for making us immigrate to Canada.

I used to tell them not to worry. Aisling is fine, busy playing hide-and-seek with the seals in the cove and grabbing handfuls of blackberries. My parents knew that, once they crossed over themselves.

Growing up a good Catholic girl, I was told I would get my reward in heaven. That God was almighty and I had to repent my sins to earn his favour. The church was an important anchor in our lives. It was reassuring to know God cared about us, especially those of us who had next to nothing. Mam prayed to God all the time. She would take out her rosary and whisper to herself as the beads slipped through her fingers one at a time. Da didn't and I used to worry that God might not pay much attention to him when the time came.

There was no need. God is grander than I ever imagined. A force so vast it never ends because it's everything. Everything I touch, everything I breathe in, the sights I see, the feelings I remember. Everyone I have ever loved is with me when I want them to be. I've decided after two hundred years of being *dead*, everyone's heaven is their own. There are no hard and fast rules here. I've interacted with enough spirits now to know that we are as different as we were when we were living, which makes complete sense to me. You can be sure my grandfather is whittling figures out of wood and smoking his long pipe, a cup of tea by his side. He's always tickled to know when I am near, but then off I go and he is content.

When I need my family, they are there. Otherwise, I am as free as a bird. A presence stays in one place only because they want to, not because they can't move on. We are not stuck. We are content. Well, most of us, anyway.

I don't wonder why I choose to be in the place where Aisling and I died. Aye, it was overwhelming and confusing, like a panicked nightmare, but it only lasted a few moments. All my inner being knew at the time was that I had Aisling in my arms and Mam would be comforted knowing that.

It was about the last time I did. That girl is as bold in this world as she was in the last. Just naughty. And I let her know it.

When I say, "Come 'ere to me now," she sticks out her tongue and goes for a ride on the back of a raven. That is not unusual, for we now understand that we are one. Not just human beings, but every living thing, animals, forests, water, the sky, the moon and stars. There is no us and them. Think of the heartache that didn't need to be, if we had known this simple truth when we were alive.

Sometimes I feel sorry for the living. They struggle and fight over small things. They are not aware of how grand they will be.

If you knew how close we are to you, you wouldn't be so wretched when we leave.

Some people do know. They have the ability to see us. Other people either seek them out or are afraid of them. We had an old crone in our village who reached out and grabbed my hand once at the marketplace. I was about ten at the time. She asked me if I believed in angels.

I nodded, too shocked to speak, as I'd never seen a woman with so many deep wrinkles on her cheeks.

"Good, child. You have one behind you."

All the way home, I looked over my shoulder. It unnerved me, so it did, and I couldn't rest. Then I got too weary to bother with it anymore. As it happens, my angel was a neighbour boy who died after falling off a hay wagon. We were all very sad at the time. He came around to my island to tell me that he'd always liked me and that's why he kept an eye on me. I thanked him and never saw him again.

You need to know that this island is harsh and soft, beautiful and varied. A surf so rhythmic and soothing your eyes close and you are lulled to sleep on the hot grass, buttercups swaying beside you while seagulls circle and glide above.

But you can often find timber and metal wreckage a mile inland amid the foliage, far from the hard granite shoreline. The southern side of the island has been battered by storms for centuries, creating salt-burned grassy barrens. The skeletons of lost ships are scattered there as well. When the storm clouds gather in the distance rumbling with displeasure, the sky will darken and great gusts will pounce on you like a furious, screaming banshee. When the rain travels sideways, you know the gale will cause spoondrifts, white plumes of spray reaching away from the mighty waves, and that power will pound against the rocks and punish anything that gets in the way.

So many of us lost our lives on nights like this. Before the lighthouse was built in the 1830s, and after. A light and a few good men are no match for Mother Nature when she's in a rage, but they did their best. I was pleased when I watched them build the wooden octagonal lighthouse with its revolving white lamp, visible for one minute, then eclipsed for half a minute. Imagine seeing that light from the ship instead of the pitch-black fury ahead of you. Where there's light, there's hope.

Most of the time.

I've occasionally watched fires set on lonely shores to bait the ship into thinking they are safe, only to have them crash on the shore. Wreckers would then strip the ship of everything they could before the authorities arrived and hide the booty to be sorted later. They were desperate and had mouths to feed as well. I see both sides now. I am nothing more than a witness.

On the other hand, I have been present while brave, upstanding, and often lonely island keepers have dedicated the best years of their lives to rescuing people they didn't know by organizing a humane establishment on the island, which meant access to a metallic lifeboat, a whale boat, and a flat which could be used to assist mariners in distress. They would jump up at a moment's notice, with little thought of their own safety, scrambling over the frothing surf and slippery rocks into freezing water to throw a cable to terrified victims.

The station had the lighthouse, a dwelling, and four outbuildings—a boathouse, a storehouse, a barn for hay, and a cattle shed. On hand were always barrels of flour, beef, pilot bread, molasses, and tea. They kept a medicine chest and blankets, clothes and shoes, mostly men's pants and shirts, caps, and drawers. Nothing for two young girls, but then, we didn't need them, did we?

I've lost count of the number of wrecks I've seen since I arrived here, every one of them heartbreaking to witness, but especially when there are families on board. Most ships are crewed by sailors who chose that life, but little ones who have to go where their parents take them and have no say in the matter are the ones my heart goes out to. I suppose because that describes my sister and me.

Life can be cruel and magnificent. You must resolve that both realities exist in the living realm.

It is not the same behind the veil. I can try my best to describe it to you, but no words do it justice, so I am content to tell you tales of the people who have lived and breathed on this patch of earth. None of their stories are my own, but I surely like to stick my nose in. Not that I can change their minds, but I do tend to gravitate to people who sense I am here. Even Aisling noticed it eventually.

"Stop snooping on old fishermen. They're afraid of you, don't you know."

I took her hand. "Come here." We skimmed over the water of Mira Bay until we were halfway across.

"Now turn. Do you see? The reflection on the water at times has Scatarie looking as if it's floating like a low-lying cloud. That's magic. And because it's magic, what does the island look like?"

She considered this, but shook her head. "Tell me."

"It's a sleeping dragon. Its head is lowered between its front legs to the west and the slope of its body rises until you get to North West Cove and after that the very long tail disappears into the water to the east."

Aisling smiled. "'Tis."

"A dragon that sleeps," I replied, "but once woken, ferocious and deadly."

"Saint Patrick cast out the serpents of Ireland. Nana told me. Maybe he sent one here."

Thinking of Nana always brings a tear to my eye. She and my granddad refused to come with us, saying they would rather die where they'd been born. Before we left Ireland Nana gave Mam her sterling silver lily-of-the-valley hairpin, the thing she valued above all else. I tormented my mother for days to let me wear it, to try and catch the eye of a lad on board. She finally relented and on that last day of mine, I was as pretty as a picture and I know the young sailor thought so too, with my red hair pulled up off my neck like a proper girl.

My mother lost three things that day that meant the world to her. That perfect silver curved strand of flowers disappeared down, down, down into greenish brown seaweed and I couldn't find it. You'd think I'd know where everything is. But I prayed to Saint Anthony and he was no help. Once I was desperate enough to look in the Spanish well. It was built by Spanish fishermen a hundred or more years before I came along. A very skillful job they did too, lining it with stone. But that shows you how desperate I was, to believe it found its way there.

I searched in the waters off Gull Cape, Hay Island, Friar Point, Fluke Cove, Little Shag, and Cary Rocks to no avail, and these are only a few of the coastal points that surround Scatarie. Looking for a wee pin in churning blue-black water was a fool's game, but I have all the time in the world. There are extraordinary amounts of tarnished silver and gold coins lying about, but they are uncovered one moment and buried by moving sand the next.

A little like Aisling. I glimpse her in a depression filled with soft-stemmed bulrushes and bog goldenrod, holding a bouquet of white beak sedge, with creamy white spikes, and then as quick as you like, she's hiding in curlygrass fern or raspberry bushes, a handful of ghost pipe clutched in her fist. I pretend I can't see her, as you do with a child, and this delights her.

I know she loves dancing with butterflies over the meadows. And she can sparkle like a firefly when she wants to; that took about a hundred years to perfect. Often, I see her on the rocks just offshore with the cormorants, spreading her arms out, imitating them drying their wings in the sun. She tells me they remind her of our priest at Sunday service. She kept expecting him to flap his arms and fly away after his sermon.

Many people over the years have caught our interest. I do tend to follow older fishermen around. They have more knowledge in their little finger than I do even now. Their cheeks have been sand-blasted by the wind, and the sun has wrinkled the skin around their eyes. Most of them squint after years of trying to escape that sharp white reflection on the water. All of them keep a smoke between their lips and their hands and big knuckles are red and swollen, calloused from pulling rope and raising killicks. They always have a dirty rag in their pocket that serves every need, and black dirt under their nails from oil and fish guts, and they reek of tobacco, seaweed, and sweat. The fishers I like best are the ones who spit and grunt and that's conversation, the ones who rarely talk. They don't need to. I can hear the whispers of their thoughts, same as I would hear them if they did natter aloud. They are in tune with the ocean and waves, keeping an eye on the horizon for trouble. Misfortune can spring on a man. The chatty types are often caught by surprise. I've seen it on their faces as they disappear below the surface. Most fishermen don't swim. The water in this part of the world is so cold, their philosophy is that once you're over the side you're done for anyway. Why prolong the inevitable?

I also have a soft spot for them because they believe in spirits. They aren't afraid to tell others what they've seen or felt, despite being spooked by us. Ghost stories abound on this island. Especially when the goulash flows. That's what they call it here. Sometimes homemade alcohol is the only thing they look forward to after breaking their backs every day.

Most of the stories, I believe. When you build your cabin over an old French graveyard, you're bound to have hurt feelings, and some spirits love to create chaos, banging away or slamming doors to let the occupants know they aren't best pleased. Why would I turn over the six covers on a stove the night of a shipwreck? Or sound a bell in the middle of the island? There was a chap who stayed at a camp alone when a storm came up and at two in the morning the door blew open and nine men came in and sat by the fire in their oilcloths. He rubbed his eyes and they were gone. The next night a boat went down and nine men lost their lives.

There are more things in heaven and earth.

But most tales aren't so convoluted. They mostly consist of someone thinking they see a shrouded figure out of the corner of their eye. They catch a glimpse. Not enough to be certain of anything. A chill running up their spine or goosebumps usually are enough to send them scurrying, especially in the dark.

Folks like to believe that their loved ones are near and they will be convinced the dragonfly that landed on their hand and stayed a while is the best friend who always loved them. And sure, they're not wrong.

If you've heard of the tradition of telling bees your family's affairs, know that this is true. The bees do deliver messages, and like to be informed because they are very nosy and extremely loyal. If you don't tell them someone has died, they will often disappear overnight to punish you.

Aisling and I used to hover around women who reminded us of Mam. Once her life was over, we didn't have to. We had the woman herself close by. And breathing in the scent of her was heaven. It still is.

But we have formed attachments to some individuals over time. People who remind us of the old country or those you know perfectly well would've been a grand friend when you were alive. Usually, we keep an eye on them and pop in and out, in no great hurry to follow them throughout their lives.

This all changed in the year of our Lord 1922. Three babies were born on Scatarie on Christmas night, only a few hours apart. Old Mrs. Spencer delivered them, running back and forth between their houses in foul weather, only sustained by cups of tea and bread and molasses. She told her husband, "We've got one underbaked, one just right, and the other so overdone he's more than ten pounds. His poor mother."

Now, whenever a baby is born, spirits rejoice because these little creatures are very close to our world and to God. They are brand new. They've been waiting in a space unlike any other and so are completely pure and innocent. They know and hear and feel more than people who have been here a long time. And they do see us, but all of that wears off after a while. Life is hard and their softness begins to fade.

Somehow, I knew these three had been wrapped up in each other before they entered our world and their fates would intertwine throughout their lifetimes. Aisling and I fell in love with them. The big boy, named Hardy, was a pudding. The just-right little fellow, Samuel, seemed impatient, with eyes so blue you could get lost in them. The underdone little girl, Mary Alice, the size of a peanut, possessed a great pair of lungs. More fascinating was the spectacular aura around her. I knew she was special. But how special surprised even me.

You might be startled that this tale will be told to you by a ghost. I prefer to be called a spirit, but it's all the same. The truth is, I have as much right to tell this story as anyone.

Scatarie Island belongs to the living and the dead.

CHAPTER TWO

My three babies were quickly absorbed into the day-to-day life of Scatarie, and believe me, the people who lived there ran from morning to night. There were about twenty families around this time. All of them with lots of bairns, so there were enough playmates to make life interesting. Both Sam's and Mary Alice's fathers were fishermen, as were all of the men on the island. Happiest when messing around in their boats wearing big rubber boots, fishermen's sweaters, and oilcloth, dealing with the weather while they hauled lobster and caught cod, haddock, and herring. Then they'd unload the fish, dry the fish, take the fish to market, repair their traps, make more killicks, organize bait, and roll their own.

Hardy's dad was the lightkeeper on the eastern end of the island, taking care of the lighthouse with its revolving white light and the building that housed the foghorn. Aisling and I love the sound of that foghorn, piercing through fog so dense you can't see a hand in front of your face. At least that's how it is for the living. We're very good at walking through walls, so a little fog doesn't deter us.

A lightkeeper has to have everything shipshape around the property, everything repaired in case inspectors show up without notice to catch them slacking. It's a demanding job. These sorts don't sleep on rough nights, too busy climbing to the top of the tower and almost being blown off the platform, making sure their lights are bright and in good working order. Lives depend on it.

I'm surprised their mothers had time to breathe, between hauling water from the well to scrub clothes and wipe dishes, tending to the wood stove, scrubbing floors, feeding and killing and plucking chickens, making meals, baking bread, knitting sweaters and mittens, darning socks, sewing, and altering worn-out clothes to fit the youngest child.

All of this by kerosene lamp. There was no electricity on the island. And they had to keep the garden weeded, can produce, even dry and cut hay to feed the pigs, cows, and sheep. For fun and relaxation, they hooked rugs and made quilts, often together to make it less of a chore. They'd shoo the kids outside for either play or chores, so they could gossip and catch up on the latest news. Not that there was a lot. The mail only came once a week in the winter, and the only phone was the one at the lighthouse that belonged to the government.

But someone was always going off in a boat to Main-à-Dieu, Louisbourg, or Glace Bay to visit a sick relative, go to a doctor's appointment, a funeral, or a wedding. And no one came back empty handed. One of the ladies delivered her baby in the hospital in Glace Bay and she took the infant back in a putt-putt boat, driven by a fisherman who was going that way with two fifty-pound bags of flour and his two German shepherds.

And keep in mind, all this was done with little or no money. Fishermen were on a barter system, "on-tick" with the fishing supply store and grocers. When their catch was tallied by the end of the season, if they had enough earned to cover their expenses with these businesses and pay the doctor too, they were satisfied.

It's like Ireland, where none of us had any money either. But when you and your neighbours are in the same boat, you don't notice what you're missing. As long as you're warm and have food in your belly, most people can carry on just fine.

But when the Great Hunger hit Ireland, it was impossible to stay. Our da said we would die. Life is never safe and Aisling and I died anyway. At least it was quick. To starve to death is a terrible thing. Mam closed our eyes on the way to the ship so as not to see the gaunt faces of people whose clothes hung like rags.

Hardy, Mary Alice, and Sam all had big sisters to help their mothers care for them, but on a Saturday afternoon in December when all the men were out hunting, either on the water for ducks or in the woods for deer, the sisters got the afternoon off, and the mothers plunked the three babies in the centre of the room on the mat with a toy.

The three ladies were secretly proud of the attention these children got from the other women on the island. They were like triplets, an oddity, and to be born on Christmas Day was special. And they were handsome babies, except for poor Mary Alice. She was still scrawny for an almost-one-year-old, but she could pull a spruce cone out of Hardy's clenched fist before he knew what happened. He'd cry, Sam would laugh, and Mary Alice would give it back to him and pat his chubby knee.

I remember this day very well, because it was the first time Mary Alice saw me in the corner, watching the ladies work over their quilts, laughing at the story of old Burt emerging from the outhouse with his shabby drawers around his ankles. His wife was more mortified by the state of his underwear than his forgetfulness.

I often sit and listen to the women talk. Aisling thinks it's boring and to a six-year-old soul it is, but I like dreaming of what might have been if there hadn't been a famine and we'd stayed in Ireland. Would I be blushing at the mention of a suitor like the new school mistress?

Mary Alice might have been scrawny, but she was walking while her "brothers" were both crawling on their knees. I saw her lift her head, with that downy auburn fluff that couldn't be tamed. Red hair like me. She felt like mine.

She wasn't looking in my direction in a vague kind of way. Her eyes stared into mine and she immediately got up and tottered over to me sitting on the trunk that held the winter clothes. She grinned and began to babble quite seriously. I smiled and nodded back to her. "I'm Cara."

Mary Alice turned to her mother, Mary, who had looked up at the sound of her voice, and the baby kept pointing at me while talking more gibberish.

"Look, it's almost like she sees someone. I wonder if it's my grandmother. She always said she would come back and haunt me if I didn't sew at least five stitches per inch."

The women laughed together, all of them agreeing that their deceased female relatives would be horrified at their lax ways. That, I couldn't understand. No one worked harder than these women.

But then, when you live on an island and have to depend on your own resources to get you through the day, your whole life and your children's lives are dictated by the effort you and your husband put in.

Later that night, I listened to the storm petrels screaming at each other over the water. The word *storm* in their name comes from superstitious sailors who would hear the birds' chattering call in bad weather and rough seas. They are surprisingly dainty, barely bigger than a swallow, dark brown birds with a white tail. They glide across oceans looking for plankton. My sailor told me that.

I have a resting place in the old spruce forest that's protected from the worst of the wind, an abandoned eagle's nest, perfect for spending time looking at the heavens, but there are no stars tonight. Bad weather is coming and those petrels know it and don't let me rest.

I feel Aisling with me, so I tell her my news.

"Mary Alice saw me today."

"G'wan now. I want her to see me too."

"It doesn't always work like that. Most of the time they can't. It depends on the person and I think Mary Alice is an old soul."

"She's a wee one."

"Even babies can be otherworldly. They can know what others don't. Ah, sure they're just new and don't know human rules, is all."

"Animals don't fuss with that," Aisling said. "That's why I play with seals and gulls. They see me all the time. Dogs and cats always know when I'm there."

"Because they live in this moment; their thinking isn't clouded with thoughts of yesterday or tomorrow. And they use all their senses and pay attention. They're grand."

That conversation came back to me when Mary Alice was three. By now her mother knew she had an imaginary friend, and she indulged her. She was the baby and still tiny, but what a firecracker. As stubborn as a mule, but oh so bright. Far ahead of Hardy and Sam. They were uninteresting lumps next to her, but endearing nonetheless.

It was unnerving at times for the family to hear her chatting away to someone in the corner or under the bed. And it spooked her siblings when she laughed out loud at nothing.

"Are you sure she's not touched in the head?" Mary Alice's older sister Rose asked their mother once.

"She'll grow out of it."

Mary sat one day in front of the wood stove and rolled a smoke, to enjoy with her tea. She watched Mary Alice play with a frayed teddy bear and an old rag doll that had belonged to every girl in the family. She was telling them what to do, of course.

Mary shook her head. "Having fun?"

"We're going on a picnic. Cara is coming with me."

"You mention Cara often. What's she like?"

"She's got long red hair like me. And she sings. She tells me not to be afraid."

Her mother scowled. "Afraid of what?"

Mary Alice turned to her mother. "When I have a bad dream, she comes and sings and I feel better."

Mary lit her smoke. "Oh."

"Ma, I need a small blanket for the picnic."

"Let me finish my tea and I'll look."

Ten minutes later, Mary came downstairs with a small flannel cloth. "I'd forgotten about this. I used to carry it around when I was small."

I glanced at the cloth and ignored the sandwiches, shocked to the core that I hadn't recognized Mary. She had seemed familiar, but I was so in love with Mary Alice, I didn't pay much mind to the rest of her family, because there were a lot of them. Five girls and five boys. So much chaos around the house.

I believe I've told you already that we keep an eye on some people but generally don't follow them throughout their lives. This is what happened with Mary. I knew her as a young child many years ago, and her grandmother Alice. I'm the only one who knows their secret, one they managed to keep from everyone. Alice took it to the grave.

Now I knew where Mary Alice got her spunk. A long line of brave women ran in her family.

Alice was getting old and forgetful. She spent most days in a rocking chair at her son's house. Her daughter-in-law was too busy to keep her company, and since Alice had trouble hearing, she gradually became cut off from day-to-day activities. Her only salvation was her little granddaughter, Mary. All the other grandkids were boys and they didn't hang around the house. But Mary was happy to sit in Alice's lap as she taught her how to knit. She didn't use a lot of words, mostly hand gestures, and this became their language, especially when they wanted to keep things to themselves. Alice at the age of eighty and Mary at the age of eight were very opinionated about the family, and loved to giggle about them right under their noses. Mary would always remember her grandmother as her best friend.

She became a lot more than that.

It was Christmastime one year and people were mummering, which had been brought over with the Newfoundlanders; dressing up in odd outfits and covering their faces with masks. They would go house to house and people would try and guess who they were. They never spoke, which made the identification even harder. Some men dressed as women and some women dressed as men. The one mask I didn't like was when someone put a chicken skin on their face, inside out, so their face looked pocked and ghastly.

On this night, a party was taking place at a house a little farther in the woods from the harbour. Mary wanted to go because there would be fiddles and spoons for making music, dancing and fun. Her brothers went but her mam asked her to stay behind with her grandmother. Mary was a little put out but knew she wouldn't have a good time if her grandmother was all alone in the house. They amused themselves playing 45s and eating Christmas shortbreads.

And then Alice asked Mary to go outside and get another bucket of coal for the fire. She insisted she put a hat and gloves on, not just her jacket. "It's cold out."

I watched as Mary did as she was told and shovelled the black coal into the bucket with the scoop, trying not to get the coal dust all over her. It was freezing. And then Mary looked up and laughed. Someone was on the road, dressed up. "Are you mummering? Come in and Grandma and I will try and guess who you are."

The masked figure walked quickly over to her, grabbed her arm, and dragged her to the shed. Mary was so shocked she couldn't speak, but she pulled against him with all her might. For a minute I forgot I was dead and rushed over to her but realized I was helpless, so I used the wind to blow in the front door of the house with a loud bang. Alice heard it and got up to see what was going on. She peeked around the corner and couldn't see Mary, so she hurried to put on her boots and coat and grabbed a spade left leaning by the door.

There was a full moon that night, lighting up the white snow. Alice went to the coal pile, shouting for Mary. She couldn't understand where she was. She was afraid she wouldn't hear her granddaughter shout for help if she was in trouble. Then she saw small and bigger footprints leading to the shed, and a blind rage took over her old limbs. I could see it in her face. She ran, yes ran, to the shed and flung the door open. A dark figure was lying on top of Mary, and he didn't even have time to turn around before Alice lifted the spade high above her and brought it down with a crushing blow to the back of his head.

She helped Mary wiggle out from under the inert body. Most of her clothes were still on, but she was crying her heart out. Alice knew she had to use her anger to stay strong.

"Mary, help me. He's dead. We're getting rid of garbage, that's all."

Mary nodded. That's what she wanted to do. Never see him again.

And between the two of them they dragged the body to the edge of the bank and pushed it off. It landed on the rocks below. With any luck, the tide would be high with the full moon and it would be gone by morning.

One thing was on their side: it started to snow, and big, fluffy flakes covered their tracks and the trail to the edge of the bank. Alice put her arm around Mary and took her back to the house and even had the presence of mind to get the coal scuttle and clean the spade. Then she and Mary crawled into bed, so as not to be awake when the family came home. They held each other and whispered in the dark.

Alice gulped and her voice wavered. "It's a sin to kill, Mary. I wanted him to stop so I hit him hard."

"I know, Gram. It's not your fault."

"Not yours either. We won't talk of him again."

The two of them fell asleep almost instantly, both worn out from the physical and mental ordeal. Alice couldn't get out of bed the next day; she was sore from head to toe. Mary spent her time by her grandmother's side feeding her toast and tea, to stay away from the family in case she let something slip. When she didn't ask about the party, her mother was surprised.

"What did you two get up to last night?" she asked as she fried gull eggs, which Mary detested.

Mary was by the stove getting more tea for her grandmother, but before she could answer her mother, her da came through the door. "Christ almighty, someone just found Jimmy Tingle on the beach."

Mary felt a ripple of shock. The body was supposed to be taken out with the tide. She looked at her grandmother through the open curtain to her bed. Alice raised her hand and placed her gnarled index finger over her thin lips. Mary understood.

"He must have had too much to drink and wandered around legless in circles. He would have been close to the house. Did you hear anything, Mary? Or see anything?"

Mary shook her head.

"What about you, Ma?" her son shouted into the next room.

"What?!" Alice shouted back.

He rolled his eyes at his wife. "Never mind. He could have been marching to a brass band and she wouldn't notice. As far as they can tell, he smashed his head on the rocks. What a way to go."

Mary's mother shook her head. "I know it's an awful thing to say, but he won't be missed. I've never met a meaner person."

People talked about it for a couple of weeks and the police came and went. It was ruled an accident, and life returned to normal.

Alice died shortly after that, as if she'd used what little life force she had left saving her precious granddaughter. Mary always felt guilty, as if she was responsible. But she kept her promise and never told a soul.

When Mary Alice, Hardy, and Sam were five, they liked to play in old Mr. Spencer's abandoned chicken coop. It was just across the road from Mary Alice's small wooden house and next door to Sam's, so they were usually the first ones there. Hardy would mosey along and join them after he had his breakfast. He never missed his breakfast. His mother was quite a cook and was always trying to convince Sam to stay for a meal. She worried about him. You could count his ribs and he had knobby knees, but as Hardy's father said to his mother, "Look at his dad. All skin and bone, but he'd beat me at arm wrestling."

One chilly March morning, Mary Alice was in a hurry to get to their meeting spot. Sam said he found treasure but she didn't believe him. He was always making up stories, and fooled the trusting Hardy all the time, which annoyed Mary Alice. She felt protective of him.

"He lies, Hardy."

"Nah, he knows stuff."

Mary Alice went right past the kitchen table and her mother called out, "Come back here and eat your porridge."

She stood by her bowl and shovelled two big spoonfuls into her mouth. Mary knew that was all she'd eat anyway, so she let it go. But when Mary Alice went to the door with bare hands, she hollered once more: "The fog's not fit this mornin'. Put your mitts on. It's some cold."

Mary Alice pretended not to hear her and ran out the door, leaving her mother to shake her head. "When your hands fall off, don't come cryin' to me."

The chicken coop hadn't been used in years and was in desperate need of repairs, but it suited the friends just fine. Inside the grey, weather-worn wood was old hay and a blanket Sam brought one morning when his mother's back was turned. They needed it because of the gaps between the slats in the walls.

Mary Alice was surprised no one was about when she crawled inside. Sam told her to meet him first thing. She waited as long as she could, until her hands were a mottled red and bluish colour. She stuck them under her armpits in an attempt to thaw them out.

"You're gonna get it, Sam Harris!"

She pushed her way back outside and looked around through the swirling mist. Neither one of them was to be seen, and this was basically the community's main thoroughfare. A dirt road, really, that went across the island to North West Cove. The houses were up on a bit of a slope but close to the shore off Eastern Harbour. All the other kids were in school, which was located halfway across the island. Our friends wouldn't start primary until September that year. The younger kids were inside with their mothers, waiting for their older siblings to get home and take them sledding or skating.

Darned if she could figure out what was going on, and then she realized there was a dog barking non-stop down by the water. Hoping it wasn't hurt, Mary Alice rushed down the hill over rocks and seaweed, as quick as she dared in the mist, and that's when she made out the boys. Hardy's dog, Buster, was causing the racket. Hardy held him by the scruff of the neck away from whatever the seagulls were trying to get at. Sam noticed her first and he waved his hands to warn her away.

"Git! Go on! Go get your pa!"

"What's wrong?"

"Just go, will ya! We need help."

Mary Alice didn't ask any more questions. She beetled back up the hill and ran back to her house, passing old man Spencer who was out by his shed coiling rope.

"Where ya goin' in such a hurry, girlie?"

"I have to get Da. There's something on the beach. The birds are after it."

The old man had a plug in his mouth and let go a spit of tobacco on the ground in front of her. "Likely a dead seal."

Alice burst through the door and startled her parents, who were finishing their breakfast with cups of strong tea and handmade cigarettes.

"Da! You have to come to the beach. Sam says so."

"Did he now? A five-year-old telling an adult what to do."

"He said he needed help."

His demeanour changed completely as he leapt from his chair, grabbed his cap off the hook by the door, and hurried out. Mary Alice tried to follow him.

"Get back here!"

"Ma! I need to go. Sam and Hardy are down there."

"You're not to leave this house until I know what's goin' on." She got up from the table and then noticed Mary Alice's splotchy hands. She reached over and grabbed them in her own. "You know what'll happen if you keep doing this? You'll get great big blue veins all over the top of your hands. You want that?"

"I don't think so."

"Stand by the fire and warm up."

The heat on her hands made Mary Alice forget all about what was going on down at the beach. With the warmth emanating from the stove, she became sleepy. The rocking chair looked cozy so she curled up in it, not realizing she'd be out like a light for three hours. Her mother let her rest, afraid she might be coming down with something. It wasn't like Mary Alice to stop moving. Mary kept looking at her as she peeled potatoes for the shepherd's pie she would make for dinner. They always had their big meal at noon. It made her feel better to know her children had something warm in their stomachs walking back to school in this weather.

Mary sighed. Mary Alice would be her last child. Mrs. Spencer told her the night Mary Alice was born that she better pack it in. The baby had been too early. "I don't think that womb of yours has the strength to keep them inside for nine months. She's your tenth child. You're asking for trouble if you continue."

Mrs. Spencer reminded Mary of her grandmother Alice, so she took it as a sign that it was really her grandmother looking out for her from beyond the grave.

Mary was smart. So many people have that thought and then dismiss it. It's very frustrating for souls like me watching your loved ones make mistakes after you try to warn them.

It was a nice change to have Mary Alice still. Her mother was able to study her face. She was sure she could see her grandmother in her, the way her eyes crinkled. She was as much a bean pole as ever, but her face was heart shaped, almost round because of her dimpled cheeks. That auburn hair of hers was now cut in a pageboy, straight bangs across her forehead and the rest to her chin. All the little girls in the twenties had this fashion, but Mary Alice refused to have a bow on her head, and her father agreed.

"She'll have that ground into the mud the second she goes outside. Don't make work for yourself."

This youngest child of hers was a tomboy. Hanging around with two little boys didn't help, but Mary Alice wanted nothing to do with dolls and playing house like some of her neighbours, and they gave up asking after a while. Seven-year-old Edith called her Mary Contrary once, but never again after Mary Alice shoved her in a puddle.

Mary Alice was still asleep when her father, Tom, came back to the house. The first thing he said was, "Is she okay?"

"Just tired. What happened?"

Tom put his cap back on the hook and poured himself more tea from the teapot that would be on the wood stove all day. Then he poured Carnation milk in the mug and lit a smoke. "There's been another wreck, a Dutch freighter. They're all gone, but one of the bodies washed up on shore. Sam and Hardy found it. The gulls and crows were pecking at it."

Mary made a sign of the cross. "Poor man."

"I'd say he was more of a lad."

Mary folded her arms across her chest. "This is something awful. A poor mother, half a world away, will never know what happened to her son. It was the same when that ship was torpedoed during the war and those three sailors were found dead on the shore by the lighthouse. Remember, old Nell thought she could hear them yelling that night? Can you imagine?"

"At least they were identified and had a proper burial here. The government even put a little iron fence around them."

"But were any of their mothers able to come here and visit those three crosses? No. We're too isolated. It makes me mad."

"This won't be the last disaster, Mary, and you and I both know it. You can't keep the kids from knowing it either. They've taken the body away. Here's hoping no more wash up. Not like the last wreck, when we were out fishing lobster and picking up floating corpses."

When Mary Alice's siblings came trooping in from school, they woke her up. But she was still groggy, as often happens when you sleep during the day. It was confusing. Everyone talked at once about the body on the beach.

"Sam and Hardy found it," she yawned. "I was there."

She was important for about a minute, and then they moved on to the story of catching the school mistress kissing one of the older Ferguson brothers before class, as he went into the trees to chop wood.

"Don't let that get around," their mother warned them. "She's a fine teacher, but if Mrs. Wadden hears of this, she'll be sacked and it will be a hard battle to get another young woman to move out here."

After lunch Mary Alice was dying to get outside and see her friends. Her parents warned her not to go down to the beach. She swore she wouldn't and wore her mitts. A few minutes later she was poking her head into the chicken coop, and there were the boys.

"Where were you at?" Sam asked.

"Asleep."

"During the day?" Hardy couldn't believe it. "Only babies sleep in the day."

"Are you calling me a baby, Hardy Campbell?" She shoved his shoulder through his plaid jacket.

"Ow."

"You missed the best part," Sam told her. "He had no eyeball. I think a crow got it."

"And he was blue!" Hardy shouted.

"Being blue is not fun. My hands were blue waiting for you this morning."

Sam's eyes lit up. "I forgot. I have to show you." He reached under the hay and uncovered the base of a ship's oil lamp. "Feel how heavy it is."

He let them both hold it and Mary Alice could hardly lift it up. "Where'd you get this?"

"On the beach down past Tin Cove when Da took me in the boat. I found it in the sand and he said I could keep it. It's treasure from a lost ship."

Mary Alice wanted treasure too. Sam always got the good stuff. It wasn't fair. And Hardy had a dog, something she'd always wanted, but her mother was allergic, and no amount of begging changed her mind.

They laughed while playing rock, paper, scissors, because Mary Alice always won and the other two could never figure out how she did it. Then they examined and exchanged their marbles before going outside so Sam could set off some caps on the rocks, but when they were done, he lost interest and said he was going home. Hardy said he was hungry so he left as well.

Mary Alice was magically awake. So awake she knew she needed to go treasure hunting and forgot all about her parents' warning not to go down to the beach. The fog had finally lifted, which made scrambling on the rocks not quite so treacherous, but bladderwrack made the surface very slippery. Mary Alice normally loved to squeeze the small pods of air with a satisfying pop, but today it was a nuisance. She needed to look under the sand and dig around.

Dreaming about pirates and treasure chests made her lose track of time. It wasn't until she heard her sister Rose yell, "Mary Alice, get home now!" that she realized how late it was. And because she hurried, she slipped on some seaweed and landed right on her bum. It really hurt, and now her pants were wet. She put out her arm to help herself up, when her fingers touched the severed hand lying on the beach.

Her screams brought Rose flying down the hill. She couldn't understand what had happened until Mary Alice pointed at the dreadful thing and promptly fainted.

This is when I came to the rescue.

Mary Alice began to have nightmares. She slept with her sisters, her parents, and even her big brothers, but she never felt safe and would wake up weeping. It was getting on her father's nerves; he'd told her to stay away from the beach. Her mother was a little more forgiving. "She's five."

But the shock was intense and Mary Alice couldn't get the sight out of her head. When she closed her eyes, she'd see fingers chasing her up the beach like hermit crabs. And I told her to get a blanket and sit in the rocking chair by the wood stove and I'd sing her to sleep. I spent many nights singing:

Sleep, sleep, grah mo chree
Here on your mama's knee
Angels are guarding,
and they watch o'er thee

Her mother woke up one night and was worried about her youngest, so she snuck down the stairs to take a peek. The chair was rocking while Mary Alice was curled up snoring softly. Mary felt a cold sweat break out under her nightie. I stopped immediately and watched Mary's face as she gingerly tiptoed over and tucked the blanket under her child's chin, keeping her eyes on the chair the whole time. It remained still.

"I shouldn't have had that cheese before bed."

She padded up the stairs and I recommenced rocking.

CHAPTER THREE

Things changed for the three friends once they went to school. Instead of amusing themselves, they were now surrounded by a group of wee ones of all ages, and their comforting dynamic was taken away.

It wasn't too bad in primary, but now that they were seven, Sam was popular with the girls and all the other boys wanted to be his friend. Mary Alice and Hardy were pushed to the side, or so it seemed. Mary Alice stormed off one day after school, annoyed that Sam hadn't even spoken to her all day. Hardy tried to catch up, but when Mary Alice was mad, she walked like a soldier.

"Wait up!" Hardy wailed, so she turned around and watched him hurry to her. Not that he moved very fast. He wasn't a jackrabbit like Sam, more like a lumbering raccoon. You'd never notice Hardy if he was in a crowd other than he was sturdier than everyone else. Nice looking in an ordinary way, with his dark curls and brown eyes. He had no outstanding features, like Sam's high cheekbones and icy blue eyes. But Hardy had a kind, freckled face, and more importantly, he was gentle. He wouldn't hurt a fly. Not for him trying to kill birds with a slingshot or dropping rocks on stranded jellyfish.

The difference between the two boys hadn't really been apparent before, but now it was obvious. At least to Mary Alice. Sam won all the foot races and could wrestle kids to the ground. He made quick comebacks while Hardy would still be thinking of what to say.

School was a torment in her eyes. She loved the work, and was smarter than everyone, but it took Sam and Hardy away from her. No, it took Sam away from her, and she was surprised at how upsetting that was. She always thought she liked both the boys the same. And she did, but school showed that Sam was one of those people who made living look easy.

Hardy had to stop for a second to catch his breath. "Why didn't you tell me you were leaving? Aren't we waiting for Sam?"

She started to walk away, hitting the fallen leaves on the dirt path with the switch she'd broken off. It felt good to smack something. "Why should we?"

Hardy followed her. "I dunno. We always do."

"Did he wait for us yesterday? No. He went home with Flossie."

"He told me he had to pick something up for his mom at her house," Hardy told her.

She swung around. "And you believed him?"

Hardy looked confused. "Yeah."

"You're thick." And she marched off, destroying bush branches as she went.

Hardy didn't understand Mary Alice sometimes. She was more complicated than his sisters. Ever since they'd gone back to school in September, she'd been grouchy. Watching her disappear ahead of him, he felt lonely. He looked back, wondering if Sam was coming, but only saw his older sister Dorothy headed his way, so he waited and walked home with her. They had the farthest to go, their house being next to the light on the very eastern edge of the island.

"Where's Sam and Mary Alice?"

"I dunno. She's mad at him and I think she wants me to be mad at him too."

She gave him a puzzled look. "Why?"

"He's not supposed to talk to anyone else but her, I guess."

She gave him a knowing look. "She's jealous."

"Jealous?"

"She's had you fellas to herself her whole life and now she has to share you."

That didn't make a lot of sense to Hardy, but he didn't want to think about it. He just wanted his friend back.

By the time they reached home, their cheeks and hands were red thanks to the wind and fog. Their house on the rocky shore was drafty, not sheltered from the elements, and during gales the wooden structure would shudder and sound like it was falling apart, the creaking got so loud.

Everything had a purpose around their place. A never-ending responsibility. The foghorn blew, the lighthouse lamp constantly turned, brightening the dark water and surroundings at night. But Hardy and his siblings knew no other life, and their house was larger than most of the dwellings on the island. They had more bedrooms. Dorothy, the only sister still home, had a room of her own and he shared a room with one older brother and one younger brother.

His dad, Len, was the son of a lighthouse keeper. He said it was a proud tradition and he hoped one of his boys would take up the mantle someday. Dorothy had objected. "I'm perfectly capable of running a lighthouse, Dad."

The thought of his thirteen-year-old daughter going out on the three-foot-wide, slightly sloping deck with only two wooden bars attached to four corner posts was frightening. It needed to be sloped to get rid of the rain. On a dirty night with ice and wind, a keeper had to clean the snow and sleet from the outside windows to keep the light bright, and in such circumstances, the footing was always precarious. He asked his wife, Annie, for a second helping so he could stop thinking about it.

Annie was more isolated than the other women, with no neighbours next to her, but she was far too busy to be lonely, and she loved to bake. She did meet with the women from time to time for quilting or hooking get-togethers, but she and Len didn't smoke or drink, which made them an oddity. They didn't go to the parties. Some of the women thought she was stuck up, being from Antigonish. That got back to Annie, and she grunted in bed next to Len. "Just because I don't suck back alcohol and fall over on someone's lap at a hootenanny doesn't mean I'm stuck up."

Len assured her she was just fine as she was. He loved cozying up to his roly-poly wife.

Hardy declared himself starved, so Annie sat him down with a glass of milk and two sugar cookies. He ate them while he watched his mother make fish cakes and beans for supper.

Annie looked over her shoulder. "Where are the other two monkeys? I haven't seen them in a while."

"Mary Alice is mad at me and Sam."

Annie grinned. "I'm sure she's not."

Hardy spoke with his mouth full. "She called me thick!"

It was all she could do to not laugh out loud. "Oh dear. I'm sure she didn't mean it."

Just then there was a knock on the porch door, and it opened. Sam appeared, looking windblown and cold.

"Come in, child. Sit down and have a snack." Annie poured another glass of milk and put two more cookies on a plate.

Sam ate them so quickly, Annie suspected he hadn't had lunch, so she sliced a thick piece of bread and slathered it with butter and jam. She put it in front of Sam and gave Hardy a warning look. "You'll ruin your dinner."

It was only when Sam smacked his lips and drained the milk that he started to come to life. He nodded at Annie. "Ta." Then turned to Hardy. "So where were you at? Why didn't you wait for me?"

"I don't know. Mary Alice told me not to."

"Do you always do what she tells you?" Sam said crossly.

Annie was enjoying this little conversation but pretended she wasn't there.

"She's mad at you for walking Flossie home."

Sam screwed up his face. "I had to pick up a bottle for Ma."

That didn't surprise Annie.

"Mary Alice is a stupid head," Sam declared. "Don't listen to her. Wait for me next time."

"Okay."

Annie pushed the pan of fish cakes over to the side of the stove, away from the highest heat. "Would you like to stay for supper, Sam?"

"Sure."

The only problem with spending time at Hardy's house was having to go home. Sam took his time walking back. He knew the way by heart, so he didn't need the flashlight Mr. Campbell offered him. Mrs. Campbell had placed a slab of apple pie wrapped in wax paper into his hand before he left. She didn't let anyone see she was doing it. That's what he liked about Mrs. Campbell. She knew what he needed without asking. He ate it as he walked.

The first stars were appearing in the sky, the sunset a thin glow on the horizon. Sam recognized the Big Dipper and knew the most important star was the North Star. His father said that because its position was constant it made navigation on the water easier. Since he'd be a fisherman like his father, this was useful to know.

He passed Mary Alice's house and heard the laughter. He peeked in the window and saw her father, Tom, dancing a jig and doing a horrible job at it, much to the amusement of his children.

Their neighbours were playing the fiddle and squeezebox and everyone was clapping. He forgot for a minute that he was angry with Mary Alice, but when he remembered he left.

His house was quiet, which meant his father, Edgar, was out, and so was Bob, his oldest brother. No doubt they were doing some chore in the fishing shack. His second-oldest brother, Ian, was at the table doing his homework. He liked school. The only one who did. His sister was at the sink.

"Where were you?"

"At Hardy's having supper."

"Mom was worried."

He knew that wasn't true. His mother was asleep on the couch. She slept a lot. She slept so much that she often forgot to cook, but she was always very sorry when she woke up. She'd pat the couch and sit him down. With her arm over his shoulder, she'd kiss him on the top of his head. "Forgive me."

"Okay."

I know what you're thinking: Mrs. Harris, Gladdie to her friends, had a drinking problem. But that wasn't it. She drank, but it was to forget about the fact that she was sick and would have to leave her family too soon. She was a private person. People who didn't know the situation had all kinds of opinions about her, but she refused to let Edgar tell anyone. "It's none of their business. I'll die without their pity."

But it was hard on Edgar. He'd gotten into a few scuffles at social events, after hearing someone insinuate that Gladdie liked her liquor. The fact that they'd be in their cups when they said it made him mad. He wanted to shout at them, "The doctor says her insides are rotten with cancer. She drinks to dull the fuckin' pain."

It was also hard on the children since they didn't know the truth, or if they did, they couldn't bring it up because she wouldn't talk about it. I thought that was the wrong decision. I could see Sam was angry with her. Mrs. Campbell didn't drink, and even if Mrs. Locke did, she never forgot to make her children lunch or dinner. He felt hard done by.

It was a month after that, on November 18, 1929, that Newfoundland was hit by the Grand Banks earthquake. It affected the entire Eastern Seaboard. It was felt as far away as New York and Montreal. That's where Aisling and I were supposed to live.

Our three friends were now on better terms, thanks to Mary Alice's realization that Sam was as stubborn as she was and if she didn't change her tactics, he'd probably never speak to her again. She gradually started to laugh at his jokes in a crowd and not make faces when he spoke to other girls. It had the desired effect...but what really helped was that the Waddens' nephew came to stay for the winter, and he was even more spectacular than Sam.

Mary Alice could see Sam's confidence wane, and he eventually took comfort in spending more time with his original friends. Hardy had no notion about what had happened, but he was pleased that something had changed and they were back to walking together after school as three.

They were nearly home when there was a huge bang or bump. Something that lasted for a minute and made them unsteady, almost knocking them off their feet.

"What was that?" Sam cried out as they looked at each other in disbelief.

Everyone started to emerge from their doorways. Mary yelled to Mrs. Spencer, "My dishes are falling to the floor. What's happening?"

No one had a good explanation, but everyone was jittery. Mothers made their kids come in the house, until someone said if there was another episode maybe the houses would fall down. It was hard to know what to do.

The men went down to the water and discussed it. Mary Alice felt better watching her father and other fishermen through the window, standing in the wake of the unknown. Len Campbell and Edgar Harris were with him. People started to shout and point, so she and the boys ran outside. They couldn't take in what was unfolding.

"Where's the water going?" Mary Alice whispered.

They watched the ocean recede from their view, leaving very little behind. They could see the ocean bed, seaweed and gasping fish in its wake. The water, always there like the sun in the sky, disappeared.

Mary Alice ran to her father and grabbed onto his legs. He put his hand on her back but kept talking to the adults. "I think this might be an earthquake. I've heard of it but never seen it with my own eyes."

Just then one of the women shouted from the hill: "It says on the radio there's been an earthquake in Newfoundland!"

That got everyone talking about what they should do.

"But Dad!" Mary Alice pulled at her father's pant leg. "Why did the water go? Is it ever coming back?"

"Oh, it will come back, all right. The question is how bad will it be."

"You're scaring me!"

Tom realized his mistake and picked her up in his arms. "Let's go home. Everything will be fine."

Of course it wasn't fine. As quickly as the water disappeared, it came roaring back in. Mary Alice's Uncle Chester arrived a few days later to tell that the Main-à-Dieu wave was three feet above the government wharf. Boats and debris along the shore were carried into the street. Louisbourg wharves and fish houses were flooded by the first major wave and the smaller waves that followed. Streets were damaged by the enormous tide. Scatarie had fish huts, boats, and equipment ruined in the aftermath. We heard news that twenty-eight people died and hundreds were injured in the Burin Peninsula when a giant tidal wave destroyed homes, ships, and businesses. It ruined their fishery for thirty years.

You see? Things happen that you're never prepared for. It was all too much for the smaller children. They couldn't take it in. The world can change in an instant?

When the Waddens' nephew came back from visiting his family in Main-à-Dieu, he told them that all the pigs had slit their own throats.

"How is that possible?" Mary Alice shouted at him. "Did they have knives?"

"No, dummy. They were trying to swim and their hooved feet kept hitting their throats."

"You're a big fat liar!"

The thought of those poor animals sent Mary Alice straight back to the rocking chair. Hardy couldn't sleep either, mostly because he kept imagining a giant wave coming straight for his house. Sam pretended it hadn't happened. His mother slept through it.

The long, hard winter hit after that, and while it was a challenge for the adults, the children were delighted. They still had chores to do, like chopping wood and taking in frozen clothes off the line, but most of the day after school was spent having fun. The older boys would shovel the snow off the ponds and they would skate until dark, all of them frozen by the time they crowded around the wood stove, drops of water sizzling from their mittens and hats hanging on fishing rope their mothers had rigged up around the stove.

A couple of Mary Alice's brothers had real skates. They'd belonged to their dad and an uncle, and were pretty beat up, but she had to make do with cheese cutters, and that was humiliating. She wanted to be a Toronto Maple Leafs hockey player like the rest of them.

It always seemed to her that the boys had more adventures. They'd put a six-foot sail on their backs or their chests, depending on the direction of a heavy breeze, and they'd rush down the ice at great speed, hooting and hollering as the sail billowed out. That, or they'd take a plank on skates with a piece of iron behind for a rudder. Once they put a spar up and sat on this ice boat, off they'd go careening over the bumpy surface, yelling at little kids to get out of the way before crashing into a snowbank.

There was a gentle slope behind Mary Alice's house that started at the back door, went past the outhouse, the clotheslines, the fence that held the sheep, and then stopped by the community well. If the snow was just right, not too wet, and the fog stayed away, it was perfect for sliding down on a makeshift sled fashioned from a piece of aluminum her father had in his boat. After many trips the route would become icy, and it was a contest to see which of our friends would go the fastest.

"That'll be me!" Mary Alice said, gloating. "I'm the lightest, so I'll fly down the hill." She dropped on top of the sheet and positioned her chest over it perfectly. "Gimme a push!" Sam shoved her feet with his own and down she flew. She was triumphant when she got up, spitting snow. "Let's see you beat that!"

She ran back up the hill, because they only had one sheet and had to share it. Sam was next, but he didn't want a push. Like Mary

Alice, he'd go face first, but he had a running start before he fell on his stomach. It proved to be the right tactic. He went at least ten feet past Mary Alice's finish line.

"I beat it!" He held his arm in the air and whooped it up.

"Show-off," Mary Alice grumbled.

Sam hurried back up and handed the handmade sled to Hardy. They both assumed Hardy would come in last, since he was heavier. His dog, Buster, put his tail in the air and his chin on the ground between his paws, waiting for Hardy to go.

Hardy sat on the sheet, uncomfortable with the thought of going head first. Sam pushed his back and away he went, Buster chasing him and barking the whole time. At one point the sheet started spinning and they heard Hardy yell, "Help!"

They realized Hardy was going faster and faster. So fast he soared right past their finish lines, left the well behind, and crossed over Jack Steele's front yard, before he went airborne and then disappeared in a ditch.

"He better not be dead!" Sam cried.

The two of them slipped and slid all the way down the slope and followed Buster's barking. They sank into the deep snow that had accumulated in the ditch and thankfully saw Hardy's boots sticking up in the air. Buster was frantically digging.

"We're coming!" Mary Alice hollered. But it wasn't easy. They were up to their waists and moving their legs was hard going. She felt sick to her stomach. The idea that something could happen to Hardy was unimaginable. By the time they got to him, Buster had dug Hardy out for the most part. At least he could breathe.

"Are you okay?" Sam asked.

"You scared us!" Mary Alice reached over and yanked off Hardy's hat that was encrusted with snow and hiding his face.

Hardy grinned at them. "I won."

Sam's mother died that winter. She was only thirty-seven. Mary Alice begged her mother to let her go to the funeral in Main-à-Dieu, said she needed to be there for Sam.

"You'll be here when he gets home."

"Why can't she be buried on the island?"

"It's just the way we do things here. Stop asking."

Hardy was told the same thing and neither one of them thought it was fair, not realizing how difficult it is to organize a funeral on the mainland when winter has descended and the ice comes in. And having children in boats is not ideal in those conditions. Not to mention maybe getting trapped over in Main-à-Dieu and not being able to make it home for weeks.

But those were adult worries and didn't mean anything to Sam's friends. They both tried to see him, but he wouldn't come to the door. His father asked them to stay away, but he accepted the baking Hardy's mother, Annie, told him to deliver.

Most of the community were in shock, not realizing the woman was ill, which in hindsight should have been obvious. But since Gladdie Harris kept herself to herself, and everyone had their own idea of what was wrong, including an unhappy marriage with Edgar, most neighbours felt mighty sheepish when the truth came out.

Mary and Tom discussed it in bed away from the children. "Why didn't she tell someone? We might have been able to help," Mary said, fretting.

"Nothin' you can do when it's cancer. I feel sorry for Edgar."

"And I feel sorry for those kids. He'll be working, and who will be looking out for them?"

"You and Annie and every other woman around here."

Mary Alice watched out the window the day Sam and his family left for the mainland. His brother Bob had his arm around Sam's shoulder. His other brother Ian and his sister Jean stayed close to Edgar. Gladdie's coffin was a wooden box, and they walked it down to the shore towards the boat with a cart and pony. It was too sad. Mary Alice looked away from the window and watched her mother making bread, with a pair of her brother's clean underwear on her head to keep her hair from getting in the dough.

"Don't die, Mama," she whispered.

Sam was never quite the same after that. I worried about him. He was mad at the world and picked fights with everyone. The worst one was just after school, when he grabbed the Waddens' nephew and threw him on the wet ground. No one knew why he jumped on top of him and punched him, but it was a spectacle for the younger crowd.

Mary Alice leapt on top of Sam to get him to stop, but he shoved her aside. It was Hardy who ended it. He had the strength to pull him off. The Waddens' nephew sat up dazed and the teacher, Miss MacDougall, came rushing out of the building.

"I'll have no more of this nonsense," she said. "Sam, I want you to apologize."

"No." And he took off running.

Miss MacDougall wasn't going to run after him. She made sure that the Waddens' nephew was okay and told everyone to get home and get home now.

Mary Alice and Hardy talked about it as they trudged along in the mud. Spring was coming and the ground was beginning to thaw.

"Ma asked Sam to come for supper yesterday and he said no," Hardy told her. "He's never done that before."

"My mother has given up trying to get him to come to our house, so she sends food over. The place is always dark now, like no one's home. It makes me feel lonely."

Hardy said, "We should pray for him."

His family were Anglican and their congregation held services in the Eastern Light boathouse, which was next to his house, so that Sunday he filed in with the rest of his family and spent the entire time with his head down, praying very hard for his friend. His brow was furrowed and he had sweat on his upper lip when he finished. Under his breath he said, "There, that should do it."

The Lockes were Catholic, and their small church was in Southeast Cove, a simple gabled building with a double front door and four windows on each side. The sides and roof were covered in unpainted wood shingles and the inside was sparse, with the studs in the walls visible. It did have a stove and the interior was divided into a sanctuary and nave by a short altar rail that went across the front. The altar was white with gold trim. Mary Alice thought gold was the best colour in the world. There was a confessional in the corner, Stations of the Cross on the wall, and a statue of the Blessed Virgin.

The priest only got over to the island once a month during the summer; laypeople performed the service in the meantime. Mary Alice was especially pious on this Sunday and she wore her best socks and put her hair back with a ribbon. She asked God to help her friend Sam and bring him peace. He needed that.

Hardy and Mary Alice met up after their mission and took a chance that Sam would be in the chicken coop. The Lord worked fast—Sam was there.

"Whatcha doin'?" she asked him.

"Nothin'."

Hardy spoke up. "Do you feel different?"

"No."

This was disappointing. "Ya wanna skip rocks?"

"No."

Mary Alice tried. "What about a picnic? I could get us sandwiches and we could eat it in here."

There was a hesitation before Sam nodded. "Okay."

"You stay with him," she told Hardy before she disappeared. She ran home and was in such a hurry she walked on her mother's clean floor with her boots. Mary screeched, "Wipe your feet!"

"I can't. I have to get sandwiches so we can eat in the chicken coop. It's the first time Sam has agreed to do something with us. I think our prayers worked. Can you help me?"

Mary Alice was back to the coop in a jiffy with three ham sandwiches, a bottle of milk, and three pieces of apple cake in a bag. "Here. Stuff your face."

The three of them munched away, and while they didn't say much, it felt nice to do something normal together.

Mary Alice took a chance. "What were you and the Waddens' nephew fighting about?"

"He said his cat died so he knew how I felt." Sam turned his head and spit into the straw.

"A cat?!" Mary Alice huffed. "What a stupid thing to say."

Hardy looked thoughtful. "Maybe he was trying to be nice."

Sam and Mary Alice threw him dirty looks. It was Mary Alice who said, "Losing a cat is not the same as losing a mother, Hardy."

Sam hung his head and big tears rolled down his cheeks. The other two weren't sure what to do, until finally Mary Alice gave him a hug. It only lasted a moment or two before Sam got on his knees and crawled out the door without a word.

"I guess we're going to have to pray again next week," Hardy said.

Aisling and I were sitting on lobster traps outside of Edgar's shack. Fishermen are always getting ready for the season if they're not fishing. But Edgar was spending a lot of time here instead of in the house, and his children were unhappy. The trouble was Edgar was miserable too, and didn't know what to do. And the men he fished with didn't have much to say other than it was a goddamn shame, and would he like a swig from their bottle?

That was the moment Gladdie appeared. She was smiling as she bent down and whispered in her husband's ear. He suddenly sat down on a sawhorse and rubbed his thumbs over his eyes, whether to wipe away tears or ease his tired mind. Then he looked up and out over the water. "I miss you."

His daughter approached with a thin sweater on. She was pale and worn out. "Da, I've nothing for supper. We need more supplies."

Gladdie held the both of them close. After a minute Edgar slapped his hands on his knees and said, "Don't you worry, I'll sort it."

Sam had a vivid dream that night of his mother standing by the end of his bed. She was beautiful, shining, and said she loved him very much and wanted him to be happy.

He got better after that. Mary Alice and Hardy assumed it was the very real mental effort they put in talking to God every week that brought about the change. Sam never told them about his mother's visit. He kept that close to his heart.

As for me, I tried to connect with Gladdie, and made an effort to be near her, but she would know I was coming and turn away, disappearing into the clouds. Her way of letting me know she wanted to be by herself. I wasn't surprised and wished her well.

CHAPTER FOUR

It was the summer the three friends were ten, in 1932, when Mary Alice saw Aisling for the first time. Perhaps Aisling broke through the veil because she was angry.

It happened on a warm, windy day. The fishing boats were out in the water as it was the end of lobster season. Because of the stiff breeze, they were tossed to and fro as the white-tipped chop slapped against their sides. The kind of sea that makes it difficult when a boat drops anchor fifty yards from the beach and you have to transfer into a dory or skiff and row to shore.

This manoeuvre can be alarming. A small dory bounces and bobs, and the men who handle these boats have to be experts, their movements flowing with the sea rather than against it. No one likes getting wet, and scrambling over rock-weeded stones at the head of the landing is slightly smoother when there's a small conch, a round of wood almost like a drum, with an iron crank that pulls a small boat up over the rocks.

Nothing is easy here.

Despite the blustery conditions, Mary Alice asked her mother to let her go swimming, she was so hot and bothered after crouching in the fields picking strawberries. She hated it, and the thought of having to harvest bakeapples in bogs full of swarming bugs in August was not helping her mood. The fact that Rose was still at it was annoying. Why did she love it so much? Sam and Hardy never had to pick berries. Their sisters did it. Not for the first time, she wished she was a boy.

Her mother was in her garden by the side of the house, picking weeds and tsking over the crows eating all her sprouting seeds. "I think you're foolish," she said. "The water's still right cold."

"There's kids down there, Ma."

"Oh, go on with ya then. You can't be told."

Mary Alice joined the others playing about near the shore. The strong wind made her skin cold when she popped up out of the water, but it was so refreshing after sweating all afternoon. Sam was messing around splashing water at Flossie and her sister, and Hardy was doing handstands in the water. He wasn't very good at it.

She propelled herself through the water like a loon taking off and stopped in front of Sam. "Hey."

"Hey."

"Wanna meet up after supper? In the new hiding place?"

Sam looked around as if not sure what to say. "I'm playing stickball."

"Can I come?"

Flossie laughed. "It's only for the boys. Don't you know anything? And you're too old to have a hiding place."

Mary Alice dove and swam away under the water so her hot cheeks didn't betray her. She wanted to give Flossie a good kick. Or maybe it was Sam, seeing as how he looked almost embarrassed and didn't stick up for her.

She bumped into Hardy and they both scrambled to the surface, wiping their wet hair out of their eyes. "Watch where you're going!" she said.

"I wasn't going anywhere. You swam into me."

Mary Alice had no answer for that, so she blurted the first thing on her mind: "Are you playing stickball with the boys later?"

"Probably not. I'm not great at it and I'm always picked last."

"They should let girls play. I'd be so good."

"They do. Anyone can play."

Mary Alice hit the water with the palms of her hands. "I'm gonna throttle that one."

"Who?"

"Never mind. I can do a handstand too, you know. Count how long I stay under?"

She held her breath and kept her legs in the air so long, Hardy got worried. He was just about to grab her foot when she came up, sputtering. "How many seconds?"

"I forgot to count."

"Oh, you!"

Hardy had goosebumps on his arms. "I'm cold. I'm going in."

"Suit yourself."

Once he left, she did another handstand. She started to count but got distracted when a large crab scuttled by. She loved opening her eyes under water. Something else her ma told her not to do. She decided to start over and took a deep breath before disappearing again.

Mary Alice felt a sharp prick on her finger. That darned crab. But there was no crab in sight. It was something under the sand. She reached down and picked up a scoop of it and watched it melt away in her hand. What was left was Ma's sterling silver lily-of-the-valley hairpin, very tarnished and forlorn, but still hers.

Mary Alice didn't know what it was, but it looked like treasure. She ran onto the beach and sat on a warm rock to examine it. Except for being mostly black, it was very pretty. Her first thought was to show Sam that she had treasure too, but she changed her mind. And then she looked up and saw a little girl with red hair standing on the water, not in it. She beckoned Mary Alice to come to her before she disappeared before her eyes.

Mary Alice ran back to the house.

The low grumbling in the distance was Aisling. She showed her displeasure by having thunder roll in. Youngsters sometimes don't know what's appropriate and will lash out. That was our mother's hairpin and she wanted it. But the truth is, I was upset too, seeing it in such a dreadful state. I'd imagined it would still be shiny silver.

My old life was truly gone.

I was always with Mary Alice, but it had been a while since I'd spoken to her. It was fine when she was younger. She wasn't afraid. But as she grew, I was aware that it would be difficult for her to understand, so I kept myself hidden. I knew she still sensed me. At times she'd say, "I'm glad you're here."

She'd never told anyone about me, afraid they would think she was odd. An imaginary friend is fine when you're three. It's not when you're ten.

She was rattled seeing Aisling standing in the water like that, but whereas she hid me from her family, Aisling's appearance was completely different. She was breathless when she burst in the front door. Her mother had finished weeding and Mrs. Spencer was over having a cuppa.

"You'll never guess what I saw!"

"What?" both women said at the same time.

"A little girl standing on the water. She was walking on the water!"

The ladies glanced at each other with smirks on their faces. "Is that so?" her mother said.

"She had long red hair and was wearing a dress down to her ankles. She wanted me to come to her."

"I'm glad you didn't. I'd miss you," Mary said.

"I think she was a ghost!"

"Plenty of spirits around this island." Mrs. Spencer nodded, before taking one last puff and stubbing out her cigarette. "You ask Old Joe. He's seen spectres everywhere. Says there's one up in that old eagle's nest, and he seen a monk behind him when he was out chopping wood."

As Mary Alice's eyes grew bigger, Mary shook her head at Mrs. Spencer, who got the message and fell quiet.

"I'm sure it was just the sun on the water," Mary said. "It happens all the time. What's in your hand?"

Mary Alice looked down, having forgotten about her treasure. "I found this. I don't know what it is but it looks old." She passed it to her mother.

"That's very old. It's been in the water a long time."

"What is it?"

Mrs. Spencer answered. "That's a hairpin. You don't see them as often as you used to. It's tarnished, but I bet a little rubbing with soapy water will take that off. But be careful. It looks fragile."

Mary Alice was delighted with the results. Her hairpin was now silver. Not exactly shining, but a vast improvement. She tried to put her hair up with it but it didn't work every well. It felt like it would break in half, so she put it on the little dresser under the window and spent quite a while admiring it. So much better than an old lamp.

In the morning, she bounced out of bed, which woke up two of her sisters. They groaned with annoyance and covered their heads with their pillows. Mary Alice went to the dresser and her hairpin was gone. She blinked and looked harder, as if that would bring it back.

"Where's my hairpin?! Who took it?" She went over to the bed and threw back the sheet covering the thieves.

Rose sat up. "No one took your hairpin. Stop shouting."

"It didn't walk away by itself." She ran out of the room and went to get her mother, who was already outside hanging up clothes. "Ma, the girls took my pin." That's when she realized she had to pee and ducked into the outhouse, with its pungent aroma of lime and waste. No one ever lingered there. She tore a page out of the Eaton's catalogue, wiped herself, and sent it through the hole into the depths. She threw open the door and continued her tirade. Her mother finally said, "Enough! The girls didn't steal your pin. If it's lost that's your fault. You were supposed to take care of it, so lesson learned."

Of course, we know who took it.

I sensed her in the billowing clouds that sat in the sky that morning. Great mounds that looked like castles on top but were flat on the bottom.

"Ah here now, Aisling! Don't you be startin'!" I was annoyed.

"It's under the bureau. It fell off, so it did."

"With your help."

"I can touch it. It's Ma's, not hers."

"And she was the one who found it so you can look at it. That must count for something."

"You sound like Ma. Don't be harpin' at me."

"Leave it alone from now on. Go swim with the swordfish."

"They're nicer than you are." The words came floating over to me as she escaped.

Aisling continued to act up. One day Mary Alice found the hairpin on the windowsill and another morning it was on the washstand. Now even her sister Rose believed her when she said the hairpin was haunted.

"There was a ghost on the water the day I found it and I bet it's her who's playing tricks."

Rose looked unnerved. She was thirteen and infinitely more mature than Mary Alice, but she didn't like the idea of a ghost. "That means the ghost is wandering around this bedroom at night?"

"I know! I'm going to stay awake tonight and catch her," Mary Alice cried.

"And what would you do if you saw a spirit?"

"Tell this one to stop trying to steal my hairpin."

Mary Alice sat up in bed in the dark, with only the lamp from downstairs throwing a little light into the small room where she and her sisters slept. She held her mother's rolling pin in case she needed it. Ma would be annoyed if she knew. She loved that thing for some reason.

Naturally she thought she had stayed awake all night. That's what it felt like, but Rose informed her that she was snoring when Rose got out of bed.

"You could've offered to help!" Mary Alice shouted.

"Not my hairpin, as you keep telling us."

Her mother yelled up the stairs. "Anyone seen my rolling pin?"

All the tasks on Scatarie ate up a day, but salting cod was a long process. Every one of them had to be split, cleaned, salted, hung for two weeks to dry, and then washed and dried again.

Women and older children helped their menfolk with this and it was extremely frustrating when a cloudburst happened. It was nothing to be in the middle of a conversation, see a dark cloud, and hightail it down to the shore to keep the fish dry. It was a fact of life. You could hang the gutted fish up dangling from rope, or place them on racks of wire in the sun, and let the ocean breeze help the process along.

Mary was down near the fishing shacks helping her husband, Tom, with his catch. Edgar and his son Bob and daughter Jean were doing the same thing. Mary stopped for a drink of water from the glass bottle she'd taken with her. She thought Jean looked tired and sweaty and offered her some.

The girl drank greedily and wiped her mouth. "Thanks."

Mary lowered her voice. "How are you fellas getting along?"

Jean glanced at her dad. "Okay, I guess. Da tries his best. Bob's a big help to him and Ian is a big help to me."

"What about Sam? He's not around as much."

Jean turned the fish fillets over. "To be truthful, he's a handful. He doesn't listen to a thing I say. Says I'm not his mother."

"It's hard for the youngest. He didn't have as much time with his mother as you and your brothers did."

"Mary, would you talk to him? He probably misses having a woman talk to him, not that Mom did a lot of that in her last year. I think he could use some advice. When I say something, he's embarrassed, but he needs to know a few things, like how to handle all the attention he's getting from girls. They don't leave him alone. Especially since the Waddens' nephew left."

"Sure, I'll speak to him. Whether he listens or not is another thing." She looked at Tom and saw that they were nearly done. "Why don't I go up to your place now, since you two are down here? Anyone home?"

"No, Ian's helping Old George with his nets. He's got arthritis."

"This is as good a time as any then."

"Thanks, Mary."

Mary took another swig from the bottle and stretched her back. She waved to Tom and went up the hill. It would give her an opportunity to see what was going on inside their house.

She knocked on the door and pushed it open. Doors were never locked here. "Hello?"

Their house was the same as Mary's. Not large, grey shingled, with one main space acting as the sitting room and eating area, the kitchen with the wood stove at the rear. Two small bedrooms were upstairs. Edgar had a cot in a small room just off to the side, almost under the stairs. There was a curtain instead of a door.

It was obvious Jean tried to keep it tidy, but living with her father and three brothers was a losing battle. Everything was dusty and drab. There was no colour anywhere. It might as well have been a fish shack, but it kept the rain off their heads. A place to eat and sleep and be with each other, so it did its job. It just felt forlorn.

Mary decided she would crochet a colourful throw for the settee and she'd get Annie Campbell to make one of her rag rugs. Why hadn't she thought of this before?

"Sam! Are you here? It's Mary Locke."

There was no answer. "Sam! I want to speak to you. Don't leave me waiting."

She heard a stirring from upstairs. It wasn't like him to be in the house on a glorious September day. She was surprised Edgar hadn't insisted he join them drying the fish, but maybe he didn't have the strength to argue with a mopey child.

Mary wished she'd thought of bringing over some cookies. She'd get Mary Alice to deliver some when the family got home for supper.

By the time Sam stood in front of her, she'd dropped into a chair. A tortoise was faster than that child.

"How are ya keepin,' son?"

He looked down. "All right."

"Enjoying school this year? I can't believe you three are in grade five."

"It's all right."

She pointed at him. "Sit down, please. I'm not the Mounties come to arrest ya. I wanted to make sure you were okay."

He sat and gave her a suspicious look. "Did Jean send you here?"

No point in lying. "She's worried about you and that makes you lucky. It means you matter to her."

He stuck out his chin. "She don't need to be worryin' about me. I can take care of myself."

"A young fella your age, things might seem confusing. Especially when you're dealing with girls. And I hear a lot of them like you."

"What's wrong with that? Mary Alice likes me."

Mary smiled. "I know she does. As a friend. Any of these other girls wanting you to kiss them, that sort of thing?"

His cheeks went blood red. "No."

She put her hand on his shoulder. "There's nothing wrong with that, but you're still young. Trouble is, you grow up real quick, and if you get too close to a girl, things can happen. You have to be careful and keep yourself to yourself until you're old enough to understand what it all means. You do know about the birds and the bees?"

"I'm not a little kid. I've been around animals all my life and there's always someone who wants to tell you all about it."

Mary sighed. "That's true. But they're usually the ones who don't know much. If you have any questions, ask your father or your brothers. Everything you're feeling is something they've been through. And your sister has your best interests at heart. She's a lovely girl. You'd do well to listen to her."

He made a face but nodded. Mary slapped the table. "Okay. That's enough yappin' for today. I'll send Mary Alice over with some cookies later." She got to her feet and started out the door when she heard, "Those ones you make with coconut in them?"

She turned her head. "Coming right up."

I love the colours in October. When you look at the island from above, it's like a muted patchwork quilt. The mainland is more vibrant thanks to their birch trees, maples, and oak. We have more spruce and fir trees, but the fields of berries and the leaves on the rose bushes turn an eye-catching scarlet, while the grasses turn yellow, brown, and rust. It's the earth's last hurrah, a gift before the world becomes cold and white. Aisling isn't as enamoured as I am with these things. She shrugs it off before she twirls away.

At least Mary Alice loved colours. She collected leaves and pressed them in her scribbler. Miss MacDougall got after her, when she picked up her lesson only to have crumbs of leaves scatter around her desk.

It took the whole month of September and halfway through October before Miss MacDougall decided that Hardy's problem in school wasn't that he wasn't paying attention, like Sam. She deduced he couldn't see very well, and confirmed it one day when she asked him to stay after class. He thought he was getting in trouble, and Sam and Mary Alice made sure they hung around outside so they could get the dirt.

Miss MacDougall was fond of Hardy. He was an odd duck in some ways, a nice boy who was quiet and kind. But because he didn't make waves, he was easily ignored by the other kids. He was the sort that might have been bullied, but he had two things going for him: He was big, and he was Sam's best friend. No one would dare touch him; Sam would knock their head off. So would Mary Alice, for that matter. She wasn't afraid to push people around.

Miss MacDougall wrote a sentence on the board with large letters: *The quick brown fox jumped over the lazy dog.*

Hardy read it out loud. Then she wrote another sentence, and another, in increasingly smaller lettering. He only got two more before he had to admit he couldn't do it. Miss MacDougall wasn't surprised, but Hardy was. She sat at her desk and wrote a note. Then she got up and handed it to Hardy. "I want you to give this to your parents. I think I know why you've been struggling of late. Your eyesight is not what it should be. Once they know, I'm sure they'll sort it."

Hardy joined the other two outside. They were digging in the dirt for worms and Sam was putting them in his pocket for bait.

"Was she mad at ya?" Mary Alice asked.

"No. She thinks my eyes are bad."

"Bad?" Sam repeated. "What do ya mean? They look okay to me."

"I couldn't see the writing on the board."

Mary Alice pushed his shoulder. "You don't mean you might need glasses like old man Spencer?!"

Hardy shrugged. "I dunno."

The three of them walked along, a bit dumbfounded. They didn't know any kids who wore glasses. That was for grandparents. They tried to make their friend feel better, because he looked a little scared.

"Can you see the crow in that tree?" Sam pointed.

"No."

He didn't feel better. Mary Alice took a peppermint out of her pocket and held it in front of her. "Can you see this?"

"Yes."

"There! Ya see? Your eyes are just fine. Here. Have the peppermint."

Hardy took it and walked beside them quietly. He didn't feel like hanging around, so he said he was going home. The other two watched him go.

"Think he'll be all right?" Mary Alice wondered.

"Yeah. Maybe that's my problem," Sam said. "I can't see the writing on the board either."

"That's because you're too busy lookin' every which way but where you're supposed to."

Sam grinned. "You sound like the teacher. Hey, Jean told me that Miss MacDougall is getting married to the oldest Ferguson brother. We'll have to call her Mrs. Ferguson."

Mary Alice picked up some yellow leaves. "Nope. Once she's married, she can't teach no more. We'll be getting someone new. Could be a man."

"I hope not."

Hardy didn't show the note to his parents until after their codfish supper. He wasn't sure why he was so nervous, but it was upsetting to think that something on his body wasn't working right. The family was working its way through his mother's famous apple pie when he passed the note to his dad.

Len looked at it, looked at Hardy, and then looked at Annie. He didn't say anything.

Annie took the note and read it. "I didn't know you were having a problem at school. Dorothy, you never said anything."

Dorothy looked surprised. "I didn't know either. What's wrong?"

"Miss MacDougall thinks he needs glasses. You can't see the writing on the board, Hardy?"

"Not really."

"Why didn't you say anything?" His mother looked concerned.

Hardy shrugged. "I thought it was normal."

"And here I thought your squinting was just a bad habit. I feel terrible. Well, we're going to have to take you to Glace Bay to an eye doctor and do it before the winter sets in."

For the first time since he'd received the news, he cheered up. "A trip to Glace Bay? Can we take Sam and Mary Alice with us? They don't get off the island much either. We'd have to take the train, right?"

"Yes, but I don't know..." Annie said.

"Please, Mom!"

So that's how my three ended up going on an adventure together. They'd all been to Main-à-Dieu at some point in their lives, visiting relatives, but trips to Glace Bay were few and far between. Annie called the eye doctor from the lighthouse phone, and because he could only see Hardy on a weekday, they had to get permission from Miss MacDougall to miss school. It would be an overnight adventure, since by the time they got to Glace Bay on the train, had the appointment, travelled back to the station in Louisbourg, and took the bus back to Main-à-Dieu, it would be too dark to cross the water.

Len's sister would put them up for the night. She said the boys could sleep under the kitchen table and Mary Alice could have the chair. Annie would share her niece's bed.

It wasn't too windy that morning, which was a blessing as far as Mary was concerned. It was a tug to see Mary Alice waving to her as the boat left the shore and disappeared from view. Annie reassured her that she would take good care of them. Their happy faces made Mary feel better. She sometimes wondered if she and Tom were doing the right thing, staying on Scatarie. The children were truly isolated. Her sons wanted to be fishermen like their da, but what of Mary Alice? Her sisters were contented souls, but she was bigger than life. Mary would do everything she could to see that she had a chance. Of all of them, Mary Alice was the one who'd go far.

One of the Waddens took Annie and the children across, since Len had to stay with the lighthouse. As they approached the tittle, an area of water between Main-à-Dieu and Scatarie, the boat really began to sway. The water was notoriously tough here. Naturally, the wee ones loved it. Annie had a hard time keeping Sam from getting too close to the side. She wasn't so worried about him falling in, he was used to boats, but he was doing his best to get as wet as possible in the spray. I stayed next to Mary Alice.

She finally got cross with him. "Sam, if I have to talk to you again, I'll put you on the wharf and leave you there while the rest of us go to Glace Bay."

He finally stopped his foolishness, but he still had a big grin on his face. Getting out of school for two days was a dream. Going anywhere was a thrill for all of them.

Main-à-Dieu came into view. The imposing wharf and the tied-up fishing boats were the first things you saw, with the houses in and around the rocky hills jumbled every which way as if dropped from a great height.

The boat pulled up to the side of the wharf and a fisherman who happened to be there took hold of the rope Mr. Wadden threw it to him and lashed it to the cleat. The iron ladder they had to climb to get to the top seemed very long. Naturally Sam and Mary Alice scrambled up no problem. Annie was a bit hesitant, so Hardy went after his mom, in case she slipped. The fisherman at the top held out his hand for her as she jumped over the edge. Then Mr. Wadden threw up her overnight bag. The fisherman caught it and passed it to her. She was grateful.

"Thank you so much!" she shouted down to Mr. Wadden.

"Aye." He came up the ladder then too. "I got a list from the wife while I'm here."

None of the friends had been on a train before. They were used to speed, from being on boats, but the train was a different animal, its wheels click-clacking under their feet. Their faces were pressed against the windows as they chugged through the countryside of endless trees and glimpses of water.

"I wish we had a train on Scatarie," Mary Alice said. "We'd get to school in five minutes."

"If we had a train on the island, the last place I'd go is school," Sam said.

Annie had packed a lunch, so she passed around cheese sandwiches wrapped in wax paper and gave them milk to drink. The conductor came to get their tickets just as Annie was passing out the crumb cake. Most of the topping landed on the floor by his shoes. He looked down and made a face. Annie's cheeks reddened. When the conductor moved away, Mary Alice looked up at Annie. "I think he's mad at us."

When they got off in Glace Bay, the noise was deafening to our friends. The only rumble they ever heard on the island was thunder or the rolling surf. Here there were cars and trams with people scurrying about. Whistles, bells, shunting trains in the railyard. It was all a bit overwhelming for them. Not for me, I've been to the big city of Montreal to visit my family many times.

Mary Alice looked around. "Can you imagine living here? Do you see how big the world is?"

"This is only a town," Annie told her. "There are cities a thousand times bigger than this. I went to Halifax once when I was a girl. Now that was big."

Instead of paying for a cab, they walked to the eye doctor's office, which was off Commercial Street. Hardy hadn't said anything in about an hour, so the others knew he was nervous. Mary Alice slipped her hand into his to reassure him. When he was finally called in, he looked back at them as if he was walking the plank. "You'll be fine!" his mother called out.

When he disappeared behind the door, she said, fretting, "Oh, I do hope he won't have to wear really thick lenses. Kids can be so mean."

"I'll take care of him," Sam informed her.

Mary Alice didn't want to be left out. "I will too!"

Annie smiled at them. "I can always count on you two."

When Hardy emerged, he looked much better. "That didn't hurt at all. I had to look at stuff through a lens. I thought they'd stick needles in my eyes."

Hardy definitely needed glasses, but his mother's fears of a thick lens didn't happen. It was only the two of them who went back to get the glasses a week later. When they got home again and stepped off the boat, Mary Alice and Sam were there. They looked at Hardy with astonishment. His glasses were round and they absolutely suited him, as if he should have been wearing them his whole life.

"Hot dog!" Sam said. "You look like you're smart."

"What can you see?" Mary Alice wanted to know.

Hardy said, smiling, "I can see your faces clearly, you're not fuzzy. Gotta show my dad, and I want to see Buster." He ran ahead of his mother as she smiled and headed home.

Mary Alice crossed her arms. "I want glasses."

CHAPTER FIVE

There is a huge difference between a ten-year-old and a fifteen-year-old. In 1937 I could barely recognize my Christmas infants.

I was in my eagle's nest listening to the night sounds. The owl nearby, the soft rustle of a deer passing through, the screech of a fox, and always, always the surf. It's my companion, my refuge, my world. And yet, lately I had been uneasy. There was something weighing on me and it was an unusual sensation. You see, we are not always blissful throughout this death experience. The world emanates vibrations and it can be an unsettled ride. We do see the whole picture and know everything will pass, but it can occasionally be a challenge to let go of earthly emotions.

And that's what I was trying to do on that dark night with twinkling stars.

Then it came to me. Mary Alice, Sam, and Hardy were now the same age I was when I died. And I realized that my earthly life was not long enough. They would now experience things I'd never partaken in. There was a childish jealousy I was trying to deny. I was feeling sorrow.

That had never happened before. I'd never been close enough. I was always very good at observing people, but now I was living with them and through them. It started with Mary Alice's red hair. For whatever reason, these children spoke to me. Some things can't be explained properly.

Their fifteen years had been fulfilling ones for me, watching them grow and seeing who they'd become. And not much had changed. They were all true to themselves. Their friendship was constant, even if it could be challenging.

Hardy was exactly the same. Easygoing, and took his time. He got new glasses, not quite as round as his first ones but they still suited him. He was over six feet tall, which irritated Sam, but Sam had plenty of assets. A cheeky personality and a natural charm that made the opposite sex swoon. His icy blue eyes were the cherry on the cake. He took risks and didn't like authority. He was still driving his sister Jean mad.

Mary Alice was who she'd always been. She was outspoken and curious and disliked people who put on airs. Her hair was divine and much thicker, but she was not. A thin straight line, with no bosom to speak of. Her long arms and legs were always moving, usually running away or towards something with equal enthusiasm. She was bright and she talked non-stop, but her conversations were interesting and thoughtful. She spent a lot of nights in her rocking chair listening to the radio. That or reading everything she could get her hands on.

Her mother gave up trying to get her interested in domestic pursuits like cooking and baking. Mary Alice usually forgot to eat. Mary every so often had to screech to get her to sit down and she'd pull up beside her until Mary Alice polished off a plate of scrambled eggs. Anything to get some nourishment into the girl.

Having her daughter come out of the oven underdone was Mary's great guilt, only relieved by seeing Mary Alice chew. That drove Mary Alice foolish. She even resorted to keeping food in her mouth and spitting it down the hole of the outhouse.

I had battles of wills with my mother, but I never won. Of course, parents in the 1830s expected to be obeyed.

It was May, a month and a half until the end of the school term. The last one for Mary Alice and Hardy. The school only offered an education to grade ten, and Mary Alice was going to miss it terribly. She even asked if she could become the new teacher. Everyone hated the man who was doing it. He wasn't that interested in them. Sam quit school back in eighth grade to go fish with his dad and brothers. Mary Alice and Hardy were surprised he'd lasted that long. Sam belonged outside on the water hauling traps.

The familiar route from school to home was the place for most of their conversations. The younger kids passed them now in their hurry to get home. This was when they missed Sam the most. It was harder to get together. There wasn't much time for lollygagging at this age. Hardy's dad was passing on his knowledge of the lighthouse to him and his sister Dorothy. Their older brother wasn't that well; he was usually tired and was finally diagnosed with an irregular heartbeat. He would not become a lightkeeper.

"Rose is getting married to Jeb Trimm. Mother is pleased, thinking Rose would be a spinster. She's only just eighteen."

"My oldest sister got married at sixteen," Hardy said.

"Ellen had to, Hardy. I'm not interested in that nonsense."

Hardy gave her a sideways look. "There's plenty of fellas who'd like to step out with you but you won't give them the time of day."

Mary Alice shifted her books to her other arm. "Everyone around here is a snooze."

"Oh, thanks."

She elbowed him. "Not you. You're my Hardy. If anything happened to you, I'd die."

"Is that so?" Hardy smiled.

They kept walking side by side. "Sam's not a snooze, is he? He's always up for an adventure. I worry about him sometimes."

"Sam will be all right," said Hardy. "He thinks of himself first."

When they got to the shore, Sam's dad Edgar's boat was in and Sam was on the beach, so they wandered down to see him. Mary Alice took in his windblown sandy blond hair, stiff from the salt breeze. With his flannel plaid jacket on, he looked like a real fisherman, now that he was filling out because of the hours of manual labour. He seemed ten years older. Whenever Mary Alice saw him now her heart gave a little bump, but she would deny it to the death.

They were chatting about nothing of consequence when Hardy happened to glance up. His face registered shock. "What is that?"

Sam and Mary Alice looked where he was pointing and they too couldn't grasp what they were seeing. It was a cross between a bloated aluminum-coloured submarine and a gigantic balloon flying slowly across the sky.

Edgar held his hand to his forehead to block out the sun. "That's a zeppelin! Unbelievable!"

It was going at a leisurely pace and low enough that they could make out the heads of people looking out the windows. There were also ropes hanging down.

By then a crowd had gathered, everyone excited to see the spectacle. Edgar pointed. "Look at the swastikas on the back of it. That's a German airship."

This sent a tremble of fear through the adults. They watched it for almost ten minutes before it disappeared. It was a marvellous, terrible sight.

"I'm gonna fly something like that someday!" Sam declared.

Mary Alice danced around. "If that's from Germany, they had to fly across the ocean! There must be beds in there, and they must have a dining room, so that means they'd have a cooker. And a bathroom! Can you imagine?"

"I wouldn't be caught dead in that thing," Hardy muttered.

The very next day, May 6, it was all over the radio that the

German airship *Hindenburg* became a gigantic fireball while trying to land in Lakehurst, New Jersey. Thirty-six people were killed but miraculously sixty-two passengers and crew survived. When everyone eventually saw the picture of it in flames in the newspaper, no one could believe anyone got out alive.

"We saw some of their heads in those windows," Sam said with awe. "I wonder if they lived or died. Imagine seeing someone just a day before they die. And they didn't know they were going to die."

"Stop saying 'die'!" Mary Alice shouted. "It's upsetting to know that they looked at us and now some of them...aren't living."

When the school year, and school itself for the graduating class, ended a few weeks later, Flossie's mother decided to have a party for the kids twelve and up, only because Flossie's sister Rita was twelve and she would've raised a stink if it was only for the graduates. There would be music and dancing and plenty of homemade goodies. Sam was invited even though he wasn't in school. The girls were hoping he would come.

Mary Alice asked her mother to put up her hair, but she couldn't use my hairpin because she had lost it. At some point it had disappeared, and she was annoyed, but life went on and she forgot about it.

I knew she would, and I was tired of Aisling's moaning. I took it and put it in the eagle's nest, so Aisling could have access to it whenever she wanted. She was right. It didn't mean very much to Mary Alice, but it meant a lot to us. It was the first time I'd done anything like that, and it wasn't easy. Moving anything in the living world requires mental strength and often I'm too scatterbrained to do it. It's easier to appear in front of an object than to move it around.

Again, a feeling of sorrow hit me when I saw Mary Alice's hair up off her slender neck. I remembered the sailor and how I felt when he looked at me. I'd been kissed before, awkward encounters in an alley and behind a barn, but the way I felt when his eyes were on me was something new. And Mary Alice's silhouette brought it flooding back.

She was excited until she realized that her dress was grey and drab. "Rose! Can I borrow your green cardigan with the lace collar?"

Rose was downstairs on a stool plucking a chicken. "Don't you get anything on it!"

"I won't."

There was a small mirror in their bedroom that only showed her face, and Mary Alice spent a great deal of time in front of it turning this way and that so see how her hair looked. She was pleased with it. She wondered if Sam would notice it.

Before she went out the door her mother called her back. Mary Alice waited impatiently, expecting to be told to eat something. But her mother came close and pulled her hand out of the pocket of her apron. She held up the only red lipstick she owned. "Want a little?"

Mary Alice was delighted. "Are you sure?"

"I'm only going to give your bottom lip a light swipe. You don't need more than that. Did you know that Hank Lahey was here the other day wondering if you were around?"

"What did he want?"

"To spend time with you, I imagine. He's a nice lad."

"He's as old as dirt."

"He's seventeen."

"Stop trying to marry me off, Ma."

As she walked to the party, our girl was in a good mood. She told the boys she'd get there on her own. Mary Alice wanted to make an entrance, so she was purposely late. She heard the music as she approached the house. It wasn't a fiddle. Of course Flossie's family had a gramophone.

She opened the door and all the familiar faces from school

were there, some of them dancing in the middle of the room. Her heart sank when she noticed Flossie and Sam cutting a rug and doing it well. Most of the others stopped and watched them and some clapped.

Flossie's mother beckoned her over. "Hello, Mary Alice. Would you like some something to drink?"

"Thank you." She took a glass and put it to her almost red lips. It was tasty but bitter too. Her mother made much better lemonade.

Hardy was standing in the corner, out of the way. He looked like he wanted to be anywhere else. As she came over to him, he gave her a big smile. "Hi. You look nice."

"Thanks. How long have those two been dancing?"

He knew who she was talking about. "Ever since I got here."

"Trust Flossie to show off her underwear in that pleated skirt."

They surveyed the raucous room together, sipping at their drinks. Hardy had a ham roll in his other hand. "These are good. Want one?"

She shook her head.

"Do you ever eat?" he said.

Mary Alice leaned over to him. "What did you say? I can't hear a thing."

"I like your sweater."

"It's not mine. It's Rose's and she said she'd kill me if I spilled anything on it."

"Don't worry, I'll protect you."

"WHAT?"

Hardy shook his head, letting her know it wasn't important.

When the song finally ended everyone clapped and took a breath. Then stupid Rita wound the gramophone up once more and played it again. Sam and Flossie resumed dancing, which irritated Mary Alice. Sam hadn't even seen her, and this lipstick was going to wear off. She put down her glass and held her hand out to Hardy. "Let's dance."

Hardy shook his head, horrified at the suggestion. "I can't dance."

"I can't either, but it sure looks easy. Just flap your arms around like those two showoffs."

He crammed the ham roll in his mouth before Mary Alice took his hand and led him to the middle of the room. Everyone was dancing now, so they blended in to a point. They tried to keep up but eventually they just laughed and began pulling their arms back and forth as they stepped on each other's toes.

That's when Mary Alice noticed Sam looking at her, but she refused to look back. She pretended he wasn't there. When the song ended, they were still laughing and went back to the corner and picked up their glasses to get a refill. Sam followed them while Flossie stood in the middle of the floor.

"Hey guys." Sam grinned. "Looks like you could use some dance lessons."

"From you?" Mary Alice laughed. "Think again." This time she poured the lemonade into Hardy's glass and then her own.

Sam said, "None for me?"

"Oh, I'm sorry. I assumed you'd be a gentleman and get your partner, Flossie, a drink. She's built up a powerful thirst."

The three of them looked back at Flossie, who was fuming by herself.

Sam threw her a look, like *two can play this game*. "You're right." He filled two more glasses and went back to Flossie.

A spot opened up on the couch. "Let's sit," Mary Alice said. Hardy followed her like a puppy and took up a lot of space beside her. She rested her head on Hardy's shoulder. "You're always so comfy. I love that about you."

Hardy looked down and resisted the urge to kiss the top of her head. She kept talking and talking through two more songs and Hardy spent the entire time nodding, like he usually did when Mary Alice was on a roll. Then Sam appeared out of nowhere, reached for her hand, and pulled her up. "Let's dance."

It was still a fast tempo, but Sam put his arm around her waist and held her hand as he twirled her around. How did he know how to dance so well? Mary Alice tried not to make a fool of herself. She was aware of Flossie and Hardy watching them and she was conscious of the fact that she was sweating too much, especially when Sam kept looking at her almost red lips.

They danced the next three dances together, pausing only while the gramophone was wound up again, and it was only when the music stopped so Flossie's mother could serve cake that they noticed Hardy had gone.

"Why didn't he stay? He loves cake," Sam said, frowning. "I'm going to get him a piece and take it to him."

"I can come with you," she said.

"Okay, you get the cake. I have to see a man about a dog."

Mary Alice got three pieces of cake (even with her finicky diet, she'd eat cake), hoping no one would notice, and waited for Sam until she refused to wait any longer. She thanked Mrs. MacCuish, who was a very good hostess, even if she was Flossie's mother. All the kids had had a great time. It was a bright spot in a life of routine. Still. Where was Sam?

Mary Alice stepped outside and it was dusk. She looked around but didn't see him. Where did he go? Maybe she didn't understand and he went on without her to Hardy's. She took a step to look around the side of the house—and there were Sam and Flossie, in each other's arms, kissing up a storm.

Blood rushed to her head and made her dizzy. How annoying that she'd had a good time with Sam, when it obviously didn't matter to him. She dumped his piece of cake on the grass and marched all the way to Hardy's.

Annie opened the door. "Hello, Mary Alice, don't you look pretty."

"Hi, Mrs. Campbell. Hardy forgot to take his cake, so I brought it for him."

"That doesn't sound like Hardy." Annie laughed. "Come on in and I'll get him." She walked through the kitchen and called his name up the stairs. Mary Alice heard loud footsteps coming down. He showed up in the kitchen without his glasses on and wasn't smiling. "You want something?"

Mary Alice was flustered. "Um, I brought you a piece of cake. You left before Flossie's mom cut it. I know you like cake. So..." She held out the piece that was now a bit mangled with hers. "Why don't you take all of it?"

"Thanks." He held the wrapped pieces and didn't move, let alone ask her to sit and talk about the party. She became increasingly uncomfortable.

"I guess I'll go, then."

"Okay, see ya."

He didn't even walk her to the door.

As she walked home, she tried to think of what she'd done wrong. They'd had a good time together. They'd danced and talked, and now he was acting like he hardly knew her.

Well, her so-called friends could go pound sand.

Her parents were listening to the radio when she came through the door. "Did you have a nice time?" her mother asked.

"No."

"Why not?"

"I hate Sam and I hate Hardy." And with that she stomped up the stairs.

Mary shook her head. "I knew this was going to happen one day."

Tom took his pipe out of his pocket. "What are you talking about?"

"They're growing up. They're not kids anymore."

"For pity's sake, woman. Those boys are like her brothers."

Mary smirked. "Once upon a time. Now it's going to be rough sailing."

He lit the bowl of his pipe. "You worry too much."

"Maybe."

Oh, mercy. I knew I would have to stop fretting also. I was more content when the three of them were little ones. Now that they were teenagers, I was in uncharted waters, and I wanted what was best for all of them. Someone was going to get hurt in all this. But then I thought I might be reading too much into it. It was one party.

The trouble is, I was a worrier when I was alive too. That's the other thing I didn't realize, and it would have been helpful if our priest had given us a hint—that the person you were is still with you here. You're not just resting in peace constantly. But then, he wouldn't have known that until he shuffled off this mortal coil himself.

And while this space is infinitely better in terms of knowing why life happens and our place in it, there's a learning curve. The longer you've been on this side, the more content you are. And seeing as how life has been churning for innumerable millennia, my fretting is understandable. I'm relatively new.

But I was invested. These particular life stories on the island claimed my heart. I would be watching. And I'd try not to interfere. Much.

The next day was Sunday. There was no fishing allowed, a welcome day of rest. Not that Sam's father ever rested. The family didn't go to church. Gladdie used to take the kids, but when she got ill, Edgar decided there was no God and stopped taking them.

Why was it that the best fishing days always happened on a Sunday? The sun was shining, the wind was nonexistent, and the water was oily. Water so smooth it was like there was a coating over it. The best waters to catch a swordfish.

Sam got up early and took his slice of buttered bread coated with brown sugar out on the back step, to look at the day. He thought about the night before. He'd kissed plenty of girls in the last couple of years, but nothing really serious. Flossie was all business. He'd heard of French kissing, but how she learned about it was a mystery. He was torn. He liked Flossie to a point. Trouble was, he forgot about her bad qualities when she put her lips on his.

This must be what Mary Alice's mother meant when she said if you get too close to a girl, things can happen. You have to be careful and keep yourself to yourself. Sam wasn't sure he'd be able to do that.

As he licked his sugared fingers he pictured Mary Alice with her hair up. She didn't look like one of the boys, even if she didn't have any curves. And for some reason it had bothered him to see her dance with Hardy.

Speaking of Hardy, he thought maybe they could go shoot some crows. People hung them up near their gardens to discourage other crows from eating their produce. Sam took the old rifle his dad gave him and walked over to Hardy's place, forgetting that the family would be in church. He had to wait out on their porch until the service was over, but he couldn't stand doing nothing, so he shot at a few seagulls, but didn't hit any.

Hardy opened the door of the boathouse and looked around. His father had elbowed him to go see who was shooting at this time of day. Sam was glad to see him.

"Hey. You almost finished in there? Wanna go get some crows?"

"Just a sec." Hardy went back in, presumably to get permission to leave church early, and reappeared just as quickly. "Okay, then."

The two of them walked the road until they got past the level, then hit the edge of the woods and tramped through the spruce, kicking at the underbrush.

Sam looked over at his friend. "You're not sayin' much."

"Nothin' to say."

"The party was okay."

"Yep."

Sam stopped. "Where did you go, anyway? You were there one minute and then gone."

Hardy pushed a branch away of his face. "I'm not much for dancing."

"You could've said goodbye. We were wondering where you went. I wanted to bring you some cake, but I got distracted."

Hardy said, "Doing what?"

Sam spun around and broke a thick rotten branch under his feet. "That Flossie sure can kiss. You should try her. You won't regret it; I nearly lost my tongue."

"Sounds unappetizing."

Sam reached over and patted Hardy's cheek, laughing, "Everything is about food with you."

"Shut up."

They kept moving forward, this time trying to make less noise, so they stopped talking and were a little more careful where they put their feet. Birds were flighty. They were at it for a good half hour. This was why Hardy hated hunting. It was as boring as hell and only a minute of guts and glory, and he didn't like that part either.

He was about to suggest they go home when Sam raised the rifle to his shoulder, pointed at the top branch of a fir tree, and pulled the trigger. A moment after that, he turned slightly and did it again. He whooped in celebration when he went over and picked the two limp crows up high. "Damn, I'm good. Wanna give it a try?"

"No, thanks." Hardy turned away and started walking, so Sam went after him and gave him a shove with the hand holding his prize. "Don't be such a sooky boy. Ya gotta kill things. These little bastards will eat everything if you don't try to stop them. If ya don't like it, why'd ya come?"

Hardy turned to him. "Habit, I suppose. I won't do it again."

Sam gave him an exasperated look. "What's eatin' you? You're my best friend and for some reason you're mad at me. What did I do?"

"Are you my best friend? The only reason you hang around me is to eat my mother's cooking."

Sam looked upset. "You're a shithead, ya know that. At least you still have a mom."

Hardy watched Sam go, dead crows swinging. Now he felt bad.

Mary Alice was outside cleaning her father's fishing clothes in a washtub with a scrub brush. It suited her mood. Rose told her to calm down. "Leave some threads intact."

Her hair was in a braid to keep it from getting wet. She saw Sam coming, carrying dead crows, but his face was like thunder. When she ignored him, he stopped in front of her.

"You should put your hair up more often," he said.

"And why would I listen to the likes of you?"

He sighed in exasperation. "What is wrong with everyone today? First Hardy, now you. What's going on?"

She kept scrubbing. "Oh, I don't know. I guess it was when you left me standing there to deliver cake by myself while you ate Flossie's face off by the side of the house."

"That's it?" His eyes widened. "You're not jealous, are you?"

Mary Alice threw the scrub brush into the tub, creating a splash, before she stood up. "Have you lost your mind? Jealous of Flossie? You think a lot of yourself, Sam Harris. I was annoyed because we made plans and you changed them and didn't tell me. That's not how friends treat each other."

He glanced down at his feet. "Okay, I'm sorry. Hardy's mad at me too."

"He was last night when I took the cake over," she told him.

"He seemed bright enough when he was dancing with you."

Mary Alice slapped her arms against her sides. "I don't care about any of this. If having a party and dancing makes people miserable, then why go? I'm not making that mistake again."

And she disappeared into the house, leaving her dad's clothes in the soapy water.

CHAPTER SIX

Their petty quarrels didn't last. The days flowed by, filled with tasks and chores and helping their families. All of it dictated by the seasons and the demands of living.

On the last few days of lobster fishing that summer, Sam was helping his dad and brother Bob take the traps out of the water. It was a blustery day, and they spent the entire time trying to remain upright, their legs splayed on the deck to stay balanced. It was uncomfortable, and Sam was impatient and in a bad mood when the rain started. He wasn't watching what he was doing and didn't notice his hand wrapped up in a rope until it was too late and he was dragged over the side of the boat. He hit the water hard, and the icy shock took his breath away. He panicked at the thought of the ropes pulling him under and he strained to keep his head above water, knowing the waves were taking him farther from the vessel.

He couldn't really see because of the churning saltwater, but he felt his arm being pulled through the surf. His father and brother were reeling in the rope and managed to pull him up over the side and get him on board.

"Ya okay, boy?" his father asked. "Damn stupid to get yourself tangled like that." They loosened the rope and Sam screamed. His wrist flopped over, obviously broken.

"Fuckin' hell," Edgar said under his breath.

They lost two days with having to go over to Main-à-Dieu, and then Louisbourg to see the doctor. The doctor could come down to the wharf in Main-à-Dieu for bad cases, but a broken wrist could be seen to in his office. Luckily the other men hauled up Edgar's remaining traps, which was a hardship seeing as how they had their own to get out of the water before the season ended. But that's what fishermen did for each other. They were one on Scatarie.

No one was more furious than Sam. He couldn't play baseball. He couldn't swim. He couldn't go duck hunting. He was feeling very sorry for himself. Mary Alice and Hardy sympathized and tried to spend time with him when their work was done, but they were always busy. Hardy's dad had him doing repairs to the boathouse and there was something wrong with a mechanism on the foghorn. It was imperative they get that sorted first. Then he had to help paint the storehouse.

Mary Alice was just as busy picking her dreaded bakeapples and cursing the flies and gods in heaven. Then she had to help her mother make endless jam from all types of the berries they had collected, enough to get them through the winter. They made relish with the tomatoes and cucumbers and onions. Beets would have to be pickled when they were ready, potatoes and turnips stored in the cold cellar, cheese and milk in the well.

At some point her father would slaughter the pig and that would provide meat for the family. But it would also mean her mother boiling the pig's head to make headcheese, a meat jelly that had a lot of nutrition and was quite tasty, but Mary Alice stayed out of the kitchen on pig-head day.

"I've said hi to that pig for months."

"You've cut off the head of a chicken. What's the difference?" her mother asked.

"The pig never pecked my shins."

She was outside on the step doing some mending for her mother while the boiling took place. Steam was coming out of the open door. Sam walked out of his place—her excuse to leave the step and get away from it.

"Hey ya!" She joined him on his step and they both sat. "How's the wrist?"

"Itchy."

"You've only got a few more weeks to wear the cast."

"If I don't cut my arm off first."

She reached over and tousled his hair. "You are such a big baby."

He smiled at her. "Keep doing that. It feels nice. I can't scratch."

"You big dope, you can so. You have a left hand."

Sam sighed and stretched his legs out in front of him. "A useless instrument. It's not effective."

Hardy came over the horizon in a hurry. It wasn't like him to be so spry. Mary Alice yelled first. "What's wrong?"

"You guys seen Buster?"

Sam shook his head. "No. When did you see him last?"

Hardy stopped, out of breath. "Yesterday morning. You know that's not like him."

His friends stood up. "He probably caught the scent of a squirrel and took off after it," Sam reassured him.

"Buster's fourteen. He doesn't run after anything now. And Da had to tell me that often older dogs will just go off when they know their time is up. I coulda hit him. I can't remember my life without that dog."

Mary Alice ran and put the mending back on her step. "We'll help you look."

They spent that September afternoon peering into fishing shacks, sheep enclosures, cow barns, anywhere they could think of, in case Buster got locked in somewhere. They called his name until they were hoarse. That's when Sam put his hands on his waist.

"If he hadn't been venturing far from home lately, most likely he's somewhere around your place."

"We've looked everywhere. Even along the shore."

"Let's go back anyway," Sam suggested. "He's definitely not here."

They walked to the lighthouse and were joined by Dorothy and Hardy's younger brother Fred. They fanned out quite a distance from the house, since there weren't any trees on the property, thanks to the rocky coastline. There was vegetation farther along, bushes and scrub. Mary Alice had her trusty stick for thrashing greenery as they searched.

The sun was getting low in the sky and they were tired and thirsty. Hardy caught up with his pals. "Look, thanks a lot but you don't have to keep looking. He's my dog."

Mary Alice whipped her stick. "He's *our* dog! I can't remember a time without him either."

That's when they heard Dorothy cry out. They ran to her in the underbrush and she pointed. Buster was lying on the ground, obviously dead.

"Oh no," Hardy moaned. He knelt down and picked up his friend. Buster's limp head fell back, revealing dried, caked blood on his neck. Hardy brushed away the fur and they saw a gaping bullet hole. "He's been shot! Who would shoot a dog?"

They were all upset and grappling with the reality of it. "Maybe someone took a shot without looking properly," Sam suggested.

Dorothy was in tears. "Then they should have come to the house and told us. Instead, they ran away and left him to rot."

Mary Alice kept wiping her eyes. "The bastard. The dirty bastard. Buster never hurt anyone."

Hardy put his head against Buster's muzzle and sobbed. Dorothy turned to Hardy's friends. "You better leave him be. Fred and I will take care of him."

Sam took Mary Alice by the shoulder and they walked away in disbelief.

"Who would've done something like that?" Mary Alice said.

Sam shook his head. "Don't kid yourself. There are lots of people who don't give a shit."

She looked up at him. "Really?"

"You and Hardy think the best of everyone, but life's not like that. It's brutal and unfair."

Shuffling along the dirt road, Mary Alice looked behind her. "I wish I could do something. Maybe I'll make Hardy some cookies."

"You hate making cookies."

"But he would like them."

Sam stopped. "I know what I'm gonna do. Find out who did this and beat them into next week."

"Wait. Shouldn't you give Hardy the chance to avenge his dog?"

"You said it yourself. He was our dog."

Mary Alice nodded. "You're right, but I don't think you should be picking fights with people. Not with a bum hand."

"Arrrrrgh. My feet work. I can kick them senseless."

When Mary Alice got back to the house, she was late for supper. Her father said, "What time do you call this?"

She told them about the events of the day. Her parents looked horrified. "You have to be a pretty miserable creature to kill a pet dog," her mom said.

Mary Alice told her she was going to bake cookies for Hardy to make him feel better. Her mother's eyes lit up. "Great. Then you can make some for me."

"I should've kept my mouth shut."

The next morning, Mary Alice suffered her way through the ordeal, getting more flour on the table than in the bowl. Her mother refused to help her. "There's only one way to learn. And sugar cookies are about as simple as you can get."

They both looked at her efforts with dismay. "They're supposed to be round," Mary Alice sighed. "How come they're not?"

"From now on, you only make drop cookies. They don't have to be round."

Mary Alice took her pathetic cookies and strolled to the lighthouse. There was a part of her that didn't want to see Hardy's sad face, but there would be no avoiding it. He'd be sad for a long time.

When Annie answered the door, she gave Mary Alice a downcast look. "He's behind the house, where Buster liked to sit."

"I'm so sorry. I made Hardy some cookies."

Annie smiled. "Why don't you take them to him?"

When Mary Alice reached him, Hardy was sitting on the ground with his arms around his knees, the newly dug grave beside him.

"Hey," she said, sitting down next to him. "I brought you some cookies."

"Thanks." He looked down at the plate. "Is your mother okay?"

She rolled her eyes. "I made them."

"That explains it." He pushed aside the wrapping and put one in his mouth. "Really ugly but really tasty."

She pushed his shoulder, like she always did when she was exasperated with him. When he half smiled, she felt better. "This must have been so hard."

"I can't talk about it."

"Okay."

They sat together and watched the water, forever moving. There were whitecaps today, and grey, wispy clouds scudding across the sky.

"Can you imagine what it would be like not to see the water?" she said finally. "I don't think I'd be able to breathe."

"Me neither."

Mary Alice tugged at the grass beside her. “Do you ever want to leave, Hardy?”

“I wanted to yesterday. But now I can’t because Buster is here. Do you want to leave?”

“Sometimes. But I’m not sure I could live in Glace Bay. It was too loud.”

“Sydney must be worse.”

Hardy ate five cookies, one after the other, and then put them aside. “I’ll save some for tonight. Thank you.”

She reached over and put her arms around his neck. “You don’t deserve this. I’m so sorry. I do love you, Hardy. I can’t stand to see you look so sad.” And she found herself leaning towards him, closer and closer, until her lips were suddenly on his. They were kissing, proper, grown-up kissing, surprising them both.

She pulled away and could feel herself blush. “I better go and help Ma.” Hardy gave her a wave as she leapt to her feet and she started to go, but she turned around and went back to Buster’s grave. “You were a good dog.” She put her hand on the freshly dug earth. Then she took off running.

Hardy watched her go. “Did you hear that, Buster? She loves me.”

Through sheer determination, Sam eventually found out who was responsible for Buster’s sad demise. He had the advantage of hanging around boats and fishing huts and overhearing conversations between the men. That’s where he heard old man Lloyd, practically a hermit, tell his neighbour he’d put a desperate-looking stray dog out of his misery. “Can’t abide seeing something suffer.”

Sam was about to confront the old fella and then he thought about it. Lloyd’s eyesight wasn’t great, and Buster did look kind of ratty lately. Hardy had told him the dog was losing weight, no doubt because of his age.

Should he tell Lloyd? What was he thinking, a stray dog on the island? There was no such thing. But then the poor old guy would feel bad. Should he tell Hardy? What could he do about it? Buster was still dead and nothing was bringing him back. He thought about it and decided to tell him anyway. It was better than thinking someone had done it out of cruelty.

Hardy was grateful to know the truth and thanked Sam for keeping his ear to the ground. But every time he went past Lloyd's shack, he stuck up his middle finger on Buster's behalf.

I wished I could tell them that Buster was just dandy. He loved watching what they were doing. He slept on the end of Hardy's bed still, and Hardy sometimes woke up thinking he could feel Buster jump up like he had when he was alive. He was right; Buster loved doing that even after his death.

Living people can be so irritating. They talk themselves out of the simplest explanation, not believing that what they are wishing for is happening. There always has to be some other explanation. Or they think they're losing their minds. Maybe they are, but their animal intuition is usually spot on. Believe what you see and what you feel. And if that brings you comfort, then so much the better. Take it and be grateful. Life is hard. To be eased for a moment is a gift.

And please know when you visit a grave of a loved one, they're not there when you're not there. You are not leaving them behind.

Now that Buster was brand new again, he was romping over the island with Aisling, and she was delighted.

Just after Christmas in the new year, yet another disaster happened. A collier ran aground off a ledge at the southeast point of Scatarie, Main-à-Dieu passage. All the crew were lost.

Tom, Edgar, Len, Sam, and the other fishermen went down to the shore in the freezing rain and were soon soaked through, hoping they could help, but had to watch the boat drift away in a helpless condition. They were too far off. It wasn't easy to watch and know that all those men were doomed. And when she did ground, the heavy seas and ice floes crushed against her. She was broadside and coated with ice.

When the wind stopped howling the next morning the men went down to the wreck and salvaged what they could. No sense in letting perfectly good items drift away. The authorities would only be able to come to the island and investigate when the weather improved.

Tom found a lamp similar to Sam's. It was still intact, except for the crown. He brought it back to the house. It came in very handy that winter, when the nights were long and dark. But whenever Mary Alice looked at it glowing on the table, she thought about those poor victims. This little jut of land was deadly for so many. It bothered her. Life was so uncertain.

She found out the hard way when Hardy's dad asked him to go over to the lighthouse on the western end of the island to pick up a piece of equipment he needed for his big lamp. The lightkeeper there was named Campbell as well, but no relation, although if you went back far enough everyone was related on Scatarie and Cape Breton Island.

Going anywhere on the island in the winter was a hard slog, especially the seven miles from end to end, but Hardy was taking their horse, Blue, and the cart, the snow wasn't overly deep, and the sun was shining. Hardy asked if Sam and Mary Alice wanted to come with him just for the adventure. Mary Alice's dad said she was allowed as long as they stayed at the lighthouse overnight, so they weren't heading home too late in the day.

The three of them set out in high spirits, as Hardy had put a bell on Blue's harness. Suddenly it felt like Christmas in February. A few little kids outside begged to get on the cart, but they had to leave them behind. Then, who should be walking along the pathway but Flossie and Rita?

Flossie stared at Sam and frowned. "Where you off to?"

"Helping Hardy."

"You better be back by tonight. We've got a party to go to, remember."

Sam waved and Hardy flicked the reins. Mary Alice wasn't above giving Flossie a smirk and a "ta ta" as they continued on their way. She looked behind her and saw Flossie stamp her foot.

Good.

Most of the road followed the irregular shore with its cliffs of bedrock, headlands, and beaches on one side and spruce fir forest on the other. The perimeter consisted of coastal bogs, barrens, and wetlands, but with the covering of snow they looked like vast fields. Hardy needed to watch where he was going so as not to get stuck in soft ground. There was no wind, so they were toasty with their knitted sweaters under their jackets. Annie had given Hardy a couple of blankets for their knees.

Mary Alice couldn't help herself. She looked at Sam. "What party were you going to? Hardy and I weren't invited, were we, Hardy?"

"Couldn't care less," Hardy said.

"The Bourinot fella...Flossie's cousin. Thanks for getting me out of it."

"Flossie will have your hide when you get home tomorrow," Mary Alice teased.

"Knock it off. She's not my boss."

Mary Alice rolled her eyes at Hardy. "If you say so."

Sam reached over and put her in a headlock.

"Hey! That hurts!" She elbowed his ribs and he let go.

"Will you two knock it off?" Hardy sounded grouchy. "You're going to unsettle Blue."

Sam and Mary Alice grinned behind their hands, but kept quiet.

It was a long ride. Thankfully their moms and sister had given them lunches, but they ate them much too early and their tummies were rumbling as the hours passed. The winter shadows on the snow were getting longer, and they were glad to finally see the light and the house before dusk descended.

The Campbells were happy to see them, as they were with any visitor; they were isolated on this side of Scatarie. Main-à-Dieu was just across the water, but there was no settlement near them on the island.

They put Blue in the barn with hay and Mr. Campbell took Hardy up to the lighthouse to see about the winding mechanism. The window lenses were rotated by a weight-driven clockwork assembly that had to be wound by the keepers. Len needed a replacement for a part that was sluggish. The new one he got some months before wasn't working right. It was faster to see if Mr. Campbell has a spare one than to wait for Fisheries to deliver him another one. Luckily, he had just the ticket, so the journey wasn't wasted.

Mrs. Campbell ladled out big servings of corned beef and cabbage to the adventurers and everyone had a grand visit, finishing off their meal with bread pudding and tea. Hardy and Mr. and Mrs. Campbell talked non-stop about lighthouses and Sam nudged Mary Alice under the table, both of them rather bored with the conversation. Mary Alice tried to ignore him, but he was looking at her the way he watched her while they were dancing, and that got her flustered. She tried not to reciprocate, but he was so attractive by lantern light, with his blue eyes taking her in, she could feel a pull and wanted him to touch her. For the first time in her life, she wanted to be Flossie.

Hardy and Sam slept on the couches in the sitting room in their clothes and Mary Alice was on top of a bed in the spare room close by, with a blanket over her. She didn't want to dirty the sheets. She wished she could get Sam out of her head and finally drifted off before she felt a hand touch her face in the dark. Before she could cry out, she heard his voice. "Shhh."

And then he kissed her softly before raising his head. "Just be with me," he murmured.

She had no idea how long they were together before she knew she could go no further. They were in someone else's house and she didn't want to get caught. She took his face away. "You have to go."

He kissed her one more time and then left as quietly as he came in.

Mary Alice spent the rest of the night not believing what had just happened, but she knew everything had changed. How would she be able to pretend things were normal between them? After she kissed Hardy things had basically been the same. They never talked about it and she still wasn't sure what had come over her. He never tried to kiss her back, which made her unsure. But these kisses had been Sam's idea, and knowing that he had his pick of any girl and had chosen her made her whole body tingle.

She'd kissed both of her best friends. If she hadn't known already, she was certain now that they weren't really like brothers to her.

All her fretting was tiring, and she knew by the light in the window that she had slept in. Throwing back the blanket she went through the door and sure enough, the boys weren't there. Mrs. Campbell was in the kitchen.

"Good morning, dear. Sit down and I'll get you some breakfast. The fellas ate earlier. They said to let you rest. I'm just packing a lunch for your ride home."

"That's awfully kind, thank you." She didn't want to eat, but she choked down about four bites of delicious oatmeal and pushed it away. "I'm sorry. I don't eat much in the morning."

"Something is better than nothing. I'll have the lunches made by the time you go and get the boys. They're down by the shore."

The first thing Mary Alice did was go to the outhouse. And then she picked up a mittful of snow and rubbed her face with it. The ice-cold sensation was just what she needed to wake up from the dream she'd had. And then her shoulders slumped. It was no dream. Damn you, Sam.

She took a deep breath and hurried to the water. But there was no water, just endless drift ice packed together like a jigsaw puzzle. Hardy and Sam were way out there, the fools, and looked like they were heading over to Moque's Head. She yelled for them to come in, but they didn't hear her, so she headed out herself, even though her parents had always told her not to walk on clampers. But it was a God-given rite of passage for children everywhere. They all risked it at one point or another because it was thrilling and dangerous.

The ice was in solid, or so it seemed. She ran towards them, but then her leg slipped through a small crack hidden by the white foam created from the tide in the tittle.

She yelled as loud as she could, "Help! Help me!" She couldn't get her leg out and was afraid it would be squeezed by the ice as it moved.

Mary Alice was in real trouble. I knew this because I've seen others crushed by ice. The only thing I could do was to stop the wind from blowing. When Mary Alice shouted again, Mr. Campbell heard her cries. He ran to her, dragging his skiff over the ice.

He blew a handheld foghorn to get the boys' attention. They turned and started back just as he got to Mary Alice.

By then she was crying. "I'm sorry!"

He never said a word, just got to work with a small hatchet to make the crack bigger. He slipped her leg out and hauled her into the boat, wrapping her in a tarp. "Can you move your leg?"

She nodded. "Yes. You were so quick; I don't think there's any harm done. I'm cold is all."

When the boys arrived, out of breath, they helped pull the skiff to shore. When Mary Alice stood up and walked on her leg, Mr. Campbell gave a sigh of relief. Then he looked at the other two. "What were ya thinkin?"

"Sorry, Mr. Campbell. It was stupid," Hardy said. "We should've known better."

Mrs. Campbell was at the top of the hill. "Are they all right?"

Her husband waved and she went back in the house.

The Campbells tried to convince the three friends to stay another night, but all of them said they'd like to get home. It would only be dark for the last mile or so, and Blue knew the way. Mrs. Campbell lent Mary Alice a pair of trousers and socks her son had outgrown and said she didn't need them back. They took their lunches, thanked the couple again for their hospitality, and left with the spare part that Len needed.

Blue was rested and ready to go. He started off at a good clip, and no one said anything until Mary Alice broke the silence. "What possessed you to go gallivanting over the ice?"

"I've crossed there before," Sam said. "I was just showing Hardy. We didn't fall through a crack, did we?"

She punched his arm. And then punched him again for good measure.

Sam knew what the second one was for.

"I like that lighthouse," Hardy said for something to say. "It's on a hill and it's sturdy. We're too open to the sea on the eastern side. I always think ships are going to run aground in front of us and keep going until they hit the house. Do you know I still think about that tidal wave?"

None of them were quite as animated as they'd been the day before. They settled into a comfortable silence and enjoyed the fresh air, the snow on the fir trees, and Blue's tinkling bell. They ate their egg sandwiches and date squares later in the afternoon.

Mary Alice was finishing her rather wizened apple when she said, "Dad told me there was a shipwreck once and the passengers and crew got off themselves but there was no one here. They lit a fire and the people of Main-à-Dieu saw the smoke and ventured over to see what was up. They found a lot of people, freezing cold and hungry. They took them over the tittle and looked after them until they could get passage. There were three people missing, and they presumed they had died. I believe it was a mother and two girls. But they found them after two weeks. They'd eaten rotten fish and stayed in one of the fishing huts. When you travel across the island this way and see how big it is, it's a miracle they were found at all."

"My da says there's one night every year when the screams of women and children are heard from a ghost ship," Sam told them.

"I've heard that story," Hardy said. "There's lots of ghost stories here. No wonder, with so many people dying off this coast. Do you believe in ghosts?"

"Who knows?" said Sam.

"I saw one standing on top of the water one day," Mary Alice said. "The day we crashed into each other in the water, Hardy. Remember? We were doing handstands."

"You probably hit your head too hard," Sam said.

"But don't you ever feel like there's someone watching you, or watching over you? I have that feeling all the time. I'm sure your mother is watching over you, Sam."

"Maybe."

He sounded glum, so she sighed, "I'll shut up about ghosts.

It's getting dark and spooky out."

But sure enough, Blue kept going on the right path even as darkness fell. It helped that there was snow on the ground, and it was seven o'clock when they pulled up to Mary Alice's and Sam's houses. They jumped down and Hardy waved. "Thanks for coming." He and Blue left to finish their journey.

She and Sam stood there. He looked down and put his hands in his pockets.

"Why?" she asked.

He shrugged. "You looked beautiful yesterday, out in the cold. Your hair..."

The door opened and her father was outlined against the lamplight. "There you are! Your ma was frettin'. Everything okay?"

Mary Alice nodded. "Yep. Hardy got the part he needed. The Campbells were happy to see us."

"Get in here. I'm lettin' the heat out. See ya, Sam."

"Yep. 'Night." He turned around and walked away.

I'm ashamed to say the weather turned dirty that night, all because I was in a rage. I flew through the storm clouds, hurled a few lightning bolts because it's so satisfying, and dove into the heaving sea, over and over again, trying to get rid of my jealousy.

Mary Alice had what I wanted with my sailor. If we had hit the rocks on Scatarie even two hours later than we did, I might have had the memory of someone kissing me softly and whispering, "Just be with me."

Now I was torn. Should I continue to spend my time with these people or fly past the moon and beyond? A welcome thought, but now that Aisling had Buster, she would remain, because Buster wouldn't leave. He told us that.

Eventually I calmed down, but I lay in my eagle's nest for days. Aisling came by to make sure I was still here. She wanted to know what was wrong. I could hardly tell her that I wanted to be kissed the way Sam had kissed Mary Alice. She wouldn't understand that. I'd love to have a friend my age. I regret never having had an older sister. This was not something I wished to discuss with Mam.

Eventually the crisis passed and I was back to my usual self. This was the first time I'd ever been so wrapped up with what was going on in the land of the living. I realized I couldn't be neutral with these personalities. I was invested in their lives and it was only natural that I would be more emotional about them. I have the mind of a fifteen-year-old. I am not wise or mature in this heaven of my own making. I would probably have more outbursts before these three were grown. I would suffer through it and forgive myself when it happened. That is the paramount canon here. Forgiveness. Of others, but mostly of your own heart. A constant, continuous effort.

I've always liked the phrase "rest in peace," but I think it's appropriate for the living, too. To quiet the mind, to stop struggling. We all deserve peace, alive or dead. That is why we feel better when we watch terns running along the shore or eagles swooping in the endless sky or loons in the water, gliding in silence. They are living in peace.

The human world is beautiful. But it's also chaos.

Flossie rapped on Sam's door very early the next morning. Jean opened it, a tea towel in her hand.

"Is he here?"

"Good morning to you too. Who are you looking for?" Jean knew darn well.

Flossie glared at her. "Sam, of course."

"Wait here." And Jean shut the door on her to make a point. Her father, Edgar, and brothers Ian and Bob looked up from the table. "Who's that?"

"Flossie."

All three of them groaned.

She yelled up the stairs. “Sam. Get down here.”

He thumped down the stairs, adjusting his suspenders. “What’s for breakfast?”

“Scrambled eggs and toast, but you can’t have any until you’ve spoken to the damsel in distress outside.”

For one insane moment, he thought she meant Mary Alice, so he yanked the door open.

Flossie had her arms folded in front of her. “How could you stand me up like that?”

“Calm down. We got there late and they invited us to stay overnight.”

“You know I was looking forward to that party. I felt like a fool arriving alone.”

“Ya didn’t have to go, did ya?”

“Why are you so mean?”

There was only one way to shut her up. “Come here.” He pulled her to him and kissed her, because that’s what she was after and he wanted his eggs. “I’ll see ya later.”

She had a goofy grin. “When?”

“I don’t know. Around. See ya.” He shut the door in her face and sat at the table. “Don’t you dare say anything,” he warned his family.

They didn’t, until his dad wiped his mouth on his sleeve. “Gonna have a hard time gettin’ rid of that one.”

Bob buttered his toast. “Why would he? He’s getting what he wants. There’s always one who obliges.”

Jean tsked. “Don’t be crude.”

There was only one kiss Sam was thinking about. After he’d had his fill, he shrugged on his jacket and said he wouldn’t be long.

When he got outside, Mary Alice was putting clothes out on their clothesline. They put them out no matter what the weather.

He walked over. “Hey.”

Before she could say it back, he took her face in his hands and kissed her properly. Despite the rush of happiness, she pushed him away. “Don’t kiss me without my permission. I’m not yours.”

Sam was put in his place, and he wasn’t happy about it. “You kissed me too, ya know. The other night. Don’t get all prim and proper now.”

“If you don’t like it, go find Flossie. She’s always available.”

And he turned on his heel and did just that.

CHAPTER SEVEN

It was that summer, 1938, when a load of liquor landed on their doorstep. There was a boat carrying alcohol, but customs were watching and the seamen didn't want to be caught. The coves of Scatarie were perfect to slip in and out of while trying to stay out of sight, but the officers were patient and the sailors quickly ran out of food and water waiting for them to leave. They ended up having to dump it all on the island.

The fishermen got a hold of it and there was non-stop alcohol for everyone. There was so much of it they ended up using it in oil lamps.

There were plenty of parties with such a windfall. Some were happy about it and others weren't. It depended on whether you had a family member who could hold their liquor, or one who became a mean drunk and used their spouse as a punching bag.

Sam, Hardy, and Mary Alice were at an age where they didn't drink in front of their parents but when together with friends in out-of-the-way spots, they enjoyed it as much as anyone. Well, Sam and Hardy did. Mary Alice gave it a valiant try, but she usually threw it all up after one cupful, which was annoying. She wanted to be as carefree and foolish as the rest of them, weaving and dancing around the bonfire.

She had enough in her one night to kiss Sam in front of everyone, and then she promptly kissed Hardy, so as to not leave him out. That's the trouble with alcohol. You become someone else. All she ended up doing was making everyone miserable. Flossie pushed her over the driftwood log, Hardy and Sam proceeded to wrestle each other on the sand, and Mary Alice stalked off, declaring them all idiots.

Rose was thankfully over, visiting their parents. She'd married Jeb Trimm in the spring and was now living in his household. She took one look at her sister and grabbed her hand. "I want to show Mary Alice something," she said, pulling her up the stairs before their parents could get a good look at her.

Their parents didn't care. They were busy listening to the disturbing news on the radio that war might be on the horizon.

Rose sat her on the bed. "How much have you had?"

"Not much. I don't need much. I'm too damn skinny. Why don't I have a bosom like you?"

"Get yourself pregnant and you will."

Mary Alice cheered up. "You're having a baby? Does Ma know?"

Rose held her stomach. "I was going to tell them when you showed up."

"Now all my siblings have kids, except Jake and Lionel. I hate being the youngest. And I'm never falling in love, anyway. Love is worse than picking berries."

Rose laughed. "I thought you had Sam wrapped around your little finger."

"That would be Flossie, and it involves more than her finger."

"Why don't you set your sights on Hardy? He's a really nice boy."

Mary Alice flopped back on the bed. "Hardy is the best. And Sam, he's...he's..."

"...attractive and dangerous. Not a good combination."

"It's not just that. He's alone. Hardy doesn't need me the way Sam needs me. I worry about Sam. Something bad might happen to him. I can feel it."

Rose tsked. "What rubbish! Just because you feel something doesn't mean it's going to come true."

Rose looked down and realized Mary Alice had closed her eyes. It was just as well. She put a blanket over her and went back downstairs.

Hardy and his father got into a war of words one night at the supper table. Len wasn't happy with the news that Hardy had been drinking with his buddies on the shore and in a derelict barn away from the main road.

His older brother James, the one with the heart condition, tried to ease the waters. "Dad, just because you don't drink doesn't mean that Hardy has to be a teetotaller. He's not up there every night like some of them."

"And how would you know?" Len shouted. "He's sixteen. He has no business drinking at all. And if I want your opinion, I'll ask for it."

James knew when to leave, but Hardy gave his brother a grateful glance. Annie sent Fred up to his room. Dorothy wasn't home. She was being courted by a Lyle Barnstable, and his mother had asked her over for dinner. Annie knew that was a good sign.

"Look, Dad," said Hardy. "I do everything you ask me to around here and then some. Occasionally I want to spend time with my friends. Yeah, sure, some of them drink, but not all of them. We just have a good time. I'm not passed out on the road every night, am I?"

"I forbid you to go. Do you hear me?"

Hardy stood up. "Are you going to keep me here forever? You don't have to worry about James, because he's always home.

Dorothy's never given you any trouble because she's a girl. I thought I was a pretty good son, always at your beck and call, but now you're treating me like a kid. You don't trust me, and I think I've earned your trust."

Annie spoke up. "He's a good boy, Len."

Now Len stood up. "I never defied my father. What gives him the right to bellyache about me? You kids today think the world owes you a living. Always doing whatever you want."

"DAD. That's not true. I work all day helping you, and you know it."

Len gave him a dismissive wave of his hand. "I'm tired of talkin'. Gotta clean the light." And he pulled open the kitchen door and stormed outside, slamming it behind him.

"I've never seen him so riled up," Annie worried. "Why don't you just tell him that you won't go?"

"Because then I'd be a liar, Mom. We have a laugh and joke around. It's harmless. Don't you remember what it's like to be young and wanting to be with your friends?"

Annie nodded. "Yes. I think your father is forgetting that. You get older and set in your ways. I'll talk to him."

"Thanks."

James and Hardy played crib, and Dorothy joined them when she came home. Fred was asleep in bed. Annie kept going to the door. She'd stand on the porch expecting to see Len. Then she got annoyed. She came into the parlour where the kids were and tapped her foot. "He's sulking out there."

"Dad?" Dorothy asked. "Why?"

Hardy moved his peg three spaces. "He doesn't want me to go to the barn with my friends."

Dorothy made a face. "Where else are kids your age going to go on this bloody island?"

"He doesn't want me drinking."

"You don't drink. Not like Sam."

"Oh dear," Annie said. "Sam doesn't drink a lot, does he? You see what happens when you don't have a mother?"

They waited until the game was over, and then Annie came out from the kitchen. "Go see if he needs help, Hardy."

Hardy sighed and headed out the door. He was annoyed with his dad and didn't want to speak to him. He wasn't in the usual places. He couldn't still be up there cleaning the lamp and trimming wicks. Hardy made his way up the curved stairwell to the top of the lighthouse. But his father wasn't there either. What was going on?

"Dad? Dad!"

That's when he noticed one of the windows was only half clean. His father would never leave it like that. Hardy opened the gateway to the outside deck and yelled against the wind. "DAD!" There wasn't a sound except the roar of the surf. He circled the deck to make sure and started to get concerned. He looked over the edge, and as the white light revolved in the direction of the sea, he caught a glimpse of something on the ground.

"Oh god!"

In his panic, he slipped on the platform and fell to his knees, so he crawled through the opening and then took the stairs two at a time trying to get to the bottom as quickly as he could. He ran to the front of the lighthouse, and in the dark, he could just make out his father's body on the ground.

"Dad! What happened?" He lifted his torso. "Are you hurt? It's okay, we'll get help." That's when his father's head dropped backwards like his neck was broken. "Dad! Speak to me." It took a few more moments for it to sink in that his father was dead, not just hurt. Of course he'd be dead, falling off the top of a lighthouse. How could he be so stupid, thinking Dad was alive?

Hardy couldn't believe it. He hadn't wanted to speak to his father any more tonight, and now he wanted only that. To hear his voice. The last conversation they'd had was in anger. Hardy put his head on his father's chest and cried.

Dorothy and James, carrying a flashlight, finally found them. It was awful, but what was worse was walking towards their mother who was still standing on the porch. When she saw the limp body of her husband in Hardy's arms, she let out a deep aching moan as if all the air in her lungs had disappeared.

Len Campbell's funeral was held in the Protestant Church in Main-à-Dieu. People were buried off the island because their family plots and most of their relatives lived across the water.

The other Mr. Campbell came over to look after the lighthouse while the family was gone. Mrs. Campbell was perfectly capable of managing theirs.

There were a lot of people who went over. A flotilla of boats bringing them to the mainland for this sad occasion. The sea was rough but not impossible.

When Annie and her children got up to the dock of the wharf, Dr. MacNeil was there, which they didn't expect. He ushered them off to the side.

"I thought you'd like to know that the post-mortem results came back. He didn't die by his own hand, which I know you were worried about, and he didn't die of a broken neck. It was a brain aneurysm. He was dead before he fell over. It was instant. He wouldn't have known."

All of them wept quietly and were so grateful that the doctor took the time to put their minds at ease. That's all Hardy had been thinking about since it happened. He imagined his father throwing himself off the tower to teach him a lesson, or imagined he slipped and was terrified as he hurtled through space, knowing his end was near. It was a huge weight off their shoulders to know that it could have happened in bed or at the kitchen table instead of the traumatic way it came about.

As they stood in the graveyard of the rural village, Hardy was comforted by the familiar faces he'd grown up with. The ones he played with, fought with, drank with, kissed, and longed for. As the sea breeze became stronger, the women held on to their hats. A few men had hats like the doctor and pastor, but the majority were bareheaded fishermen, taking off the caps they spent their days in.

Hardy could see Sam and Mary Alice standing together with Flossie. What a strange triangle that was, but he was grateful for their concerned faces. Of course, Sam would know what this felt like, but they hadn't had a chance to get together since it happened.

The parson told them there was a cup of hot tea, sandwiches, and sweets in the church basement, and most made a move to leave. Annie put her hand through Hardy's arm.

"Can James take you, Mom? I want to be alone with Dad for a minute."

She nodded and followed the others.

As he stood there, he knew that his life was now the lighthouse. No wondering about what life would be like somewhere else. His father had trained him well. And he made a pledge to himself that he would never drink again. As an atonement for that awful final night.

His dad was a good man. Hardy wanted to make him proud. He would be responsible for his family now. His older brother couldn't do manual labour and Dorothy was a big help, but for how long? She'd get married and be off somewhere else. Meanwhile his mother and Fred needed protecting.

Standing there, he felt like a man. His childhood was gone.

Joining the others, he was pleased that his mother was smiling at the people who surrounded her and gave her hugs. The room was crowded and their neighbours were enjoying the lunch. The Main-à-Dieu church ladies always put on a good spread.

He saw Mary Alice and Flossie hurrying over to him with plates of sandwiches and squares. It was like a race. He knew Mary Alice would win; when she put her mind to something there was no stopping her.

He was right. Mary Alice said, "I thought you might like something to eat, Hardy. To keep up your strength."

Flossie was right behind her. "These brownies are my mother's. They're so good."

"Thanks," he sighed, "but I'm not hungry." And he made a beeline for the door.

Flossie looked confused. "He's never not hungry."

Mary Alice looked at her as if she was a simpleton. "His da just died. Of course he's not hungry."

"So why are you trying to feed him?"

"I'm not. This is mine." Mary Alice stuffed an asparagus roll in her face and walked off.

Hardy sat on the wooden steps of the church. It was too hot in that room and he needed air. The door opened behind him and Sam came out, joining him on the step.

Sam shook his head. "A damn shame." He reached into his pocket and took out a rolled cigarette. "Want one?"

Hardy didn't smoke. "Yes."

Sam lit it for him and passed it over, lighting one for himself.

Hardy inhaled and automatically started to cough. He looked at it. "Yeah, this is real good."

"You'll get used to it. Just take short puffs at first. It helps take your mind off things." Sam bumped his shoulder. "Need anything? Just say the word."

Hardy took a shorter drag and blew out the smoke. "Nah, I'll be busy with the inspectors coming to see about the light. They said they'll send someone out to see if I fill the requirements for being a keeper and if they deem me worthy, then I'll have an assistant. I'm gonna stick around the house for now. Fred is having a hard time, waking up with nightmares. And my mom is showing a brave face today, but she and Dad were always together and this is hitting her hard. I think she's afraid to be alone."

"It took my da forever to stop mopin' around. But he eventually did it. It's not going to last forever."

"That's good to know." Hardy flicked the cigarette away. "Can't say I enjoyed that."

"You've always been a goody-two-shoes."

"Shut your face."

It was always difficult when someone died on the island. The people who made Scatarie home were like an extended family. Annie was suddenly inundated with food and women taking time to visit with her. She started to feel badly that she'd been a bit standoffish with some of them. They were a real help and Annie felt like a tribe member now. They asked her to pick blueberries with them, which was an excellent way to let someone talk about their sorrow. She was grateful.

But there was more heartache to come that year, one of the worst tragedies to ever befall the residents. One September night when all the boats were in for the night and supper had been eaten and everyone was winding down from a busy day, there came the sudden sound of an explosion and the smell of smoke and crackling flame lit up the evening sky. The men raced towards it, hoping it was just a shed or fishing shack, though they'd still have to get the blaze under control; all their houses were made of wood.

Edgar and Sam were the first on the scene. It wasn't a shed. It was their neighbour little Sandy's house. Before Edgar could stop him, Sam ran in the door, yelling. Edgar found Sandy reeling outside with burns. Others approached, all of them with buckets of water and blankets, Bob and Ian among them.

"Your foolish brother is in there!" Edgar shouted.

Just as he said that, Sam came teetering out with Sandy's wife, Mildred, under his arm. They were coughing and trying to take a breath. Everyone shouted at each other, trying to figure out what to do. Then the fire flickered in the upstairs window and a little face appeared.

"My babies!" Mildred fought against Sam's tight hold with everything she had and ran back into the house. Just a few moments later the entire structure was on fire and no one could get near it. People were crying and trying to stop the flames.

She and her three youngest children never made it out.

The entire community was devastated. But every one of the women said they would've done exactly the same thing. No mother is going to let her babes die alone if she can possibly help it. Mildred was a hero in their eyes. Some of her kin recounted her saying that if anything happened to her, she wanted her children with her. Most thought that was an odd thing to say. Did she know something? There was an old lady on the island who was said to have second sight. She claimed she saw flames over that way a week before it happened, but things like that are said and no one knows what to believe.

In the end Mildred got her wish. She was buried in the same coffin as her little ones.

Because there was an explosion, everyone knew what had happened. Sandy had been sealing up bottles of goulash with wax in the kitchen, and a lit candle came too close to the alcohol fumes. There was a fireball. It was a tragic accident, made worse by the fact that it didn't have to happen. Sandy was in the hospital for a long time, and when he came back, there were hard feelings for years among the relatives. Everyone wanted to assign blame, but in the end what good does it do, except to make a bad situation worse?

Those four souls were gone but never, ever forgotten on Scatarie.

I'm certain you are wondering about them. I've seen the four of them holding hands, but they didn't stay near Scatarie for long. As someone who was without her mother for a long time, I'm grateful Mildred is with them. She made the right choice. How would she have carried on? When the only thing you have in this world are your children, to lose them is the ultimate cruelty. Your spirit dies and some women can't make it. The ones who do have dependent children to take care of, so they have no choice but to suffer it out. My mother was one of them.

Sam had a hard time, thinking he'd failed her—if only he'd held on!—but in that moment, Mildred was stronger than he was. He'd never felt strength like that before.

It didn't matter what people said to him, assuring him he'd done all he could; Sam went into a malaise of sorts. Hardy was busy now that he was the lightkeeper, and the only person he could talk to was Mary Alice. Flossie tried her best to help him, but he didn't seem to care, which got her back up.

One night Mary Alice happened to glance out the window and see Sam in his window. He gave her the signal he used to give her when they were kids, his thumb and two fingers straight in the air. She nodded.

"I'm going to visit Rose," she said, putting on her sweater.

Her mother was in the rocking chair darning and Da was looking through the *Cape Breton Post*.

"Mind you don't keep her talking too long. She'll get tired in her condition."

"Don't worry."

Once out the door Mary Alice looked behind her to make sure they weren't spying, because she was headed for the chicken coop across the road. It was a tighter squeeze than when they were young, but plenty roomy once inside. They still had a blanket out there, and Mary Alice made a promise to herself to wash it.

"Hey," she said.

"Hey."

"What's wrong?"

"Jean has some friends over and they're talking about the fire. No one can shut up about it."

Mary Alice drew her knees to her chest and encircled them with her arms. She rocked back and forth. "That's understandable, a shock like that. I still cry over those kids."

Sam put his hands through his hair. "Maybe I should've gone upstairs and gotten them out first."

"Oh, Sam. Don't do this to yourself. You were the only one who went inside. Doesn't that count for something?"

He rubbed his forehead. "I can't think anymore. Or I'm thinking too much. I wanna get out of here."

Mary Alice reached over and touched his cheek. "Please. It's not your fault."

He grabbed her hand and kissed her palm. "Don't touch me if you don't mean it. I can't deal with it."

She wanted him to feel better so she reached over and put her lips on his. He laid her back on the blanket and they disappeared into each other, as much as you can in a chicken coop with old hay. He pushed up her shirt, and that brought her back to reality.

She said against his neck, "If you're expecting Flossie-sized breasts you'll be disappointed."

He raised his head and grinned. "There is nothing disappointing about you, my girl."

After a bit, Mary Alice was once again the one to stop the proceedings. "Look, as much as I like what's happening, this is the least romantic setting I can think of. And I'm having flashbacks to when we were five and I thought you were my brother and that's really uncomfortable."

With that he laughed out loud and sat up. "You're right."

They adjusted their clothes and picked hay out of each other's hair.

"Do you feel better?" she asked.

"You always make me feel better, when you're not hitting my arm."

"But what is this?" she wondered. "I know we're friends, but this feels like more."

"Why do girls always have to label something? You sound exactly like Flossie."

That snapped her out of it. "God forbid. This was fun, nothing more. Next time I see you I might not even speak to you."

He reached for her hand again. "You have my permission to never kiss me again, but please don't ever stop talking to me. You and Hardy are my closest friends. I'd die if that happened."

She squeezed his hand. "It will never happen."

I know that Mary Alice hated when he said things like that. She felt responsible for Sam's happiness. She could still picture the picnic in the chicken coop they had shortly after his mother died, and the big tears rolling down his cheeks before he ran out. That had stayed with her. Sam was all bluster and confidence, but she knew inside he was lonely and afraid, and she wanted more than anything to help.

CHAPTER EIGHT

Every household was glued to the radio on September 1, 1939, the night war was declared. The adults who had lived through the Great War were horrified, knowing what was to come. Mothers of sons wept. Two young island men had joined the military in the Great War, Henry Trimm and John Steele. Henry had come home, but John hadn't.

Mary Alice felt sick. She had five brothers. Jake and Lionel couldn't wait to fight the Huns. Tommy wouldn't be able to go because he'd lost the use of his arm in a fishing accident, never mind his young children. Fabian and George had young families too and it would be a hardship if they left. At some point they might have to go, but not now.

Hardy was safe. He was the head of his family and had an important job. He never said if he minded that. He kept it to himself. But Mary Alice knew Sam was itching to get over there.

Immediately.

The same old argument was going on in the Harris household. Sam wanted to enlist. His father shook his head. "You have to be eighteen! You're only sixteen. They won't take you. You're not going."

"I'm seventeen in three months, Da. Lots of guys my age are going."

"Who?"

Sam was pacing around the kitchen table. "Maybe no one here, but there's plenty in Glace Bay and Sydney. I hear things. When I was over in the Bay visiting Uncle Charlie, he told me."

Edgar lit another cigarette. "Uncle Charlie is a shit disturber. You know that."

"I've never been anywhere! I want to see the world."

"You'll get your face blown off, and then what will you see, lying in a muddy trench?"

"Jesus Christ. I'm goin', Da. You can't stop me!"

Edgar knew that was true. Ian could go now. Bob was needed on the boat. The thought of losing another family member gave Edgar an ulcer.

"Then you're not goin' until you're seventeen! Ya hear me? You try to sneak out that door before your birthday, I'll kill ya myself."

He'd have to cool his heels a little longer. Sam dreamed of being a pilot or a navigator but knew he didn't have the education. Now was when he wished he'd thought about his future. Still, being a soldier in the army and wearing a uniform was exotic enough. And he wanted the army, not the navy; to run on dry land with a gun and see a Nazi up close, not on a ship in the distance or hidden in a submarine. He'd spent his whole life on the water. If he took a boat and kept going, he would land on the beaches of France. There was no land mass between Scatarie Island and Europe.

Sam was young enough to not give a thought about how his decision affected those who loved him. He was full of bluster and excitement.

It got to the point where his friends had had enough. "For God's sake," Mary Alice screeched at the end of November. "Just shut up, will you! We all know you're going. You can't wait to get off this island and leave everyone behind. We get it."

He was helping with the woodpile behind her house. When she covered her face with her mitts, he took a step towards her to put his hand on her shoulder. She shrugged it off. "Just leave me alone."

"So, if I go and you're mad about it, then you're not going to write to me? I'll be the only soldier to not get letters from home. Hardy's not going to write, my dad isn't going to write, Jean isn't going to write because she's too gaga over that Brewster fella in Port Morien. Bob might, but his life is so boring it won't be worth reading."

She took her hands away. "Have you forgotten the epistles you'll be getting from Flossie swearing her undying love for you? She'll send letters, cookies, mitts, pictures, and anything else she can fit in a parcel. You'll be well loved up."

Now he wanted to shake her. "Listen, I have no interest in Flossie. You know it and I know it. The only one who doesn't know it is her. She could send me a letter every day for years and it would mean nothing. I'm going to need your letters, to tell me the stuff I want to know about what's going on here."

Mary Alice stamped her foot. "Then stay and find out for yourself. The war is supposed to be over in six months anyway. You can miss it altogether if you wait until you're eighteen."

"I'm going to do my duty."

"Oh, spare me. Don't go. You can't go."

"Why?"

She bent down, picked up a piece of wood, and threw it at him. He caught it, which made her angrier. "You have got to be the stupidest boy in the world. Go. Have a great time killing people and being killed. I'll make sure your gravestone reads *He died for nothing.*"

She stomped in the house and left him there.

"Goddamn it," he said under his breath, but he stayed and finished the wood for her. Mary Alice was one stubborn mule. If only she knew how much he was going to miss her.

Sam was counting down the days until Christmas. He asked Jean for her help in pulling off a birthday party for the three of them. All their friends were welcome. Jean did it because it might be the last time she did anything for him. She didn't think Mary Alice would show up, however. And Hardy might be too busy, but his new assistant was now installed in the spare room, so he'd probably make it. Flossie would be there with bells on.

To make sure Mary Alice was there, Sam went to see Hardy. His mother was pleased to see him. "You sure you're eating enough?" Annie worried.

"You'll have to send me parcels of cookies when I'm overseas fighting the Germans."

With that, Annie covered her face with her apron and ran up the stairs.

"Sorry," Hardy said. "She's still emotional. She did the same thing when she found out I wouldn't be going." He passed Sam a mug of tea.

"Are you sorry you have to stay?" Sam asked him.

Hardy shrugged. "I have no idea. I wouldn't mind crossing the ocean with you, but who knows where we'd end up. Not together, I don't imagine. And if I don't like killing critters, I can't say I'd enjoy killing a man."

"We're talking about Nazis. And if they were pointing a rifle at you, you'd be squeezing the trigger real quick."

"Not going to find out, am I? But you better come home and tell me all about it. Don't do something stupid and try to play the hero. I know you. Keep your head down."

"Yes, sir." Sam took a sip of his tea as Dorothy walked in. "Hi, stranger. I hear you're having a party and all your cohorts are invited. Does your dad know?"

"Of course he knows. He'll be the one sitting in the corner drinking and not saying a word."

"Have some pity for the poor man. It's terrible for a parent to watch their young lad go off to war."

"People have got to stop making me feel guilty about my decision," Sam sighed. "I'm not even sure Mary Alice will show up." He looked at his friend. "You have to make her come to her own birthday party. It won't be the same without her."

"You know her. Once she makes up her mind, she's not likely to change it, but I'll talk to her."

"Thanks, buddy."

Dorothy agreed to show the new assistant around so he'd get used to the place while Hardy took a stroll to Mary Alice's. It was a glorious winter day, with snow draped over tree branches and smoke rising from chimneys. It was cold enough you could see the breath of the horses in the field, looking like they belonged on a postcard with the light blue sky and the navy-blue sea with whitecaps in the background. The bright red holly berries scattered about completed the picture. What a beautiful, heartbreaking place this was. How long could families live here? The fishery was changing, and now, with war raging, who knew how things would play out?

Hardy stood and took the scene in to remember it. This was the perfect day before Christmas when the three of them were still together.

He knocked on the door.

"Come in." Mary was at the table kneading bread dough on a floured board. "Hey, stranger. How's the family?"

He pointed at her head. "Are those..."

"Underpants, yes. They're my hairnet. Don't worry, they're clean."

"We're doing okay. Holidays are hard."

"Of course, dear. I must go down and visit your mother. She

tends not to wander over here."

"I think she's afraid she'll fall, which sounds odd, but ever since Dad died, she acts older."

Mary put more flour on her sticky dough. "She's alone now. I mean, she has you kids, but it's not the same when your man leaves you."

Hardy rocked back and forth with his hands in his pockets.

"Listen to me, goin' on about nothin'. I assume you want to see Mary Alice. She's cleaning the cow shed. She says it helps her think."

"That sounds like something she would say. Thanks."

Mary wiped her hands on her apron. "It's none of my business, but I have a feeling Sam asked you to talk to her about going to the party. But don't push her too hard. She's having a terrible time thinking of him going. She'd be the same if it was you."

"Okay." He went out the door, thinking, *No she wouldn't be the same if it was me.*

When he got to the cow barn the doors were closed. Maybe she'd gone. He checked anyway and opened one side of the door. "Mary Alice? You in here?"

"No."

He opened the door a little wider to let in some light. She'd already mucked the place out. Their two cows seemed to be dozing. Mary Alice sat on a few stacked bales of hay and leaned back on another one by their pen. Hardy hopped up and sat on the bale with her.

"This is a surprise," she said. "I never see you anymore now that you're busy doing grown-up stuff."

"It's a fine day. Wanna walk?"

"Nope."

"Too busy sulking, I guess."

She chewed on a piece of hay. "You know me too well. And I know you and that other brat who sent you here. This is the mission to make me go to his damn party."

"It's our party too."

"What are we? Six?" She was getting wound up. "Why can't he respect my decision? I don't want to go."

"Why can't you respect his? He does, and you're punishing him for it."

Mary Alice grunted. "Like he's ever cared about what we think. He bulldozes his way past everyone to get what he wants. He always has and you know it. He doesn't need my approval except to make himself feel better."

Hardy sighed and leaned back on the hay. "I'm thinking of you. I'm thinking about how you'll feel if you stay mad at him and he goes off and gets killed and he never got to say goodbye to one of his best friends. That will eat you alive."

She picked up more hay strands and broke them.

"It's not your life, Mary Alice. It's his, and whether we agree with him or not, he has to know we love him before he goes. We're not just his friends; we're his family too."

"Why are you making this so hard for me?"

Hardy put his arm around her. "Because you're not that girl."

She tilted her head and snuggled into his shoulder. They sat like that for quite a while, not speaking.

"You make my life better."

"Remember that, please." He gave her arm a quick squeeze and jumped down. "See ya tomorrow night." He walked out and closed the door behind him, leaving Mary Alice in the gloom with shafts of sunlight peeking through. She laid her head on the hay.

"I'm not that girl."

When Mary Alice came down the stairs on the way to the party, there was a houseful of Lockes, who came visiting after their own family Christmases were over. Her sisters Tilly, Eileen, Susan, and their kids were there, and three of her brothers, Jake, Lionel, and Tommy. Rose had begged off, afraid to fall on ice at this stage. She was due in the new year. Fabian and George were at their in-laws'.

It was Jake who spotted her first. "Where's my baby sister?"

Her sisters made a fuss over her hair up and the new pink blouse, her one gift under the tree. Her mother brought out a cake and everyone sang "Happy Birthday" to her. "Make a wish!"

She paused for effect, then dutifully blew out the candle. Her mother made her eat two bites of cake before she let her go. Before she could get her coat on, her dad went into the story of the night she was born and how she was named after the Virgin Mary.

"Go on with your nonsense, Tom. I'd had nine kids by then!" Mary shouted.

"You guys tell this story every Christmas," Mary Alice sighed. "It's getting old."

"And we'll do it again next year!" her father chuckled. "Now don't get lost goin' twenty steps across the road."

"Da." She finally gave them all a quick wave and took a deep breath in the frosty air once she'd closed the door. By the sounds of it the party was going strong over at Sam's. Okay, she could do this. Sam was here tonight. That's all that mattered.

She pushed the door open. Everyone their age on the island was having a blast. Some danced, some were in their cups already, others were eating and laughing. It looked like a fun time, but not for Edgar, who was sitting at the kitchen table drinking while Jean hovered over him.

Sam and Hardy were deep in conversation while Flossie stewed beside them. They saw Mary Alice at the same time and they both smiled and hurried over. "Happy birthday!" they said together.

Mary Alice held her hands over her head. "Happy birthday, boys." And she hugged them both at the same time.

"You look sensational," Sam said. "I always tell you to keep your hair up. Thanks for coming, and thanks, Hardy, for your part in all this. What did you say that changed her mind? She wasn't having it last week."

"That's between us and a couple of cows."

Flossie ventured over so as not to be left out. "Hi, Mary Alice. I thought you weren't coming?"

"You were misinformed. We've spent every birthday together."

"You won't next year if the war keeps going," Flossie reminded her.

Mary Alice glared at her nemesis. "You have the unique ability to always add a drop of black ink into crystal-clear water. Were you aware of that?"

Flossie put her hands on her hips. "And you always talk like you're better than everyone else."

"That's because she is." Sam grabbed her hand and led her away. "Come with us, Hardy. I need to speak to both of you."

Flossie was sick to death of these three. It was impossible to crack their bubble. But she still had time. The evening wasn't over.

They sat together at the back of the room, trying to get away from the worst of the noise.

Sam pointed at Hardy and Mary Alice. "I'm depending on you two to stay exactly as you are until I get home. I don't want anything changing, ya hear me? I don't want you running off and moving somewhere else. You need to be here when I get back. I have to imagine you still here just like this, when I'm over there. Do you promise me?"

Hardy and Mary Alice were confused and looked at each other. Mary Alice waved her hand. “Let me get this straight. You get to move on, but we have to stay here like statues until you come back? Are you listening to yourself? What if this war lasts for years? Wars tend to do that, you know. Ever hear of the Hundred Years’ War between England and France?”

“No.”

“You shouldn’t have quit school in eighth grade.”

Sam looked desperate. “I’m not explaining it right. I know I pushed for this and I have to go now, but the closer it gets the more I’m dreading everything being gone when I get back. You’ll change and I’ll change and maybe we won’t even know each other. Ever thought of that?”

Hardy shook his head. “We will always recognize each other. We’ll always be here for each other. Nothing’s going to change, Sam, even if we do move away or it takes years for you to come back. This little circle will always be.”

Sam wiped his eyes with his sleeve. “Okay. Okay. I needed to hear that.”

“Do you want to change your mind, Sam?” Mary Alice asked. “It won’t matter a hill of beans if you do want to wait an extra year. No one will think less of you.”

He shook his head. “No, I’m okay. I just panicked this morning thinking about being on the other side of the world. This island is the only world I know. That’s why I need you. I need to know my world is still here. Christ, this is the longest speech of my life. I sound like a nut job.”

“Sorry,” Hardy said. “You’ve always been a nut job.”

Sam grabbed him around the neck and pretended to choke him.

It was a long, hot, frantic party. Jean put poor old Edgar to bed. People drifted away couple by couple, all of them wishing

Sam good luck. Flossie started to cry. She was drunk. Sam asked Hardy and Mary Alice to stay while he walked Flossie home. He wouldn't be long.

Hardy waited a few minutes and then looked at his watch. "I need to get back. I don't like leaving Dorothy alone with everything. Tell Sam I'll see him before he goes."

"Maybe I should go too."

"You stay. You're the important one. Goodnight."

"Goodnight." Mary Alice looked at her hands. She wished Hardy wouldn't say things like that. She loved him as much as she loved Sam. Hardy acted like it was a contest he was always losing.

I was cross at Mary Alice. Hardy was shy, and just because he didn't kiss her in the middle of the night or grab her and let her know he was attracted to her didn't mean he wasn't. But what do I know? I've never had two men love me.

Jean was straightening up in the kitchen, collecting dishes and debris. Bob and Ian had headed up long ago. Jean yawned and threw the dishtowel by the sink. "I'll do this tomorrow."

Mary Alice got up. "I can help you."

"No, no. Sam will be back in a minute. Tell him I've gone to bed."

"Okay."

Jean headed up the stairs but turned around. "You look very pretty tonight, Mary Alice. No wonder Sam is going to miss you." And with that she headed to bed.

Mary Alice blushed as Sam walked through the door.

"Where's Hardy?" he asked.

"He had to go. He left Dorothy too long. He'll see you before you go." They sat on the couch together. "When are you leaving?"

"Before New Year's. I have to report to Sydney, get my medical, and sign a bunch of stuff..."

"...and lie about your birthday."

"Among other things. Then we leave by train for Halifax. I have no idea where I'm going after that. Some sort of boot camp in Ontario, I think they said. It might take me a long while before I actually head overseas."

She looked down at her hands, not wanting to look at his face. "Flossie okay?"

"I left her on the couch. No one was up. She was snoring by the time I got to the door."

"You have to hand it to her. She's been devoted to you since second grade."

Sam pulled his hair back from his face. "Do you know what it's like to be hounded like that?'

Mary Alice wagged her finger at him. "No, no, no. You don't get to say that. You've taken great advantage of what she was offering over the years. You can't pick and choose, saying she was a burden. If you really thought that you would've stayed away from her."

"You've always been my conscience, Mary Alice Locke. I'm going to miss you."

She sighed. "Same."

He moved closer and rubbed his thumb over her cheek. She leaned into it and then kissed him with everything she had. She savoured it for longer than she should have, but it was too little, too late, and she knew it. She lifted her head and whispered, "I have to go."

Sam groaned, "Don't do this again. Please."

"I am not going to be with you on a couch in your father's house with everyone sleeping upstairs. I'm not that girl."

"Let's go to the chicken coop."

"In the dead of winter? That's obviously your pecker talking, and I'm worth more than that." She went to get up and he held her arm.

"You're right. You're right. I apologize. Here, let me get your coat."

He stood up and brought it over to her. She buttoned it up.

"I'll walk you home."

They both grinned. Out the door they went, took twenty steps, and arrived at her door. She threw her arms around him and he gave her a long hug.

"I'm saying goodbye to you now," she whispered against his neck. "I'll be there to wave you off on the day, but this is my farewell. Stay safe. We love you. Come home to us in one piece. I promise I'll write."

He wept silently against her coat, his shoulders heaving. They were there forever. Then he straightened up, took a deep breath, cupped her face in his hands, and kissed her forehead.

"Bye bye, my little Spitfire."

CHAPTER NINE

Strange as it may seem, the war showed up on Scatarie. That's what happens when you live on the coast. Not every day, but enough to make you edgy.

A submarine was spotted off of Bateston. That was very unsettling, and it set off gossip about spies everywhere. There was a rumour that two German soldiers were hiding under the beached hull of a boat off of Main-à-Dieu. But it was never proven. Not that people need proof when tongues are wagging. And the details get more and more implausible as time goes on.

Clearly convoys of ships met at Scatarie on their way overseas. That made everything very real. Mary Alice would stand by the water and say a prayer for all the young men aboard until they disappeared out of sight.

And then there was the day a plane fell out of the sky.

It was a warm July afternoon in 1942 when a Canadian bomber plane crashed at Eastern Harbour. Mary Alice was weeding their garden, something else she hated doing. She realized that anything that made her stay still was extremely irritating. Weeding, picking berries, canning, baking, sewing. She had a list a mile long.

Her mother would get cross. "You've told me twenty things you hate doing, what is it exactly that you like doing?"

"I like reading."

"You have to sit still for that!"

"No! You go on adventures in your mind. That's as good as doing something."

So while Mary Alice was wishing she was somewhere else instead of pulling up carrot shoots, she became aware of a drone sound that was far away but seemed to get louder as time went on and eventually turned into an ungodly roar. She got up off her knees, went around to the front of the house, and put her hand up to shield her eyes from the sun. It was a plane, a bomber, and it was dropping down to the ground. How was that possible? With her heart in her throat, she expected to see a huge ball of fire, but it landed on its wheels and its front just plowed ahead uncontrollably taking everything in its path—sod, dirt, Jerry Spencer's outhouse and shed, a wheelbarrow. Mary Alice had to run because it was coming her way. *Please don't hit the house* was all she was thinking.

Luckily the plane shuddered to a stop before that happened. It was a miracle it didn't hit any houses. The pilot obviously aimed for the road as best he could.

By now everyone was running out of their homes or from the shore and fields towards the plane, not believing their eyes. When two pilots crawled out of the wreckage, they had a lot of help. Fortunately, aside from a few bumps and bruises, and a gash on each of their foreheads, only their pride was hurt. But they were dazed, and because the plane was sitting right outside Mary's house, she told the neighbours to bring them inside.

Mary Alice was put to work making tea, while Mary cleaned up their wounds. Her mother told her to make tea with plenty of sugar in it, and they were down to very little, so Mary Alice hightailed it to the small store the MacCuishes ran and came home with a pound.

She was happy to keep refilling their mugs as they smoked Mary's cigarettes and ate some oatcakes. Mary Alice grabbed her own tea and sat with them.

"I'm Mary Alice."

They looked so good in their uniforms despite their bandages.

The bigger one said, "I'm Malcolm and he's Eddie. I'm from Newfoundland and he's from Alberta, the poor bugger."

"What were you doing flying over Scatarie?" she asked.

"Looking for U-boats."

"My da is out fishing today. Should they be worried?"

"Nah, not unless they want lobster for supper."

Once the two men had caught their breath, they went back outside to take a look at the damage. Then Malcolm asked if there was a telephone on the island.

"At the lighthouse," Mary Alice said. "I'll take you there."

Eddie stayed with the plane as Malcolm walked side by side with her. "Why's a great-looking gal like you living in this backwater? You shouldn't be hiding yourself away."

"And you shouldn't be talking nonsense. I'll put it down to the bump on your head."

He put his head back and laughed. "Oh yes, you're wasted here. You should come to Newfoundland. I'd see you right in no time."

It was fun to flirt with this nice young man. She realized how lonely she was.

Malcolm and Eddie stayed with the Lockes for two nights before they were whisked away by their superiors, who arrived on the island to take a look at the damage. Mary Alice walked down to the water's edge to wave them goodbye, when the cheeky Malcolm ran back up to her and kissed her smack on the mouth.

"That's for good luck!" He smiled. "And to make you come to Newfoundland."

She kissed the one from Alberta too.

She often wondered if they made it through the war.

Mechanics were dispatched to the island and they worked on the plane for three days before they declared she was in good flying order. Getting her off the island was tricky. Another pilot steered her down closer to the lighthouse and took the same route out, only going the opposite way. Everyone talked about how he had only twenty feet left before he soared in the air and just over the treetops.

The place looked empty without it.

They heard from Sam now and again. He was over in England after months of basic training in Ontario, but still nowhere near the front. He complained about the constant marching and manoeuvres.

If I'd known how obsessed they are about rules and obedience, I woulda told them I'm not their guy. They made it seem like we'd be fighting Germans from day one. Two and half years later and I haven't seen a German yet! But we do have to clean up the mess their bombs make every night in London. And for that I want to kill every one of the bastards.

Mary Alice wrote back to tell him about the plane, but that was about as much excitement as she could think of, which was pathetic. She told him his family was well. Jean was getting married to Terry Brewster from Port Morien and would be moving there. That meant Edgar and Bob would be the only ones in the house, since Ian had enlisted too and was now in Italy.

And then she remembered:

You'll never guess. Flossie got married! To Hank Lahey of all people. The fella who was always at our door looking for me. So you're off the hook when you get back. No more canoodling with her, although knowing Flossie, it might not be out of the question.

Flossie couldn't wait to tell her. She had casually dropped in one day saying her mother needed a spoonful of vanilla.

"Really? You run a store."

"Never mind. Be like that, then." She turned around to leave but looked back. "Oh yes, I have news. While you'll be pining away for years for a fella who may never come home, I'll be getting married and having a family. Looks like you're about the only spinster in the class."

"I wish you every happiness, Flossie. You deserve ten kids, while I will keep my girlish figure."

"You're a bitch, you know that!" Flossie had quickly flounced out the door.

Mary Alice knew that was quite true. Especially where Flossie was concerned. Mary Alice was still acting like the day Sam went over to Flossie's house in grade school. She didn't want to think too hard about that. She was obviously being very immature.

Sighing, she dropped the pen and flopped on her bed. She was languishing here, doing nothing of importance. Is this what her life was going to be from now on? What was she waiting for?

She knew what she was waiting for, but it might not happen. Then what?

That night she had a vivid dream. She saw herself teaching at the new school they'd built in 1940 with the Credit Union's unfinished building. Her old friend Cara was in a seat. She sat up instantly. That's what she'd do, she could be a teacher. No one read more than she did.

She went to Mrs. Wadden and told her that she intended to be the new school mistress on Scatarie in the fall. Mrs. Wadden's mouth dropped open. "How did you know Miss Turnbull is leaving? I haven't even written up the notice."

A completely fortuitous coincidence. She pretended otherwise. "I'm well informed about everything, as you know, Mrs. Wadden. No one can stump me. I have energy and drive and I live here. I'm not going to move away like these other teachers when they decide they're too lonely here or want to get married. I have no intention of getting married. I will be a spinster until I die. So your problem is solved. Don't even circulate that notice."

It turned out to be a little more complicated than that. Mrs. Wadden did have to consult the education representative and Mary Alice did have to write a test to judge her abilities and yes, she scored a hundred out of a hundred. Mrs. Wadden shook her hand. "Welcome, Miss Locke."

The first thing she did was run all the way to Hardy's house. She burst into the kitchen without knocking. Hardy was at the table with a white-and-brown cocker spaniel puppy on his lap.

Mary Alice screamed. "Where did you get this little doll? Give him to me."

Hardy grinned and handed him over. She lifted him up under his front paws and his round tummy was perfect. He kept trying to lick her. "Oh, I love him. Please say you're keeping him."

"That's the plan."

"Can I name him?"

"No."

"Meanie. Make sure it's something cute."

Hardy shook his head. "Umm, no."

Mary Alice sat down and kept the puppy on her lap. "Okay then, these are just suggestions. I made a list once of what I'd call a dog if I ever got one. Let's see if I can remember...Alfie, Bingo, Buddy, Casey, Happy, Jack, Oscar, Otis, Toby..."

"Toby."

She laughed and raised the pup in the air again. "Toby! You look like a Toby. Oh, I love you." She kissed and hugged the little creature until he started to whine so she let him down on the floor.

He promptly peed.

Hardy made a face. "Stop getting him so excited." He reached over to the wood stove and grabbed an old newspaper to sop it up. Then he picked Toby up and put him back in his towel-lined box. The little puppy fell over and was instantly asleep.

"Where did you get him?"

"I went to Main-à-Dieu and had to go to Mullins's to pick up a few things and someone had come in with a box of them. Eight in total, all with those big brown eyes. Peter said they were gone in an hour. Toby was the last one, so I grabbed him."

"Thank goodness. Toby was meant to be here."

"We all love him." Hardy smiled. "How does one little bag of fur cause such intense devotion after only one day?"

"Because dogs are the best things in the world. When I finally leave home, I'm getting one of my own."

"You're leaving home? I thought Sam told you to stay put."

"I'm not leaving Scatarie, but I hope to make enough money to build my own place."

Hardy folded his arms across his chest and stretched his legs out in front of him, crossing his ankles.

"Why are you looking so skeptical?" Mary Alice said. "You don't think I can do it?"

"I believe you can do anything, but where's the money coming from?"

Mary Alice sat up straighter in the chair, remembering why she'd come in the first place. "As of September, you are looking at the new teacher on Scatarie."

Hardy clapped his hands together. "Wow! Those lucky kids.

You'll be fantastic."

She got up and curtsied. "Thank you, kind sir. Until that happens, I'll just love Toby. I better run and tell Ma and Da."

"I'm the first to know?"

"Yep. See ya."

Out the door she ran. Hardy looked down at the sleeping Toby. "You're going to love that girl," he said. "Almost as much as I do."

Mary Alice was over-the-moon happy with her new situation. She couldn't believe she hadn't thought of it before. That's why I'd given her a nudge. Dreams are very important; visions that carry messages and speak to you. Usually things you know subconsciously but can't articulate in the real world.

And it's an easy way for spirits to come and visit you. What you'd never believe in real life you can accept in a dream, because dreams have no rules. You can fly, fight off a bear, be in a palace with the king, or become a mouse. It's all normal.

On Mary Alice's first day, as she sat at the desk in the front of the room before fifteen children came in, she said, "Thank you, Cara." That made me incredibly happy.

I didn't like to think of her wasting her life just cleaning fish and washing clothes. Most girls her age were married and busy from morning till night. She didn't have a young man to spend time with. Those who didn't get far with her told the others not to bother. Her reputation was that she thought too much of herself. That she was better than the rest of them. She was snooty. A snob. Who did she think she was?

Mary Alice was blissfully unaware of this. She kept her head down and helped her students in any way she could. They loved her, because she would take them out on field trips to study plants and look at the geography of the island. Things she thought might have helped Sam stay in school instead of fidgeting behind a desk until he couldn't stand it anymore.

She had a curriculum she had to follow, but she also incorporated periods where she would let the children paint, even the older grades, and she'd hang up their work. It was always something to do with their everyday life on the island, in case Mrs. Wadden dropped by.

When she organized the school Christmas pageant, she had them all make their very minimal costumes out of patterns so they could use math in the real world. They practiced singing while they worked, and she'd lead them in exercises outside at recess so everyone got a chance to stretch their legs. Especially her.

Mary Alice had never been very maternal, except when it came to dogs. She never thought about having babies like her sisters, but she came to love these little ragamuffin students of hers, who never had a lot and wore hand-me-downs. She became aware of the ones who didn't say much and always tried to take them aside in case they needed her. Often they didn't, but there was always one who sought attention, one way or the other.

She had indeed found her calling, and I like to imagine I assisted with that.

Buster was very jealous of Toby at first, but when he realized how much happier everyone in his family was because of this critter, he gave his approval, and even moved over when Toby would get on Hardy's bed at night. Toby would often zoom around the living room for no apparent reason, but of course he was playing with Buster.

The sky was spectacular on this late November day. There

had been rain showers earlier so there were grey clouds mixed with white ones dotted across the island and the winter sun made the light mellow, the shadows long. On days like this Mary Alice sometimes thought November was her favourite month, and not many people said that, especially when the weather was miserable. But when it was glorious like this, with rime on the leaves sparkling and the air cold, crisp, and clean, it was a wonder to be alive.

Normally.

But Mary Alice was in trouble. Sam was gone. Hardy was always working and so was she. It hit her quite hard to realize she had no friends. No girlfriends, specifically. Her mother had a wide circle of women she depended on, and her four older daughters were always running in and out, but her sisters looked on Mary Alice as the baby, who knew nothing of their lives, and had nothing in common with them seeing as she had no husband or children.

She'd always been closest to Rose, but now Rose was busy with her little boy and another baby on the way. Still, she was the one Mary Alice sought out on this Saturday morning.

A quick knock on the Trimms' door and she went inside. Rose was feeding the little guy, a roly-poly. Her mother-in-law was frying up something on the stove. She had a kerchief over her hair tied up like bunny ears on top. She seemed rabbit-like with her protruding teeth, but a nicer woman you'd never meet.

"Hello, Mary Alice! You're a stranger. Never out of the classroom, I hear."

Mary Alice smiled at Irene. "I'm a prisoner."

"Well, from what I hear, you're doing a fine job. All the mothers like you because their kids like you. No more whinin' at the breakfast table in the morning."

"Thanks, Irene. I do enjoy it."

"Why are you here?" Rose asked.

"Can't I come to see you?" Mary Alice sat in the chair beside her sister and leaned over towards Jeb Jr. "Hey there. Hello."

Jeb frowned, opened his mouth, and wailed. His aunt fell back in her chair.

"You have a way with babies." Rose shushed her son and held out another spoonful of mashed-up potato and turnip.

"I'm lonely, if you must know, and I don't know what to do about it."

Rose shook her head. "When a fella asks you to go out with him, GO."

"I don't care about that. I don't have any girlfriends." Mary Alice put her elbow on the table and leaned her cheek against her hand.

"Why are you surprised? You basically ignored every little girl you came across growing up, too busy running around with Sam and Hardy. Boys are all well and good, but you need another female in your life to tell your secrets to."

Mary Alice surprised herself by saying, "I suppose I have Cara."

Rose reached over and wiped Jeb's chin with a cloth. "Who's Cara?"

"Remember when I used to talk to an imaginary friend when I was little?"

"Yes. It was spooky."

"She's real."

"Okay. If you say so." Rose kept her eyes on her baby.

Mary Alice sat up. "You are a lousy friend. Too busy with your baby to even acknowledge me. I'll go find someone else." She got out of the chair and said, "Goodbye, Irene," before she went out the door.

Rose looked at her mother-in-law. "Why is she so difficult? She's always been the odd one in our family."

Irene turned over the haddock. "She's a special soul. Always has been. Didn't you know that?"

"No. You try living with her."

Mary Alice thought about going to see Hardy so she could snuggle with Toby, but that wouldn't solve her problem. She knew her mother would find some chore for her to do if she went home, so she kept walking and eventually ran into Flossie's younger sister Rita with a couple of her friends.

"Hi, Rita."

Rita looked leery. She knew the history between her sister and Mary Alice. "Hi."

"What are you girls up to?"

The one chewing gum answered. "We're going to Kenwood."

She had no idea what possessed her. "Mind if I tag along?"

These three were too old to be her students, but they were so shocked that the local schoolteacher wanted to come with them they didn't know how to say no.

Kenwood was a dance pavilion in Mira Gut. It hadn't been there long, but was already popular because of the live music. It was a place for everyone to go and have a good time and it wasn't as far away as Sydney or Glace Bay.

It wasn't going to solve Mary Alice's problem of finding a friend, but she could burn off excess energy on the dance floor.

She said she'd meet them at the boat and ran back to tell her mother she was off to the mainland for the afternoon. She didn't say where. Mary was just glad she was doing something.

The girls quickly realized that Mary Alice wasn't interested in them, they were just a handy way off the island and back. That was fine. Who wanted to be caught dead with the spinster schoolmarm, anyway? She would put a damper on everything.

Kenwood looked like a very long, narrow cow shed. It was

white with lots of small windows and a large one they could open for people who wanted to buy cigarettes, pop, and chips. The door opened, and inside there were tables and chairs around the perimeter and a large dance floor in the middle. The band played at the back. No one cared that it wasn't dolled up or fancy. It served its purpose, letting young people be together and have a laugh. Who didn't love music, and who didn't want to forget about the war for a time? The news was always so bleak. A few young men from the area had already been killed or were missing in action. No one was getting off scot-free in this situation.

What started out as a mission to find a girlfriend ended up a whirling good time with a lot of fellas. She knew a few of them, but most were total strangers, and they were the ones she could let down her hair with. It seemed to her she went from one to the other without a break, except to drink from a glass occasionally. You wouldn't think it was cold outside because everyone was sweating from the exertion.

For one afternoon, Mary Alice was able to escape her dull life. This was what she needed. Never mind girlfriends. Having a man put his arms around her was something she'd almost forgotten. Not that she had much experience. Oh god. Why wasn't Sam here? What if he never came back?

Mary Alice wondered if her life would've been worth it if she drowned later, on the way home. She'd never done a wrong thing, as in worthy of being sinful. Had she ever lived anything but a humdrum routine? Where was the excitement? The ecstasy? She was going to be twenty-two and she had nothing to show for it.

There must have been rum in that cola she had, or her courage came from her desperation. She looked out over the sea of faces and saw one who was looking at her the way Sam used to. He was the complete opposite of Sam: dark-haired, brown eyed, and taller.

When she didn't look away, he approached her.

"Hello, beautiful."

"Okay, that's cheesy."

He laughed and held out his hand. "Let's dance."

They cut a rug for a good half hour, knowing nothing about each other but the feel of their hands as they twirled and their arms as they swayed. Eventually a slower song played and they rested their bodies together, her head on his shoulder.

"What's your name?" he asked.

"Cara." She didn't even think about it, the name just came out.

"I'm glad you came, Cara."

"So am I."

"Wanna go outside and catch our breath? It's too damn hot in here."

She nodded, so he took her hand and they shrugged their coats on but didn't button them up as they went through the door. He offered her a cigarette and she took it. This girl did smoke. Or at least tried to. He grinned when she coughed so she took another drag but blew it out right away.

"You don't have to smoke, Cara."

She threw it away. "Fine. I can think of something else I'd rather do."

He immediately threw his cigarette away and pulled her around to the back of the pavilion. They leaned against the wooden structure and kissed for a long time until he was sure she meant business. That's when he picked her up, reached under her dress, and pushed himself against her. And the craziest thing was, she was glad that she was doing it, glad they might get caught, happy that it felt good. She'd denied herself with Sam and she could kick herself now. She'd earned this moment.

They were breathless when he finally slid her down and they

laughed together as they arranged their clothes.

"It's a little chilly out here. Let's go in," she said.

Once more he took her hand and led her back inside. They danced cheek to cheek, even as the band played "Boogie Woogie Bugle Boy."

When the song ended, she declared she was thirsty. "Let's go to the canteen."

They were zigzagging through the crowd of dancers when Mary Alice saw Rita come towards her. "We have to leave. Now."

Mary Alice turned to her dance partner. "Oh, I'm sorry. I have to go."

He looked shocked. "Wait! You're not Cinderella. I don't know anything about you. And you don't even know my name."

"It's better this way. Thank you for the dance."

Before she went out the door, Mary Alice looked back and saw him still standing where she'd left him.

The gum chewer's cousin drove them back to Main-à-Dieu and her brother was waiting in a boat tied up at the dock.

"Hell's bells. I told you to be here before four thirty. Get in."

They hustled down the ladder and he took off before they were even seated. The sun was setting, a glowing pink. Mary Alice put her hand over the side and felt the spray as they bounced over the waves. It would be dark before they got home.

With the sea against them, it was rough going. And the wind felt ten times colder on the water. Normally this would have bothered Mary Alice, but tonight she didn't care if she drowned. She'd finally done something she should be ashamed of, but she wasn't.

"I *am* that girl."

The wind took away her words.

I'm thinking I am too, since he was with Cara and not Mary Alice.

CHAPTER TEN

The war for Sam was an endless wait for something to happen. First, he was sent to a basic training centre, Camp Borden, northwest of Toronto, but all they did was forever march, learn to make beds, polish shoes, and clean guns. He wanted to shoot something.

I have to admit it was boring, so I didn't stick around for long.

He spent time in London cleaning up the mess from German bombs and was finally sent to a large training base for minor landing craft training set up in Inverary, in the west of Scotland, where he met Nick and Denis, who became his good pals. Nick was from Pickering, Ontario, and Denis was from Moncton, New Brunswick. They were the class clowns, and all the men got a kick out of them. But they knew when to rein it in, and they learned all there was to know about the latest amphibious landing techniques, including embarkation and disembarkation on landing beaches. Little did they know all that knowledge would come to nothing.

Then things started to get serious. I was with Sam when he was sent to the front in the first wave, with a contingent of Canadian soldiers who landed on Juno Beach on D-Day June 6, 1944, during the invasion of Normandy.

He and Denis ended up with thirty-six other nervous soldiers on the same landing craft, close to Courseulles-sur-Mer. Their mission was delayed a day because of weather, and that dawn the water was still very rough. The landing craft was supposed to ram the beach. They'd practiced in Inverary how to exit, but on the day, they were told just do their best, because there was a loud explosion and their craft started taking on water. They'd hit a mine.

It was a mad scramble of men, with ships, smoke, and the deafening sounds of shells detonating in the water while German rifles shot at them. Add to that the incendiary grenades that contained white phosphorus. Men were popping out of the water on fire, while other poor wretches were hanging on to the scramble net over their ships, trying to jump into the landing crafts but not making it. They were crushed between the two vessels before they even got to shore.

Some were dropped near the beach, and soldiers stepped into a couple of feet of water, but because their craft was compromised Sam and Denis had to leave with heavy mortar packs on their backs, carrying spades, and jump into water that was at least nine feet deep. Essentially, they had to swim to shore. Denis struggled as he wasn't a good swimmer, and he was stunned when the craft hit him on the head as he jumped. Sam went back for him and dragged him along as best he could until he could touch the bottom.

"Don't leave me," Denis panicked, water covering his face.

"I got you, buddy. Just hang on to me."

Of course, Sam knew the longer they struggled in the water, the more they were sitting ducks for the Germans, but he kept hold of Denis even though he was running out of steam. Luckily another soldier going by saw their predicament and grabbed Denis's other arm and between the two of them, they gave Denis the traction he needed before the fellow had to keep going.

The two friends crawled out of the surf, soaking wet and freezing cold. They'd lost their equipment and couldn't protect themselves.

"We have to get out of here," Sam yelled at Denis. "Let's go." Sam started ahead and turned around to see Denis try to stand on his feet. Denis looked at him with dismay. "I think I hurt my leg. Merde, you go."

"Goddamn it." Sam turned around and went back to help him. He was only a foot away when he watched Denis's face disappear in a mist of red blood and bone as he fell backward into the sand.

"NO! Denis! Get up." Sam was pulling him by the arm when another soldier yanked Sam away. "Get off the fucking beach or you'll be next. You can't help him now."

Sam huddled behind the sandbank for protection, waiting for the next wave of men. Meanwhile more soldiers fell to the left and right of him. An officer came by and ordered them to pick up anything they could use off the dead. He turned over a body and it was Nick. Sam was too numb to feel anything. "I'm sorry." He took his helmet, grenades, and Sten gun.

He finally knew what war was. It's when your bowels loosen from fear and your guts heave but you're trained to keep moving forward, take cover, and do your job.

The survivors soon realized that when their tanks finally rolled in, all the dead men lying on the beach would be run over, so they did their best to drag the bodies out of harm's way.

The rest of that day was a kaleidoscope of unimaginable images that became a blur. Sam couldn't fathom that he was still alive by the end of it.

I couldn't believe it either. The suffering was unbearable for those who were still alive. Denis and Nick were enfolded into their families and taken away from the bloody mess of their last moments on earth.

Sam's ordeal continued. The next objective was Putot, with orders to follow the Oak Line. They marched along fields of wheat four feet high, stopping for the night, but the Germans had infiltrated the surroundings without being seen, and on June 7 and 8, three companies lost two hundred and fifty-six men, either killed or injured. Sam saw fifteen from his platoon lined up and shot in the back of the head. That just about killed him.

They pushed on into France and fought street battles with the Germans for weeks, trying to head for Belgium. Sam was hit by shrapnel, and buried twice in ditches along the way, covered in dirt from the explosions. He had a grenade detonate behind him that blew him into a glass window. His hearing was never the same.

And then his luck ran out and their convoy was ambushed by Germans hiding in a ditch by railroad tracks. Quite a few of his unit were killed by grenades, and he was sent flying through the air. The ones lying on the ground not moving were picked up and shot, to make certain they were dead.

The rest became prisoners of war, taken to a camp in Germany. Sam had never been somewhere so awful, so unrelentingly cold, so empty of food and joy—until the Germans sent them on a death march through Europe, heading for Poland.

Sam never knew where he was and couldn't remember much afterward. It was just putting one foot in front of the other to make it through one day and doing that for months. The other spirits and I did what we could, gentle winds behind them as they walked and warmer air around them when they slept—in churches, in barns, even out in the open some nights at twenty-five below zero. But we could only do so much, and the ones who didn't die of starvation or cold were in very poor condition by the time they arrived at another camp surrounded by barbed wire.

Sam would talk of home at night, as they lay in the dark. Anything to distract himself from their reality. "There was an old fella on our island. Archie Spencer. He'd yell 'Lord flyin' dyin'!' every time he lost a fish, and he once threw his rubber boot in the water because he said that fish deserved a good kick."

The other POWs appreciated his stories. He talked to keep from going crazy. There were no letters from anyone, obviously; no misshapen cookies or ugly socks. How he wished he had those socks now. Prisoners of war were supposed to receive packages, but it often didn't happen.

There were times when he daydreamed about Mary Alice teaching at the new school or was curious to know how Hardy's dog, Toby, was getting along. He'd be big now. Not that cocker spaniels were big. Not like a black lab. When he thought of Buster the tears would come unbidden. That dog represented the happiest days of his life, spent with Mary Alice and Hardy. Looking back, he only saw the wonderful things about Scatarie and embellished it with more nostalgia than truth. He was allowed to do that. It was only thoughts of the island that kept him from stepping out of line and running towards a German guard.

There was one guard who took particular pleasure in making life as difficult as he could. He would slam the butt of his rifle into the back of someone who wasn't moving fast enough and when they dropped to the ground he would stomp on their hands, anything to add a little more pain. Sam would watch him. When the soldier became aware of this, he turned his attention to Sam, but no matter what he did, Sam refused to react or cry out. He wouldn't give him the satisfaction. Sam got to the point where he'd be damned if he'd die. Nick and Denis were still lying on a beach in his mind. He'd outlast these bastards for their sakes. He'd let their families know they died heroes. All of them on that beach that day were bloody heroes. He needed to live to remember them.

But deciding to live took more courage than he realized. It would've been much easier to give up.

The soldier moved on to another victim when he eventually decided Sam wasn't worth his time, making living day to day slightly easier, until one morning Sam opened his eyes and saw the same ugly window he'd been looking out for far too long. He wiped the crust off his eyes. At some point he'd gotten an eye infection. He just hoped he wouldn't go blind as well as deaf. Then he looked at his sinewy, bony arm reaching over his face and thought, no, he'd probably starve to death before that happened.

But something was different. Not that his hearing was great, but he still knew it was quieter than normal. He was the only one awake. Years of getting up before dawn to fish was hard to break. He went to the door of their bunk room and took a peek outside. There was no one around. No guards with their dogs, no sentry in the tower. He stepped out in the middle of the yard. "Anyone here?"

Why would they run and leave them? Was the war over? It was too much to take in. Sam didn't want to give anyone false hope, but he needed to tell his mates.

News travelled in an instant, and all the POWs who were still mobile milled around in the yard. No one tried getting over the barbed wire fences. It could still be a trick. And where would they go? They had no idea where they were except somewhere in Poland. Where was the nearest town? They were surrounded by trees.

Sam and some of the others ventured into the inner sanctum of the operation. It was a hole, like everything else here. The Germans who guarded this place must have hated it too. But it looked like they took all the paperwork, to leave no trace of the travesties committed.

There was no food. At some point the POWs were going to have to figure out what to do, but they were exhausted. It was enough that the Germans were gone.

The next morning a rumbling noise came closer. They poured out of their bunks and stood in the yard.

"Jesus!" Sam cried. "I think that's a tank."

"Maybe it's German," someone shouted.

"Shut your gob!" Sam yelled back.

The rumbling became louder and then voices were heard and a line of British tanks appeared over the horizon and crashed through their barbed wire fence. When they finally came to a stop, one of the troops on top yelled, "Did ya miss us?"

"Hell no!" Sam shouted.

"Cheeky bugger. Good news, fellas. It's over!"

The euphoria was too much. While they laughed and tried to dance around, most of the prisoners just sank to the ground and cried. Soldiers emerged from the tanks with blankets and water and food. Sam put his hands over his face and thought of Nick and Denis.

"We made it, boys. We made it."

It was incredibly difficult to move from one world to another. For five years, the war had been a looming storm cloud over everyone, their hopes and dreams drifting away in a maelstrom of human misery.

And now, with peace, they were supposed to get on with it, live an ordinary life, but everyone had a story that pierced their heart. Not all made their way across this great divide. Others did what they had to. Pretending it was fine. It was all fine.

Jane Sinclair was one of those people.

You might remember I told you I can be everywhere at once. I am also entangled in the future as well as the past. And I wanted to go back and meet Jane, before.

The only way she could cope was to make believe nothing had happened when she was nineteen. She didn't lose her mum and dad and younger brother in the largest air raid over central London on May 10 and 11, 1941, three of the almost fifteen hundred civilians killed over two nights.

There should have been four in that house, but her dad had sent her out to the shops to see if she could find brown sauce. They'd laughed about it as she left.

On her way back she was herded into an air raid shelter with everyone else when the sirens went off. As she sat with the others along the floor of the long underground tunnel, they looked at each other nervously. The lights were flickering and the sounds were horrendous. The entire structure shook. This was a bad night.

It took hours before they were given the all-clear to leave. Everyone crowded up the stairs in a hurry to get a glimpse at what had happened over their heads and to get to their loved ones as soon as possible.

Jane was still holding the bottle of brown sauce as she made her way under a bright full moon along an obstacle course of downed bricks, splintered wood, firehoses, and burnt-out cars. The acrid smell burned her nostrils. She turned to go up her street and on one side, half of it was missing. The missing section was a smouldering mess of debris, in the middle, where her house was. She called out for her parents as she stumbled along, hoping against hope that they'd somehow survived and would crawl out of the rubble and run to her. A fireman heard her screaming and stopped her from going any farther.

"Sorry, pet, we can't let you in. There are still fires to be put out."

Jane couldn't remember what happened after that. At some point she was in a police station drinking a cup of lukewarm tea. And then she was on a Red Cross cot with lots of others in a large room, everyone crying. She curled up and put a blanket over her head to drown out the sorrow that threatened to destroy her.

What was she going to do? How would she do it? She had no money. Only the change from the brown sauce. Immediately, she sat straight up in a panic. Where was the brown sauce? She started to search through the blanket and when it was finally revealed, she grabbed it and held it against her chest. This was her dad's. She'd keep it at all costs.

One of the Red Cross ladies let her use the phone to call her father's older sister in Dorking, a market town in Surrey about twenty miles away. After she and Aunt Lou cried and cried, her aunt said, "I'll come and get you."

"No. I doubt you'd get through. It's an unbelievable mess."

"Then you come to me."

"Thanks, Aunt Lou, but the authorities think I should be available to...um...if I need to identify..."

"Oh my god. This is too much for you to handle alone."

"I'm okay. The only thing I need is money."

Her aunt said she would wire her some funds through the Red Cross, and Jane promised to keep in touch and let her know what was happening. Aunt Lou was a tough old bird and Jane had always been a little afraid of her, but right now she was her only family and Jane was grateful.

Jane stayed close to her cot in the facility that week. At least there were people around. And she made herself useful, bringing tea to other survivors as she'd pat their backs and hold their hands. She was about to go back for more tea when a man at the entrance called her name. She hurried over to him.

"Jane Sinclair?"

"Yes."

"Did you live at Holford Square in King's Cross with your parents, Jim and Doris Sinclair, and brother Billy?"

She didn't trust herself to speak, so she nodded.

"Would you come with me?"

This is when her make-believe world started. She didn't attend the morgue and identify her parents by the rings on their fingers. She didn't see the burnt body found between her parents, assumed to be her brother. She didn't go through the rubble to collect anything salvageable like her mother's dented stainless-steel teapot and she didn't go to their funerals in her mother's neighbourhood of Camden Town with Aunt Lou.

Again, her formidable aunt insisted she come home with her, but in Jane's mind that would mean her parents were dead. She wanted to stay in London to fool herself all was well. It was the first time she really stood up for herself.

"I appreciate the offer, I do, but I'd like to stay here. I feel closer to them."

"You never were a sensible girl, but be that as it may, I'm always here if you need me."

She did take Aunt Lou's money to hold her over until she got a job. She'd been to secretarial school but never really liked it, so no office work for her. She was much happier at a bistro in Islington. And she managed to rent a room in a boarding house not too far away. She could take the bus to work. And the other young women there were great for taking her mind off her troubles. When they would come home from their dates, they would sit on someone's bed and brush out their hair while gossiping about the young sailors and soldiers in the city, or moan about trying to find stockings. One of the older girls asked her why she never dated.

Jane put her hand through her hair. "I used to, but I don't have the heart for it now."

"Child, you've got to start living. Otherwise, why are we going through all this?"

Now Jane thought she must be doing everything wrong. That's when she took up smoking. All of them smoked. But she never could get the hang of drinking. She tried but she immediately got tearful and bad thoughts came back, so she nipped that in the bud. She wasn't like her dad, all gruff and disciplined, as a bobby should be. She was airy fairy like her mother. A dreamer. Billy they used to call Goat, because he was so stubborn.

Time to stop thinking.

Time to stop thinking.

Of Nick and Denis, of Scatarie, Mary Alice, Hardy, his dad, his siblings Ian, Bob, and Jean, the boat, the water, a feed of lobster. Round and round and round Sam would go, wishing, dreaming of going home.

In the summer of 1945, the repatriation process was already bogged down. First in were supposed to be first out, but it didn't always work like that. Married men were able to jump the queue and there were seemingly endless other reasons. It didn't help impatient men like Sam. He was ready to jump out of his skin. He'd given enough of himself to this cause. All he wanted to do was stand on a cliff on Scatarie and breathe in the sea. When he saw himself do it, he was always screaming.

He and other Canadian soldiers stationed in and around London were just biding their time until they were given the go-ahead to board a ship, in his case to Halifax. He'd become fast friends with a fellow from there, as Maritimers tend to do when they meet each other in another part of the world. Stuart Campbell was a great guy. They decided Stuart must be a distant relative of Hardy's, because he was big and tall too. It was a good excuse to chum around, anyway.

The only saving grace about having to wait was that, little by little, Sam was starting to look like himself again. If he'd walked off a boat looking like the day he'd left the prison camp, not a soul would have known him. Even he had a hard time looking in the mirror when they got back to civilization. There was no way he looked twenty-three anymore. But as Stuart pointed out, the ladies still gave him a second look.

"They're looking at you, mate, all six foot four of ya. I think I'll do myself a favour and find someone shorter to hang around with."

It was the end of July when Sam happened to be on a bus in Islington, looking for a barbershop. He didn't want to use the one at the base. It brought back memories of his first military haircut when he was seventeen. It had been hard to get over the shock. He'd looked like a skinned rabbit.

The bus made one of its frequent stops, so he closed his eyes. When he opened them again, a young woman was walking towards him down the aisle. At first, he thought she was Mary Alice because she had the same auburn hair and wore it up, but she was a finer, more delicate version. There was nothing determined or no-nonsense about her. He wanted to put his arms around her and protect her from the world. She looked lost, her eyes haunted. He recognized that in a person.

She sat on the opposite side of the bus. Sam was so taken aback, he just sat there and tried not to stare at her. She eventually glanced at him, or more likely looked out his window, but she did smile a little before she looked straight ahead again. His heart was pounding and his mouth was dry. Sam hadn't felt like this for a very long time. He'd forgotten he could. And while still thinking what a miracle it was, she pulled the cord and got up to leave.

Forgetting completely about his haircut, Sam rose quickly and disembarked to watch the woman walk up the street. He didn't want to follow her, but he didn't want to lose her either. This was ridiculous. He felt like he was thirteen years old. Or maybe it was that this feeling belonged to another life. One he'd almost forgotten.

She walked almost two blocks before disappearing into a corner bistro. What luck. Anyone can walk into a bistro. Everyone has to eat. But she didn't sit down. She disappeared through the door at the back. Was there a rear entrance? Maybe she was trying to get away from him.

He hurried out of the building and ran around the corner. There was a back door, but she wasn't standing in it or running for her life down the street. Now that he had established that, he realized that while he was standing there, she could be leaving, so he hustled back to the bistro and walked in again. She was serving a customer.

The relief was enormous.

He settled into a small table by the window and tried to be calm.

"Would you like a menu?"

He looked up into the eyes of a tired-looking older woman. "Sorry?" He realized he wasn't sitting at the right table. "Do you mind if I switch my seat? The sun is in my eyes."

"Be my guest." And she moved away.

There were no unoccupied tables around this new Mary Alice, so Sam dithered until finally a couple got up and left. He scooted right in behind them, despite the crumbs and empty teacups. He was happy to sit there and watch her. She had her back to him. The curve of her neck with the sun catching the copper highlights in the tendrils of her hair caused him an intake of breath.

She was home.

He was too busy wiping his eyes to notice her standing beside him. "Good morning. Are you okay?"

Sam nodded and then shook his head. "Are any of us?"

His answer took both of them by surprise. She immediately sat down hard in the chair beside him. "Thank you for saying that. All I hear from everyone is how we have to buck up, carry on, and have a stiff upper lip. I'm tired of hearing it."

He nodded again. "How are we supposed to live a normal life now? We need to be sad for as long as we want. We've all been though the fires of hell. I swear if I ever told anyone about what I've seen, they wouldn't believe me."

Jane was talking to a kindred spirit. "Have you heard of the Hardest Night? I lost my whole family in the Blitz, in 1941." She had never said it aloud before. She couldn't believe what she was hearing out of her own mouth.

His face registered shock and then the other waitress tapped her on the shoulder. "What's this? Get back to work."

Sam immediately took the blame. "It's my fault. She's an old friend. I asked her to sit down. I'll have a tea and an egg salad sandwich, please. We'll get caught up another time."

She gave him a grateful look while she cleared the teacups and wiped his table. "I'll be right back."

Sam felt lighter somehow. He watched the kitchen door for her to come out again, and she did but headed to two more tables before she approached him with his sandwich and tea.

"Thank you." He smiled. "What's your name?"

"Jane Sinclair. You?"

"Sam Harris. Would you like to meet me somewhere to have another cup of tea, Jane?"

She nodded. "Yes."

And that's how it started. They met each other as often as they could. The older girl at the boarding house was pleased with Jane's change of heart. "Goin' to see that dishy bloke again?"

Sam and Jane mostly talked about their experiences in the war while walking around the city, in cafes, on park benches, at the pictures (but they got in trouble for that). After so long avoiding even thinking about their deaths, Jane was grateful to have someone to talk to about her family, someone who'd seen awful things too. And Sam didn't just tell her to move on.

He took her to a nice restaurant one night and she ordered salmon. When it came to the table, Sam looked at her plate.

"You call that a piece of salmon? That's been scraped off the deck of a dory, Jesus, b'y. We'd use that for bait."

She laughed and laughed. "You have a different accent."

"This is my true accent. I've just been hanging around you lot for too long."

"And why don't you like my salmon?" She took a bite. "It tastes like salmon."

"I'm a fisherman."

Jane looked up at him. "Are you? That's amazing. And what do you fish?"

"Halibut, haddock, sole, mackerel, lobster, herring, swordfish. I don't fish salmon, but I know what it should look like. Thick, moist, and reddish-pink with a crispy skin."

"That's fascinating."

"Not that special. If I was wearing my usual clothes instead of this uniform, you'd walk right by me."

She doubted that, as she sat back in her chair, completely unaware of the other people in the room. "And what do you wear?"

"Baggy pants, plaid flannel shirts, a knitted fisherman's sweater, oilcloth, big rubber boots, and a cap. And work gloves to keep my hands from being cut to pieces by the rope."

He took a breath and ate more of his chicken breast covered with some kind of sauce, reminding himself that food supplies were still iffy. He was sure this was a rooster.

"I assume you live near water."

"I live on an island."

She couldn't imagine that. "But how do you get anywhere?"

"By boat, obviously. You city girls really are stunned."

He made her laugh. Something she never thought she'd do again. He had a refreshing, unfussy way about him. She'd never met anyone like him.

After taking another bite of inferior salmon, she took a sip of water. "Tell me about your island."

His eyes lit up. "Oh, my girl. You never seen the like of it. Granite cliffs, sandy beaches, fields and woods, lakes and bogs. And the wind howls over the land when a storm brews. The waves swell with whitecaps and the fog rolls in and covers everything until you can't see your hand in front of your face. That's when you hear the foghorn moan. My best friend, Hardy, is the lighthouse keeper and keeps that light shining on dark nights, so ships at sea don't end up wrecked on shore."

"That sounds...romantic."

He grinned. "We got that too."

That was the night they held each other and kissed for the first time. Both of them realized they might have a future after all.

When Jane called her aunt three months later to tell her she was going to marry a boy from Canada, the poor dear bellowed, "Over my dead body!"

Jane expected this reaction, which is why the next words out of her mouth were, "Would you like to meet him? We're coming by train tomorrow. He's dying to meet you."

"Have you lost your senses, Jane?"

"Ask me that after you've met him."

Sam and Jane held hands on the train as they travelled to the pretty market town of Dorking. This is where her dad grew up. Aunt Lou was still living in their childhood home. She had planned to marry her young fiancé and move to Cornwall, but he was killed in July of 1916 in the Battle of the Somme in the First World War. She'd never married.

They walked from the station since it was a lovely October day, the kind that had you take off your sweater and carry it. Aunt Lou lived in a brick terraced house with a walled-in front garden filled with shrubs and flowers. They opened the wrought iron gate and used the knocker. There were stained glass windows in the door, so they saw Aunt Lou's large shadow before she opened it.

Sam was instantly afraid of her. She had that strict teacher look, the type that taps a switch in front of the class to see who's not listening. She would know all the rules of etiquette and expect others to adhere to them. Sam would rather wrestle with a shark, but he put on a brave face and reminded himself he'd faced worse.

Not by much.

"Well, well. This is the young Canadian who thinks he's going to drag my beloved niece across the ocean and marry her."

"We want to get married here, Aunt Lou, so you can be with us," Jane said. "We need a witness, and I think Dad would like you to be there."

Aunt Lou did not seem moved. "Come in, the both of you. I've set the table."

They walked through a very flowery sitting room with a gas fire. There were three fat cats in front of it. Why it needed to be on, Sam couldn't figure out. He was already sweating. He knew his shirt would have wet marks under his arms, so he'd keep his uniform jacket on regardless of how hot it got.

She ushered them into the dining room, which had more dishes on the table than Sam had ever seen in his life. Now he was really nervous. Jane sensed his panic and squeezed his hand before they sat down.

"This looks very welcoming." Sam smiled at Aunt Lou. "I appreciate you going to so much trouble. Jane talks about you all the time."

Aunt Lou took her napkin and gave it a shake before she put it on her lap. "Save your effusive comments until after tea."

He wondered if she meant *offensive*. He had no idea what *effusive* was. This was nerve-racking.

Aunt Lou poured the tea and they helped themselves to crustless fish-paste sandwiches.

Sam took a bite. "This is cod. My favourite. Do you know I once caught a cod that weighed over a hundred pounds?"

"You fish in your spare time?" Aunt Lou asked.

"No, all the time. I'm a fisherman."

Jane didn't look up, so she didn't see the glower on Aunt Lou's face. "Really. And is that lucrative?"

"Must be. I love it."

Jane knew this was going downhill. Her confident, funny, endearing man was like an uneducated schoolboy.

"And what do you bring to the table, young man? You can't possibly expect me to let you marry my niece without getting to know you. This seems very premature. And thoroughly unwise. You are basically a stranger from a strange land."

Sam got annoyed. "You might not know me, but Jane does, and she's the one I want to marry, not you. I'm sorry if that sounds rude, but I don't have time to argue about this. I left my friends dead on a beach. They had their whole lives ahead of them and now they're in the ground like so much garbage. For some reason, I was spared that day and then managed to live through a death march for months, watching guys give up, lie down, and die in front of me. I have no idea why, but surely someone wants me to live and be happy. And Jane makes me happy."

Lou took a sip of tea to collect herself. Jane took advantage of that.

"Aunt Lou, we've come to tell you our plans because you have been kind to me, especially in the early days after...that night. We didn't want to leave the country without your knowing. I need your blessing. I finally have a future I can look forward to, which I didn't think was possible until I met Sam. He understands loss. He has suffered too."

Putting her napkin to her lips, Aunt Lou felt outmanoeuvred.

Jane touched her aunt's hand with her own. "We're in love. You know what that's like. Don't feel like you have to be Dad, asking questions about money and housing. We're young and strong and smart. We've been through the worst and we'll deal with life as it comes."

Now Aunt Lou gave a great sigh, and her shoulders, which had been up around her ears, lowered. "I wanted to be your father. I feel I owe him that. But I also know what it's like to be denied a normal life because of war. I do understand. But you'll be an ocean away. What happens if you decide you don't like it in Canada?"

"I'll come home."

Sam smiled. "I'll row her across the Atlantic myself and bring her back to you."

"You have to write to me every week and send me pictures. I need to know where you are. I don't want you to disappear and never come back."

Jane patted her aunt's hand. "I won't. I promise."

The plan was that as soon as Sam got his marching orders to return home, they would marry at the local church in Dorking, and Jane would stay with her aunt until she was able to book passage across the Atlantic. She wasn't allowed on his ship. There were too many soldiers trying to get home. But he promised Aunt Lou that he would stay in Halifax with his friend Stuart until Jane's ship docked and he would take her to Cape Breton himself, so she wouldn't be travelling alone in a foreign country. And he would send Aunt Lou a telegram when they arrived safely on Cape Breton Island.

Jane stayed at the bistro working until Sam got his long-awaited ticket home. It didn't come until January of 1946. By then they'd had many visits to Aunt Lou's, and Jane could tell she got a kick out of Sam, now that she knew him better, and she took a real shine to Stuart immediately.

They tore up to Dorking with Stuart as Sam's best man, and Aunt Lou as the maid of honour. A local photographer took a picture of this odd wedding party in front of the church, Jane in a navy suit with an ivory headpiece and short gloves, wrapped in a fur jacket, the two handsome fellas in their uniforms, and Aunt Lou looking like a figurehead from the prow of a ship.

Aunt Lou had saved all her butter and milk coupons so she could make a wedding cake and invited the neighbours to come and toast the happy couple. Stuart said goodbye, as he was catching the train back to London that night. He kissed Jane and her Aunt Lou goodbye. He liked the old doll. He shook Sam's hand.

"See you on the dock in two days."

Sam and Jane booked a room in a local hotel for their wedding night. Jane bought a pink negligee for the occasion. As they said goodbye and thanked her for the lovely party, Aunt Lou took Jane aside. "I assume you know what's coming? Your mother did prepare you?"

Jane tried not to laugh. “She did. She said I’d have the happiest night of my life.”

Aunt Lou made a face. “Trust that woman to offer no practical guidance whatsoever. For what it’s worth, take my mother’s advice. If all else fails, lie back and think of England. Or hide in the bathroom.”

Finally, everyone was gone. They’d done it. They were alone standing in front of each other, as Sam slipped the negligee straps off Jane’s shoulders and watched it fall to the floor.

There was no thinking of England. Sam turned her around, came up behind her, and put his lips on the nape of her neck. She leaned her head forward and to the side so he could kiss below her ear.

He held her close. “Thank you for loving me. I’ve been so lonely.”

She turned to face him and put her cheek against his. “We have each other now. It’s all over. We’ll be fine, Sam. Just fine.”

CHAPTER ELEVEN

While all that was going on, I was also preoccupied with my charges on my island. In early January 1944, a telegram from Western Union arrived for the Lockes. The postmistress, Mrs. Theresa Wadden, knew what it was. When she saw Mary Locke walking up to get her mail, she tried to keep the tears out of her eyes. She didn't know if it was news about Jake or Lionel. Maybe one of them was injured. Maybe it wasn't terrible.

"Mornin', Theresa. Some cold out there, wha'?"

Theresa nodded and held out the telegram. Mary also knew what it was instantly. The two of them looked at each other, both of them shaking. Mary tore it open.

"I regret to inform you..."

"Oh no, oh no," she moaned. "It's Jake. He died on Christmas Day in the Battle of Ortona. I don't even know where that is. Poor Mary Alice. He died on her birthday. How can I tell her? How can I tell his father?"

Theresa hugged the poor woman. Normally she loved her job, but not today.

As soon as Mary Alice got home from school she was confronted by her weeping parents and sister Rose. She froze in the doorway. "Which one?"

Rose's face crumbled. "It's Jake. He died on Christmas Day while we were eating a fat goose. How is that fair?"

Mary Alice tore off, running over the ice and snow to get to the lighthouse. Hardy was coming out of the shed when he saw her stumble and fall and get up again, still running. He knew it was bad. But who? He held out his arms and she grabbed him around the neck. "It's Jake. He died on our birthday!"

Mary Alice wore herself out crying at his kitchen table, Annie hovering in the background, sniffing into tissues. She laid her head on her arms, hiding her face. Hardy put his hand on her back. "Let's get you home. Your parents need you."

He was right. He was always right. Together they walked back to her place, his arm around her shoulder the entire time. She hugged him before she went inside. "Thank you."

There were times when I wanted to throttle Mary Alice. For such a smart creature, she was very shortsighted. Who did she run to at the first sign of trouble? Who was always there for her? And yet she still saw Hardy as a dear pal, someone strong enough to not need her.

She was going to need him when Sam came home. I fretted about what was to come.

There were other young men who went overseas from the island. James Parsons, John Steele, Henry Wadden, Joseph Bourinot, and Herbert Harris. Joseph and Herbert never made it back. Everyone on the island felt the loss deeply. It was such a miserable waste.

But Edgar Harris was a lucky man. While the Lockes across the road from him had to mourn their son Jake, a wire was sent in July 1945 to say that Sam was alive and had been a prisoner of war. A quick letter from the man himself was delivered shortly thereafter. He didn't say much, just that he was looking forward to coming home.

And then Ian showed up with no warning a month later, in August, and surprised them all. He'd fought in Sicily and then throughout Italy, a bitter campaign made more difficult by the mountainous terrain and fast-flowing rivers. After years in the Mediterranean sun, his skin was bronzed, his hair bleached. Once more, females on the island were swooning over a Harris, but all of them were married. He would have to go farther afield to look for a mate.

It only took him two months, and he was married to a girl named Judy from Marion Bridge. Her father owned a store and asked Ian to join the business, which Ian was very happy to do. No more fishing for him. His left arm had been damaged in a fiery explosion and he didn't have the strength needed, or the range of motion, to haul fishing lines or traps.

That was his official excuse, anyway. The real reason was that looking out over the water reminded him of drowning men. Sure, it happened on the island too, but watching a sinking ship with more than a hundred men in the water getting caught up in a flaming oil slick was something else entirely.

His father was disappointed that Ian was not going back in the boat, but he could hardly complain. At least his son was alive. Every time he saw Mary Locke's sad face, he was reminded of what might have been. Poor Mary's heartache was eased when Lionel came home shortly after that, although no one recognized him. All his hair was gone and no one knew why, not even Lionel.

Finally, a letter showed up at the post office in January 1946. It was from Sam. Edgar waited until Bob came in for supper to open it. After all this time you'd think he would have something to say, but again there were only a few lines. That was Sam for you. Always hated school and writing. He was letting them know that he was finally being shipped home on the *Île de France* at the end of January and might stay in Halifax for a bit with his friend Stuart Campell before coming to Cape Breton. He hoped all was well and he'd let them know when he landed.

Bob stared at his dad. "What the hell? He's been gone since 1939 and he's staying in Halifax for a while before he comes home? What for? Now that he's seen the world, he can't stomach coming back? As true as I'm sittin' here, I'm gonna give him a piece of my mind when he shows up. Does he even know how hard it was to not hear from him? Imaginin' all sorts. Selfish bugger."

Edgar didn't say anything. Bob had said it all for him.

Hardy and Mary Alice were playing their usual Thursday night game of gin rummy. Mary Alice was delighted with the news that Sam was returning but bewildered as to why he was staying in Halifax first.

"I'm going to hug him and then kick him for being so miserable and making us wait even longer. He's not even going to recognize us after five years." Mary Alice put down a card in the discard pile. Hardy picked it up, melded his cards, and knocked. "Gin."

She threw her hand down. "Why do you always win?"

"Because you talk through the whole game and don't concentrate." He gathered up the playing cards and put them on the sideboard. He was tired. Of what, he wasn't sure.

"It's not even eight o'clock. Are we finished?"

Hardy pulled on his ear. "Yes. I can only talk about Sam for an hour and a half at a time."

She put her elbows on the table and held up her cheeks with her fists. "I suppose that's a dig."

"If Sam knew how often you talked about him, he'd be annoyed."

Mary Alice sat up straight. "I'd do exactly the same thing if it was you over there."

"You think so?

This wasn't the first time Mary Alice wondered if Hardy was jealous of Sam. That was nonsense of course. She loved them both and they knew that. "Think what you want, then. I need an early night anyway. I have a field trip planned for tomorrow."

"You're always dragging those kids outside. When do you teach them spelling and arithmetic?"

She ignored the question and got up off her chair. "Can I take Toby with me? The kids would love that."

Toby lifted his head at the sound of his name. He was curled up under Hardy's feet. "No, you may not. He's fine where he is."

"You're so mean. See ya."

Hardy walked out on the front porch and watched her go. He didn't realize his mother was peeking at him from the window.

Annie shook her head. She worried that Hardy would always be alone. He had never looked at another girl. Dorothy arrived one day with a friend from Little Lorraine, hoping to pique his interest, but mother and daughter had to admit it was an abject failure. He barely grunted at the poor friend.

That was Hardy's problem. He never pushed himself forward for attention like Sam. Always content to not rock the boat. Instead of telling Mary Alice outright how he felt about her, he watched and waited. But he was going to wait too long. He would become just like his uncle Ted, a lifelong bachelor. And Annie didn't want that for him.

At night, when Annie said her prayers, she'd talk to her Len. "I wish you were here. Maybe you'd have some practical advice. I'm beyond knowin' what to do with that boy."

But I knew there was nothing to be done. Hardy loved who he loved and would never change his mind. Having Mary Alice as a best friend might be all he could hope for. Unless I could think of something that might change their destinies. But as I'm not God, as you call her, my options were limited.

The *Île de France* had been a French luxury ocean liner. It was now a troop ship heading for Halifax with seven thousand men on board. There was nothing luxurious about that, other than the fact that they were finally heading home.

All of the soldiers knew they were the lucky ones, and they thought about their buddies who hadn't made it as they leaned over the side and watched the Atlantic Ocean below. Sam and his best man, Stuart, were excited to see each other on the day they left the English pier, but for Sam it was bittersweet. He was leaving Jane behind.

Over the five days it took to cross the great divide, Stuart couldn't help noticing that Sam was becoming increasingly quiet. It worried him. He joined Sam on the deck for a smoke. "Out with it. What's got you so glum? You're goin' home!"

Sam looked out over the grey horizon. He couldn't tell where the ocean stopped and the sky began. He took a long drag. "You know how you dream of home? You make it better than it is. Especially when you're missing it after so many years."

Stuart shrugged. "We all do, I suppose."

"I'm just realizing that Jane is from another world. I have no business making her come here."

"She loves you. She wants to be with you."

Sam flicked the ash off his cigarette. "I was so caught up in our dream world, I forgot to prepare her for the one she'll live in."

"For Christ's sake, are you dragging her to a cave? You're making a mountain out of a molehill."

He shook his head. "You live in Halifax. I live on Scatarie, an island with no running water, no electricity, no telephone, and no indoor bathroom."

Stuart slowly turned away and looked out over the churning sea. "Jesus."

"I know. What have I done?"

Everyone was delighted when they sailed into Halifax Harbour and stepped onto Canadian soil for the first time in years. The troops were sent up to the Halifax Armories, where their families and loved ones were waiting for them. Stuart brought Sam with him and Sam watched as Stuart's parents and siblings embraced him and jumped around in their excitement. Mrs. Campbell then gave him a big hug, and for the first time in a long time, Sam missed his mother.

There was utter chaos as the families reunited and slowly left the building to go their separate ways. Life was about to begin again, and everyone could take a deep breath for the first time in years and be happy.

The Campbells lived in a really nice house with a landscaped property on Connaught Avenue. Just the kind of place Jane would probably be delighted with. Sam felt sick to his stomach. He'd never envied anyone in his life, and now he felt second class. What the hell?

He asked if he could use their phone to get in touch with his family. He didn't tell them he was calling the government phone at the lighthouse. Thankfully it was Hardy who picked up.

"Hey, buddy. It's me."

"Sam?"

"You forget me already?"

There was a long pause. "Sam, I'm happy to hear from you, but I have bad news. Your father had a stroke two weeks ago. Bob wants you to come home immediately. They're going to need help."

"Oh my god. Okay. Tell them I'm on my way. I'll get the train tomorrow morning. Thanks, Hardy."

"It's good to hear your voice," Hardy said. "We've all missed you."

"And I've missed you. Tell Mary Alice. See you soon."

When Sam hung up his mind was racing. He told Stuart, and the whole family felt terrible that Sam's happy homecoming was so short. He took Stuart aside. "I promised Aunt Lou I would meet Jane in Halifax, and now I won't be here. How's that going to look? My first promise broken."

"You can't help that your father's ill. Don't worry about Jane. We'll get in touch with her and tell her the plans have changed but I'll meet her at the pier and take her to the train myself. All you have to do is pick her up. She'll be fine."

That decided, the next morning Sam was on the first train to Sydney, giving Stuart a warm embrace before he boarded, to thank him for being such a great pal. Honestly, he was never so grateful to anyone. And to think they'd met so recently. It felt like they'd been friends for years.

Sam had envisioned this train ride through Nova Scotia to be nothing but joyful. But now he was full of doubts. Why didn't he tell Jane more about Scatarie? He'd just assumed she'd love it as he did, but that was insane. He'd grown up in that situation. She was raised in the city of London. Their worlds couldn't be farther apart.

That's when he knew he was crazy. His entire war experience had made him lose his mind. Or maybe he was at a loss because she wasn't with him. Maybe she'd love it as he did. He felt adrift as he watched the spruce and fir trees go by, and then it dawned on him that his breathing had slowed and he was aware of the feeling of a hand in his. He didn't know who it belonged to, but he was glad of it.

Maybe it was his father. Maybe his father had died already. No. It couldn't be his old man. He'd never held Sam's hand, except for the time he pulled Sam out of the water when he broke his wrist while fishing.

At some point Sam was so exhausted from fretting, he put his head back and let it sway to the rhythm of the locomotive until he fell asleep. He woke up in Mulgrave, where there were rail and car ferries to take people across the Strait of Canso to Cape Breton Island. He slid open the back door and stuck his head out to take a great lungful of air. It smelled like home. He was grateful. This time he stayed awake and watched the scenery go by.

He'd forgotten how beautiful Cape Breton really was. Not that he'd been everywhere, but from what he'd seen of the world, there was nothing to compare to it. Especially with the snow covering everything like lace. Hopefully there was no ice in to keep him from getting on Scatarie. He hadn't even thought to ask Hardy.

He arrived in Sydney and got the next train to Louisbourg. It was late in the day when he arrived. Bob was standing on the platform. Sam was almost afraid to see him. He wasn't sure he'd know him anymore. But once he got off the train it was an automatic response to put his arms around his big brother.

Bob patted his back. "Good to see you. You're still a skinny little shit."

"You can thank the Germans for that. How's Da?"

"He's home now. Jean is with him. There's nothing they can really do for him. He's lost the use of his left side and he can't talk. It's miserable."

Their cousin Danny was taking them by car to the wharf in Main-à-Dieu. He lived in the village. He was mighty glad to see Sam and shook his hand vigorously. "We thought you were a goner there for a while."

"So did I," Sam shot back.

They piled into Danny's old Ford pickup. It smelled like fish and gasoline.

"Now that your da is probably never going on a boat again, you'll have to help Bob with fishing," Danny said, grinding the gears down a hill.

"I plan on it."

"You were gone a long time." Bob looked over his shoulder to address Sam in the back seat. "Things have changed with the fisheries. Everyone wants fresh fish now, instead of salted, because it's better money and no work to it. By the time we get in from fishing and then take our catch over to the mainland, it's late and there's no time to rest. People are starting to talk about getting off the island."

"Da saw the writing on the wall and I'm glad we left," Danny added. "You don't realize what a chore it is to live there until you stop doing it. Mind, I still miss the place."

They pulled up to the pier and only took a few minutes to say goodbye to Danny before they set off in Bob's boat that was tied up to the side of the wharf. The sun was going down and they wanted to sail before it got rough. They went into the cuddy and the engine roared to life as they headed out.

"The ice didn't come in yet," Sam said. "God, it's good to be on this old girl. You must have put a fresh coat of paint on her."

"Aye. At least twice since you've been gone. Are you sorry you went?"

"I can't answer that, because I met some great people."

Now that they were alone, Bob had his chance. "Gotta say, it hit Da like a punch in the gut when you wrote to say you were going to stay in Halifax for a while. What the hell was that all about? Your family missing you for years, not hearing from you for a year. Do you know what it was like to wonder every day if you were dead?"

"Are you telling me that's what led to Da's stroke? My letter?"

"No..."

"It sure sounds like it from here. I had my reasons for wanting to stay a little longer, but it's not something I want to discuss right now."

Bob's hands gripped the helm tightly. "You always were cocky."

"Frig off, Bob. I just got back. I'm exhausted. I have news that

I will tell you in my own good time. Right now, all I want to do is see Da. I came as soon as I could, didn't I? Does that count for anything?"

Sam left the covered wheelhouse and sat on the back of the boat, despite the frigid air blowing right at him. He'd dreamt about this in that damn prison camp, the feel of the wind, the splash of the waves, the familiar rhythm of the boat. This is what had kept him alive all those months, and now here he was.

Realizing he had to go back to being part of a family, instead of a lone wolf.

Sighing, he got up and went back to his brother, putting his hand on the back of his neck. "I'm sure it was tough for you too. I'm aware of that, and I'm sorry. This war has made me angry, deep-down angry. I'm going to have to come to grips with that."

Bob nodded. "We've all changed. Times have been tough, and it's about to get worse. What are we going to do with Da? If you and I are on a boat all day, come fishing season, who's going to look after him? Jean has two little kids now, with another one on the way. We can't expect her to take him on."

"She does? Holy shit. Where's Ian?"

"In Marion Bridge playing store with his new wife. He says he's never coming back here."

Sam felt a heavy weight sink in his gut. "I thought everything would get better when I got home."

Bob turned to look at him. "Lordy, b'y, when have we ever had it easy?"

When they approached Eastern Harbour, there was no one on the shore. "Looks like no one missed me."

"I told Mary Alice and Hardy to come and see you tomorrow. Tonight belongs to us."

Sam saw the sense in that. He was too tired for an exuberant homecoming, which is what would happen if Mary Alice was involved. They shut off the engine and anchored the boat, dropping Sam's duffle bag into the dory before the two of them scrambled over the side and oared to shore, something they had done thousands of times. When Sam put his feet down by the water's edge, he experienced a moment of dread. He was back to dragging Denis onto the beach in Normandy. Just the sensation of his boots mired in the sucking sand was enough to take him there. He lost his breath and gulped for air. Bob came up behind him with his duffle bag and pushed him along. "No sense standing here getting your boots wet." He didn't see the sweat rolling down Sam's face.

Sam wiped his sleeve across his forehead and upper lip, waiting for the moment to pass. He willed it gone, and proceeded to walk up the hill towards the old house. All he really wanted to do was knock on Mary Alice's door and hug her until he felt better, but Bob made it clear that tonight was about them.

But Sam knew her. She'd be peeking out from behind the curtain in her upstairs window. While he didn't look up, he waved his hand over his head and walked in his own door.

Jean ran to him and put her arms around his neck. She cried and cried. "It's so good to see you, you miserable brat." She put her hands on his cheeks as if trying to memorize his face. "Don't ever go away again."

"Thanks, Jean. Bob tells me you have two and a half kids already. I'm surprised you found time to miss me."

Jean laughed. "You see, that's what I've missed. You cheeky devil." She took his hand. "Come and see him. He's been waiting."

His father was in his bed in the room off the kitchen. Sam tried hard not to react when he saw his dad. It wasn't just that half his face had drooped, sliding down a few inches, or that his mouth was crooked. His face was full of deep wrinkles, no doubt caused by the worry of having two sons overseas. For the first time Sam realized how his actions must have hurt his dad, and he felt ashamed.

"Hi, Da."

Sam sat on the side of the bed and his father grabbed his arm with his right hand and started to mutter a lot of nonsense, bits of spit dripping down his chin. It was painful to watch.

"I'm sorry, Da."

Edgar nodded and opened his mouth once more but gave up when it was obvious he couldn't say what he wanted to. Instead, he kept hold of Sam's jacket and pulled it back and forth, like a frying pan on the stove. He was still remarkably strong. His one good arm, anyway.

His brother and sister left him there, no doubt appreciating the break. Jean made some tea and put scones on the table, before coming back in the room with her father's cup filled with lukewarm tea, which he managed to drink through a straw. Sam wasn't eager to see him try to eat.

This was a nightmare.

His father's eyes started to close and he let go of the jacket, and Sam almost jumped off the bed to get away. He went through the curtains and had to hold his thumb and forefinger to his eyes to keep the tears away.

"Sit down and eat something. You must be hungry," Jean said. "I know it's a shock."

Jean poured tea for both her brothers and gave Sam a chicken sandwich, while she and Bob ate the scones. Sam tried to eat but his stomach was upset. He managed to sip some tea. "What are we going to do?"

Jean put down her mug. "I'll help as much as I can, but I can't stay here endlessly. I could come a couple of afternoons a week depending on the ice. I don't want to get over here and not be able to get back to the kids. Terry's mother said she'd step in if I needed her, but she's not in great health either."

Bob sighed. "I don't suppose Da could go live with you?"

Jean made a face. "Do you really think Dad would leave this island? To go to Morien? You know better than that. And excuse me, but why is it always the daughter's obligation to look after the parents? You two are single men with no responsibilities who actually live in this house. Does that make sense?"

"We'll be fishing," Bob reminded her.

"That's at least four months from now. You'll spend the rest of the winter close to home gearing up for next season."

"I have some money from the army," Sam said. "We could pay someone to watch him when the time comes. Would that help?"

"That's very kind, Sam." Jean smiled. "That would help a lot."

"What did the doctors say? Is he ever going to get any better?"

Both his siblings shook their heads. "His heart is bad too," Bob said. "They don't understand how he survived."

"He was waiting to see you," Jean offered by way of explanation. "So, thank god you came. Why were you going to stay in Halifax, anyway? He couldn't understand it, and frankly neither could we."

Sam really didn't want to get into this conversation tonight, but it looked like he had no choice. "I want this to stay between us for the time being. I don't want Mary Alice or Hardy knowing until I've told them myself. And I don't want anyone on the island knowing until she gets here."

"She? Who's she?" Jean asked.

"My wife."

Bob and Jean's mouths dropped open.

"Wife?" Jean whispered.

Bob couldn't believe it. "You have a war bride?"

Sam nodded.

"And she's coming here?"

Sam nodded again. "That's why I wanted to stay in Halifax. She wasn't allowed on my ship, so she has to book passage on another one, and I didn't want her travelling from Halifax by herself. I promised her aunt."

"Where is she from?" Jean sputtered.

"London."

"She's going to take one look at this place and get on the first ocean liner back to England, you foolish boy," Jean said.

"She loves me."

"I'm sure she does," his sister said, "but is she prepared for this?"

Bob slapped his hands together. "Hey, we don't have to hire anyone. This little wife of yours can look after Da."

"Don't talk shit," Sam grumbled. "I'm not having Jane look after an old man she's never met. And the look of him is enough to scare anyone. She's been through a tough time. She lost her whole family during the Blitz."

"How awful," said Jean.

"What does she look like?" Bob asked.

"Kind of like Mary Alice."

His brother and sister glanced at each other and then down at their plates.

"What? She's got the same hair colour, that's all."

Bob raised his head. "If you wanted a Mary Alice, all you had to do was come home. The real one's been waiting for you for five years."

Sam was confused. "Stop talking nonsense. Mary Alice is my best friend."

Jean looked at him sadly. "Who has always wished she was more than that. Didn't you know?"

Now he was angry. "We had a crush on each other when we were kids. Everyone outgrows that nonsense. She's not going to make a big deal about it. She's always wanted me to be happy. And Jane makes me happy."

There was nothing else to say. Jean got up and put the dishes in the sink and then checked on her father before bedding down on the couch. Bob went to bed and Sam walked out the back door to look at the shining stars.

And he was sick all over his boots.

CHAPTER TWELVE

Mary Alice saw Sam's waving gesture before he disappeared into his house with Bob the night before, but he never looked up. She tossed and turned over that all night.

Luckily it was a Saturday so she didn't have to rush off to school. She sat on her hands until ten o'clock. Surely they'd be up and about now. Suddenly Sam felt like a stranger instead of a part of herself. She'd never had to wait to see him. He was always just there, and now he was behind a door. This was foolish. She was going over there.

As she was putting on her clothes, her bedroom door slammed shut and made her jump. "Ma?" She opened the door and expected to see her mom standing there, but there was no one, so she looked back at the window to see if a draft had come through, but it was shut tight.

It was a mystery, so she ignored it.

Her mother made her sit down and eat a slice of toast with a piece of cheese. "Ma! I'm twenty-four years old. If I don't want to eat, I shouldn't have to."

Mary wiped her hands on a tea towel. "While you're living with me, you'll do as I say."

Mary Alice choked it down because she knew it would go faster. She stood up. "There. Ya happy now?"

Her father sipped his tea. "She's trying to make you leave the nest. Any chance it will happen before we croak?"

"Oh, hardy har har." Mary Alice put on her old brown coat and flipped her hair out from under the collar.

"Take your mitts!" her mother reminded her.

"Lord jumpin'." Mary Alice grabbed a pair from the box by the door.

Her dad lit a smoke and grinned. "Say hi to Sam."

Mary Alice had no privacy at all. She was getting fed up with it. Of course, Rose said it was her own fault. She could've been married years ago, but she was a like an old toad hiding under the mud in a bog.

She took twenty steps across the road and knocked on the Harris's door. Normally she would have barged in, but because poor Edgar was ill, she didn't want to presume.

Jean opened the door and Mary Alice thought she gave her a sad look. "Is your dad okay?'

"The same. I assume you're here to see Sam."

"I've been waiting years to see him and I can't wait any longer. How's he doing?"

"Go see for yourself. He's down on the rocks by the shore. Said he needed to breathe."

Mary Alice smiled. "That's so him. Thanks Jean."

And off she went, unaware of Jean grimacing as she closed the door.

The air was frigid and damp and Mary Alice could see her breath as she hurried along. It reminded her of when she'd seek out the boys and find them in the chicken coop. Where did all those years go?

She stood on the top of the rise. There he was, skipping rocks, something he always did when he was thinking.

"Samuel Hugh Harris!" she yelled.

He turned around and smiled at her. She ran down the hill and he caught her by the water's edge. They hugged each other tight.

"I've missed you so much," she said against his coat.

"You and Hardy were never far from my mind." He pulled away, still holding her arms. "Let me look at you. You haven't changed a bit. Still a string bean with freckles."

She gulped. "You look different. Much older, and sad, which is to be expected. You can't go through a war and not have it change you. I'm just so grateful you survived."

"Jean told me about Jake this morning. I'm really sorry. Our family got lucky. But now there's Da to take care of."

"Life doesn't stop being difficult." She sighed, before putting her arm through his as they walked along the shore. "How did you manage, Sam? How did you make it?"

"By not thinking. Not wishing. Not hoping. Just breathing."

She leaned her head on his shoulder. "I'm so sorry. It must have been awful."

"I can't talk about it, Mary Alice."

She straightened up again. "Of course. I'm sorry. I shouldn't have asked."

"Let's go see Hardy. I can't wait."

"The three musketeers, together again!"

As they strolled to the lighthouse, Sam pointed out all the things he'd missed. "See that rock we always called The Wolf? For some reason I'd dream about it. The strength of the stone. And that lone tree that's been bent by hundreds of storms over the years but has never broken. I'd think of that tree when times were hard and it kept me going."

"I prayed for you every night. I prayed for all of you."

As they approached the lighthouse, Sam smiled. "I missed this as well. Hardy and his mother's cooking! That woman kept me fed."

"Wait until you meet Toby. He's delightful."

"I still miss Buster." Buster was in fact doing his best to trip Sam as he wound in and out of his feet, tail wagging.

One thing about having no trees around the lighthouse is that you can see people approach a long way off. Hardy, Annie, James, and Fred waved from the front porch as Toby ran up to Mary Alice and jumped on her so she would pat him. She picked him up and let Sam put his hands around his face. "He is pretty cute."

And then he let the dog go and ran up the stairs to give Hardy a big bear hug. They clapped each other's backs and grinned like fools. Then it was on to hug the others. Everyone was talking at once and Annie ushered them all in and had food on the table in an instant. It was like a party. Now this was a homecoming. It cheered Sam up after the sombre return to his place.

The best part was that no one asked him anything about the war. It was a given that it was awful and if he wanted to talk about it he would. Instead, they filled him in on the gossip.

Hardy cut a piece of his mother's apple pie and put it on a plate in front of Sam, who wasted no time putting it in his mouth. "I used to dream of this pie, Annie."

She blushed and looked as pleased as punch. "I have another one. You can take it home."

"I feel sorry for everyone across the ocean. They're still dealing with shortages and rations. I feel guilty eating this, but god, it's good! So rich. I better not eat a lot."

Hardy licked his fingers. "Listen to this. Hank Lahey went duck hunting one day and came back with a mess of birds. Twenty-two in all!"

"How's that even possible?" Sam asked with his mouth full.

"He startled a huge flock and as they lifted off the ground, he just kept shooting. Even he didn't know how many he got at first.

He shared them with all of us, even though Flossie didn't want him to. What was she going to do? Eat them all herself?"

Sam nodded. "Oh yeah, he married Flossie. How's that going?"

"She's got two sets of twins." Mary Alice laughed. "You know her. She's got to outdo everyone."

Sam said, "You're still not friends then?"

"No, thank you. She's been a pain in my side since we went to school."

"And you're still in school. I'm sure you're a wonderful teacher, but how do you stand it?" Sam shook his head. "I couldn't wait to get out of there."

"I take the kids outside a lot. It helps."

Sam shook his finger at Hardy. "Speaking of outside, I'm hoping to have a chopping party before too long. I'm dying to get into the woods to get some firewood."

"And who's going to feed the men at your chopping party?" Mary Alice asked. "Are you going to cook? You can't keep Jean hostage for weeks at a time."

"I could help with that," Annie chimed in. "But how will you and Bob cope with your father so ill? Especially during fishing season?"

"We talked about a few options last night. I really don't know at this stage."

"Practically, I'm not sure what I can do, but if you ever need anything, you know I'm here for you," Hardy said.

"I do know that. This is what I love about home. We're in it together."

They sat around for two hours talking and laughing. It was like Sam had never been away. He wished it could stay like this, but he was aware of the time and that Jean would be expecting him.

He also knew he had a bomb to drop that would probably change everything. One he didn't realize would be so traumatic until last night. He had to be the most dull-witted man alive. Yes, he and Mary Alice had fooled around some, but had he ever uttered the words *I love you*? Did he ask her to wait for him? Not that he could remember.

He felt like shit. And it wasn't going to get any better, was it? He needed to get it off his chest now, because life was complicated enough with his father and the worry that Jane would leave him the minute she arrived.

"This has been grand, but I better get back. Thank you everyone."

"I'll walk with you," Mary Alice said.

"Would you come too, Hardy?" Sam asked. "The three of us together, like we're going to school. The only time I ever liked school. I used to dream about it."

Hardy smiled. "Sure. Mom, I'll be back in a bit."

"Take your time." Annie kissed Sam goodbye and handed him a pie. "Just for you."

When they went out the door, Sam looked awkward holding the pie, so Mary Alice took it from him, and she was glad she did. The pie was still warm and her fingers were grateful.

They were about halfway home when Sam turned to face them. "I have something to tell you both and I don't want anyone else to know for now."

Hardy and Mary Alice looked at each other. "What's wrong?" she said. "Are you ill? Were you hurt? Is it bad?"

Sam tried not to show his annoyance. Mary Alice always jumped the gun and didn't give anyone a chance to explain before she started peppering them with questions.

"No, I'm not ill. I'm married."

There wasn't a sound between them. Sam looked at Hardy first for some reason. Hardy's eyes were huge and his mouth open.

Then he dragged his eyes to Mary Alice's face. Except for the fact she looked deathly pale, her demeanour betrayed nothing.

"Congratulations," she said and walked off with the pie.

Sam and Hardy watched her go. Sam put his hands over his face. "I never wanted to hurt her. She'll hate me now." He took his hands away and grabbed Hardy's jacket. "I didn't know. I didn't know she was in love with me. You have to believe me."

Hardy's face got stony. "Everyone else on this island knew it. Are you really that brainless?"

Sam let go of his jacket and turned away with his hands on his head. "I swear to god. She never told me she loved me like that. We kissed each other a few times, but that's it. I love Mary Alice, but I'm not in love with her. Should I have told her that? I didn't even know I had to. Would you ever say that to a girl?"

Hardy looked down at his feet and put his hands in his pockets. "This is not good."

Sam poked his finger into Hardy's chest. "If everyone on this spit of land knew about this, including you, why didn't you say anything to me?"

"It was none of my business."

"Of course it was! Everything we've ever done together has been *our* business. We're supposed to have each other's backs, damn it."

Now Hardy pointed his finger at Sam. "Wait a minute. Don't you dare get mad at me. This whole mess is not my fault. If you feel bad about it, then apologize to her. Ask her to forgive you."

"I didn't know I needed forgiveness! I just met a girl and we fell in love and got married. People do it every day, and now I'm being condemned for it."

"And this girl from England is going to come and live here? Does she know what she's getting in to?"

Sam clenched his fists. "You know what? I'm really sorry I came home." He turned around and walked away.

Hardy couldn't think. He whistled for Toby and went back inside. There was his mother by the window.

"What's going on out there? I thought you were walking each other home."

"Mom, mind your own business, please." And he disappeared up to his room with Toby and shut the door.

Mary Alice didn't want to go home, so she placed the pie at the Harrises' front door, after resisting the urge to throw it, and kept going all the way to the school and let herself in. It was lightly snowing, which normally was enchanting, but she didn't care. She sat behind her desk and wept.

Her anger was at herself. How could she have been so stupid? She thought about all their encounters. Not once had Sam ever told her he loved her. She'd taken her first crush and made it into something it wasn't. But why did she have to wait this long to find out? Everyone was probably laughing at her.

She still loved Sam, but she wanted to beat him to death. She went back and forth blaming him, blaming herself, blaming the world in general. At the age of twenty-four, when all the other girls she'd grown up with were married and had families, she had nothing. She'd pinned her hopes on what? Smoke and mirrors.

How was she going to cope, seeing this new wife live only twenty steps away? She hated her already, which she knew was childish, but so what. Apparently, she *was* a child. Her mother still made her eat breakfast and reminded her to put on mittens before venturing outside.

Something had to change. Mary Alice lifted her head and gazed around the schoolroom that had been her solace during the war years. It was a stopgap to keep herself from going mad. Did she want this forever? According to tittle-tattle, there might not even be a school here in five to ten years, if everyone moved away to the mainland. They were already down to sixty-five people on the island, only twelve children coming to school, a small group of boys leaving early like Sam, to help their families fish.

There were no more tears. Her mind and body and spirit were done in. She had no energy to think, so Mary Alice got up and went out the door, locking it behind her. The snow was coming down faster and accumulating. How long had she been inside? She put one foot in front of the other and stared at the path at her feet. Normally she would have tried to catch the falling snowflakes or looked for fat black crows sitting on snow-covered branches, hunched over like gangsters.

The surf was muffled by the snow, but she caught sight of the pewter-coloured water, where a long roll of wave far out crept under the surface, getting closer and closer before bursting forth on the rocky beach.

That's how Sam's news had felt. She had had no warning. She never saw it coming.

When she finally made it home, she was soaked through and very cold. Her mother met her at the door. "Where were you? I went across the road, but Jean didn't know and Sam said he'd last seen you three hours ago. I almost sent your father out to look for you."

"I'm glad you didn't. That would have confirmed my suspicions."

"What are you talking about?"

Mary Alice shed her coat, boots, and mitts; her hair was completely soaked because she hadn't worn a hat. "My suspicion that I'm still a child. Sam's not. Sam has a wife. A war bride."

Mary's hand flew up over her mouth, but she quickly removed it after glancing at Tom, who shook his head at her.

"But—"

"Don't ask me anything else, Ma. I don't know the answers. I'm going to lie down. I don't feel well."

Mary insisted on towel-drying Mary Alice's hair before she crawled into bed, and then she placed a hot water bottle beside her daughter and brought up a cup of tea. Mary Alice stayed there, not because she was moping, but because she had chills and a fever and a raging sore throat. Mary put a cold cloth on her daughter's head during the fever and fed her hot water and honey when she was chilled. She also smeared goose grease on a piece of brown paper and laid it as a poultice on Mary Alice's chest to help with her cough, because that's what her grandmother Alice used to do. Mary tried to give her daughter a spoonful of goose grease for her sore throat, but Mary Alice said she'd jump out the window if she tried.

While she lay there for the first week, Mary Alice thought how pleasant it was to not rush to school every morning. Like a child. She hadn't even asked who had taken over for her. She didn't care. The world would go on without her. Being in this bed was perfect because she didn't have to face anyone. Her mother told her that Sam and Hardy had both been by to see her, separately. She didn't care.

As usual, her favourite sister, Rose, showed up to get the skinny and relay it to their mother at a later time. She wasn't fooling anyone, least of all Mary Alice.

"It's all over the island that Sam's bride is coming in March. Can you imagine arriving here in the middle of winter if you've never been here before? If she knows what's good for her, she'll stay where she is. What a madman. Apparently, she's from London. Imagine."

When Mary Alice didn't comment, Rose put her hand over hers. "Are you okay? You must be very disappointed. I know you loved him."

"How do you know that? Have I ever told anyone I loved him?"

"I've got eyes. And the fact that you've never been with anyone is a dead giveaway."

"Shows how much you know. I've been with boys behind Kenwood, as it happens."

Rose slapped her hand. "Stop lying."

"I'm not. I've done it with three boys against the building. It was fun."

If Mary Alice had set herself on fire, Rose wouldn't have been as horrified as she was hearing this bit of news. "Have some self-respect. Only trollops do that!"

"And girls named Mary Alice. Or Cara."

Rose put her hands up to her cheeks. "And you never got caught?"

"Nope."

"And you never got pregnant?"

"Obviously not."

Rose reached out and held her sister's hand. "I'm sorry that you felt that desperate. I'm sorry this happened to you. You don't have to stay brave for me."

Mary Alice turned and hid her face in the pillow. Rose reached over and rubbed her back. They never said another word. A while later Rose kissed the back of her head and left, closing the door behind her.

Since her father was listening to the radio, Rose and her mother walked over by the kitchen.

"Well?" Mary asked. "How do you find her?"

"She's in a bad way, Ma. I wouldn't push her. Don't let her go back to school until she's ready."

Mary wrung her hands. "She always was a sensitive little thing. What if she really breaks down?"

"I think she already has."

"But how can I help her?"

"By doing what you're doing. Don't ask questions. Keep feeding her and let her rest. She doesn't want or need company. I think you should tell the school board that she'll be out for a month. Tell them it's pneumonia if you have to."

Mary took a tissue out of her apron pocket. "Can you believe this? He broke her heart."

"It's for the best. Maybe now she can move on."

Oh dear, oh dear, oh dear. I was after getting all worked up because my three favourite living beings were hurting. They lived so close to each other but they were in separate worlds. Mary Alice was suffering the most. I could tell by the dull colour of the aura around her, and the fact that it was much smaller.

Sam was nothing but nervous energy flying all over the place. Guilt was looming over him. Guilt over Mary Alice and Jane. At that point he was selfishly dying to see his new wife, but worried she'd hate him soon enough. He was right to be worried.

Hardy was hiding in his work. His only concern was Mary Alice's state of mind. He was neglecting his own feelings in all of this. He had spent his whole life not dealing with his needs. There's a fine line between being kind to others and cruel to yourself. I do wish the living would see themselves as worthy, but most of them don't. I was the same way, always occupied with what others thought of me, when I should have been more aware of what I thought of myself.

Again, I hate the word *died*, because I didn't really. I became a whole new being, and this being has come to know a few things since my shipwreck. I know that the human heart is a fragile thing, so it is. It needs protecting. It needs to be hidden away at times. And while Mary Alice thought she had failed because she was lying in her bed, she was doing exactly what she should have been doing. Stepping back. Resting instead of performing. Gathering her strength.

I always think of animals at times like this. They know how to lie down and just watch the world go by. Because they don't speak with words, they don't trip themselves up, trying to figure out what they've done wrong. They've done nothing wrong. They are content to spend every day living. Life is just as dangerous for them as it is for us, but they don't spend years worrying about the inevitable. And don't tell me they don't know they're going to die someday. They do.

So, who is the smarter creature?

Aisling was annoyed with me because I was spending so much time with Mary Alice.

"All you do is look at her. How is that helping?" she said, frowning. "You're always in that room. Why don't you come to Hay Island and hang out with the gulls?"

"Tempting, but no. I'm doing more than watching her. I'm filling the room with words and ideas that might help."

"You're not God," she huffed.

I smiled at her. "Yes, I am. And so are you."

"I hate grown-ups." She left through the wall.

It was all over the island that Mary Alice had a breakdown because Sam loved someone else and was bringing his new wife over to live right next door to the poor girl. Everyone sat over their dinner tables and chewed the bone over this bit of news. And they all had different reactions. If Mary Alice had known what was going on behind closed doors, she'd never have believed Flossie's take on it.

"I think he's a miserable snake to do that to her," she said to her husband as she buttered bread for her four little girls. Hank pretended to listen. "Everyone knows how much she ran after that boy."

Now Hank's ears perked up. "A little like you, then?"

Flossie put her hand on her hip. "Listen here. Every girl on Scatarie was after Sam Harris. I can't help it if he took a shine to me."

He went back to not listening. Flossie brought the buttered bread over to the table and put a piece in front of each daughter. "She waited for five years for that man. I told her not to be so foolish, that she'd be pining away for a fella who might never come home. But did she listen? I think she'd rather see him dead in the ground than bringing home another woman and throwing it in her face every single day. Who could have imagined that? I feel sorry for her."

Sam started to get dirty looks from the women in his community. It was bad enough he was stuck inside a lot of the time looking after his father, which never got easier, and had to chase Bob around to do his part and try not to bother Jean too much. But he had to deal with the weight of condemnation as well.

He was wiping his father's chin after giving him scrambled eggs when there was a knock at the door before it opened. He peeked around the curtain to see his neighbour Evelyn carrying a casserole. "Just me. Thought your dad could use a home-cooked meal. God only knows what you two are feeding him." She placed it on the table.

"Gosh, thanks, Evelyn. He'll enjoy that. So will we."

"Now don't go eatin' it all up on him. He could get a few meals outta that."

"All right."

She turned to leave and then faced him again. "I gotta say it and I probably shouldn't, but what you did to Mary Alice is not fit. We all knew she was in love with you. She waited for you through the whole war, and this is how you repay her."

Sam glared at her. "I had to come home to find out what a shit I am. You can think what you want. I love Mary Alice, but not like that. If she thought it was more, that's on her."

"But bringing the other woman to live right next door?"

Sam threw his hands in the air. "Jane is not the 'other' woman. She didn't cheat on anyone and neither did I. And where else do you bring your new wife but to your home? I live here, Evelyn! I'm not camping out on Mary Alice's doorstep to be mean. I wish you and everyone else on this island would just leave me alone."

Evelyn walked to the door and hesitated. "I shouldn't have said anything."

"You're sayin' what everyone else is thinkin'. I'd rather that."

She turned to look at him. "I'm sorry, Sam. You start listening to gossip and make judgments without knowing the other side."

"Thanks."

"And thank you for the five years of your life you'll never get back. Don't worry. Things will calm down."

Sam walked closer to her. "Could you tell everyone that Jane is not to blame? I don't want people being cross with her. She's an innocent victim in all this and she's going to have enough to deal with."

"I'll do that." And she left.

Sam punched the wall and cracked the plywood. His father did his version of shouting, no doubt wondering what the noise was. Sam poked his head in. "I walked into something."

His dad looked like he didn't believe him, even with his melting face.

An hour later Bob finally returned from whatever he was doing. Sam was out the door before he crossed the threshold. "Where are you off to?"

"Going to see Hardy. Evelyn brought a casserole over, but don't eat it. It's for dad."

Sam glanced up at Mary Alice's window, where the curtain was still shut. Flippin' 'eck, as his mates overseas used to say. He ran through the snow as if it wasn't there. He needed his friend, even though they were mad at each other. This had gotten way out of hand. How could he have known this would happen?

He saw Hardy going into the pump house and was glad. He couldn't face Annie and the boys and their wonderful kitchen. He needed to be cold and tired and alert, not lulled with apple dumplings.

He threw open the door and shut it again, leaning on it. Hardy said, "Fred?" from behind the pump itself.

"It's not Fred. It's your asshole friend who has apparently killed Mary Alice with his shocking behaviour. My lynching will be tomorrow at dawn. Everyone welcome."

Hardy emerged from behind the machine Sam knew nothing about. He was wiping a bit of grease off his hands with a rag.

"I'll be first in line," Hardy said with a smirk.

Sam was so relieved. All was not lost. "I need to talk to someone."

"Grab yourself a bucket and sit your arse on it. And need I remind you that it's always you who wants to talk. About himself. Have you asked me what's been going on since you left?"

Sam grabbed the nearest bucket, turned it over, and sat. "What's been going on with you since I left?"

Hardy sat on his bucket. "Nothin'."

Sam laughed. "God, I missed you." He took a cigarette pack out of his pocket.

"That's one thing I did. Learned how to smoke."

He offered one to Hardy before taking one himself. Once they lit up, Hardy said, "No more roll-your-own? You're getting fancy with store bought."

"I'll be back to it soon enough. This is my last pack. A special duty-free Macdonald's Gold Standard. Look at the side. It says *GIFT to Canadian troops on active service, not for re-sale*. I swear, sometimes it was only a cigarette that kept us from losing our minds."

"It was bad." Hardy said it as a fact.

Sam confirmed it. "It was so bad."

Hardy nodded. "Once Mary Alice and I went to see a film at the Savoy. They played newsreels before the show and one of them was soldiers landing on the beach at Normandy. You could see some of the soldiers die before they got out of the water. Mary Alice burst into tears. I almost did too. I kept thinking those poor bastards."

Sam looked away. "I was there. I lost two buddies. One shot in the face as close as I'm sitting to you. It never leaves my mind."

"Bloody hell."

Taking another drag off his smoke, Sam sat up. "Enough of that. I don't know what to do about Mary Alice. I tried to see her but her mom said she wasn't having any visitors. Have you been able to get to her?"

"Nope. She's well and truly hiding."

Sam stomped his foot. "She's always so friggin' dramatic. Do you know all the females on this island now hate me? And Jane, who hasn't done a thing wrong other than fall in love with this idiot."

Hardy blew a smoke ring. "Don't panic. As soon as Mary Alice shows her face, it will all blow over. Right now, they picture her in bed sobbing. Mary Alice is beloved here now because she's a good teacher and the kids love her. People are upset that she's sad. They're not going to hate Jane. You'll see. However, they might hate you because you've always been a fathead."

They chuckled together. It felt good. For the first time Sam felt a glimmer of hope.

"Now come to the house. It's freezing in here. Mom cracked open two jars of cherry preserves and made a pie."

"I love your mother."

After four weeks in bed, Mary Alice knew that was enough. It was the first of March. Sam's wife would soon be here and she needed to prepare herself, and not languish like a wretched victim for the rest of her life. She was almost at the point where she was very cross with her hibernation but decided, upon reflection, she should be kind to the young woman known as Mary Alice Locke.

And she knew what she wanted to do.

When she came downstairs dressed and put together, she could tell her parents were more relieved than anything else.

"Good to see ya, girlie," said her dad. "I was missin' your saucy mouth."

Mary Alice knew what was coming next. Her mother hurried to the stove. "I've got a nice pea soup warming up. Would you like a bowl?"

She wasn't a kid anymore. "Yes, that would be nice."

Mary almost fell over with that response, but she didn't want to jinx it, so she said nothing and just brought it to the table, along with thick slices of soda bread.

Mary Alice had to admit the soup was really good. Her appetite was much better now that her mother had been making her regular meals. What her mother didn't know was that she never ate lunch when she was in school. She was always too busy to go home, and forgot most of the time. She'd either give it to one of the kids or spill it out on the grass in the woods for whatever animal happened by. Childish behaviour.

She even had a cup of tea and slice of fruitcake. Her mom couldn't wipe the smile off her face.

Mary Alice put down her mug and cleared her throat. "I've made a decision."

Her parents were all ears. Anything was better than having her live in bed.

"I'm not going to be a teacher anymore."

"Oh no!" her mother cried. "You love that job."

"I did love that job, Ma, but not anymore."

Her dad squirmed in the rocking chair. "What's changed?"

"What's changed?" She rose from the table and looked out the window. "I've spent five years in that school dreaming of Sam coming home to me. Now it all seems so juvenile. I was one of the kids spending time there until I could head out the door and start my real life. I'm not prepared to do that anymore. It would make me feel sorry for myself and I want to be free of those memories."

Her parents didn't say anything, which Mary Alice took as a good sign. They seemed to understand her reluctance to stay in the past.

Her mother finally said, "But what will you do?"

Mary Alice started to put on her coat, a hat, gloves, scarf, and boots like a real live adult. "I'm going for a walk to think about it."

She took a deep breath of the frigid air and rejoiced in how it made her feel. She'd been cooped up in that room so long she forgot what it was like to breathe real oxygen. It was a sparkling day; the sun glinted off the snow and there wasn't a cloud in the sky. The kind of day when she, Sam, and Hardy loved to go skating on the pond, their cheeks a bright apple red by the end of the day, Buster underfoot the entire time. They were good memories.

She wanted to make more.

It didn't take her long to get where she was going. She knocked on the door and Annie answered. "Mary Alice! It's so nice to see you dear. How are you feeling?"

"I'm fine, Annie. I need to speak to you-know-who."

"Fred? James?" Annie laughed. "Sorry, you-know-who is up in the lighthouse. You'll probably have to holler."

"Thank you."

"When you're finished, come on in for some strudel."

Mary Alice shook her head. "Do you ever stop baking, Annie?"

"Does Hardy ever stop eating?"

They both smiled before Annie closed the door and Mary Alice walked over to the lighthouse. She'd forgotten how big it was. It looked enormous up close. When viewed from out on a boat, it seemed like a toy during the day. But in the dark it was vast, its light shining out over the water searching, searching for wayward souls. She thought that Hardy was like a lighthouse, big and strong, quiet but steady.

She opened the door at the bottom and walked up the stairs to the first floor. "Hardy?"

He wasn't there, so she kept climbing. Now the lighthouse seemed gigantic. There were too many stairs, and she'd had no exercise in a month. The next level housed equipment needed for the light. She yelled for him again but no answer, so she kept going, because that's what adults did. She finally got to the level that housed the light itself. Such an impressive apparatus. She felt tiny next to it.

"Hardy!" No answer, but then she saw him around the back of the slanted deck. He was reaching down for his sponge. No doubt he couldn't hear her because of the wind. She thought about going outside but quickly nixed the idea. Hardy would have a heart attack. But he'd probably have a heart attack if she knocked on the window. While she was dithering about what to do, he knocked on the window first with an incredulous look on his face and hurried over to the door. He had a hard time pulling it open, so thankfully she hadn't tried that herself.

"What in blazes are you doing here? Are you crazy? You could fall."

"Sorry. I just wanted to see you."

He put his fingers through his tousled hair to get it out of his face. "And you couldn't wait until I got down?"

She looked at his familiar, caring eyes. Hardy had always been her lighthouse. Of course!

"Hardy, will you marry me?"

Immediately he said, "Absolutely not."

That was a kick in the teeth. "Why not?"

He took a deep breath and sighed, taking off his glasses. She knew that meant business.

"You've had a shock and lain in bed for the last month. You're flailing around for something to make you feel better. Maybe you even want to stick it to Sam, to let him know you don't need him after all. I don't want any part of that. I won't be anyone's consolation prize."

Mary Alice walked over to the wall and slid down onto the floor. Hardy joined her. She put her head on his shoulder. "It's so annoying that you're always right."

"I'm not always right. I'm just looking out for you."

Mary Alice squeezed his arm. "You always have. I love you, my dearest friend. I guess I'll keep teaching while I figure out what to do. That way I don't have to watch the happy couple during daylight hours. Is it awful that I hate her? I don't even know her."

"She's coming here with no friends or family. She has no one but Sam to rely on. She's going to need someone like you."

He let that sink in. Mary Alice finally looked up. "I'm freezing. I think I'll go home to my hot water bottle."

Hardy helped her up. "Do you want me to walk you home?"

"No. I'm not a kid, even though I act like one." She kissed his cheek. "I'll see you later. And thanks."

He stayed by the window to make sure she made it to the ground. She knew he'd be watching so she turned and waved, blowing him a kiss.

Hardy put his forehead against the cold glass. "I'm a fool."

CHAPTER THIRTEEN

It was a harder wrench than she thought, leaving Aunt Lou. The two months she spent with her after Sam left brought them closer together, and it was distressing to see the tears stream down Aunt Lou's face as she waved goodbye.

"I don't think it's a good omen that Sam won't be there to greet you." She sniffed.

"He's looking after his sickly father. Stuart will collect me. We can rely on him, and what's more, you like him."

"I don't like the idea of a sickly father. You better not get roped into taking care of the old fella."

"Aunt Lou, this isn't helping. I'm already nervous about getting on this huge ship."

"It better not sink."

At that point Jane gave her aunt a big hug so she'd stop talking and was glad to go up the gangplank to get away from her doom and gloom. She didn't care if the ship sank or not.

On March 4, 1946, Jane boarded the ship *Letitia* and after two long weeks, went through Pier 21 in Halifax with hundreds of other war brides. She'd been terribly seasick for most of the journey and was determined to never tell Sam about it, since he lived his life on the water.

The Red Cross and Salvation Army were there to greet the ladies and children, giving them gifts of food and clothes as a welcome to Canada. It was a thoughtful gesture and all of them were grateful.

Jane had the piece of paper with Stuart's phone number and address on it clutched in her hand, in case she couldn't find him in the mob. It was all rather bewildering, and she envied the women being grabbed by their husbands and kissed in front of everyone. Stuart had said he'd be by the front door, and when she heard a loud whistle coming from that direction and saw a man a head taller than everyone else waving frantically, she recognized him instantly. She was so thrilled to see him she gave him a huge hug and kiss on the cheek when they finally managed to make their way through the happy families.

"You have no idea how glad I am to see you." She laughed. "I worried the whole time that you might get hit by a coach and not show up, and then what would I do?"

He grabbed her suitcase and parcels. "And have Aunt Lou cross the ocean to hit me over the head with her handbag? Are you nuts? How is the old doll, anyway?"

"She's heartbroken that I left, and I feel like a heel."

"Come this way." Once again, they wove through a sea of people and made it outside to the parking lot. "The car's over here."

Jane had to hurry to catch up to his long strides. "You have your own car?"

"It's my dad's."

He ran around and opened the door for her. "Your chariot awaits, m'lady."

They were stuck in traffic endlessly, as there were so many people trying to leave the area, but that was all right. They talked the entire time. Jane knew Stuart was a great guy, and she appreciated what he was doing for her.

"My mom said I should bring you home and she'll cook you a nice roast beef dinner tonight before you set off tomorrow. We have an extra bedroom, so don't worry."

"Are you sure? I could always stay at a rooming house."

"Never. She'd have a fit."

They pulled up to a very nice house. It surprised Jane how every house was unattached. She was used to row houses for the most part. The entire set-up felt foreign and new. Everything seemed so far apart. The roads were wider, and the pavement. There was more breathing room everywhere. She was nervous walking around in so much space.

Stuart's family was lovely, but they were loud and boisterous and she was still feeling slightly sick. She ate as much roast beef and gravy as she dared and thanked her hostess thoroughly. His mother showed Jane her room and pointed out the loo.

"Get some sleep, dear. You look tired. You have a long journey tomorrow."

Despite her nerves, Jane slept well for the first time since her journey began. She didn't take a shower that morning, not wanting to impose. She'd do that tonight. But she freshened up and put on her mother's red lipstick to give her courage, the only other possession she'd found in the rubble besides the teapot. The blue enamel lipstick tube with a picture of three mallard ducks flying over water had stood out among all the grey ash. She considered it a sign that her mum was still with her, but she didn't use it often, not wanting it to run out.

Stuart's mother gave her breakfast and then passed her a paper bag. "This is your lunch, in case you get hungry." It was something her own mother would have done. "Thank you."

All of them wished her good luck and said they hoped she and Sam would be able to come and visit sometime. Jane could tell Stuart wanted to get going. He kept looking at his watch, so she hurried down the stairs and he put her belongings in the back seat this time. More waving goodbye before the house disappeared.

"Your parents are lovely," she said. "What does your dad do?"

"He's a doctor. I'm going back to school to become one too. I'll probably be close to thirty before I'm finished, but I know that's what I want to do, because I kept getting in the way of the medics every time one of my friends got shot."

That brought back memories of the war and they both wanted to avoid that, so he said, "You've still got my number, right, in case you ever need it?"

"Oh yes, thank you."

"I sent a wire to your Aunt Lou saying you landed in Halifax safely."

Jane beamed at him. "Thank you! I forgot all about that. She'd be worrying."

"Make sure you send one when you land in Cape Breton."

She nodded. "I will. I'm sure Sam will know where to go."

Stuart kept his eyes on the road and his hands on the wheel but he was biting his lip, something her brother used to do.

"You'll get a cold sore if you keep that up," Jane said.

Stuart shook his head. "Cold sores are caused by viruses. I know because I'm a doctor."

They both laughed and then he said, "How much did Sam tell you about where he lives?"

Jane's eyes sparkled. "He says it's beautiful, with the ocean and the sky and the waves. He can never stop talking about it. He does love the place. I hope to love it too."

They were almost at the train station, so Stuart kept his mouth shut. He was torn. He didn't want to betray his buddy, but he felt like he was leading a lamb to slaughter. But maybe he wasn't giving Jane enough credit. She'd managed to live through the Blitz.

"We're here." He took her suitcase and bags, one of them carrying the kettle and her jar of brown sauce, and brought her inside the station and stood with her while she bought her ticket to Sydney. That's where Sam said he would pick her up, not wanting her to make the connection to Louisbourg in case it mixed her up.

They sat down together on a bench, waiting for the announcement of the train's arrival. Stuart shook his legs and Jane was determined not to get upset when she had to leave him. Sam was waiting for her. She'd be fine.

The announcement was made and they both stood. Stuart took her bags to the door and handed them over. "I'll wait here until I see you get on and I'll stay until the train leaves."

That's just what she wanted to hear. She hugged him again. "You've been such a good friend. Thank you for everything."

"You tell that bonehead to treat you right, or he'll answer to me!" He gave her a quick salute as she headed off and found a conductor who pointed out the car she was to get on. He put her bags up on the train and she followed, turning around briefly to wave to Stuart again.

He was as good as his word. Jane saw him waiting by the window the entire time before the train finally left about thirty minutes later. She waved again and kept her eyes on him until he was finally out of sight.

He walked back to the car, trying to figure out if he'd done the right thing.

The train ride seemed endless. How big was Nova Scotia? Jane was used to a quick thirty minutes or an hour to get anywhere. This was taking all day. And there were so many trees, and lots of snow. Everything looked cold and bare, but huge tracts of fir and spruce trees filled in the landscape with dark green.

She didn't speak to anyone and no one sat down beside her, but there was a cute little girl asking her mother all kinds of questions about everything under the sun. It would be wonderful to have a baby, but the idea made her sad, too, because her mother would never meet her child.

They finally made it to Mulgrave, and the conductor told her to stay in the train car because they were going to be put on a ferry. Who could ever imagine such a thing? It was a bit of a procedure, but off they went. A train on the water. Jane was nervous as they crossed and was very happy to finally land on the other side.

So, this was Cape Breton Island, the island she'd be living on. As she got closer to Sydney, her stomach was fluttering. It was like a dream to soon be able to put her arms around Sam again. She missed him desperately, and how he always made her laugh.

Sam had said Sydney was a city. It didn't look like a city to her. It was rather drab, but then, she was in a railyard. Jane gathered her things and kept looking out the window as she went down the aisle, in hopes of seeing Sam, and got a little panicked when she couldn't pick him out. She opened her purse to make sure Stuart's piece of paper was still in it.

Now a nice conductor helped her down the stairs and put her bags on the platform. She nodded her thanks and stood like a scared rabbit, trying desperately to see Sam's face.

Then she heard him laugh. "I told you that you wouldn't recognize me." He was maybe ten feet away from her, wearing ordinary old clothes.

"Sam!" They grabbed each other and all was right with the world. Jane breathed in his scent as he put his hands through her hair. There was really nothing to say. They simply wanted to melt into each other and all the passengers had to go around them. And they did, smiling. Happy reunions were quite common these days.

And who would begrudge young lovers after all their generation had been through?

He held her face. "I've missed you so much. I can't believe you're here. Sometimes I thought you were a dream."

"I'm real." And she kissed him again.

Eventually they realized they had to get off the platform and out of the way. Sam reached for her bags and she put her arm through his as they walked towards an old truck. "Sorry, this is my cousin's truck. I don't have a car, since you don't need one living on an island."

She looked around, confused. "But all these people have cars. This is Cape Breton Island, isn't it?"

"Never mind all that. We're spending the night here in Sydney. I didn't want my first night with you to be at the house with my dad and brother."

"Oh, they live with you?"

Sam's mouth began to dry up. "Oh yes, didn't I mention that?"

She shook her head. "Maybe you did, but I don't remember."

"Let's just go to the hotel. I can't wait."

"I'm a bit peckish. Can we get something to eat first?"

He piled her belongings into the back seat. "Of course. I should have thought of that."

Jane got in the truck and the smell of fish was very noticeable. She tried not to wrinkle her nose.

After a hurried sandwich at a local diner, he took her to the Isle Royal Hotel, a tall brick building downtown. Jane got a kick out of him signing *Mr. and Mrs. Sam Harris* in the register.

The man behind the front desk recognized her accent and smiled at her when she spoke to Sam. "Welcome to Canada, Mrs. Harris."

She beamed at him. "Ta, very much."

Their sleepless and wondrous night together was too short, and neither one of them wanted to get up in the morning, but they eventually made their way downstairs and returned to the diner for breakfast before hitting the road. That's when Jane remembered she had to send her Aunt Lou a telegram, so they stopped at the telegraph office.

I'M HERE IN CAPE BRETON. SAM IS WITH ME. ALL IS WELL. LOVE JANE

"I wonder if she's stopped crying," Jane said as they left. "I felt terrible leaving her."

"She'll feel better once she gets that message," Sam assured her.

"How far do we have to travel before we get home?" she asked, trying not to let the smell of gas give her a headache.

"It's a bit yet."

There were snow squalls on the way to Main-à-Dieu, and the landscape was getting more and more rural. At one point Jane shivered and Sam realized he should have put a blanket in the truck for her. "It's not always this cold," he said. "Why don't you take my jacket?"

"But then you'll be cold."

"I've got a sweater under this."

Sam wiggled his way out of his jacket while still driving on rough roads, and Jane was grateful to put it on. Sam asked her how Stuart was and how her trip went and she filled him in on what it was like to travel with nothing but women and children on a ship. "You know how you see lines of pennants and flags on ships fluttering in the breeze? We had lines and lines of diapers everywhere. It was like an obstacle course trying to get through them all. I think the sailors were fed up after a while, but they were all good-hearted about it."

He grabbed her hand and kissed it before changing gears. "How was the train ride?"

"It was so long! Just how big is Nova Scotia, anyway?"

"It's one of the smaller provinces. Some of those war brides will be travelling out west to British Columbia, and that will take at least five days on a train."

"Five days! Oh, those poor women and little children."

"You see? This wasn't so far after all."

Sam talked non-stop, aware that Jane was chatting less and less as time went on. Never had the drive to Main-à-Dieu seemed so endless. And the weather didn't help. He'd been hoping for a fine day, and all these flurries weren't making it easy to see the landscape.

Finally, they made their way into Main-à-Dieu. Jane was shocked at how small it was, but all she said was, "It's very pretty."

He pulled into Danny's place, with fishing clutter taking up a lot of real estate around the house. "Let's go in and get warmed up," Sam said.

"Is this our place?" she asked.

"No, no. I'm just bringing back the truck." They hurried into the house and Jane was very grateful it was warm. Sam introduced her to his uncle and his family and they were on their best behaviour in front of Jane. His aunt asked her to sit and have a cup of tea and his smaller cousin, Ruthanne, asked if she was a princess.

Soon there was a plate of squares on the table and then his aunt thought maybe she should put on a bigger spread. "You'll need your lunch before you go."

Jane looked confused. "Where are we going? I thought we were here, close by somewhere."

Danny, who never was too bright, slapped his hand on the table. "Lord love a duck. You've still gots to get over to the island."

Sam was ready to brain him.

"The island? I thought we were on the island."

"No, missus. You still gotta get on a boat."

The look Jane gave Sam chilled him to the bone. "It's not far, I swear. Just a half an hour to where we're going."

"Can someone point out this island to me?"

Again, Danny was more than happy to oblige. "Look out the window. You see the wharf? Look past that and across the tittle and then you see that dark shape out in the water? That's it, except you have to keep going almost seven miles to the other end."

Jane did not want to show herself up in front of Sam's relatives. "I'm sure it's lovely."

Danny drove them back to the wharf; they gathered Jane's things and Sam put her belongings on the boat after taking them down the dock ladder.

"Am I supposed to climb down there?" Jane asked him.

Sam hurried back up the ladder. "I'll be right behind you. You won't fall."

It took everything Jane had to put one foot over the edge and onto the first rung. "Okay, I've got you. Now put your other foot over."

It was taking her so long, she was freezing again. She wasn't dressed properly. Her city boots were no match for this boat, especially as it kept moving. It was frightening, but she tried to keep a brave face. Sam gave her a hug to reassure her.

"Come in the wheelhouse out of the cold."

Danny let go to the rope and gave them a wave goodbye. Sam turned over the engine and it sprang to life with a very loud rumbling that seemed to reverberate right through Jane's body. She tried to say something to Sam but he couldn't hear her so she had to shout: "Is this a good day to be on a boat? Is it calm?"

"These Cape Islander boats are the safest out here," he shouted back. "Don't worry, I know what I'm doing."

And he did look like he was in his element. She loved watching that gorgeous face as he held the wheel. Now he was confident, unlike the boy who sat at Aunt Lou's dining room table. He looked like a man. She was frightened but felt safe. It was time to be brave. Jane didn't want to make his life difficult. This wasn't what she'd expected, but now was not the time to bring it up.

He increased the speed and they left the harbour behind. It wasn't exactly snowing, but there were large, ominous clouds threatening just that. The water was much choppier as they continued on, and to Jane's horror her stomach started to revolt. She wasn't sure what to do, be sick in here or out there. She wanted to stay close to Sam. Again, there was too much space on the boat.

"Are you okay?" he yelled.

"No. I'm going to be sick."

"Put your fingers below your wrist and press hard. It helps."

She tried it but knew it wasn't enough, so she bolted out of the wheelhouse and was sick over the side, getting wet in the process from the spray. At one point the boat rolled down into the trough between waves and Jane thought she was going to go over the side. Her chin started to tremble again and she was sick once more.

"Are you okay?" Sam yelled over his shoulder. "Do you want me to stop the boat?"

At first, she thought yes, but that would only prolong the agony. "I'm okay," she shouted. She walked unsteadily back into the wheelhouse and Sam put one arm around her as he steered.

"I'm so sorry. I wish it was a nice calm day, then you'd be fine."

She hid her face under his arm. "Just get us there."

It was the longest ride of her life. It felt endless, as journeys always do when you don't know where you're going. They gave up trying to talk to each other over the engine. She didn't want to talk, anyway. She was afraid she'd start crying, so she kept her jaw clenched and held on to Sam for dear life.

Sam thought he was going to be sick for different reasons. The fact that his wife couldn't even look up to see her new island home, or didn't want to look up, was upsetting. Everything he took for granted as normal, he was now seeing through her startled face. He could only hope that things would get better. He now wished they'd waited for her to come in the summer, when everything wasn't a complete ordeal. Well, at least when it was warmer and prettier.

God. This wasn't even a difficult day.

When Jane felt the boat slow down, she lifted her head and saw a clearing with primitive unpainted wooden houses dotting the landscape in and around a natural harbour.

"This is it," Sam said before he turned off the engine. Jane was thankful when it stopped. Her ears hurt. Sam went onto the deck and gaffed the buoy in the water and used a length of rope to tie the boat to it. There was a small skiff attached to the buoy as well.

She emerged from the wheelhouse in a bit of a daze. "Where's the wharf?"

"We don't have one."

"But how are we going to get off this boat?"

Sam realized the ordeal wasn't over. Why had none of this occurred to him? The only thing he could think to do was to take her in his arms. "Do you trust me?"

When she didn't say anything, he had his answer, so he did what he did best. He went to kiss her, but she turned away. "I was just sick." He stroked her hair instead. "I won't let anything happen to you. You're safe. I've got you."

She nodded.

Sam saw Bob come down the hill. He got in another small skiff and rowed out to them. He stayed in the small boat, Sam hanging on to the rope Bob threw him.

"Bob, this is my wife, Jane."

They said hello, but it was awkward, Bob bobbing in the water and Jane up above him.

"Now this is what's going to happen," Sam said to her. "Bob will steady the boat and I'll help you in it and he'll take you to shore. I'll put your belongings in the other skiff and row them in. Then we'll all have a nice cup of tea."

"I need a drink," she replied and Bob smirked. "So how am I supposed to crawl off this boat into that little thing? Does everyone do this? I'm never going to leave here if this is how it's done."

Once again, Sam hadn't even thought this would be a problem. He'd grown up doing it, and it was second nature.

"I'll keep ahold of you and Bob will steady you when you get in. Sit down quick."

Jane was worried that the whole world was going to see her knickers. What was she going to do with all her dresses? She obviously needed trousers for this type of activity. The only reason she wasn't bawling was that she was too afraid of landing in the water. Fear was keeping her focused.

Sam told her to go over backwards, with her chest and stomach against the side, so while he held her under her arms, her legs were dangling as the boat was going up and down with the waves.

"Help!" she screeched. And then she felt her new brother-in-law put his hand on her bottom and then her legs and pull her down with a thud onto the seat at the back. There was no time to react before he was rowing away towards the shore.

"That was awful," she told Bob.

"You get used to it."

"I'm sorry, but I will never get used to that." She looked at him, trying to see if he resembled Sam, and he did a bit, but his eyes were brown, which looked odd to her. One thing about Bob was that he didn't mess about. He had them to the shore a minute later, and he hopped out into the water as if it were nothing, but then he was wearing big rubber boots. He pulled the skiff up as far as he could, but the sand was still very wet and the minute she put her feet down, a wave came up higher and went over the toes of her suede zip-up boots.

Bob pointed at them. "You're going to need something better than that."

Jane adjusted her hat and wiggled her clothes back to rights. "I'm realizing I'll need a lot of things to live here."

Sam was on shore right behind them and Bob took her belongings and walked away with them. Sam took her by the shoulders. "I'm proud of you. You did it."

"That was terrifying. I never want to get in a boat again."

"Tough to avoid if you ever need to get out of here." He took her by the hand and led her up the hill.

She glanced at him. "Why didn't you tell me? I thought you'd have a ferry or some normal way to get off and on an island. One that didn't involve getting your feet wet and hanging over the open sea."

He stopped and closed his eyes before facing her. "Forgive me. I missed home so much I forgot that someone who's never been here would find it challenging. I should have written to you as soon as I got to Halifax, because it was on the way over that I realized I was asking a lot of you. I'm sorry, Jane."

He looked so sad and she loved him too much. "It will be fine," she said.

A group of teenage boys were obviously watching them as they approached the road. Sam waved his hand. "Nothin' to see here," he laughed.

Clarence, who was eight years old when Sam left, stood with

a cigarette dangling from his lips. He pointed at Jane. "That the new Mary Alice?"

Sam walked over to them, taking Jane with him. "Boys, this is my new wife, Jane. She comes from London and doesn't know a soul here. Please make her feel at home."

"Hello, boys. It's nice to meet you," Jane said, smiling.

"Hey! You talk funny!" one of them said, and they all laughed.

Sam took a quick step towards them and gave them a hand gesture that meant get the hell out of here. They knew better than to make Sam mad. His reputation was legendary for taking no shit, so they moved along.

The incident was upsetting for Jane. They had laughed at the way she talked, and she wanted to know, "Who's Mary Alice?"

"Remember? I told you Mary Alice and Hardy are my best friends. We were born on the same day and have hung around together all our lives. I'll be happy to introduce them to you when we get you settled in."

"Where is the house, anyway?" She hoped it wasn't one of the small houses here in the harbour.

He pointed. "It's that one."

Dismay washed over her as she stared at the unpainted structure. It looked like an overgrown shed. So far, everything wasn't as she'd imagined. She was trying not to panic, but she couldn't swallow. It was so small, and he said his father and Bob lived here too.

For the first time Sam was seeing the house through her eyes, as he remembered the pretty town of Dorking and the warm comfort of Aunt Lou's home, with its fenced garden and stained-glass doors.

He tried to be brave. "Shall I carry you across the threshold?"

"No."

He opened the door and a foul smell hit them in the face. Bob yelled for Sam. "Get in here. The old man shit himself."

That's when Jane's unshed tears burst forth and everything that had happened that day became too much for her.

What had she done? What was she going to do?

Sam ran out the door, knocked on Mary's door, and opened it. Mary and Tom were surprised and looked up from the table where they were having lunch.

"Ya gotta help me, Mary."

"What's wrong?"

"My wife Jane just got here and Da shit his pants and she's crying and I don't know what to do. I wish Jean was here. Can I bring her over and you can give her some tea or at least a place to cry while we deal with Da?"

Tom stood up. "My cue to leave. I'll be over at Yomie's."

Mary stood up too. "Go get her."

"Thank you." Sam dashed back across the road and bundled the crying Jane in his arms. "You're going to sit with Mary until we deal with this. She'll take care of you."

Jane couldn't stop crying and just followed along. Sam sat her at Mary's table and said, "I'll be back soon."

Mary went over and squeezed the poor girl's shoulder. "Go on. It's better out than in." That set off Jane again, so Mary took the time to pour a cup of tea and made her some toast with honey. She kept peeking over at Jane, and was amazed at how similar she looked to Mary Alice. Her hair was almost exactly the same colour. She didn't think that was a coincidence. Oh, what a tangled mess.

She sat down beside Jane and offered her a wet facecloth. "Now, wipe those eyes and get somethin' in ya. You'll feel better."

Jane took it and wiped her face, tears still falling down her cheeks. "I'm so sorry. What must you think of me?"

Mary loved her accent. She kind of sounded like the young Princess Elizabeth. "I think you're a long way from home."

The gates opened and Jane told Mary the whole story of her bewildering day. "I didn't know I was coming to this island. I thought Cape Breton was the island. It's so far away from everything. And I was seasick on the ship all the way over and then on Sam's boat, and had to drop into that skiff out on the water, and his house is so small..."

She hesitated when she realized Mary's house was too. "I mean, I didn't know his sick father and brother would be living with us. It's all too much."

Mary nodded. "I raised ten kids in this house, but it's different when they're your own. Child, this place is too much for most people on the mainland. Can't for the life of me think how it must seem to you. I couldn't believe it when Sam said he had a war bride. Not many young women from a city as big as London would want to move here."

Jane's hand hit the table. "That's just it. He didn't tell me you had to get off one boat into a smaller one while still out on the water. He just said it was beautiful and he made it sound so romantic. I believed him."

Mary pointed at the mug to remind Jane to take a sip, which she did. She even picked up the toast.

"There is nothing romantic about this place. Granted, there's beautiful scenery, but you're usually working too hard to enjoy it."

"Why did people come here in the first place?"

"Fishing. It's the only thing that keeps most poor folk going, and when your pa is a fisherman, chances are your sons will be too."

Jane chewed her toast before she leaned forward. "I don't mean to sound rude, but is Sam poor? Does he have any money?"

Mary smiled. "We're all needy, girl. But when everyone around you is in the same boat, you don't notice it. And no, he doesn't have any money, although I imagine he earned some in the army.

The thing is, we don't need money here. We trade our fish for the things we need. Over in Main-à-Dieu, Peter Mullins is a fish buyer and merchant. He kits the men out with supplies, and at the end of fishing season, they pay him back with their catch. As long as he's paid, and the doctor, all is good. We've got our own animals for food and we grow vegetables and eat fish and pick berries. The kids all wear hand-me-downs, but there's always something in a tin jar to buy things on occasion, flour and sugar from the MacCuishes down the road. It's different here. A world away from where you grew up."

Jane took another swig of tea. Her tears were drying up. Mary was doing her job.

"He should have told me before I came here."

"Yes, he should have, but if he did, would you have come?"

Jane rubbed her forehead. "I don't know. Probably not. Or maybe. I love him. He's so different from the boys I knew. He's worldly, but naive. Confident, but not. This explains why he was always so nervous around Aunt Lou."

"It's not going to be easy, but if you love each other, that helps."

Jane drank more tea and then said, "I'm sorry, I need to use the toilet."

Mary pointed. "Out the door to your left."

"An outhouse? I haven't used one in years." Jane went outside and stumbled along, with the wind grabbing the door and banging it against the side. It was freezing and the cold draft from the deep hole on her bare skin was a shock. The only outhouse she had ever used was tucked away in a protected corner of a back garden. This was open to the elements. She noticed a catalogue on the bench beside her. She searched in her coat pocket instead and found some tissue and then got out as quickly as she could, shutting the door behind her. It smelled like Sam's house and she cried all over again, but she waited until she was more composed before going back inside. Mary was being very nice to her and she didn't want to be a burden.

By the time Sam came back for her, Jane was at least calm. She didn't want to leave and Mary sensed that, so she spoke up. "If you'd like, why don't you and Sam come and have dinner with us? That way you can meet Mary Alice and perhaps Hardy could join us. Get the introductions over with in one fell swoop."

Sam could have kissed her. "Thanks, Mary. We'll be over later."

As they walked across the road, Jane gave a big sigh. "I like Mary."

"Everyone likes Mary."

Then she looked him right in the eye. "I like her more than I like you."

Oh dear. This wasn't going to be easy, and I didn't know what to do. Not that I could do anything, really, but my heart was sore for Sam. He'd been building castles in the sky and now reality had fallen in on him.

And I felt for Jane. She was a sweet girl, and I knew she loved him, but she was a fish out of water here.

It was adding Mary Alice to the mix that most concerned me.

CHAPTER FOURTEEN

Tom returned from Yomie's a few hours later. He peeked in the door. "All clear?"

"Ya big coward," Mary said, turning to him as she stirred the fish chowder for their supper.

He came closer and looked over her shoulder. "That's a jeezly amount of chowder you're makin', woman. Who ya feedin'?"

"You, me, Mary Alice, Hardy, Sam, and his new wife, Jane."

"You want Mary Alice to scratch this gal's eyes out over the supper table? I'm goin' back to Yomie's before I get heartburn."

Mary hit the side of the pot with her wooden spoon. "This is the easiest way to have them meet each other, all at once, instead of sculling around. And with us there, none of them will make a scene."

"Have you met your daughter?"

Fortunately, the snow was hard and squeaky on Mary Alice's journey home. It made walking so much easier than having her boots punch through soft snow. She'd had a hard day in the classroom. Two of the older boys got into it and frightened the little ones. She grabbed the troublemakers by the ears and pushed them out the door. "Go have your little bust-up out here where we can't see you." It took a while to settle the young ones down. The rest of the kids only wanted to look out the window to see the fight continue, with the two fellas rolling around in the schoolyard. They looked like two snowmen after only a couple of minutes. She'd have to go out there if they didn't let up, but they stopped throwing punches and resorted to pointing and name-calling. Tired of that, they walked away together, and she couldn't call them back in. Effectively an afternoon off.

She got home and kicked the snow off her boots against the door before going inside. Just the way her parents looked at her when she came in, she knew something was up. There were also more plates on the table than they needed.

"Okay, what's going on?"

"I'm inviting a few people for supper."

"Oh, Rose and the kids?" Mary Alice began to unwind her scarf when her mother pointed at her. "No, not Rose, but I want you to see if Hardy would like to come. Sam and his wife, Jane, will be here as well. I met her earlier and thought I'd make her welcome, since she had a rough first day."

Mary Alice stood stock-still and then rewound her scarf and headed back out the door to tramp to the lighthouse. She didn't look across the road at Sam's house. By the time she banged on the Campbells' door, she wanted to wring her mother's neck.

Hardy and little Toby greeted her, and she went right by them and sat on a kitchen chair. Hardy's assistant keeper, Gerry, took one look at her and disappeared out the door. Toby had to jump up and down to get her to notice him. She finally gave the top of his head a pat.

Hardy folded his arms across his chest. "Spill it."

"I've come to invite you for supper."

"And this makes you furious? I don't have to go, you know."

She made a face at him. "It's not you making me mad, it's my mother for inviting Sam and his wife over too. You better sit beside me so I don't hurl a fork at her. Or a knife at him."

He sat in the chair beside her. "Well, this will be fun. Makes sense, though. We all meet at the same time. I wonder why she thought of it, other than the fact that your mother has more sense than most."

"My mother wears underpants on her head to make bread, don't forget. And apparently Mrs. Harris had a hard first day, poor thing."

Hardy slapped the table. "Stop sookin' and let's go." He took his jacket from the back of the chair and hollered into the parlour. "Ma, I won't be home for supper. Feed Toby, will ya?"

There was no answer so he raised his voice. "Ma?"

"Yeah, yeah, I will," she said.

He pointed his thumb towards her voice. "She got a load of crosswords from Auntie Bea, who can't do them anymore because her eyes are so bad. She got nothin' done all day."

"She's allowed to do nothing all day for once in her life."

Toby wasn't happy that they left without him. He crawled under the kitchen table, gave a great sigh, and laid his head on his front paws.

The two of them walked back to the house side by side and didn't say anything. But before she opened the door, he said, "Be nice."

Mary and Tom were very relieved to see Hardy, especially Tom. "Hey, big guy. The muscles on ya! You're startin' to look like a brick shithouse."

Mary hit Tom with a dishcloth. "Watch your mouth. Jane is a city girl."

Mary Alice hung her coat up on the hook. "But you can be crude in front of me. I'm not that sophisticated."

"Take it down a notch," her mother growled at her.

"This was your stupid idea," Mary Alice growled back. "Don't expect me to be happy about it."

Her father glared at her. "Don't talk to your mother like that."

Hardy took a deep breath. "Can we all just remember that this girl's entire family was wiped out and Sam spent five years of his life fighting in a war? I think they deserve some peace and understanding. They've dealt with enough misery to last a lifetime."

All of them looked at Mary Alice. She threw her arms in the air. "Fine! I'll be as good as gold. Butter wouldn't melt. I'm going to get changed."

She went upstairs and Mary squeezed Hardy's arm. "Thank you for being here."

Mary Alice poured some water out of a pitcher into the wash-bowl by her bed and held the cold facecloth to her face. It helped ease the pressure behind her eyes and gave her the chance to take a minute. She looked in the mirror and a voice said very clearly, "You're acting like a child." She knew this voice. It was hers, but it wasn't. "Okay," she said. Then she put on her pink blouse. It was still in good shape because she never went anywhere fancy. Then she brushed her long hair and put it back in a bun. She looked older like this and hoped she could compete with the city girl named Jane.

She thought it was odd that Sam's wife was named Jane. Mary Alice had always loved that name. Even thought about naming a daughter Jane, but then she remembered she was a spinster and never wanted kids. Who needed them if all they did was fight and hit each other in the snow?

The front door opened downstairs and she heard Sam's voice introducing Jane to everyone. Mary Alice didn't want them to think she was hiding, so she hurried downstairs and walked right over to her. "Welcome to Scatarie."

She caught Hardy's eye and knew he was thinking what she was thinking. Jane resembled her. Their hair was exactly the same colour. Instantly, she wasn't mad at Jane anymore. She felt badly for Jane. Sam went and found himself a British Mary Alice. He must have loved her in more than a friendship kind of way after all. It was obvious, at least to her. She hoped Jane wouldn't figure it out.

Sam flashed her a big smile of appreciation and Mary called everyone to the table. Mary Alice had a chance to look at Jane while her mother meted out the bowls of chowder. She was a very pretty girl, but at the moment she looked lost and tired. She was making a valiant effort to appear carefree, but she wasn't fooling Mary Alice or Mary.

Hardy was right. Jane was going to need a friend. Her mother had recognized that instantly. Now Mary Alice felt even worse. She was lucky enough to still have her mom. Jane's mother was blown up.

God in heaven.

Sam looked delighted that Mary Alice was being friendly to Jane. He kept giving her grateful looks. And now here they were, telling Jane all about their adventures together as kids and laughing at the recollections.

Mary glanced at her husband, who gave her a quick nod to acknowledge her role in this successful evening. She knew that Jane had a rough road ahead, but hopefully meeting Sam's friends would reassure her she wasn't alone. And Mary had to admit she was very proud of her daughter. She'd done something right with that girl.

Mary rose from the table to gather the bowls and Jane asked if she could help. Mary Alice waved her away. "Sit and relax. You're our guest," and she brought the rest of the bowls to the sink. Her mom handed her a butterscotch pie and Mary Alice cut it into six pieces while Mary poured the tea.

Mary Alice took her first forkful of pie and then said, "I suppose you get asked this all the time, but have you ever seen the King?"

Jane swallowed her mouthful and nodded. "I have, actually. My father was a bobby, a policeman, and he was asked to be part of a security detail for Trooping the Colour, which is a military parade to celebrate the King's official birthday. Mother took us down the mall to Buckingham Palace and we tried to find Dad but there were so many people and horses and soldiers and flags waving, it was all a bit of a blur. But then the royal family came out on the balcony and waved to all of us and we were so excited. Dad was really tired by the time he came home, and my mother carried my brother because he fell asleep." Her voice caught then, and she looked down at her lap. "Sorry. I still have trouble talking about my family."

Sam reached over and put his arm around Jane's shoulders, kissing her forehead. "It's okay."

Mary Alice wanted to kick herself. "I'm so sorry. I didn't mean to upset you."

Jane held up her hand. "It's fine. I like talking about my family normally, but today has been a bit overwhelming." She looked at Mary. "Your mother was very kind to me. I'm glad she's my neighbour."

"You need anything, child, just walk right in," Mary said.

"I think we'd better go," Sam said. "Thanks, Mary. It was a great meal."

"Yes," Jane said softly as he steered her out the door. "Goodnight."

Mary Alice had to blow her nose. "I'm such an idiot. Why did I ask her that?"

"You weren't to know," Hardy said. "I think you handled the situation beautifully. I know Sam was pleased."

Her parents nodded. "Good job," her mom said. "I'm sure it wasn't easy."

She wiped her eyes and then leaned forward. "She looks like me, don't you think?"

All three of her tablemates took big bites of their pie and said, "Mmmm," just to get out of answering. Hardy went so far as to point at it with his fork. "This is delicious. Just as good as my mom's."

"Well, that's saying something," Mary laughed.

"Ignore me then, you all know I'm right," Mary Alice said, sighing. "Not that it matters anymore, because I like her."

Once the pie was gone and the teapot empty, Tom went to his chair and lit his pipe. Mary started on the dishes. Mary Alice grabbed her coat.

"I'm going to walk Hardy home."

"Because I'm afraid of bears."

"I need some air, you big goof."

Hardy put his jacket on too. "Thanks for the great meal, Mary."

Mary raised her hand but didn't turn around.

More snow squeaking as they walked the road under a crescent moon. "Looks like the clouds moved off. But we're in for a blow tomorrow. Gerry and I will be on shifts."

"You be careful up on that galley with the freezing rain and all. You pretend it's so easy, but I worry about you."

He smiled in the dark. "That's nice to know."

"So did you like her?"

"Who?" he teased.

"Knock it off."

He put his gloved hands in his pockets. "She's a very sweet girl, and I'm assuming she's our age, but she seems younger."

She nodded. "Yeah, I thought so too. We were never young. Too much hard livin' here on the island. And what about Sam? I think he's changed, more unsure of himself."

"Of course he's changed."

"I worry about him too."

"You know where worrying gets you?" He put his gloved pointer finger on her nose. "Absolutely nowhere." They were approaching the lighthouse. "Let me get you a flashlight."

"Hardy Campbell. The day I can't walk home from your place at night will never come. Remember, be careful tomorrow. See ya."

She turned around and was soon gone, a small shadow disappearing in the dark.

Sam installed Jane in his upstairs bedroom, where she could have some privacy. It was basically just a bed and a dresser. She didn't unpack because it was dark and the lamp didn't shed a lot of light. Something else her husband forgot to mention. No electricity. Or gas outlets. Although apparently a neighbour had a generator. Fat lot of good it did her.

Sam waited until after dinner to introduce her to his father, which in hindsight wasn't good thinking. She had to see his sagging face in the shadows, and she jumped with fright when his father extended a shaking hand towards her. She knew she'd have to shake his hand and tried not to let her alarm show, but instead of taking Jane's hand he grabbed her whole arm and squeezed it and wouldn't let it go. Sam had to reach over and take it away with some effort.

"He doesn't mean it," he whispered. "He can't control his movements very well."

Jane took a deep breath and said, "It's nice to meet you, Mr. Harris. Thank you for inviting me into your home."

Edgar tried to speak, but only spat and then moaned.

Sam put his hand on his father's chest. "It's okay. She knows you're glad to meet her. I'm going to take her upstairs because she's tired. We'll see you in the morning. Bob is sleeping down here tonight in case you need anything. I'm hoping Jean will be able to come tomorrow to stay a night or two. Goodnight, Da."

Jane felt ashamed of herself for her reaction, seeing Sam being so considerate to his father. The poor man couldn't help his situation. It's just that everything today was too much. And now she needed to pee again.

"I have to go outside. Do you have a torch handy?"

Bob was at the table reading an old issue of the newspaper. "A torch? Jesus, don't take a torch. You'll burn down the bog hole."

"It means flashlight," Sam said impatiently.

"I never heard it called that."

"Because you didn't go to war, did you?"

His brother looked up. "Fuck off. Pardon my language, Jane."

They went out the back door and Sam held her hand over the crooked ground. She stopped and looked at him. "Please tell me you have tissue paper in there?"

"Sorry."

"You're sorry about everything, aren't you?" She grabbed the flashlight and took it in with her. Somehow, as she tried to manoeuvre off the high seat, she managed to knock the light down the hole. She screamed with frustration.

"Are you okay?" Sam shouted and he tried to open the door, but she'd locked it with the small piece of wood that swivelled on a nail.

"NO! I'm not okay. I've never been so not okay in my life. I can't see a thing and I can't find the lock."

"Use the—"

"Oh, the torch I just knocked into the smelly abyss? I can't say I want to rummage around in shit to find it." Just as she said that, her fingers found the small lock and she turned it to open the door.

Sam opened his mouth but she spoke first. “Let me guess. You’re sorry.” And she stumbled back to the door and let herself in. “Where can I wash my hands?” she asked Bob.

“In the bucket there.”

“So you don’t have a tap and running water? No, don’t answer that.” She dipped a small pot into the bucket and took it up the darkened stairs with her. She wanted to wipe her face as well as her hands. The lamp in the bedroom gave off a pretty glow. It was a bright spot in a very bleak day.

Jane was so disheartened she lay facing the wall on the far side of the bed with all her clothes on and a sweater and her coat over her. She didn’t want to get under the sheets. She didn’t know this place. She was lost and alone. She thought of crying, but she was all out of tears. Her eyes felt swollen and dusty dry.

She was glad that Sam didn’t come upstairs. If she heard the word *sorry* from his lips one more time she’d have to slap him. Her body vibrated with indignation but it took up too much energy after a while and she needed sleep. She knew she was going mad when she heard someone whisper the Irish tune “Hush Now Don’t You Cry.” *Don’t even wonder about it*, she thought before her eyes finally closed.

At some point in the night, Jane woke with a start. The lamp was still glowing but low. It gave off enough light that when she turned her head, she saw Sam’s back and shoulders heaving up and down. He was quietly weeping, trying not to wake her.

This was the saddest thing of all.

She turned over and put her hand on him. “I’m sorry.”

Sam groaned and faced her, pulling her into his arms. They didn’t speak, just moved as close as they could to one another until they felt like one animal. That’s when rest came.

CHAPTER FIFTEEN

Jane cried at least once a day every day for a month. She didn't mean to, but everything was a chore. Keep the fire going. Go to the well to get water. Heat the water to do dishes. Learn how to wick the lanterns. Wash the clothes in a tub, not a wringer-washer. The day Bob said, "You don't know how to make bread?" she felt useless.

And then the worst happened. Bob scrambled some eggs and opened the jar of brown sauce that was sitting on the windowsill keeping Jane company. She grabbed a broom and, screaming, chased him out of the house. He ran down to the fish hut and hid behind Sam. "She's a fucking lunatic."

Sam picked her up where she fell, out of breath and spent, then carried her back to the house. She sat on his lap while she whimpered. He got the jar and put the lid back on really, really tight. "No harm done."

When he told his brother why the brown sauce was so important to her, Bob stood in front of her like a little kid, cap in his hand, and apologized.

She eventually said all was forgiven. How could he have known? But she made sure the jar was near her side of the bed after that. And Bob made sure to check first, to see if she had any emotional attachment to whatever else he wanted to eat.

Sam was in and out all day with his brother, getting ready for the start of fishing season in a month. All their equipment had to be in tip-top shape—lines, nets, buoys, as well as the boat and its engine, not to mention making new lobster traps. Jane was often left alone with their father and that was daunting, feeding him like a baby. She was incredibly grateful to meet Jean and have her stay overnight a couple of times a week if the weather allowed, and when it didn't, it was depressing.

The storms here were frightening. The sound of the surf roaring at night made Jane think a train was headed in her direction. When Edgar was asleep, she often skipped over the road to Mary's, more for company than anything. She told her what Bob said about her not knowing how to make bread, so Mary set to work to show her.

Jane sighed. "It's so complicated."

"You're not the only one to think so. Mary Alice refuses to make bread and most everything else. She's gonna have a hard time when I kick the bucket."

"Please don't die, Mary."

"I'll try not to."

As the weather got a little warmer, more women came to the door with a plate of something to welcome Jane. They were kind, but since they had nothing in common the conversations were somewhat stilted and didn't last long. They had heard through the grapevine that this English girl was a real softie and hated everything about the place. Most understood, but it was still off-putting that their way of life was miserable in Jane's eyes.

Flossie wanted to see for herself, so the minute both sets of twins were down for a nap, she recruited her mother-in-law to keep an eye on them. Walking over to Sam's, she got her boots muddy, since the frost was coming out of the ground and made things soggy.

She knocked on the door and had to knock again before a flustered-looking Jane opened it. Flossie's eyes got wide. "Well, hello there. You must be Sam's new wife. I'm Flossie, a very close friend of Sam's."

"Hello."

Since she just stood there, Flossie had to point into the doorway. "Shall we sit and get acquainted?"

Jane looked behind her. "I'm trying to do the laundry, so the place is a tip."

"Don't bother me." Flossie moved right past her and sat at the table. "A cup of tea would be nice."

"Oh. Yes." Jane dipped a small potful of water out of the bucket and poured it into her mother's kettle and put it on the stove. She stood near it to give herself some comfort.

"Well, I'm just going to have to state the obvious. You and Mary Alice are the spit of each other."

"We are?"

"Oh yes. Your hair, for one thing."

Jane touched her head. "I'm sure there are many people with this colour."

Flossie nodded but didn't look convinced. "Mary Alice was always chasing Sam. It was embarrassing the way she went after him. But it looks like you won the prize, so good for you."

Jane was confused. "I know that Mary Alice and Sam are good friends. I didn't think it was more than that."

"Well, they'd hardly tell ya, would they?" Flossie laughed and then pointed at the wall behind Jane. "Did you see that?"

Jane turned around. "What?"

"As God is my witness, there was a girl just standing there a second ago!" Flossie got up from the table, her face ashen. "Mother Mary. This place is haunted!" And she ran out the door.

Edgar began to make noises, so Jane put her head through the curtains. She was getting the hang of what he wanted by hand gestures. He pointed in the direction of the front door and then closed his fingers up and down.

"Who was here talking? I think she said her name was Flossie."

Even though Edgar's face wasn't very animated, he managed to express his dislike. He rolled his eyes and then twirled his finger by his temple.

"She's crazy, is she?"

He nodded his head.

Jane smiled. "She must be. She just said she saw a ghost."

Now he waved his hand in disgust.

It bothered Jane that Edgar was lying in that bed all the time. They did get him up and about if both the boys were holding him to give him a little exercise, but in the month since she'd been here, she saw him get frailer. Jean mentioned it on her last visit.

"It's such an ordeal to get him to the doctor, but we'd do it in a heartbeat except he refuses to go. Why are old men so stubborn?"

"Maybe he doesn't want to live like this. Would you?"

"I think you're right, Jane."

After the upsetting visit with this Flossie character, Jane finished the endless wash and put on a pair of old rubber boots that Jean gave her and took the clothes outside. She'd learned quickly you had to wear mittens to do this, because the wind off the water combined with the wet material made your fingers freeze.

She'd never heard of hanging clothes out in weather like this, but it seemed they all did it. She watched Mary take in a pair of Tom's overalls when they were stiff as a board. It looked like she was dancing with him.

While she struggled with this task, Sam whistled from the beach, where he was bent over some piece of machinery and blew her a kiss. She waved and then jumped when Mary Alice came up behind her.

"Sorry, didn't mean to frighten you. Thank goodness school is over. It was the longest day ever."

Jane pursed her lips and then faced Mary Alice, a pair of wet jeans still in her hands. "Was he blowing a kiss to me or you?" she said.

"What?"

"Someone named Flossie came by today and mentioned that you've chased Sam all your life. She assured me you weren't just best friends."

Mary Alice was livid. She clenched her hands into fists and hit one into the palm of her hand. "Wait till I get my hands on that miserable bitch. Don't listen to a thing that one says. She was so in love with Sam that she was jealous of anyone who even talked to him. She used to drive him crazy. You can ask Sam yourself. Or ask Hardy. He'll tell you. Although Hardy tends not to point out people's bad qualities, unlike myself. What else did that witch say?"

Jane continued hanging the jeans. "Not much. A minute after that she pointed behind me and said there was a young girl standing by the wall. She declared her a ghost before she ran out yelling the place was haunted."

"Typical. Flossie is also a drama queen. You know the type. Always wants attention."

Picking up the basket, Jane said, "Want to have some tea? I get lonely for female company."

"Love some."

They went in the back door and Mary Alice immediately stuck her head between the curtains. "Hey, Edgar. Hope Jane is treating you right."

He gave her a thumb's up.

She went back to the kitchen and whispered, "That poor man."

Jane nodded and set about putting her kettle on. "So how was your day at school? I should wander over there one day to see it, but I'm kind of stuck." She nodded her head towards Edgar's space.

Mary Alice gave a big sigh. "I'm getting weary of being a teacher. I mean, I love the kids, most of them anyway, but it's so depressing when some of them drop out for one reason or another. Donald Phillips was only in grade three and he left. Had to help out his family because his father died. Can you imagine?"

Once the tea was poured Jane put some cookies on a plate. Mary Alice nodded. "Mom's oatmeal cookies. She must have given you the recipe. You did a great job, they taste just like hers."

"No, she brought them over. I'm not much of a baker and that wood stove scares me."

Mary Alice took a sip of tea and nodded. "I'm a terrible baker. I have no interest in it."

"I still can't wrap my head around not being able to go to the shops to buy a package of biscuits without hopping on and off boats and climbing up slippery ladders."

"Believe it or not, you'll get used to it."

"I doubt that."

It was the way she said it that caught Mary Alice's attention. "Are you sorry you came here? You can tell me. I won't breathe a word."

Jane nodded sadly, her bottom lip quivering.

Mary Alice wasn't expecting her to be so candid. She leaned forward. "It's okay. I know you love him."

Jane put her arms on the table and hid her face. Now Mary Alice took to patting her back. She'd never had a close girlfriend, so she hoped she was reacting properly. Eventually Jane raised her head and looked towards Edgar's room before dropping her voice.

"He's everything I've ever wanted and I'm trying to adjust, but I can't get over my resentment about him not telling me exactly what I was walking into. Did he do that on purpose? And now he's starting to get exasperated with me if he thinks I'm going to cry about something. Not overtly, but I can read his face. I don't mean to cry, but sometimes it's all too much. He's not around most of the time."

She again looked at the curtain and leaned closer to Mary Alice. "And lately, Sam's been having terrible nightmares. He's always moaning or shouting in his sleep. When I ask him about it, he says he doesn't want to discuss it, that he's fine. Does that sound fine to you?"

Mary Alice was concerned. "No doubt memories of the war bubbling up. He won't talk about it, you know. From what I've heard from some of the other families, their lads are the same way. Hardy said he spoke to him briefly and then Sam shut it down. Do you blame him? Would you want to relive the worst days of your life?"

"How do I help him when I can't even help myself?"

Grabbing Jane's hand, Mary Alice reassured her. "I'm here and so is Ma. She'd do anything for Sam and Hardy. She considers them her sons too. And I've loved them both my whole life. You're not alone, Jane. I know this wasn't what you imagined, but you're here now and so is Sam and it's obvious he thinks you're wonderful. Getting annoyed with each other is a part of being married. If my parents had walked away every time they had an argument, they'd only have one kid, not ten."

"Oh yes, I think she mentioned that."

"Scary, isn't it?"

Jane didn't look as desperate as she was when they first came in. She dunked her cookie in the tea and chewed thoughtfully. "May I ask why you're not married?"

"I'm basically lazy. I can't be bothered."

"But you're so pretty. You must have had fellas come to your door."

"I told them to bugger off."

The two of them laughed, and it was just what Jane needed. She gave Mary Alice a big smile. "I like you so much. I hope we'll be good friends."

"You can't be if you bugger off too, so you better not. You're the first girlfriend I've ever had. Most of the time my sisters couldn't be bothered with me because I was the youngest and looking after me was a burden. Only my sister Rose has kept tabs on me. I like her the best. But I promise I will be a faithful friend to you."

They held hands across the table. "I feel better already," Jane told her.

Mary Alice eventually left, and instead of walking twenty steps home for supper, she hightailed it to miserable Flossie's house and banged on the door. Hank opened it and blushed straightaway, like he always did when he saw her.

"I want to speak to your wife."

"She's not feeling well."

"Oh dear, did she see a ghost?"

Flossie stormed to the door. "Don't you dare make fun of me. I did see a ghost, as alive as you standing there. Sam's place is haunted, I tell you."

"Shall I tell you who else will be haunting you? Me! If you ever say anything to Jane again about me and Sam. Why you need to make that poor girl more miserable than she already is boggles my mind. Is your own life so tedious that you can't wait to inflict heartache on other people?"

"Hey now," Hank said, "watch your mouth."

"Why should I, Hank? You've been watching my mouth for years and years." She pointed at Flossie. "You heard me. Keep away from that girl."

Mary Alice became breathless and slowed down on her way back home. She doubted that Jane would ever have a problem with her again, because Flossie was a bully and bullies were cowards.

But she did believe her about the ghost.

"I don't know if you did that for me or Jane, Cara, but it worked."

I did it for both of them. I was becoming very protective of Jane. She didn't have her mother either. Motherless children run around the world with no skin on. Their first layer of protection vanishes too soon.

And that's why my heroines, my banlaoch, are women like Mary and Annie. They gather these chicks and push them under their wings with their own, with no thought of reward or compensation. It's enough that a lonely and needy child is nourished with food, affection, advice, or attention.

Every little soul needs a friend. That's a founding principle, a doctrine of this afterlife. No one can get through life or death alone, and that's a comforting thought for people wondering if they will be floating around by themselves in their heaven. No one is ever left behind. You can be physically apart if you wish, but you are tethered to the source. No more getting lost, like so many walking on this earth.

Like Sam.

Edgar died in July, in the middle of fishing season, which was unlucky. Fortunately, Jean and her husband, Terry, handled all the arrangements from Morien so the boys could stay on the boat and fish, but there was no getting around going to the funeral. They wanted to go, of course, but it still meant less profit at the end of the season, missing even one day.

None of them wanted to admit to each other that their lives going forward would be much easier without Edgar. But it was true.

Jane, on the other hand, was sorry to see him go. At least he was a living soul breathing in the next room. Now that he was gone, there was no one with her until her husband and brother-in-law came home stinking of fish. Mary Alice was at school all day. Hardy occasionally dropped by to ask how she was doing and deliver some tasty treat his mother had whipped up, but he mostly worked. Mary told her to come over any time, but Jane knew she couldn't bother the woman every day.

There was a lot to keep her busy, but there was no one to talk to while she was doing it. She waved and passed the time of day with her neighbours, but other than talking about the weather, the conversation wasn't that interesting.

There were a few house parties. Everyone danced their jigs to lively music thanks to fiddles and spoons, and Fred Steele was an excellent squeezebox player. The liquor flowed and the guests became more animated, some of them stumbling around and declaring their undying love for each other.

Everyone told her that Sam had always been the life of the party before he left home. Now he didn't like to dance and sat beside her on a couch, nursing glass after glass of hooch. Jane didn't like to say anything because he never got to sit still, but it bothered her when he put his arm around her and basically staggered home with her propping him up.

He'd say stupid things like, "Do you still hate me?"

"No, I don't hate you."

He wagged his finger at her. "But you don't like me. You told me that."

"I was upset, I didn't mean it. Now stop talking nonsense."

They never went back to another get-together after someone had the bright idea of setting off fireworks outside, and with the first blast, Sam instantly threw himself on the floor and cowered with his hands over his head. Since Hardy didn't go to these parties, it was Mary Alice's father, Tom, who quickly gathered him up as everyone watched, shaking their heads.

Tom took Sam out the door and Jane turned around before she followed them. "Have any of you ever had a grenade or bomb go off beside you? You don't have a clue what people went through overseas, so leave him alone!"

Mary Alice and Hardy heard what had happened after the fact and didn't say anything to him, but they made sure they were with him when the family left for the funeral. Jane was so grateful that Mary Alice was with her on the boat. Since it was a calm summer day and not a stormy winter one, she didn't get sick, and watching how Mary Alice and everyone else got on and off the boat made things easier.

Bob drove the boat and Sam went up on the front deck away from everyone. He knew Mary Alice would be there for Jane and no one else would bother walking on the edge of the boat to get to him.

He lit a cigarette, which wasn't easy with the wind in his face, and stared at the water as the boat pushed through it. Another funeral for another parent. So far, he was two for two; Hardy had one under his belt, and Mary Alice was lucky enough not to know what it was like.

Everything since he'd come home was not what he imagined. The carefree days of his youth had disappeared in a puff of smoke, and the idyllic life he'd imagined with Jane was stuff and nonsense. He knew she was trying, but looking at her face when she was unaware he was watching told him the truth. She looked older and constantly worried, as if she needed to pass every test the island threw at her. There was no joy, and she didn't smile often, except when she was with Mary Alice or Mary.

The only thing that saved them both was when they lay under the covers together at night, and even that was a silent affair because Bob was next door. Having his wife still willing to be close to him was Sam's reassurance that she did love him.

But he'd failed her. He'd acted the big man in London, filling her with romantic stories of this island and what a paradise it was. When he was a kid, maybe. Because everyone around him lived the same life, he didn't notice the hardship. Not until she was hanging off the boat scared to death when she first arrived did he realize that not everyone could handle this.

Sam's guilt consumed him. Anger at everything eating him whole.

He felt the boat slow, so he got up and came around the side and jumped down beside Bob in the wheelhouse. "I was thinkin', maybe you could sleep downstairs from now on. To give us a little privacy."

Bob smirked. "Soon you'll be having me sleep in the fishing shack."

"I know it's tough..."

"I don't give a shit where I sleep."

Sam dipped his head. "Thanks, buddy."

Bob grunted. "I just want this damn day to be over."

Sam turned his attention to Jane, who was sitting between Mary Alice and Hardy on the back of the boat. They scooched over to let him in beside her. "You okay?" he asked.

Jane gave him a small smile and nodded. "Don't worry about me."

He put his arm around her and squeezed. "I want to tell you how much I appreciate you being there for Da. He really liked you, and my father didn't like a lot of people."

"I came to like him too. I'll miss him."

Their brother Ian and his wife, Judy, along with Jean and her husband, Terry, were on the wharf to greet them. Ian, Judy, and Terry had never met Jane. This was the first time she'd been off the island since she'd arrived. Now that Jane saw all four siblings together, she could see a resemblance. She didn't feel quite so lonely. There was family here after all. She'd have to make more of an effort to see them and not rely on everyone coming to her.

The ceremony at Immaculate Conception was supposed to be short and sweet, since Edgar wasn't a man of God at the end of his life, and Jean had told the priest they would appreciate a pared-down version, but Father O'Gorman had his own ideas and must have read every passage in the Bible that pertained to fishermen and the sea. They were well and truly ready for it to end when he recited Lord Tennyson's poem "Crossing the Bar." That had the four of Edgar's kids snivelling and the Father felt vindicated. No one was going to tell him how to conduct a funeral.

The food and tea were very welcome, but those from Scatarie had to be making tracks. The Harris family hugged each other and promised to get together more often, and then it was time to crawl down that ladder and back in the boat.

Going home was chillier, so Jane stayed in the wheelhouse with Bob and Sam. Mary Alice put her arm though Hardy's and leaned on his shoulder. "I hate funerals."

"Can't say I know anyone who likes them," Hardy commented.

"Just dig me a hole like you did for Buster and leave me be."

"Okay."

She grunted. "You're awfully accommodating. You'd throw me in a hole without a second thought."

"Sure. Because I know, without a doubt, you'd be outta that hole in five minutes telling me I didn't dig it properly."

Smiling, she said, "I really am a pain, aren't I?"

"This is not news, Mary Alice."

"I don't know why you put up with me."

Hardy looked out over the water. "I don't know either. I must be mad."

When they were getting off the boat into the skiffs, Mary Alice again showed Jane where to place her feet for a smoother transition.

But Jane still ended up getting her shoes wet onshore.

"Well, that's just a given," Mary Alice told her.

The two of them walked up the hill together, Mary and Tom behind them talking to the fellas. Jane pulled Mary Alice close. "While I've got you here, I want to point something out."

"Okay, shoot."

"Hardy loves you."

"Of course he does. I love him too."

"No. He's madly in love with you."

Mary Alice laughed. "If he was madly in love with me, he would have told me before now."

"Would he, though?"

Mary Alice stopped and looked at her. "What do you mean?"

"From what I've seen, Hardy takes his cues from you. He's not going to confess anything until he knows where you stand. I think he's the type of person who suffers in silence."

Looking behind her to make sure the others were still by the shore, Mary Alice held her hands up, as if to push away the words. "Wait a minute. You haven't known us very long, and you can see all this?"

"Sometimes it takes an outsider." Jane put her hand out and touched Mary Alice's forearm. "He is a wonderful guy. Stop taking him for granted. He might get really fed up one day and propose to someone else."

"But I asked him once if he would marry me and he said no."

"Did you mean it?"

Mary Alice squinted. "Sort of."

They heard the others come up the hill, so Jane said, "Food for thought," and disappeared behind her door.

Well, hallelujah. Thank you, Jane. This is why women need girlfriends; something Mary Alice had been missing her entire life.

Even Aisling knew Hardy loved her. She told me one day that Hardy looked at Mary Alice the way Toby looked at Hardy.

Out of the mouths of babes.

CHAPTER SIXTEEN

August brought a marvellous spell of great weather. Now Jane could see the beauty of her surroundings. She'd walk along the cliffs and sit to take in the unending sky and vast, dancing ocean at her feet. Watching the birds swoop and soar, carried by the wind, everything with the scent of salt, sunshine, flowers, and berries. Buzzing bees made their way around her as they worked. She picked up a leaf and found a perfect little ladybird with her brilliant red jacket and black spots. Sam told her they were called ladybugs here, but there was nothing buggy about them.

She was a little less lonely. Looking out, knowing the next port of call would be England or France, was still fascinating. They truly lived on the very edge of the continent. There was nowhere to go if she stepped off and let the current take her.

She sat this morning to read her latest letter from Aunt Lou. That was one thing she did love—going to the post office, run out of Theresa Wadden's home, and seeing if she had mail. In the summer, they had two mail deliveries a week instead of just one. Today was a bonus. She had two letters. One from Aunt Lou and one from Stuart Campbell. She opened Aunt Lou's first.

Dear Jane, I can't believe you've been gone six months. Are you sure Sam isn't going to row you back some day? You seem a little better. For a while I wondered if you were desperately unhappy, but your last letter was cheerful enough.

I do love when you write. Not that you have anything really interesting to say, but I imagine living on an island doesn't afford you much in the way of entertainment. Then again, there's not much going on here either. We're still dealing with food rations, which is tiring but one must be grateful. I've been losing weight lately, which my GP says is a good thing, cheeky devil. I still host our bridge club and fix the flowers for the church. Oh dear, I must tell you one of my dear companions, Fluffy, died peacefully on her favourite chair. I'm afraid I didn't notice until bedtime. Such a sweet cat. Petunia and Biddy miss her. Well, not much else to report. Do send a few more photos if you can. I miss your face. All my love, Aunt Lou xo

Jane chuckled. "I miss your face too, Aunt Lou." Then she opened Stuart's letter. She'd written when she first arrived to thank him for his kindness and he'd surprised her by writing back. She showed his letter to Sam, who was pleased to hear from him. But he was busy and she ended up writing to Stuart from time to time just for something to do, and every time she did, he would respond. He was a pen pal.

Dear Jane, it was nice to hear from you again. I'm glad things are getting easier. You sound better. I was very sorry to hear about Sam's father. That must have been a tough blow. All is going well here, school wise. Always busy and constantly studying. No time for anything else interesting. Both Mom and Dad say hello and wonder if you two are coming for a visit. I keep telling them it's not quite so easy to pop round!

My sister Liz is getting married so she and my mom and sisters are all in a tizzy about wedding plans. Fortunately, we all like the guy but he's always crowing about the fact that he was a fighter pilot. Still, let him boast. They were a godsend to all of us. Well, this is rather dreary, so I'll end it here. Do take care of yourself. You and Sam know where I am if you ever need me. Take care, Stuart

She smiled as she tucked the letter back in the envelope. He always made sure to include Sam's name, but Jane knew instinctively that he was trying to tell her if things got bad and she did need someone, he was out there. It was comforting. He was definitely a friend and everyone needed one of those. Which reminded her that she'd agreed to meet Mary Alice to go pick bakeapples, a berry Jane had never heard of. Mary Alice said Jane needed to come along with her so she'd have someone to curse with while she did it.

She ran back to the harbour and Mary Alice was sitting on her step with a giant bucket.

Out of breath, Jane laughed. "How big are these berries?"

"They're tricksters. You can pick a whole bog's worth and suddenly they disappear to nothing in the pail. Never seen the like. But I have to admit they do make great jam. Take a hat and a sweater you can drape over your head. There are bugs galore where these things grow."

Jane ran into the house to get what she needed. There were plenty of big buckets around, but most of them smelled like fish, so she took one of the water pails. She left a note in case Sam returned for lunch. He was usually too busy, but he inevitably made time when she suggested a picnic. They would traipse off somewhere private and enjoy each other, as well as the food. At first, she was reluctant, until Sam reminded her that this was a very big place with very few people. The chance of being seen was low, but he didn't count on the chipmunk in the tree branch above last week, staring at them the entire time. Jane couldn't stop laughing.

The two gals set off arm in arm, and for the first time since stepping foot on the island, Jane felt carefree. Mary Alice chattered away like a little squirrel, and she was so funny most of the time, Jane spent the whole day trying to catch her breath. Not for the first time did she thank god for Mary Alice. Life would be much bleaker without her.

Jane had never been to this part of the island. She realized the difference was with Edgar gone she was free to wander. And it was fascinating how the landscape changed and changed again, depending on which direction they took. Mary Alice told her that was because the land close to the coast was open to the direct assault of the wind and seas, while the inner island was protected somewhat.

They reached an area that was field-like but wet. "This is where the little jerks are. The berries and the flies," Mary Alice told her.

"It smells like apples here. And are these berries orange? That's all I see, everywhere you look. It's so pretty."

"Don't let that fool ya. That's how you're lured into their evil web."

Jane stopped. "You should be a writer."

They were there most of the afternoon. They'd started out talking, but as they headed in different directions, they concentrated on the task at hand, Mary Alice cursing at regular intervals. And she was right. Every time Jane thought she was nearing the top of her bucket, it was as if the bakeapples decided to hunker down and make themselves cozy near the bottom.

As the sun lowered, Jane stood up and held her hand to her back. "I think I'm done. My back is killing me."

"I'm surprised you lasted this long. Good going for your first try. I only lasted five minutes, to my mother's horror."

Then Jane put her arm across her chest and cupped her left breast. "Even my breasts are sore."

Mary Alice jumped up. "Sore breasts? Are they bigger too?"

Jane made a face. "I'm not sure. Why?"

"Is your period late?"

Now Jane looked alarmed. "I'm never regular. You don't think..."

"All I know about pregnancy is that Rose's breasts always swell and she says they're sore and have big blue veins all over them in preparation for being milked like a cow."

Jane unbuttoned her blouse and peeked. "Oh god. What do you think?"

Mary Alice took a look and gasped. "You've got a road map going."

"A baby? A baby here? With no hospital? How will I take care of it?"

"Don't ask me. Ask Ma. Are you happy?"

Jane was shocked more than happy. "We've never even discussed having a family."

"Well, girlie, I don't think there's much you can do about it now. Baby is coming, I think. But don't quote me, because I know nothing. Just wait and see. You're going to find out eventually."

"Shouldn't I see a doctor?"

"I believe so. We can go over and talk to Rose if you like. She's had babies more recently than Ma. Sam, Hardy, and I were born here with a midwife running around from house to house on Christmas Day! My oldest sister, Tilly, said I ruined Christmas that year because they didn't have a turkey and Ma was too busy to spend time with them."

"I have to get out of here. I need to sit." Jane took her bucket and went to the edge of the bog and plunked down on the solid ground. She looked dumbfounded, so Mary Alice gathered up her pail and sat down beside her.

"You'll be all right. Women do this all the time."

"I've never done it. What if I'm no good at it?"

"You're smart, kind, and hardworking. A mother any kid would love."

Jane burst into tears. "I'm always crying, but this time I really mean it. I miss my mother." And she howled, rocking back and forth, holding her stomach. Mary Alice began to tear up because she felt so helpless. Why did she say anything? She didn't know for sure if a baby was on the way. It wasn't her business to poke her nose in. When would she ever learn to stop mouthing off?

The only thing she could do was sit with the distraught Jane and keep her company. She vowed not to say a thing until Jane spoke, and as a consequence they sat there for at least a half an hour, Jane getting it all out of her system. Then she lay back in the grass and looked up at the white and grey clouds drift by, completely spent.

"Poor little thing," she finally said. "What a way to be greeted."

"Fortunately, babies have terrible memories."

Jane turned her head and smiled. "You always know what to say."

Mary Alice lay down in the grass too. "I don't always know what to say."

"What do you mean?"

"Remember what you told me about Hardy?"

Jane squinted her eyes. "Yeah."

"I've made a point of staying away from him."

Jane got up on her elbow. "You haven't seen him in three weeks?"

Mary Alice sat back up and pulled at the grass around her. "No. I'm afraid to face him. I didn't even show up for our Thursday night card game. He's probably mad and that's why he hasn't been over to ask where I am."

Jane looked off in the distance and didn't say anything for a minute. "How come our own problems are so hard to fix but we can offer limitless advice to someone else?"

"I'm going to have to do something soon. I miss him. Especially since I never really see Sam anymore. There was a time when not a day went by that I didn't run around with the two of them, and tell them what to do. I miss those days."

Jane sighed. "I better get back. They'll be home soon and I have fish cakes for supper. They're sick of them because I make them all the time, but they're easy."

"Make macaroni and cheese. That's easy too, and Sam loves it."

The two of them helped each other up and walked back with their berries. Before they parted, Mary Alice said, "I won't tell a soul about the maybe baby. It's your news."

I could have told them if they'd asked me. Sam's son was on the way. I knew this little boy would go far; it was already written in the stars. There are no babies born by accident. All of them are meant to be here and have the mothers they were meant to have, even when they don't see life outside the womb or have to leave when they are small. They will continue their journey another way, but always in love and connected to the woman who loved them first.

For no reason whatsoever, Mary Alice got up three days later and knew this was the day to stop messing around and have it out with Hardy. Too bad it was drizzly, windy, and raw. But it mirrored her mood. This had been hanging over her head, making her irritable, something her mother mentioned quite often.

"You're like a bear with a sore head. No wonder no one comes to see you. Now sit down and eat your sandwich." Or "Sit down and eat your porridge." Or "Sit down and drink your milk."

This morning it was "Sit down and eat your kippers."

This is when having a dog under the table would have come in very handy. But again, childlike behaviour. "Ma, you know I don't like fish for breakfast. Give me toast and jam."

It was easier than arguing, so while Mary set about browning bread in the frying pan, Mary Alice poured herself a mug of tea and put two spoons of brown sugar in it. She was going to need fuel.

Mary put the toast in front her and moved the dish of butter closer, before reaching for a jar of strawberry jam on the counter. Then she sat down with her tea and a smoke.

"Where's Da?"

Her mother gestured over to the window. "Went to Peter Mullins to get his account straightened out now that fishing season is over. He had a pretty good year for an old-timer. But at some point, he's going to wear out, and then what will we do?"

"Da's as strong as an ox."

"Even an ox bites the dust."

Mary Alice spread jam on the toast. "Why are you killing off Da this morning?"

Mary looked out the window through a haze of smoke. "In case you hadn't noticed, your father and I aren't getting any younger. At some point something has to change. And I'd like to see you settled before it does."

"What do I have to do with it? I can take care of myself."

Mary gave her a sideways glance and said nothing.

"Do you really think he should stop fishing? He'd hate that."

Mary blew smoke over the table above her daughter's head.

"You don't hear him at night moaning and groaning with arthritis. They say the last place people with arthritis should live is by the ocean. The damp makes you ache. I should know. Look at my fingers. I can hardly knead bread anymore."

This made Mary Alice even more annoyed. "When did you and Da become old people? Stop it!"

"If we stop getting old, we're dead. Would you rather that?"

Drinking down the last of her tea to help wash down the toast, Mary Alice put the mug down with a thump. "This is what's called being morose. You and Da are still fine specimens."

"You see what you want to see, child. Time to grow up."

Mary Alice frowned and headed for the door. "I'm going to visit Hardy." She plunked an old yellow sou'wester on her head. "See ya."

Her mother sighed and put out her smoke.

Going along the old road she'd walked a million times, Mary Alice felt uneasy. This nagging little fear of something happening to her parents had never seriously occurred to her, which was ridiculous but true nevertheless. She realized she didn't want to grow up. Maybe that's why she was always hiding. What a hopeless specimen.

She really missed Hardy and his advice, but remembered he was probably annoyed with her for vanishing suddenly. It couldn't be helped. She'd face his wrath and accept it. Not that Hardy was ever wrathful with anyone.

Once again, she knocked on the door and opened it a crack. "Yoohoo. Just me. Annie? Anyone?"

There wasn't a soul around. There was always someone home. It was disconcerting. She even yelled up the stairwell. "Anyone here?"

The assistant lightkeeper, Gerry, said groggily, "I'm asleep. We're taking shifts."

"Oh, I'm so sorry. I'll go. Sweet dreams."

Damn. She crept out, but not before taking an oatmeal cookie off the baking rack in the middle of the table.

Hardy and Toby were around here somewhere; the light couldn't be unattended. She finally found them in the boathouse checking on the equipment in case a rescue was needed. Everything had to be attended to. One old rope snapping in two while Hardy was trying to get people off a sinking ship would be a disaster.

Toby was thrilled to see her. "Hello, buddy boy! Hello, my little man!" He wagged his tail until it was a blur and licked her hands while going in circles.

"At least someone is glad to see me. Hi, Hardy."

He glanced at her. "Hi."

"Okay, I know you're mad. I'm sorry I haven't been around for game night. I've been spending a lot of time with Jane, which is something you told me to do."

"Oh, it's my fault you dropped me like a hot biscuit." He went back to coiling his ropes.

It seemed he really was put out. Usually, she could jolly him along, but this felt different. She changed tactics.

"Where is everyone?"

"James had a doctor appointment, so Mom and Fred went with him."

"Nothing wrong, I hope."

"Just the usual shit he deals with every day but never complains about. Some of us aren't as lucky as others."

"He's very brave."

"He has no choice." And then Hardy threw the ropes on the floor. "Like I have no choice when you decide to disappear whenever it suits you. Do you really think I won't be hurt when you ignore me? I'm getting really tired of being your friend, Mary Alice. I think you see me as part of the background of your life. A great guy to have around when you want some advice or reassurance, but not someone you're interested in sharing your life with."

"I have spent my whole life with you..." she said, before she realized what he was talking about. "And need I remind you that I asked you to marry me and you said no!"

"I don't want to be with someone who thinks I'm second best."

Mary Alice looked away and then turned back. "Jane says you're madly in love with me. Is that true?"

"So a perfect stranger arrives on this island and sees what you've been refusing to see your whole life." He stepped closer to her and grabbed her arms. "Yes, you incredibly stupid girl!"

She was in shock. "But you never said anything."

"I have been telling you in my own way my whole life, but the spectre of Sam has always lurked in the shadows. I knew you were in love with him. So, what was I going to do? Make you choose? I wanted you to come to me of your own free will. Not that pathetic solution you came up with to keep yourself occupied when you found out Sam had a wife."

He let her go and took a step back.

Toby was whining, knowing Hardy was sad. "If you must know, that really hurt. I would've loved to have said yes, but your heart wasn't in it, and I would rather live the rest of my days alone than spend it with someone for their convenience."

Mary Alice wasn't the sort to cry easily, but she felt herself coming apart at the seams. "If you want to know the truth, I've always been more afraid of losing you than Sam. I didn't want to risk it. You're my lighthouse, Hardy. If something went wrong between us and you walked away from me, I couldn't live with that. I couldn't live in that darkness." She wiped her eyes. "The two of you have driven me crazy my whole life. Sam would kiss me and ask me to be with him. I thought that meant he was in love with me and he needed me. And you never did. So I thought that meant you weren't in love with me and didn't need me. I can't know a person's true feelings unless they tell me. I'm not going to take all the blame for this."

He took a step towards her. He was so furious about everything; it all came out in a jumble. "Pay very close attention to this, Mary Alice. I'm telling you now. I want you to be my friend, my lover, and my wife for the rest of my days. I want to have it all with you."

Mary Alice was so tired of being alone and lonely, without this man's arms around her. She took off the ridiculous sou'wester, walked to him, and jumped up, putting her legs around his hips, her arms around his neck, and her mouth on his. She held him so tight there was no space between them, and forceful enough that they nearly fell backwards.

Years of pent-up desire that had lived in both of them for different reasons came crashing down. He leaned her against the wall but she said, "No. Not like that, like this." She pushed him to the ground and straddled him, neither one of them caring who heard or saw them. It was pure electricity and Toby ran to a corner of the room to stay out of its way.

They gazed at each other in amazement and then rolled over and did it again, because they were not done. This would never be over. This clash of bodies speaking for their hearts, where words didn't mean anything. It was beyond their imaginations and so much dearer when they realized it was real, not a dream. What they were creating together would keep them bound to each other.

When they finished once more, Hardy lay over her and gently wiped the damp hair off her face before saying, "Well, it's about time."

Mary Alice laughed. "I thought you were going to tell me you love me."

"I just did."

I confess I was jealous, which set off a terrible rumbling of thunder in the distance before I realized that Hardy didn't need the distraction of a storm on that particular night. He deserved to lie in his bed and relive that incredible moment in time. That's what I'd planned to do, imagining my sailor until it dawned on me (after only two hundred years) that he's never come to seek me out. So, no love lost there.

Finally, these three souls had sorted out their affairs of the heart.

I wish I knew what that was like.

Forgive me, I should keep their secret, the one they didn't even know yet, but I was thrilled about their baby girl starting her journey. And no, the two babies would not end up together. Their stars didn't align. But both mothers would love the other's child as their own.

Annie and her sons found Hardy and Mary Alice at the kitchen table with a pot of tea and a table full of oatmeal cookie crumbs.

"You're not after eating that whole batch?" Annie said with dismay. "I'll have nothing for dessert."

"Sorry, Mom. How was the appointment, James?"

"Encouraging. No changes with the heart. A bit of improvement, actually. He's pleased."

"Good man. You're unlikely to have a heart attack when I tell you that Mary Alice and I are getting married."

Annie screamed and threw her arms around Mary Alice, almost strangling her. James and Fred looked very pleased for them both and thumped their brother on the shoulder. Annie moved on to Hardy and took him around the waist, burying her face in his chest. "I'm so happy. If only your father..." She didn't finish the sentence before she looked up. "Do Dorothy and Ellen know?"

"You can have the pleasure of telling Dorothy, Mom, but we'll have to wait to fill Ellen in, unless you want me to row over to Morien tonight."

Poor Annie was in such a state she said she couldn't make supper and they could all have sandwiches and pie. Hardy told her they were stuffed and going to the Lockes' to tell Mary Alice's parents, and that Gerry was on duty.

His mother was still buzzing around when they left hand in hand. The trip back along the road Mary Alice had walked a million times was vastly different, and the thought that she wouldn't be alone if something happened to her parents made the fright go away. She was adding up the benefits in her head at this change in circumstance when she realized something else.

"I can't be a teacher anymore. That chapter is well and truly closed."

"Do you mind?"

She shook her head. "I'm ready for something else and I'm glad it's you."

Hardy put his arm around her as they walked. "You've made me very happy."

She relished the feel of his strong body against her. "Thank you for waiting for me. I'm obviously thick."

They chuckled together, remembering the time she called him thick when they were kids.

When they walked in the door of her place, Mary Alice was happy to see that her father was home, resting in the rocking chair after his journey to Main-à-Dieu. "Hey you two," he said. "What's goin' on today?"

"Hardy and I are getting married."

Her mother spun around and nearly knocked a pot of soup off the stove. It wasn't often she was at a loss for words, but her mouth remained open and nothing came out.

Her dad struggled a bit to get out of the chair, saying, "Well, well, well. This is very good news indeed." He shook Hardy's hand. "You know we love ya, son. Always have. Just been waiting for this silly child to come to her senses."

"Thank you, Tom."

On a normal day, Mary was never as animated as Annie, but on this day, she almost skipped across the kitchen floor and hugged Hardy first. "Thank you for being so patient, you dear boy."

Mary Alice put her hands on her hips. "So, if you knew too, why didn't you say anything?"

She reached out and held her youngest tight. "When have you ever listened to me, my girl?"

"Gonna have this wedding soon?" her father asked.

"As soon as humanly possible," Mary Alice answered. "A justice of the peace and Annie's parlour is just fine, since it's bigger."

"But what about a reception? Or a party."

Mary Alice looked at her soon-to-be-husband. "I for one do not want a party. Neither of us drink. A bridal lunch is fine. And I'm not wearing a white gown. They're hideous."

"This is a celebration," her mother reminded her. "You're buying a new dress, we'll have lots of flowers and a big cake. Our family alone will be a crowd."

"That's the other thing. If anyone asks, it's only for family and friends."

Hardy finally spoke up. "Am I going to have any say in this?"

With a wave of her hand, Mary Alice gave him the floor. He grinned. "I agree."

Tom laughed. "Oh, my son, you're off to a bad start. Don't let her get away with that. Now she'll be thinking she has the upper hand."

"Tom, your daughter has always had the upper hand, and I expect it will continue throughout my lifetime."

Mary Alice jumped up. "Let's go over and tell Jane and Sam."

Hardy did as he was told.

She gave a quick rap on their door and opened it. "Jane?"

Sam replied, "She's hanging clothes. Come on in."

He was at the table, which was covered in newspaper, gutting fish. He looked up, a cigarette between his lips, squinting because of the smoke. "Oh, hey, Hardy. Didn't know you were here too. How's life treating ya?"

This time Hardy delivered the good news. "Mary Alice and I are getting married."

Sam dropped his knife and took the cigarette out of his mouth, flicking it into the sink. "You sneaky bastard." He grinned so wide and ran over to Mary Alice and twirled her around. Then he went up to Hardy and put his hands on his shoulders. "Ya lucky bastard."

"So far, Hardy is a bastard." Mary Alice laughed. "What am I?"

"A very lucky woman." Sam started to get choked up. "Goddamn it. I couldn't be happier. It's about time you two got yourselves sorted."

"Will you be my best man?"

Sam seemed shocked. "But your brothers?"

"Will understand."

"Ya wonderful bastard." Sam reached over and hugged his oldest friend. His head was under Hardy's chin. Mary Alice sniffed and looked away.

Jane walked in with the laundry basket. "Oh, hi. What's going on?"

Before the other two could say anything, Sam shouted, "My two best pals are getting married! Can you believe that?"

Jane put the basket down and walked over to hold her friend. "Oh yes, I do believe it. And I'm so glad. You're perfect for each other."

"I'll always have you to thank," Mary Alice whispered.

CHAPTER SEVENTEEN

Word spread like wildfire, and by the time Mary Alice knocked on Mrs. Wadden's door a few days later, she'd already heard the news.

"I thought you were never getting married." She smiled. "Come on in."

"That's what I thought when I was young and stupid, but things change."

They sat at her kitchen table, which had a red-and-white checkered plastic tablecloth on it. The height of fancy.

"Well, dear, congratulations. I wish you two all the best, but we're really going to have a hard time replacing you. The kids all love you, and I feel sorry for whoever comes next."

"They'll be okay. But I hope it's a woman."

"Why's that?"

"The little ones are always a little afraid of a man, and the older boys don't like to be challenged head on. They don't seem to mind a woman giving them what-for when they act up, but take exception to it when it's another male."

Mrs. Wadden cocked her head. "Is that so?"

"Maybe it's different now. All I know is that we hated that male teacher when I was in school."

"Well, he was a pill. I should never have considered him, but my sister-in-law talked me into it. Would you like some tea?"

"No thanks, we're going to Main-à-Dieu so my aunt can take my measurements for the dress. By the way, whatever happened to your handsome nephew?"

"He's a teacher."

They burst out laughing. Mary Alice had always been a little afraid of Mrs. Wadden, but not anymore.

"I'll clear out my desk before school starts."

Mrs. Wadden got up and held out her hand. "Thank you, dear. You were an exceptional teacher."

"That's kind of you to say."

That bit of business over, Mary Alice met up with her mother, Jane, and Rose down by the shore. Her dad was driving their boat to take them over to the mainland. Dorothy hitched a ride over so she could visit her sister Ellen in Morien. She'd take the bus. And old Bailey Bates needed a ride to go to a doctor's appointment. His daughter would meet him at the wharf and drive him to Louisbourg.

Everyone on the island was everyone else's taxi. It was considered rude to not ask if someone needed a lift. No journey over the water was ever wasted.

Tom pulled up alongside the wharf perfectly, and another fisherman grabbed the rope and secured it. Up the ladder they went, poor old Bailey having to take his time. Jane felt like a pro. Once Bailey was picked up and Dorothy hopped on the bus, both of them staying overnight with their relatives, the small gang walked to Tom's brother Fabian's house, who Tom's own son was named after. The house that Sam and Jane went to when she arrived.

Tom and his brother immediately went out to the garage with Danny. No hanging around with the women doing women stuff. His wife, Lucille, and their daughter, Ruthanne, were very quick to congratulate the almost-bride and welcome Jane back to the house.

The women arranged themselves around the table. Lucille had it all prepared. She was a seamstress from way back. "I've gathered every pattern I own and even borrowed some from friends and neighbours. You'll have as much choice here as any store. Let's look through them and see if one catches your eye."

Some of them were godawful and so old-fashioned Mary Alice, Jane, and Rose had a hard time keeping a straight face. Ruthanne was in on it too, trying not to laugh. Finally, Lucille caught on.

"This always happens with people who don't know how to sew. You don't look at the picture with its fabric that is obviously not suitable for the occasion. You look at the lines. Sleeves can be added and taken away. Flounces removed. Necklines altered. It makes a world of difference when you tell me what you like. Then I can choose the best pattern for your dress. I want lines."

Now they peered at the patterns again and realized what Lucille was saying. Mary held one up. "This looks nice. I know she wants simple."

"I don't want a potato sack, either."

Mary stuck her tongue out and put it back.

They were still at it when the men came in sniffing around for something to eat. Lucille shooed them out with a pan of gingerbread and three forks.

They were slowly making three piles. The "wouldn't be caught dead" pile, which was the thickest, the "maybe" pile, and the "fingers crossed" pile. There were only three patterns in that one. All of them were getting cross-eyed, so Lucille told Ruthanne to make the tea and take the egg salad sandwiches she'd made out of the ice box. "And take away all the patterns except these three. We'll decide after lunch."

Mary Alice realized how wonderful it was to have her aunt take charge of this mission. She'd still be flapping around like a headless chicken. And having her be the leader eliminated her mother and the inevitable fights they would've gotten into.

Once they were feeling refreshed, they tackled the problem with renewed vigor. Lucille placed the patterns in the middle of the table, as if she was a tarot card reader. "We all agree we like these three the best. But I'm going to take one of them away and I'll tell you why. You don't want a fussy garment and you'd like to wear this dress for years to come." She pointed at the first one. "You would have to wear a crinoline underneath to get this shape in the skirt."

"Never. Imagine me in a crinoline?"

Lucille dramatically handed the rejected pattern to Ruthanne. "I'm going to rule out this one because it has a peplum at the waist and would look too fancy in an everyday situation."

"True."

Lucille picked up the last one. "This one has a roll collar, buttons to the waist, with three-quarter sleeves and a skirt that folds into soft pleats. Now imagine it in soft green or blue. It's simple, but on your wedding day you can fancy it up with a hat. And when you're holding flowers, all dresses look special."

Jane got excited. "You've seen our wedding pictures. I wore a Juliet cap with a birdcage veil. You can borrow it if you like."

Mary Alice had seen the pictures, and Jane's headpiece was divine. "Sold! And I'll take the dress in a mossy green."

They clapped and hooted. A difficult part was over. Now Lucille got her tape out and had Ruthanne write down Mary Alice's measurements as she went along.

"But where will we get the fabric?"

"That requires a trip into town. Just you and me. You don't want a thousand opinions."

They were done for today. "How long will it take to make?"

"Once we get the material, give me a couple of weeks. I don't want to rush and you never know what will come up with this lot."

"You're the best, Aunt Lucille. I'm going to pay you for this."

"Don't you dare. Your mother already tried and I told her the same thing. This is our wedding gift to you."

In short order, the dress was done, the wedding cake made, the justice of the peace found, and Annie had her home spic and span, with a couple of tables put together in the parlour covered by a white tablecloth.

Hardy had made plans of his own.

The accommodations in the lighthouse itself were divided into two spaces. The Campbells never really needed the other side except for storage, Annie declaring it too much work when her kids were little. But Hardy was determined to make this end of the structure into a home for his wife. It had the basics in it, in case it was needed for an inspector's overnight stay, or an assistant's family, but since Gerry was a bachelor, he never wanted to be there alone. Not when the smell of Annie's baking filled the house on the best side.

His mother made a few rag rugs for the floor, and Mary gathered a couple of items that she knew her daughter liked. The little ceramic rabbit Alice had given Mary years before, and the soft blanket from the back of the rocking chair.

Hardy also took a trip into Sydney and bought a ring with some of his savings. A delicate Art Deco gold band that would look like a ring of tiny flowers on her finger.

Mary Alice was blissfully unaware of everything. She asked Rose and Jane to stand with her. That was about all she had to do. The two mothers and sisters were handling the food. And despite her mother's objections, she decided to create her own bouquet with flowers from the island.

Mary Alice woke at sunrise on her wedding day in early September and headed off alone to some of her favourite haunts. It was really just an excuse to wander about and remember her girlhood. She stopped at the top of one cliff that had been weathered out by wave action. There was a sea cave, and when exposed to the waves, the pressure carved a hole in the top and created an opening where the water spews up in a jet of spray and, depending on the wind, creates the most ungodly moaning, a *wooo*ing that sounds exactly like a ghost. The three of them had heard it one early evening when they were seven and took off like shots, thinking they were being chased by phantoms.

Then she remembered when they were ten and they slept under the stars after her father took them on a hike to Gull Head. They settled in around the campfire he made, and he told them ghost stories after they kept bugging him. He was very good at it, making it very dramatic.

"You know, this island has a sad history of people dying along these shores. When the worst happens, and it's been happening for hundreds of years, sometimes the bodies are washed up. You three know all about that. Well, there was one shipwreck where everyone on board was lost and the people here had to bring them ashore and tried to cover their bodies with anything they had, tarps, sails, blankets. And as you know, things like that are scarce, since the people living here need them, but they were trying to do their Christian duty. Shortly after the tragedy, this would have been in my great-grandfather's time, he and his buddies went out to Scallop Cove..."

"That's not far from here," Sam noted.

"You're right. They were camping and had settled down for the night in the grass by the beach. When they woke up in the morning, none of them had their blanket."

He waited for that to sink in, the kids looking at him with big eyes. "My great-grandfather swears he felt someone tugging at him in the night."

Mary Alice gasped. "The dead wanted his blanket."

It took them a while to settle down, but they eventually fell sleep. In the morning, when they woke up, their blankets had disappeared. The three of them screamed and carried on until Tom put them out of their misery, and brought the blankets out from behind a rock.

Mary Alice went by the big pond where they skated, and followed the path to Cranberry Heath. Everywhere she went she had a memory, especially when she took the road to the school. How many times had they run along, galloping home for lunch? Sam beating up Mrs. Wadden's nephew, the earthquake, the *Hindenburg*. The three friends were always together.

What a lucky girl she was. They never had much, but they had everything.

If she'd married a month earlier, her selection of flowers would have been plentiful, but she managed to create a delightful nosegay with pink wild roses and morning glories, purple orchids, yellow evening primrose, and blue harebells. She smiled at the cream pearly everlasting. They peeked out of grassy meadows, gathered in clumps of bushes, and thrived by granite rocks near the ocean. Such tiny things that were remarkably sturdy. She'd seen them all her life and thought they were weeds of some sort. Ordinary. But as she tucked them into the flowers in her hand, she knew she loved them best of all. Just the name, pearly everlasting, was enchanting.

It was only much later, when reading a book about species native to Cape Breton, that Mary Alice learned the flower was associated with remembrance and nostalgia, and symbolized eternity and immortality due to its long-lasting blooms. Perfect for her wedding day.

Her family and Sam's gathered at the house, a big milling crowd waiting for her, Rose, and Jane to come down the stairs. When she did, no one spoke until a little voice said, "There's Mommy, Sam's wife, and a fairy queen."

The mob was excited and talking over each other while Mary Alice stood there, perfectly serene, knowing in her heart that when Hardy laid eyes on her, he would cry.

Her father came forward in his best shirt and tie and held her hand. "My little rug rat has turned into a lady. Well done, sweetheart." Then he held out his arm and they walked out the door first, with everyone trailing behind.

They'd hoped for a little less wind. Rose had to hold her flowers so Mary Alice could keep her birdcage from flying away. But it wouldn't be home if everyone didn't look a little dishevelled.

Annie had said she'd keep Hardy away from the windows so when his bride walked into the parlour, it would be a surprise. She greeted everyone at the door and squealed at the sight of her new daughter-in-law, but did it quietly. She ushered the rest of the crowd into the next room while Jane, Mary Alice, Rose, and her father stayed in the kitchen.

Tom shook his head. "Our last chick. Who can believe it? And you were the most annoying."

Mary Alice smirked. "Is that something you should say to your daughter on her wedding day?"

He patted her hand. "A high-spirited lass who was fun to be around. I wouldn't have changed a thing."

They heard the strains of Jeb Trimm's fiddle. When Rose was helping her on with the wedding dress, she told Mary Alice that her husband had practiced a slow version of the "Banshee Reel" on his fiddle. "Which he obviously did on purpose," Mary Alice huffed.

Jane gave her a thumb's up and walked into the room first,

carrying a small white Bible. Rose followed a few steps behind, with a nosegay of Scatarie roses.

Still on her father's arm, Mary Alice caught her breath at the sight of Hardy in a suit. In that instant she saw him as the grown man he was and not the little boy she remembered. He was by far the nicest looking man in the room, confident, calm, and clearly very, very happy. As predicted, as soon as he caught sight of her, Hardy lowered his head and brushed a few tears away before he collected himself and locked eyes with her. There was no one else there except the two of them. Hardy and Tom shook hands and Tom didn't bother to kiss his daughter because of that net thing she had around her face. Pretty to look at, dangerous to touch.

That's when Mary Alice noticed Toby, being held up and away from the many feet by Fred. Dorothy had made a bow tie and wrapped it around his neck.

They held hands and listened to the vows and said the right things at the right time, before Sam reached into his pocket and gave Hardy the ring. When Hardy put it on her finger it seemed familiar, like her flowered hairpin of long ago. Mary Alice adored it. She kept looking at it even as the ceremony continued, but came out of her fog when it was time to kiss.

The birdcage wasn't dangerous at all. Hardy gently raised the delicate netting and gave his bride a sweet kiss. She was dying for more but that would have to wait until after they cut the cake.

They turned around to face the crowd and were mobbed. Sam got to them before anyone. "I'm so goddamned emotional all the time, but this nearly sent me over the edge." He laughed as he hugged them both at the same time. "All the best, guys. All the best."

Mary Alice had more fun than she thought she would. She had been hoping for a quick escape, but then she realized all these people were celebrating her and Hardy and that would never happen again, so she relaxed and let it happen. She especially looked at her parents, surrounded by their children, minus one. All of them decent human beings raised on this jut of land out at sea, thanks to their hard work and sacrifice.

Someone brought a camera, so they piled outside and onto the steps of the house. That photo would float around the family for decades. A brief moment captured in time when everyone looked young and happy.

It was finally over and her family made tracks. Annie, with her daughters Dorothy and Ellen, refused to let Mary Alice anywhere near the cleaning up. Hardy ran over to the lighthouse after Fred came and asked him about something, so she and Toby sat on the steps and waited for him.

"Do you like my dress, Toby?"

Toby wagged his tail.

She saw her husband return and just that thought alone gave her a shiver. He sat down beside her and gave her a proper kiss. "Would it be rude," she said, "if we just moseyed over to the boathouse?"

He grabbed her hand and pulled her up. "We don't have to. Let me show you." They went up the stairs of the porch and walked over to the right door. He opened it, picked her up, and carried her over the threshold. "Welcome home."

"But...but..."

"If ever an inspector shows up, he'll get the good bed, but until that happens, it's all ours."

She wiggled to get down. "Is that my mother's rabbit? What's it doing here?"

"She brought it over, along with your blanket off the rocker too. Thought you might like it. We all mucked it out."

She stared at him. "All this went on under my nose?"

"You're thick, remember?"

Pointing, she said, "Shut that door, Mr. Campbell. Mrs. Campbell needs some urgent attention."

Sam and Jane meandered back home, both buzzing from the excitement of the wedding day.

Jane sighed. "She was so beautiful in that dress. And my headpiece was perfect."

"She was almost as beautiful as you were."

Jane glanced at him. "We do look alike, don't we?"

"Nah. Except for the hair, you don't look anything alike. I should know. I've been staring at her all my life."

"I'm selfishly happy that she won't be teaching anymore. I know she won't be next door but it's only a hop, skip, and jump to their place."

Sam put a long piece of grass in his mouth. "It's getting kinda crowded over there. Might put a damper on...you know."

Jane laughed. "They could always go on a picnic and entertain chipmunks."

Just as they were about to go in the house, two rifle shots rang out from the woods and Sam instantly crouched down and covered his ears with his hands, the crack reverberating in his head. "Fuck!"

"It's okay," Jane said. "Let's go inside," and she hauled him in the door. He was shaking and breathless.

"Goddamn it. I can't live like this! Every time I hear a gunshot, I see Denis's face explode in front of me. I'm never going to be able to go hunting again."

Jane tried to think of something. "Maybe it's because you're always startled. If you know you're going to shoot, it might be easier."

"Bloody hell." Sam went over to where he kept his stash and pulled out a bottle, drinking it down in one shot. Jane hated when he did that.

He paced from the front door to the back door. "You know, it was a great day and then this happens and it's ruined." He walked over and took another bottle.

"You don't need that," Jane said.

He faced her. "That's where you're wrong. I fucking do. Now leave me alone." He went out the back door and slammed it behind him.

Jane sat down slowly on the kitchen chair. This wasn't the Sam she'd married. He was still with her, especially when they were holding each other, but his anger was becoming a living thing and was brought to the surface by startling sounds and flashbacks. Bob said it was to be expected, which wasn't comforting. Obviously, alcohol would take it away for a moment, but that could get out of hand too.

Jane felt defeated, and after such a lovely day. Watching Mary Alice with her father had brought back a longing. How she wished her father had been able to walk her down the aisle. It never left, the occasions where a dad should be at the forefront. It was going to happen again when she gave birth to this child. Her parents would have been at a christening. She'd wanted to tell Sam tonight, after the happy day, but his mood had spoiled everything.

Mary Alice's sister Rose had taken her to Louisbourg to see a doctor and he'd confirmed what she knew in her heart. Rose had given Jane practical advice and said she would keep her secret. Now that Jane knew she was responsible for a little soul, the uncertainty about her life choices ramped up. Why hadn't she listened to Aunt

Lou and just married a boring man down the street?

She had wanted to tell Sam tonight because she was looking forward to writing to Aunt Lou. Lou would be chuffed at the thought of her brother being a granddad.

It didn't take long for her to become annoyed. She went upstairs and took off her good clothes. They were never going to wear out; where could she go in them? Once she had her old slacks and sweater on, she went out the back door to confront Sam. She knew he'd be in the fishing shack by the water. A miserable, reeking place. He seemed to love it.

There he was, sitting on a lobster trap that needed mending. He gave a startled jump, surprised to see her.

He'd never seen her really angry, and she wanted to use that to her advantage. She'd rehearsed it walking down the slope. It would be good to act and sound like a miserable harpy, as Aunt Lou called the woman who lived two doors down.

Jane pointed her finger at him. "I realize you've been through the wringer and I should be sorry for you. And I am. But not when you curse at me and tell me to leave you alone and waltz out the door like I'm a nobody. You and I both know that getting drunk will not solve your problems. And I refuse to put up with it. I will not bring up our child with a father who runs away and wallows in his pain. I need a man. And if you're not prepared to be one, I'll book my ticket back to jolly old England."

He slapped his hand on his knee. "Oh great, hang that over my head. You'll leave if things don't go your—wait...what did you say?"

"I want the father of my child to be strong and happy and know that life is good. You came home from the war. Don't go back there. We need you, the ghosts you left behind don't."

He stood up and put the bottle down. "Did you just say you're having a baby?"

"I did."

He looked at her sheepishly and opened his arms, but she didn't run into them. She stayed where she was.

"That's wonderful," he said.

"Is it? Is it truly? Does it make you happy? Tell me the truth."

He wiped his hand down his face. Then scratched his chin and rubbed his earlobe.

She wanted to scream "Well?!" but she didn't. She'd have to wait him out.

He placed his hands on his hips. "I'm scared, but I think this is the best thing that's ever happened to me since the day I got on that double-decker bus."

Now she ran to him.

Dear Aunt Lou, I hope you are well and your two pussycats are still alive and kicking. I finally have some un-boring news. I'm having a baby! Sam is very excited and so am I. The baby should come in mid-February, close to the date when I arrived in Canada a year ago. How quickly life changes. I am surrounded by women who all have babies and they are giving me good advice. Don't worry, I've seen a doctor and will have regular appointments. How I wish Mother and Dad were alive. They would have been thrilled to be grandparents! And now you'll be a great-aunt. I promise I will visit one day and bring the child with me so you can meet him or her. I'll let you know how I'm doing. So far, no morning sickness, just an increased desire for apples. Lots of love, Jane xo

It was early October, and just as Mary Alice and Jane were in Annie's kitchen getting a baking lesson, James came through the door with a big smile on his face. "You'll never guess. The new teacher had a meltdown and said she never wanted to step foot on this island again, so Mrs. Wadden asked me if I'd step in for the meantime."

"You're perfect!" Mary Alice cried. "Why didn't I think of that before? I basically told her not to hire men. What a numbskull."

"I know. Mrs. Wadden told me."

"That I was a numbskull?"

"Among other things."

"Are you sure it won't be too much of a strain?" his mother asked.

The look he gave her answered her question. "Continue on." And he left as quickly as he arrived.

Annie gathered her wits. "Okay girls, this time it's not a pie but a tart."

Mary Alice pressed her lips together to keep from giggling. "Aren't tarts just small pies?"

Annie held up her wooden spoon. "Pie crusts are made from flour, fat, water, and salt. Likewise for tarts, but they usually include sugar, which results in a thicker, crumblier shortcrust."

"I did not know that," Jane said.

"Pies are baked in a pie dish with sloped sides, while tarts are baked in a shallow-sided tart pan. Tart pans often have removable bottoms and fluted edges."

Mary Alice nodded too. "Interesting."

Annie was encouraged by their enthusiasm. "Pies are served in the same dish they were baked in, while tarts are usually removed from the pan and served on their own. Pies are covered on all sides by a top and bottom crust, while tarts are open on top and the filling is visible." She took a breath. "Not to mention that tarts are generally more delicate than pies. Pies are firmer because of the upper and lower crust. And lastly, pie crusts shrink slightly while baking and tart crusts maintain their shape."

"Wow," Jane said. "And here I was thinking they were exactly the same."

Annie waved her spoon around. "Not at all! We'll practice now and see who makes the best crust. A healthy competition never hurt anyone."

When they were finally released into the outdoors, they looped their arms together. "I always knew you were a tart, Jane Harris."

"And I always knew you were useless, full stop."

Mary Alice smiled. "Has it sunk into Sam's scattered brain that he's about to be a dad?"

"Yes and no. He gets excited when he finds his old fishing rods and says they're for the baby. But when I ask if we can get a cradle, he says he slept in a dresser drawer and it didn't hurt him any."

"Well, to tell you the truth, that's what a lot of families do here. When you have eighteen kids, sometimes it's even a clean box."

"Oh lord."

"Don't worry. It'll all be sorted in plenty of time. There has never been a baby sleeping on a rock in this community."

"Oh, while I think of it, can we run to the post office? I'm hoping to get a letter from Aunt Lou. I'm dying to know what she thinks about the baby coming."

They set off, both of them wishing they'd taken a sweater. The fog was rolling in and the temperature dropped drastically. They hurried into Theresa Wadden's home to get out of the mist.

"Hi," Jane said. "Just wondering if I got a letter."

Theresa looked. "Yes, one from England."

"Oh, that will be Aunt Lou." Jane held out her hand. "Thank you." She headed for the door and then took a second look. "This isn't from Aunt Lou. Who else would be writing me?" She started to open the letter when Mary Alice said, "Why don't you wait until you get home?"

Jane looked up, confused, but did what she was told. On their way to her house, she asked why.

"Only because if it's bad news, you don't want to be in someone else's home."

"You think it's bad news?"

Mary Alice shook her head. "No, I'm just saying it might be difficult for Theresa always being in on personal business."

"Of course." They hurried into Jane's house and Bob was at the table eating out of a can of beans. They acknowledged each other and then sat down at the table too. Jane ripped the rest of the envelope and took the letter out. She started to read and then put her hand to her mouth, before she threw it down and ran up the stairs.

Mary Alice stood up and wasn't sure what to do. Bob pointed at the letter. "Read it. So you'll know how to help."

September 12, 1946

Dear Mrs. Campbell, I am Herbert Hampton, Miss Sinclair's solicitor, and regret to inform you that your aunt Louise Marjorie Sinclair passed away peacefully of natural causes at home on September 4, 1946. As you are her only living relative, it was her dearest wish that her estate and assets go to you. Please contact me so we can come up with a plan moving forward. You have several options, but I'm sure you'd like to have some time to digest this news. Looking forward to helping you through this painful process. Regrettably, H. Hampton, LLB

"Oh no. Her aunt Lou died."

Bob pushed the can away. "Oh, shit."

"I'll go up and be with her."

As soon as Mary Alice ran up the stairs, Bob went out the back door and walked down the hill to the fishing shack. Sam was painting buoys. He looked up.

"Jane's aunt Lou died."

"Oh, shit."

I know you're wondering, and yes, Aunt Lou and I met. Not in the way the living do, but we know each other. She is a force and was now together with Jane's family, so her loneliness eased. They were all watching over their girl, and they knew about the baby. They'd met his little soul and were eager for Jane to hold him in her arms, so her heart would feel better. And because this child was meant to be, Aunt Lou was glad Jane had followed her man across the sea.

It's a terrible thing to watch our loved ones suffer when we die. We try and send signs that we are here, but most are lost because our brains get in the way of our instincts. All we can do is wait. They'll know someday.

CHAPTER EIGHTEEN

Hardy got the foghorn up and running, its mournful sound reaching through the mist to help the lost. He kept whistling even as the weather made things difficult to work around the station. He couldn't even see Toby, but knew he was near. Nothing got him down anymore. Not with Mary Alice by his side.

God, he loved her. He didn't think he could love her more, but every day just got better and better. It was waking up in her arms. It was watching her sleep. It was when she'd run up the stairs and jump on the bed, giggling. It was watching her burn eggs, and scrub his shirt collars, and romp around the yard with Toby.

He knew deep down that he'd never seen her happier and he was responsible for that, which made him proud and confident. Now he felt alive, after years of something missing, always pining for a girl he couldn't have, and here she was. She'd belonged here the whole time.

Everyone in the family seemed to be in better spirits. His mother was over the moon to have another woman about the place and she kept pinching Hardy's cheeks whenever she ran into him. "I wish your dad was here. He loved Mary Alice. Said she was a spritely girl, a breath of fresh air."

It was getting later in the afternoon and he wondered where Mary Alice was. Probably with Jane. He popped in the kitchen to ask his mother.

"Oh, the two of them were here earlier for their baking lesson."

"Their baking lesson?"

"Darn. Mary Alice didn't want me to tell you. She's trying to learn how to bake, but I'm afraid she's not a natural. Still, she does try."

"Did they say where they were going?"

Annie kept stirring water into whatever she had in a bowl. "Nope."

Time was passing and for some reason, Hardy was getting anxious. He wasn't worried anything had happened to her. Mary Alice could walk around this island blindfolded. He just hoped her parents were okay.

It was Toby who alerted him to her whereabouts. He began to bark and run towards the path. Hardy saw her coming out of the heavy mist, holding her arms with her head down. He knew something had happened. Hurrying to her, he took off his jacket and put it around her shoulders. She laid her head on his chest.

"Jane got a letter saying her aunt died. Her only living relative in England. She's distraught, because now Aunt Lou will never know about the baby, and that was her dearest wish."

"Let's go inside. You're freezing." Hardy put his arm around her as they walked.

"I'm worried about her. She was almost hysterical at one point, blaming herself for coming here and leaving her aunt to die alone. Not being at her funeral. She tore a strip off Sam, asking him why he brought her to a place that doesn't even have a phone. She has to find out almost a month after the fact. It was awful. Almost as if she blamed him. Said Aunt Lou probably died of a broken heart because she was so lonely."

They got to the house and Hardy took the jacket off her and replaced it with the soft blanket she liked. Then he brought a towel over so she could dry her damp hair as she sat by the stove.

"Sam looked terrible. He let her yell and watched her pace back and forth and tried to comfort her but she wouldn't have it, and told him not to touch her. I wanted to help him too, but she needed me more; laid her head on my lap and wept. She's inconsolable."

"I imagine the guilt of not being there is going to eat her up."

"That's just it. And she doesn't need this right now. She's got a baby in her belly." Mary Alice held the towel to the ends of her hair and squeezed. "I think it's the fact that she's lost the last member of her own tribe. I'm sure she feels alone in the world. She's blaming herself for coming here."

"And she'll take that out on Sam," Hardy said.

Mary Alice put the towel down. "You're going to have to help him. Go talk to him. He needs a friend right now. He feels responsible for all of it."

"I will. But not tonight. Neither one of them is in a state to hear anything anyone says. Let's go over to Mom's for supper. You look worn out."

It was such a comfort to be able to sit at the table and eat with family. As soon as Annie heard what happened, she said she'd make chicken soup and Hardy could bring it over to them. He dearly loved this little woman, who spent her life trying to make people feel better by giving them nourishing food. She would say it was nothing, but Hardy knew better. He'd seen what her caring had meant to Sam over the course of his life, and it was not nothing.

That night in bed, Mary Alice's back against Hardy's chest, he put his arms around his wife as if she was a gift. "I love you."

"If you didn't, I'd have to hit you in the shoulder."

He chuckled. "My poor shoulder is seriously damaged with the abuse it's taken in the last quarter century."

She wiggled around to face him. "Let me kiss it better."

His whole body felt better once she was done. She lay on top of him. "Hardy, promise me something."

"Okay."

"Don't die before me."

"All right."

Hardy woke at sunrise and knew Gerry still had a couple of hours on his shift, so he carefully got out of bed so as not to wake Mary Alice and got dressed. He threw some water on his face when he got downstairs and went out the door. A fine day was brewing, if the fogbank offshore would stay there.

He knew Sam got up with the birds, so he walked to the road, and who should he see coming towards him but Sam, his hands in his pockets, looking at the ground.

"Hey, buddy."

Sam lifted his head and nodded. "Hey."

"I'm sorry about Jane's aunt. Mary Alice was worried about how upset she was."

Sam pointed. "Let's sit on our rock." They settled on the big flat one that had always been their place for conversations. "I don't know what to do, Hardy. She hates me."

"She doesn't hate you. She's distraught, and people say things they don't mean when they're in that state."

Sam stayed quiet before blurting, "I think she's hated me all along. Ever since I brought her here. She'll deny it, but I know. And yesterday it all came up to the surface. She can't forgive herself for leaving Aunt Lou behind, and thinks she's failed her father in the process."

Hardy looked out over the water. It was picking up, so maybe not such a nice day after all. "She's having a baby. Her emotions are all over the place. But she feels safe enough to tell you all this, so she needs you to stay calm and take it. Don't react. Just agree and say you're sorry. That you understand why she feels this way."

Sam shook his head. "You're wasted as a lightkeeper."

"Just don't tie yourself in knots like you always do."

"Hey!" Sam poked him in the ribs with his elbow. "I'll have you know the only reason I'm alive is because I stayed calm on that march through Europe. I kept my head down and followed my feet. A lot of the others couldn't do it."

"Well, there's the tactic you should use. Keep your head down and let her grieve. You can't change it for her. Just be there."

"Not always possible when I'm on the boat trying to make a living."

"But when you are home, let her know you're listening. Don't be cutting bait. Look her in the eye. Mary Alice, Mary, Rose, and my mother are all here. She'll have plenty of support. These first days are the worst. We both know that."

"Okay. Thanks."

"Any time." He pointed. "That damn fog is rolling back in."

"I'll let you get to work," Sam said. "Talk to ya later."

Sam breathed a lot easier as he walked away. He went over what Hardy had told him and tried to remember everything he said. It was unusual for someone to have all the answers, but Hardy always had a solution. Sam wondered if the man ever felt unsure about anything.

He went back in the house. Bob was gone, traces of his quick breakfast on the table. Sam had slept downstairs because Jane hadn't wanted him near her. He couldn't hear anything upstairs, so he hoped she was sleeping. She needed it. He needed it. He'd tossed and turned on the couch. Bob's snoring didn't help.

He stood by the door and made himself look at the place through Jane's eyes. She was living with two men, neither of whom cleaned up after himself. One of them snored. Maybe Sam did too, but she never said anything. Everything was drab and worn and old. The only bright thing was her mother's kettle, because she shined it every day.

She had nothing to occupy her at the moment, but that would change. And the minute he had that thought, he knew what he would do. He left a note, knowing she didn't want to see him first thing this morning, and grabbed the stash of army money he kept in an old tackle box and ran down the hill.

Bob was mending nets. "We goin' out later?"

"When I get back." Sam jumped in the skiff and rowed to the boat.

"Where ya goin?"

"Shopping."

Bob made a face and looked at the cat who always hung around the sheds. "I think I'm going deaf. I thought he said *shopping*."

Once again, Danny's truck was put into service, and Sam sprung for the gas. "Where we headed?" Danny asked.

"I'm buying a cradle."

Danny didn't take his eyes off the road. "Jesus. Where we buy that at?"

"Don't have a clue. We better go back and ask your ma."

Aunt Lucille offered to loan Sam an old cot that was in their back shed, but Sam said he needed something brand spanking new. She suggested Crowell's in Sydney.

"It might be costly," she said as they ran back out the door.

"Doesn't matter."

The large brick building looked very intimidating. Sam had never been in a store like this, here or in London. Danny didn't want to go near it, so he stayed in the truck. But then Sam had to stay in the truck too because it wasn't open yet. At the stroke of nine he was in through the doors, but had no idea where to go. It had at least four floors. He didn't need perfume or gloves. Wandering around, he was rescued by a pretty young sales associate who asked if she could help him.

"I need a cradle," he said.

"Oh, congratulations. You'll find furniture up on the top two floors. You can take the elevator."

Sam had never been in one. He looked over and saw an operator in uniform, closing a folding gate across the elevator door, trapping the people squished inside. If that jammed, how would they get out? "Do you have stairs?"

"Sure." She pointed in their direction.

"Thanks."

Dashing up two flights of stairs, he quickly walked through a maze of departments and finally gave up and asked another woman if she could help. She took him to the only place he hadn't looked. Now he was faced with another problem.

"My wife wants a cradle. Is this a cradle?"

"This is what we call a bassinet. It's white wicker and a popular choice."

He wasn't sure. "It's awfully small."

"Babies are small."

"And the cradles?"

She pointed him to little beds made of wood. "These are small too. But they rock."

He went back to the bassinet. "Does this one rock?"

"As a matter of fact, it does. Not all of them do."

The brown wooden ones were rather drab, like his house. A sparkling white bed would look so much more impressive, he thought. "Does the stuff in there come with it?"

"The bedding? No, but you're welcome to buy it."

It was absolutely fascinating when the salesgirl went to her counter and put the receipt and his money in a brass canister. It shot up a tube and disappeared, as if a giant vacuum got ahold of it. He didn't want to seem ignorant but he had no idea what she was doing. She didn't seem bothered, and before he knew it another brass canister shot out of the tube and inside was the receipt and his change. He pretended this was normal, like he'd seen it done a hundred times.

He hurried out to the truck carrying the white bassinet and a bag of bedding. He knocked on the window and Danny rolled it down. "I'm going to sit in the back of the truck. I don't want it to stink like fish."

"You're going to freeze your balls off."

"Can't be helped."

Sam was nearly frozen by the time he got to the wharf. He got aboard first and Danny reached down and handed him the bed, once Sam made sure his hands weren't dirty. Then, thanking his cousin once more, he beat it back to the island as quick as he could. Thankfully Bob was still on shore, so he whistled and gestured for him to come to the boat. Bob jumped in the skiff and rowed over.

"Are your hands clean?"

"What?"

"Are your hands clean?" Sam picked up the bassinet. "I can't get this dirty."

Bob took off his work gloves, then Sam passed it and the bag down to him. "Don't take it out until I get there."

Bob rolled his eyes but followed instructions. Sam jumped out of his skiff and grabbed the precious peace offering. "Thanks, pal."

"For baby, I assume," Bob guessed.

"For the mama."

Now that the ordeal was almost over, Sam was excited and hoped Jane wouldn't be downstairs when he came in. He wanted to set the bassinet up first. Luckily, she wasn't anywhere in sight, so he placed it in the middle of the room and opened the bag of bedding, arranging it like he'd seen in the store. It was all white too, and so very pretty, but then he thought maybe it was all too white. Would you be able to scrub stains off something that white?

He was overthinking it. He ran upstairs and opened the bedroom door slowly, thinking she might still be asleep, but she was sitting up in bed with a book on her lap, using it as a steady surface to write on a piece of paper.

"Hi," he said.

"Hello."

"What are you doing?"

She took a deep breath and looked at him. "I'm writing a letter to Stuart."

"Stuart? Now?"

Jane put down her pen. "Stuart is the only other person in my life who actually met Aunt Lou and I'd like to share my sorrow with someone who'd care. No one else around here ever met her except you. I think he'll be sad when he hears the news."

Hardy's face sprang to mind in Sam's head. "I completely understand why that would be important to you."

She paused and then continued writing.

"Um, could you come downstairs for a minute? I have something to show you."

"Can it wait? I'd like to finish this."

"Okay."

He went down the stairs and waited for thirty minutes. After a while he was sure she was doing it to piss him off, but he stayed calm because that's what Hardy told him to do. He finally went over and grabbed a slice of bread and butter. He hadn't eaten anything.

He had the last mouthful to chew when Jane came down the stairs. She stopped and stared. "Is this mine?"

"Yes. I bought it this morning. I hope you like it. The lady at the store said this bassinet is very popular because it rocks and not all of them do. I looked at the cradles but they weren't as nice as this one. And I bought the bedding too."

Her face crumpled and she put the heels of her hands over her eyes. Sam rose from the table and went to her. "Do you like it, Jane? I want to make you happy. I can't bring Aunt Lou back, but I want to make you happy."

He put his arms around her and she stayed as she was, holding her eyes, until she let out a long sigh and held her face to his chest. They stayed like that until Bob came in looking for lunch.

A bassinet would not solve everything, but it did go a long way in letting Jane know that her husband cared about her feelings. She knew it had been an ordeal for him to get one, but he went anyway. And she was delighted with how sweet it looked. It made her realize that the baby was actually coming.

Rose came in carrying a pot of soup, but said she'd found it on the step and she couldn't take credit for it. She squealed over the bed, saying she was jealous, but she also said that Jane shouldn't spend too much time crying because it wasn't healthy for the baby. Which made sense.

Jane knew the soup had to be Annie's or Mary's. No one wanted to disturb her. She ate the chicken soup and felt better. Then she went over to Mary's, who said she didn't make it, and then advised her, "Cry if you want to. Nothin' ever happened to my babies and there wasn't anything I didn't do. Cried, yelled, argued, jumped up and down. They're tougher than you think."

Mary Alice spent a lot of time with her, just letting her talk about her memories of spending time with Aunt Lou as a kid when her dad would go over to visit. "I'm also feeling guilty that she frightened me sometimes. Only because she wasn't used to kids and had a fit if we broke something. Now that she's gone, I'm happy I lived with her before I sailed away."

As the weeks went by, Jane got many letters from the solicitor, Herbert Hampton, asking her to sign papers for legal purposes and wondering what she was going to do with the estate. She didn't discuss it with anyone. She wanted the decision to be hers alone. Sam never even asked.

Mr. Hampton told her yes, the cats had been rehoused with a friendly neighbour and yes, he'd taken money out of the account for the funeral and grave marker at the cemetery. He could forward her the sum she was owed out of Aunt Lou's bank account, but he needed to know about the house and property. Was she planning on selling? What should he do about her aunt's possessions?

Jane went for a walk one day over to Northwest Cove and sat on the top of the dunes that gave her a view of the smooth, curved, sandy beach and watched the grass blow in the steady breeze.

She noticed something in the sand, an interruption of its continuous glint. Curiosity got the better of her, and she went to look at whatever it was, half buried along the beach. She brushed it with her mitt and realized it was the vertebrae of some enormous animal. Maybe a whale? Sam would know. It was completely bleached from exposure to the sun. She could use it as a stool. She thought it would be heavy, but she picked it up easily. A little awkward to hold, but it was a treasure and belonged to a fabulous creature who once roamed the waters here.

Jane was so pleased with it she decided to decorate the house with more natural gifts that were all around, like white driftwood twisted into shapes that resembled birds. And by the time she got home she knew what she wanted to do.

October 23, 1946

Dear Mr. Hampton, I've decided I would like to keep my aunt's property and not sell it. I do not wish to sell her belongings either. Would it be possible to arrange for the house to be a furnished rental home? I imagine I can retain you to arrange a property manager who will keep an eye on things. I request that only families with no children are considered. Aunt Lou was fastidious and the thought of little ones roaming around her house and breaking things would upset her. Feel free to give her clothing away to a charity shop and save any photos. If you could, let me know if this is possible. I appreciate all your help. It's hard to be so far away, but I feel confident that you have my best interests at heart. I know Aunt Lou would have vetted you thoroughly before hiring you as her solicitor! At the back of my mind is the thought that I might return to England one day and it makes me happy to know I have my grandfather's house, in case I do. Thanks again, Jane

She licked the envelope, addressed it, and put three stamps at the top. Then she walked to the post office and mailed it. There was a letter for her from Stuart. She waited until she got home and sat on her whale stool to open it.

The sympathy card was exquisite. His mother must have helped him pick it out. A cascade of fall flowers filling the entire front. The card read:

Dear Jane and Sam. Thinking of you from across the miles. Our deepest sympathy, The Campbell family

Then she opened the note included. It was in Stuart's handwriting.

Dear Jane and Sam,

I'm sitting here thinking of the fun we had with your dear Aunt Lou. What a character she was! I remember you were scared to death of her, Sam, but we both came to know her as a real pistol, and someone who, if given her due, could have stopped the war three years earlier with her glare alone. I know you're heartbroken, Jane, and thinking you shouldn't have come here and left her, but I want you to know that she told me in confidence on one of our last visits that she was proud of you for getting on with your life and having the guts to do what she couldn't. I think that speaks volumes. She knew she would miss you but was certain your destiny lay in a new country. So please don't agonize about your decision. Prove her right. I'll raise a glass tonight to that charming British lady.

Fondly, Stuart

She held the letter to her heart. "Thank you, Stuart. That's just what I needed."

Are you aware of what a few kind words can do for a person? All of us are capable if we have a mind to. You don't have to be educated, or worldly, or someone important. I watched these individuals from above, living their lives and seeing how someone can come in and completely change the other's course. A quiet talk, a listening ear, holding someone close. Warm soup. None of that takes money or power or brilliance.

Perhaps that's why I loved it there. I was in a community that could only depend on each other. They were a separate world within the world. They didn't have access to a lot. But then, you don't need a lot. You need love, and love is a letter. And a white bassinet. And a punch to the shoulder.

And a dog.

Mary Alice couldn't sleep. The storm outside was making a racket. She had never believed Hardy when he said that his house made more noise than theirs did, but boy, was he right. The wind whistled through the cracks. And they were in the line of fire. There was no land or trees helping to protect the place from the wind. There was only the sea coming straight at them because a lighthouse has to be on the edge, so mariners have the best chance to see it. And the coast on this point of the island was almost nonexistent.

That dragon's tail that disappears into the water.

And now that she was a lightkeeper's wife, storms were deeply scary. Hardy was out there tonight. If it was really bad, he'd stay up with the light. A cold, miserable watch, with the wind howling so loud he couldn't hear himself think, and the lighthouse swaying enough to make him uneasy.

She gave up and put the lamp on the end table beside her so she could play solitaire. A perfect game to play when you're alone in bed. She tried to keep the blanket over her, but her shoulders and arms got cold. She'd have to put her long underwear on under her flannel pajamas. She crawled out of bed and put the lamp back on the bureau. The one thing about this place was that the mirror was a lot bigger. She could see down to her waist. After opening the drawer, she threw her pajama top off and went to put the thermal shirt on when she stopped and looked at herself.

Never once in her life had she stood in front of the mirror and said, "My, what a fine pair of tits you have, Miss Locke."

But that's what she was staring at right now.

"Merciful god! Really? Really?" She cupped them. "Why didn't Hardy say anything? He truly is thick."

And then she realized she was, too. Had she missed her period? She couldn't remember.

Forgetting she was cold, Mary Alice just stared, and the longer she stared, the wider her smile became. There was a movement in the mirror behind her, a quick shadow. "I see you, Cara. You're happy for me, aren't you?"

The flame in the lamp flickered and shone brighter.

"Will you promise to look after this baby too?"

"Why are you standing in the mirror with no top on?"

Mary Alice hadn't even heard Hardy come in. She turned around and faced him. "Do you notice something different?"

"You're naked from the waist up and that makes me happy."

She walked over to him with her beautiful big breasts in her hands. "And these fine specimens don't look different to you?"

"They're softer and rounder, and if you don't put them away, I'm going to take you right here with my rain gear on."

"So, you agree they're bigger?"

"Yes. Putting on weight from all my mother's desserts?"

"No, not because of that." She pulled him over to the bed and said, "Close your eyes, Cara."

Hardy was busy tearing off his duds. "Who is Cara and why is she here? Don't answer that."

It was a good half hour before they could resume talking. Once again, she sat over him and put his hands on her swollen breasts.

"You and I are having a baby, Hardy."

He instantly pulled her down and lay across her. "Tell me again."

"A baby. A little you and me."

He held her head and kissed her slowly, before looking into her eyes. "You are literally my life. It all begins and ends with you."

She rubbed his cheek. "Do you remember what you said to me?"

He shook his head.

"'I want to have it all with you.' This is me, giving you my all."

CHAPTER NINETEEN

In late January 1947 Tom was outside piling wood. Mary glanced out her window just as he clutched his chest. She managed to get him inside the house before he collapsed. She ran over to Sam's first and he took off to get to the phone at the lighthouse to call the doctor.

Jane, heavily pregnant, gingerly waddled over across the ice and snow, holding her belly, to see if she could help. Shortly after Mary Alice arrived, holding her smaller tummy, and Rose and her husband, Jeb, showed up. Soon everyone knew. A community crisis.

Tom remained conscious and was in a lot of pain but told everyone it wasn't that bad. Looking at him didn't inspire any confidence. He was ashen. Sam and Hardy came in to tell them the doctor would be at the wharf if they could get him there. The men conferred. There was no way they could take a boat as the ice was packed in solid. They'd have to take him by horse and cart across the island and pull him on a sled to Main-à-Dieu.

There was no time for long goodbyes. Tom told Mary to stay at home and she told him to bugger off, she was going with him. The girls packed a bag for her to take and held Tom's hands for a moment and then the men got him in the cart, wrapped up as warmly as they could, helped Mary in beside him, and headed out. They took two carts, so more men could help with the dragging across the ice.

Those left behind would have to wait for hours and hours, not knowing what was happening.

This was the reality of life on the island. But thanks to the teamwork, strength, and sheer stubbornness of Tom's wife, friends, and two horses, they drove the seven miles to the other shore, and slowly walked the sled a mile across the uneven ice pans to safety. The doctor was on the wharf as promised and had a vehicle ready to take Tom to the hospital. Off they went, and the men turned around and walked back across the ice. Their trusty horses took them home.

He survived.

Mary came home once Tom was out of danger. He would be in the hospital for a couple of weeks. She gathered her children around her and told them the news.

"Your father went through hell. That trip across the island in an old cart and then the ice was brutal and I didn't know if your Da would make it. We aren't getting any younger and we've decided to move off the island. We all knew this day was coming and now it's here."

Mary Alice couldn't blame them, but the thought of not having her mother around when the baby was born in early May was upsetting. They'd always been there. It was going to be heartbreaking walking by the place and not stopping in, but then Rose and Jeb decided to make it their home, which made Mary Alice feel better. They'd always been a little cramped at the Trimms'. Jeb was mighty happy.

The boat was the only fly in the ointment. Tom had four living sons, and they started to squabble over who would get it. In the end, Mary told them to put a lid on it. Their father was selling the boat because they needed the money. They planned on moving in with Mary's widowed sister in Baleine. She could use a man about the house, even one with a wonky heart.

The incident shook Jane up. She ruminated about it at night, as she tried to get comfortable.

"Sam, what am I going to do? What happens if something goes wrong when I'm in labour and I have to get to a hospital? We'd die trying to get across the ice."

"I told you I'll take you to my aunt Muriel in Glace Bay. She said you're welcome to stay with them until the baby comes. You can have it at the Glace Bay General."

"But I don't know these people. When should I go, and how long before I can get back?"

Sam pushed himself up on his elbow. "I'll do whatever you want. What bothers you more? Being here if something goes wrong, or being there if something goes wrong?"

"But you won't be with me if I'm in Glace Bay."

"What the heck am I going to do? I can't go with you into the delivery room."

She turned onto her back and sighed, rubbing her protruding bump. She was due on Valentine's Day, which was getting ever closer. "Look at me, I could pop open any time. Maybe I should go soon."

"You get your stuff together and I'll keep my eye on the weather and hopefully we'll get a break in the ice and I'll take you over. I think you'd feel better in the hospital."

"But the bassinet?"

"You can take it with you if you want."

A week later, the ice broke up enough that Sam was able to take Jane over to Glace Bay. She and Mary Alice had an emotional goodbye.

"You'll do great! And I'll be here when you get back."

For some reason Jane had forgotten that she had to get on the skiff to get on the Cape Islander and climb the ladder at the Glace Bay wharf. She stood on the beach and stared. Sam knew what she was thinking.

"Bob's here. I'm here. We're going to get you on."

She had no choice. And they did get her up. Her larger ass was a great handhold for Bob, and Sam had wiry arms that were stronger than they looked. He also had adrenaline on his side, because he wasn't nearly as confident as he let on.

Bob rowed back for the bassinet and her suitcase and delivered those. Sam reached for them. "Ask Hardy to call Aunt Muriel and tell her we're coming. Get Uncle Howard to meet us at the wharf."

Bob waved. "Good luck, Jane!"

"Thanks, Bob. Don't burn the place down!"

Sam had a folding chair for her to sit on in the wheelhouse. He also put a bucket beside her just in case. He wrapped her in a blanket and off they went. It wasn't exactly a smooth ride, but it wasn't terrible. She didn't end up needing the bucket.

He looked down at her and shouted over the engine. "When you come back, there will be three of us in this boat."

"There's three of us in here now," she laughed.

"What do you think we're going to have?"

"A girl."

Sam shook his head. "It's a boy. I had a dream."

Jane shivered with excitement and then called out, "What should his name be?"

He didn't hear her and she had to repeat it. "Not Sam! I never really liked it. Anyway, sounds like Spam."

She mulled things over for a while. "I've only been thinking of girl names. Louise, Mary, Annie, Alice, or Rose. I'd name her after my mother, but she hated the name Doris. And you told me your mother never really liked her name, Gladys. If it's a boy, would you mind James or William? They were my dad's and brother's names."

"Sounds good to me."

Jane was getting tired as they approached Glace Bay Harbour.

She'd had a few cramps but nothing serious, so she didn't say anything to Sam. She knew he was nervous enough.

There was more ice along this shore. Glace Bay was originally named Baie de Glace by the French. Bay of ice.

As Sam pulled up to the wharf, he pointed. "There he is."

Jane stood up with Sam's help and rubbed her back. She wasn't sure which old man was Uncle Howard, but as soon as Sam cut the engine, the man who looked like Santa Claus reached down to catch the rope. "How she goin', b'y?"

"Great, Uncle Howard. Thanks for meeting us. This is my wife, Jane."

He doffed his cap. "Pleased to meet you, Jane. Your tummy is almost as big as mine!"

She liked him instantly and breathed a sigh of relief.

"Now, how are we hauling this poor girl outta there?"

Sam said, "I'll push and you pull."

Uncle Howard turned his head and whistled for a couple of young, strong men by the warehouse. "My pulling days are over thanks to a bad back."

Sam steadied her at the start of the ladder, keeping his body close to hers. She grabbed the rungs slowly, and when she was close enough, the two men reached under her armpits and pulled her up until she was able to put her feet on the edge of the wharf and stand on her own, but they didn't let go until she was far enough away that she didn't topple backwards.

"Thank you," she said to these strangers as she smoothed down her coat.

"No problem, darlin'. Good luck with the little one." And they disappeared into the warehouse doorway.

Sam had handed the bassinet and suitcase to his uncle and got off himself. They shook hands.

Uncle Howard looked serious. "I hate to tell ya, but the ice is coming back in. If you don't leave soon, you'll be stuck here for who knows how long."

Jane panicked. "You could stay for a few days, right, Sam?"

He made a face and pulled at his chin. "Bob's expecting me back and he can't be without the boat for days. And it could be weeks before I can get out. You never know."

"That means *I* might be here for weeks! Oh, I shouldn't have come."

Uncle Howard put a reassuring arm around her shoulder. "Now don't you fret, Jane. Muriel and I will take good care of you, and when baby comes and is doing well, Sam will be back here and take you home. I believe I heard that you'd feel better going to a hospital. Isn't that right?"

She calmed down a little. "Yes."

Sam pulled his wife over to a more private spot and held her close. "You're going to be fine. I'll come back and get you as soon as I can and as soon as you want. I'm dying to meet this little chap too. You're going to do brilliantly, as my English buddies always said." He kissed her. "I love you."

She grabbed him tighter. "I love you too. I'm going to miss you. I haven't been away from you in a year."

"You can do this. Aunt Lou thinks so too."

With a final squeeze, Sam let his wife go and shook his uncle's hand once more before he jumped back down onto deck of the boat, started the rumbling motor, and left the harbour behind.

Howard and Muriel lived in a smaller house on Amelia Street. It didn't matter how small it was, it had electricity and hot water and an indoor bathroom. Jane had completely forgotten such things existed.

Muriel was as round as Howard and just as welcoming, so Jane asked them if there was any way she could have a bath, as she hadn't had one in a year.

"You must be awful dirty then," Howard joked.

Muriel was the practical one. "Do you think you'll be able to get in and out of the tub? I can help you if you like."

"If I can get in and out of rocking boats, I think I'll be all right, but I'll certainly yell if I need a hand."

Jane laid her head on the curved rim and lowered her whole body as far as she could. Her belly still stuck out, but floating like this was such a relief on her aching back. The luxury of immersing herself in a claw-foot tub with hot water she didn't have to heat up herself, in the privacy of a bathroom instead of a galvanized tub in the kitchen, was so blissful she stayed in it for at least an hour. She kept adding hot water as needed. Muriel would come to the door every so often to check if she was all right, and she would yell, "This is heaven! I can't thank you enough."

"There's bubble bath you can use."

She'd already put it in. "Oh, thank you. I won't use much."

"Take as much as you like."

Eventually, Jane knew she had to get out and socialize with the two souls who were allowing her to stay here. It took several tries turning this way and that to see if she could manage on her own, and she did, once she rolled over on her knees and lifted them one at a time, holding on to the side.

Jane felt like a different person when she finally joined her hosts. She was glowing with pleasure and relaxation. "That was perfect."

Muriel made her sit and eat a bowl of Scotch broth, with crackers and butter. "We put your belongings in your room and set up the bassinet as well. I'm so glad you brought it. It's a lovely little bed."

Jane held her spoonful of soup in the air. "Sam bought it all by himself. He surprised me."

"That was very thoughtful," Howard said with a mouthful of crackers. "He always was a good kid."

They chatted happily until Jane began to yawn, as much as she tried to hide it. Muriel noticed and ordered her to bed. It was only six o'clock, but it was dark outside and felt like night. When she got out of the bathroom after brushing her teeth and having yet another pee, Muriel was in her room pulling down the sheets and coverlets. "There are more blankets on the chair. If you need anything through the night call me, I'll hear you. Howard won't. And there's a nightlight in the hall."

Jane startled the poor woman by giving her a hug. "Thank you. It's been so long since someone put me to bed."

Muriel patted her back. "Enjoy these last free days. You'll be putting baby to bed soon enough and getting no sleep at all. Just get up when you feel like it. Goodnight, dear."

"Goodnight." Jane manoeuvred herself under the covers and relished the comfy mattress. "I am definitely a city girl." She went out like a light. The kind she never got to use on Scatarie.

The minute you hope one thing, another thing happens. Jane was looking forward to another week of pampering after finding her hot breakfast on the table in the morning. "Oh, this looks yummy. I'm feeling guilty letting you do all the work."

"It's no trouble at all. I hope you had a great sleep." Muriel put some homemade bread in the toaster.

Jane happily tucked in to her bacon and eggs. "Can I live here?" The minute she said it, something felt amiss. She looked down at her tummy and felt warm liquid start to run down her legs and puddle on the kitchen floor. She was mortified. "What's happening? This is too soon. What do I do?"

Muriel shushed her and told her to get her things. They'd take her right to the hospital.

It only took five minutes to get there. "I'm not due for another week," she told them.

"Babies come when they feel like it."

They went in with her, and Muriel told her she would stay, but she sent Howard home. She had her book of crosswords and didn't need him yapping in her ear. While Jane was bent over with contractions, Muriel filled the nurse in with details. Then the nurse pushed Jane down the long hall in a wheelchair and she looked back at Muriel, who waved at her. "You'll be fine!"

Jane wasn't fine. She was scared to death, lonely, in pain, and embarrassed. It wasn't until the real show began that she stopped caring about anything else. It was just her and agony. An older doctor came in wearing a gown and mask and barely grunted at her. It was like she was a slab of meat and he was about to carve her up.

"Don't scream," he said at one point.

Thank god for nurses. One of them leaned over and whispered, "You're not doing anything wrong. Just try and keep that energy inside and not waste it. You need it to push. Hold my hand when you want to screech."

It must have helped. Fifteen minutes later the doctor lifted a bloody bundle in the air and said, "It's a boy," with little enthusiasm. He cut the cord and passed the baby to another nurse, who took him to a table and worked on him. Jane was dismayed. "Shouldn't he be crying?"

When her son did make a helpless little wail, it was as if someone had started her heart again. A different heart that belonged only to him. "Give him to me. He's mine."

The sullen doctor was doing something between her legs and she didn't care. She held out her arms as the baby cried again. "Please!"

Finally, after the nurse had cleaned him off and wrapped him in a flannel baby blanket, she turned around and, smiling, handed the baby to Jane. "He's perfect."

When her baby was placed in her arms, Jane recognized him. He wasn't a surprise to her. She even knew his voice, as she cradled him and kissed his forehead. "It's okay, baby. Mommy's here." He stopped crying and gazed at her as if he understood. Maybe she was imagining things, but he looked a little like her brother. Her eyes filled with tears. "Oh, Sam, I wish you were here."

When the doctor left the room, Jane said thank you anyway. He gave her a little wave. The nurse who held her hand said, "He's not the obstetric doctor. He was filling in."

"I don't care if he was abrupt. He brought my baby into the world safely, so I'll always have a soft spot for him."

When Jane was settled in her room, Muriel came to see her. "It's a boy, I hear. Congratulations! I'll try and get a peek at him on my way past the nursery."

"He's adorable. Soft blondish hair, but not much of it, and a little round face."

"How much did he weigh?"

"Six pounds, eighteen and a half inches. I thought he'd weigh more."

"Well, he is slightly early. Anyway, dear, I'd better go. I've been here all day, but I'll come and see you tomorrow."

"Thank you for staying. It was nice knowing you were close by. Could you get word to Sam somehow to tell him he has a son?"

"I will indeed." Muriel patted her hand. "Goodnight."

Jane lay back, marvelling at the timing of the whole thing. If they had waited one more day, her son would have been born on Scatarie, and although it seemed like the birth went well, if she had been in that much pain lying in her own bed, she would've thought she was dying. She'd made the right decision.

The nurse brought the baby in with a cart and checked mother and baby's ID bracelets before she left. She said she'd be back to give Jane something to dry up her milk and get the baby used to a bottle with water at first. Jane didn't pay much attention. She was busy unwrapping the blanket so she could see every inch of her son's little body and breathe him in.

This was a love like no other. And as she held his tiny fingers, his name came to her. Louis James William Harris. She'd call him Louie, after Aunt Lou. It suited him. The names James and William seemed too grown up for a six-pound boy, but Louie was perfect.

Sam celebrated the birth of his son by getting stinking drunk with Bob. He'd asked Hardy and Mary Alice to join him in wetting the baby's head and they came over to be with him, but Mary Alice couldn't touch the stuff and Hardy wouldn't. That didn't mean they weren't delighted for them both. Sam said he understood as they left but he'd had a few by then, and as soon as they disappeared, he moaned to Bob, "Great pals they are. How often does this happen to a man? A first-born son." He drank another glassful and waved it in the air. "Let's go tell people."

So, the two of them lurched their way around and stopped at everyone's house, getting more and more plastered as they went. Everyone was pleased for him. At the last house, when they were truly in their cups, the woman of the house suggested her husband accompany them home to make sure they didn't fall down, pass out, and freeze to death.

They wouldn't hear of it and said their farewells. The husband followed them far enough behind that they didn't notice him. They weren't noticing much, and they both fell down a couple of times but managed to right themselves. He was able to go back home and report they were in the house. "They better not burn it to the ground," his wife mumbled.

In the morning, they both swore they'd never do that again. A phrase often uttered but never acted upon.

The ice didn't let up and two and a half weeks went by with still no way to bring Sam's wife and son home. Why the hell did they have to have this baby in the winter? He thought about walking over to Main-à-Dieu, even just to visit them, but while the ice was indeed there, now it wasn't quite strong enough to walk on. Bob told him, "That's a great way to greet your son, dead at the bottom of the tittle."

Mary Alice and Hardy did their best to keep Sam's spirits up, but he was in a foul mood. Mary Alice finally marched over there, slowly mind you, and pushed the door open. Sam and Bob were at the table eating the cornbread she'd brought over the day before. They both swivelled around when she screeched.

She pointed at them. "You say you want to go get your wife and son and bring them home?! Why the hell would she want to come back to this dump? You've got dishes in the sink, clothes everywhere, a layer of dust on everything, dirty sheets, and the foul smell of garbage coming outta that bin by the back door. If you don't have this place shipshape in two days, I'm calling Jane and telling her to stay in Glace Bay. I mean it, Sam. You're wallowing again and feeling sorry for yourself."

She picked up the newspapers that were draped over the furniture. "You know who I feel sorry for? Your wife. She's living with other people and trying to handle a newborn by herself. Give your head a shake. I'm furious. I can't imagine her reaction if she were to walk into this filth with an infant."

Mary Alice went to the door and spun around. "Did you hear what I said, Sam?"

"Bloody hell, the whole island heard you."

"Good. Now get off your ass and prove you're a loving husband and father."

She slammed the door for good measure and then carefully picked her way home across the icy snow.

I'm quite certain you can understand why Aisling and I love the soul named Mary Alice. She's not afraid to say what needs to be said. And that needed to be said. Their sister couldn't get over to visit at the moment, their brother Ian pretty much forgot about them most of the time. Their parents were dead. All their relatives were on the mainland. There was no one around to expect anything from Bob and Sam Harris now that Jane wasn't in the house.

Mary Alice shouldn't have had to go there and remind them of their responsibilities, but she was doing it for Jane's sake. I also knew very well that Hardy would never put himself or others in that situation. Sam and Bob were behaving like my teenage brothers, except they never got away with it because my father would take off his belt.

I love Sam, I always have, but there were times when I wanted to strangle him. Not a very nice thing for an angel in heaven to say, but then you'll notice I've never called myself an angel. Similarly, I refer to Aisling as a little imp, which is a polite way of saying a devilish child. Which is exactly what she is.

Sam and Bob were in for a heap of misfortune if they didn't mend their ways.

Mary Alice and Hardy took a walk over there two days later, during Gerry's shift. She wanted Hardy with her, so he could beat up Sam if she was greeted with the same misery. Hardy said he couldn't promise anything.

"Coward."

She took a deep breath and barged in like she had before. The first thing that hit her was the smell of clean. There were no dishes in the sink, the garbage can was out of sight, the table was cleaned off, and there were no clothes hanging off the furniture. Even the throw rugs were straight.

"Looks good to me," Hardy said. "Clearly the Harris brothers are afraid of you."

"Sam?!"

"I'm upstairs putting clean sheets on the bed."

"Well done."

"You better leave. I've got things to do."

The two of them backed out the door and practically skipped home.

Jane was so grateful to Sam's aunt and uncle for their hospitality. Especially when Louie would be awake every few hours and she'd have to go to the kitchen to make formula in the middle of the night. They never said a word about it, but when you know you're putting people out for an extended period of time it makes you anxious. And as much as Jane loved having hot water out of a tap and a warm, un-smelly bathroom, she was never able to get in the tub again. She was a new mother and didn't have the luxury of floating around. It was a quick sponge bath standing by the sink.

And she missed her husband. She knew he was probably distraught about not being able to get to her.

The phone rang in Muriel's kitchen and the way she twirled around to look at Jane, she knew it was about her. She held out the phone. "It's Sam."

Jane was so glad to hear his voice. "I miss you. Louie misses you."

"Who's Louie?"

"Your son. Louis James William Harris. Do you like it?"

"You could've called him Davy Crockett. I don't care. Listen to me. I can come and get you tomorrow because the ice is gone, but something happened to the motor and I can't drive the boat right now, so I'm going to borrow another boat and I'd like Uncle Howard to drive you to Port Morien and I'll pick you up there."

Jane repeated everything he said and Howard stood up. "Tell him I'll drive you to Main-à-Dieu." Jane told Sam and then she put her hand over the receiver. "He says that's too far and you've done enough already."

"Give me the phone." He grabbed it. "Will you just do as I say? Let me worry about the gas in my car."

So that was it. It was all arranged. Muriel packed up all the baby clothes she bought Louie despite his mother's protests. "Rose has loads of baby clothes she's going to lend me."

"I want him to have a few new outfits. Some of these will be too big for him now, but you'll see how fast he grows into them."

She insisted on coming for the ride out to Main-à-Dieu, more so to hold Louie a little longer. Jane was thrilled to be going back home. She never thought she'd say that about returning to the island, but she had good friends there now, not just her husband.

When they got to the wharf, Sam ran to the car and had Jane's door open in a flash. They kissed each other quickly because she wanted to show him the baby and he wanted to be shown.

"God love you two," Sam said as he leaned into the back seat. "I can never repay you for your kindness."

"Our pleasure, my boy," Uncle Howard laughed. "I'm going to miss the little man and I know Muriel will be boo-hooing all the way home."

Sam took his son into his arms, turned away from them, and held him close, whispering in his ear. He'd missed the first precious days of Louie's life and wanted him to know that he would always be with him from now on.

He turned back, his rough hand cradling Louie's head, and smiled at Jane. "He's perfect."

"Okay, let's get this show on the road," Howard said. "You don't want him to get cold."

Jane took Louie, Sam took the bassinet, Uncle Howard had the suitcases, and Aunt Muriel held the plastic picnic bag she put Louie's bottles in. They were still warm.

They got to the edge of the wharf and Uncle Howard said, "Where's your boat?"

"I told Jane the engine is frigged at the moment but I borrowed another one."

"That?" Uncle Howard pointed at a large enough boat, but it had a motor on the back and no cover from the elements.

"You're going to take that baby on the water with nothing to shield him?" Aunt Muriel cried with dismay. Jane got upset. "Sam! This is crazy. I'm going to get back in that car."

Sam held his hands up. "Look. I've made a cozy nest in the front for Jane to lay down on the bottom and hold the baby. She can lean against the front seat. I have blankets to put over them and a tarp to cover both mother and child. I'm not a complete idiot. And this was the only boat available or we would've had to wait another three days, and I've already missed his whole life! Now let's stop arguing. The sooner we leave, the sooner we get into a warm house."

Before any of them could say anything, Sam gave the baby to Aunt Muriel, and made Jane go down the ladder and position herself where he wanted her. Then he took the baby and put him inside his winter coat and scooted down the ladder as quick as you like, before Jane could even open her mouth to shriek. The bassinet was next, the suitcases and the picnic bag put next to Jane. He blew Jane a kiss before he covered them up with the tarp and tucked it down.

"Thanks again, you two! You saved our bacon."

Sam's aunt and uncle waved from the pier. "You better call us!" Aunt Muriel yelled. "I don't care if it is the government phone!"

The motor started, Uncle Howard untied the rope, and off the little family went.

As predicted, Aunt Muriel blubbered all the way back. "Someone up there better be looking out for them. I can't believe he's taking them across like that."

"Sam is an excellent boatman. He wouldn't risk his family if he didn't think it was safe."

Out on the water, Sam yelled to Jane as they crossed the tittle. "Kick your foot if you're okay under there."

He saw the tarp move. "Good, if you need help, give me two kicks. In the balls if you like!"

Underneath the plastic-smelling tarp, Jane had to admit it wasn't bad, except for the pounding of the waves under her bottom. He'd put enough padding down, thankfully. Maybe she should travel like this more often. Not seeing the height of the waves coming at her made it easier. She could pretend she was on a train and not in deep, deep water. And miraculously, the whirr of the motor and the rocking boat put Louie right to sleep. Jane kept looking at him wrapped in her coat, under her chin, as he placidly sucked on his soother.

"You must be your father's son. You like being on the water."

She was more than ready to have it over with when she felt the boat slow down and the engine soften. She heard Sam whistle for Bob and then he started to unwrap her and Louie. He had a big grin on his face when he saw them. "Thank you for being so brave."

"Louie loved it. He's fast asleep."

"That's my boy!"

Because this boat was shaped differently, Sam was able to manoeuvre it close to the shore and Bob pulled it up with a rope, the front end out of the water. "Welcome home," he said.

"Hi, Bob. Ya miss me?"

"You have no idea."

Bob held the boat steady and Sam helped Jane and the baby up off the bottom, and then he picked her up in his arms and carried them both to the dry sand.

"Could you grab the stuff, Bob?"

He grinned. "As always."

Mother and father walked up the hill with Louie and went in the door. Jane gasped. "It smells so clean! And looks clean! It *is* clean! Oh, thank you, Sam. This is the best gift you could've given me."

"You can thank your girlfriend Mary Alice, who came over here one day and threatened to tie us to a burning stake if we didn't have this place spotless when you walked in."

That night, as Louie lay in his bassinet in the bedroom and the lantern was low, Jane and Sam held each other close.

"I'm so happy," she said.

"I love you and our little boy."

She sighed contentedly and then sat straight up. "We forgot to call Aunt Muriel!"

CHAPTER TWENTY

Mary Alice spent the rest of the winter and spring watching and learning about babies. She was in love with Louie and kind of hoped her baby would be a boy. They were so darned cute. And Louie had startling blue eyes like his dad.

It was quite something to watch Sam bounce Louie up and down and throw him in the air and catch him again. His son's rumbly giggles were adorable.

It was also quite something when things went wrong, like a fever, or a croupy cough. Luckily the island mothers, with their combined knowledge, had a remedy for most of it. But life was still busy and hard, and didn't stop just because a baby was around. Mary Alice often listened to Jane complain, or fondly reminisce about Muriel's tub.

"Do you think Sam will ever leave here?" Jane asked her.

Mary Alice said, "Who knows? If he does, he'll be one of the last ones to leave. No one wants salted fish anymore, they want fresh now, and fewer boats are coming out to the island to get it. It's easier to pick them up from Main-à-Dieu and for the fisherman there's more money in it and the work isn't as hard. It makes sense to leave. But it's a terrible shame for those of us who've lived here and love the place.

"You won't. Someone has to stay and look after the lighthouse."

"Would we want to stay if no one else is here? I don't want this baby growing up with no friends."

Hardy was like a mother hen. He had everything arranged for

baby's arrival. Dorothy came over one night for supper after Lyle went to his hunting camp for a few days, and she teased him about it.

"You should have been a nursemaid."

"No finer job," he countered.

"Are you having the baby here or in town?" she asked Mary Alice.

"Here, after the nonsense that Jane went through."

Annie took another roll out of the basket. "But there's no ice in May."

"I've got Ma saying she's coming to stay with Rose for a couple of weeks, and between the two of them and you, Annie, I'm sure I'll be fine. You've had eighteen kids between you. There's not much you don't know, and the doctor said everything looks good."

The whole month of April was surprisingly uneventful. No big storms, no cold fronts moving in and bringing rotten weather with them. There was a lot of rain and a whole week of thick fog, which made things damp and dreary, but they had enough sunny days to make it feel like spring would come eventually.

In late April, Hardy received a call from the maritime weather station advising him of an intense nor'easter making its way up the coast. It was hardly news. Hardy knew it was coming because of the gloomy skies and the dark towering clouds gathering offshore. The wind picked up dramatically and flashes of light and thunder were heard in the distance, but advancing quickly. The barometric pressure fell dramatically.

It was early in the afternoon but looked like twilight. Gerry was in the yard making sure everything was locked up when the heavens opened and rain pelted down so hard it was painful. Hardy was in the tower with the light shining and the foghorn on, peering out to sea with his binoculars. And that's when he saw it. A ship, trying to make it to shelter, but the wind and surf were causing havoc.

Its steering was out of control and it looked like it was coming for the rocky shore.

Hardy flew down the lighthouse stairs and grabbed Gerry, the rain and wind making it almost impossible to talk or hear. "We've got a ship on the rocks. Get Fred to let the men know, then meet me in the boathouse."

Gerry tore off, and almost instantly Hardy saw Fred running for help. As Hardy opened the doors of the boathouse, James was behind him.

"Don't do any lifting," Hardy told him. "Get the oars and flashlights and rope. And get the cables."

Gerry rushed back and they worked the winch so the large rowboat slowly made its way outside. The fishermen arrived and worked like a team to get the boat into the water. For the time being, they put all the equipment in it and ran it along the shore until they came to the floundering ship. It was hard going. The rain and the pounding surf made things hellish.

They could barely see the sailors on the listing ship gathered by the bow, their hands gesturing to hurry. Hardy knew he had to get the boat over to the ship so they could rig a cable from ship to shore. Without that to hang on to, the sailors would be bashed against the rocks if they went in the water.

The men tied a rope to the boat, and had the cable wound, ready to throw. Hardy and Gerry got in and grabbed the oars, trying desperately to make their way through and past the rolling surf. The fishermen on land let the rope out slowly, trying to give the craft some stability in the water. Sometimes all it took was a slight pause in the wave action and they could gather steam with their giant oars and make headway, but it was more of a dance. They'd get ahead and then be rushed back.

After what seemed like forever, and what must have been an

eternity for the men on the deck, Hardy got close enough and Gerry threw the cable as far as humanly possible. Luck was on their side. One of the men caught it and threw the other end back. They would have to return and anchor it on shore, but not before getting as many men as they could in their boat.

Because it was almost on its side, the drop into the rowboat wasn't far, but it was still a tricky business in these conditions. They managed to get five off before they headed back, the men on shore pulling the rope as fast as they could. They almost went over a few times with the fury of the wind, but they righted themselves and made it. The sailors got to land and helped the others rig up the cable.

Sam was almost up to his knees in water, trying to get to Hardy. "Are you okay? Can you go back out there?" he shouted.

"We're good. Be here when the men start using the cable!"

Sam couldn't hear him, so he said it right in his ear. Sam gave him a thumb's up.

He and Gerry went back out and took six more men off the ship. "How many are you?" Hardy yelled into the wind.

"We're thirty."

Hardy cursed. He knew he didn't have enough strength to go out that many times. He and Gerry would have to pass it off to Sam and Bob after one more trip.

Back out they went, and now there were men hanging on to the cable as they tried to make it to shore, hand over hand.

Hardy didn't dare take more than six this time. If their boat went over, everyone would be lost. While they headed back, they saw two sailors let go and land in the water. Hardy and Gerry were able to drag one of them for a bit before a wave took him. The other one disappeared instantly, but a third man behind them made it all the way to shore under his own steam.

Back on shore, Hardy and Gerry could hardly get out of the boat themselves, their arms limp. Sam and Bob jumped in and off they went, battling over in conditions that were, unbelievably, getting worse.

Before long, they were back with six more. Hardy was trying to count in his head. They took seventeen off, Sam got six more so that was twenty-three. Two went in the water, made twenty-five. The one on the cable made it, so twenty-six. He went up to Sam and yelled, "There's only four more. One more trip."

Sam nodded and they pushed the boat out. Two men were trying to get started on the cable, but just then, the ship lurched over on its side, dumping the men into the sea. Immediately, the fishermen dropped the cable into the water, hoping the sailors could grab it and hang on. Sam and Bob rowed out to try and pick them out of the water one at a time, but they all knew it was unlikely.

James and Fred took the miserably cold and wet sailors along the shore and up to the house. Annie would know what to do. She'd done it before when Len was alive.

It was an absolute miracle that the brothers managed to get two of them out of the water. The other two were gone. Before they returned, Hardy thought he saw something and shone a light on a large rock near the beach. He could hardly make it out, but it looked like someone hanging on for dear life. He took off down the beach, Fred and Jeb with him.

A sailor, half-dead and bleeding, was splayed out on the rock's round surface, his fingers curled around the one sharp edge that kept him from being pulled back out. It was a team effort that got him off that rock, with the churning breakers hitting them in the face. Fred and Jeb had to pry the sailor's frozen fingers from his handhold and Hardy held him until they could put their arms under his armpits and drag him to the beach. Hardy took a step to follow them and his foot slipped on seaweed and down he went in the water, hitting his head on the rock.

The water was so turbulent he didn't know which way was up, and it tossed him around like a limp doll, every time bashing him against another hard surface. He needed air and had a moment of terrible regret, thinking of Mary Alice and the baby he might never see.

And then someone pulled him up. "Ya miserable bastard! Don't you dare die on me!"

Well, he knew that was Sam, and relief filled his entire body. They had to crawl out of the water since the whitecaps kept knocking them down. Hank Lahey and Lyle helped them.

Even though they were soaking wet despite their rain gear and chilled to the bone, the men of Scatarie stood on the beach, hoping for a miracle like the sailor on the rock. God forbid someone went under only to pop up farther along and have no one on the beach to help.

Eventually they had to go. Jeb patted Hardy's back. "Twenty-seven out of thirty rescued. Keep remembering that."

"A job well done, boys," Sam shouted.

The men just wanted to get home. There were enough hands at the Campbell place to help the sailors for now. They would be available to put them up if need be after the storm was over and the authorities came for them.

Sam turned to Hardy before they got to the house, still shouting. "I've got to get back to Jane. She was terrified when we went out the door and she's alone with the baby."

"Thanks, Sam. Don't tell Jane about coming out to get me. I don't want Mary Alice to know."

"What?"

He told him again.

When Hardy walked in to the kitchen, there was pandemonium. Annie, Fred, and James were passing out blankets and clothes that were stored for just such an occasion. Mary Alice was making tea and sandwiches while bandaging men with cuts and bruises. She looked over at her husband with relief and said, "Thank you, God." She tossed her head. "The fellow on the rock doesn't look good. And you've got blood on your forehead."

Hardy nodded and went to the phone. He called the doctor and asked him to be on call when the storm was over, and told him they had a badly injured sailor. Then he called his superiors and told them about the wreck, but had to hold the phone to his chest. "Can someone tell me the name of the ship and your destination?"

The nearest fella with a wrapped hand told him it was the collier ship *Sea King*, from Halifax, headed with coal for Louisbourg. "We almost made it, too."

Hardy relayed the message and then said, "Twenty-seven survivors, one of them badly injured, and three souls lost. Let me know when to expect the authorities."

He stripped his rain gear off and went up the stairs to get dry clothes. Gerry was coming down after putting his on. "I'll go out to the light first."

"Thanks, Gerry. Great work."

He forgot his dry clothes were next door at his place. He pilfered some from Fred. Only when he was undressed did he see the extent of the bruising over his whole body. He'd be sore, and Fred's tight clothes didn't help.

He went back down to check on the badly injured man. One look at him and Hardy knew he probably wouldn't live through the night. It was sad, but seeing friends around him, one of them holding his hand, he was grateful they were able keep the man from dying alone on a damn boulder.

The sailors were subdued. Glad to be in a warm house with a cup of tea in their belly, but their brush with death was too fresh to think of anything else. Hardy went over to one of them sitting on the floor. "What went wrong?"

"We had a hydraulic power failure. Once the steering goes, especially in these weather conditions, you're screwed." He shook his head. "The captain thought we could make it to Louisbourg before the storm. Money often trumps common sense, but I can't speak ill of the dead. He was one of the four still on the ship when it went over."

The storm blew itself out sometime in the night, taking the poor sailor's life with it. Everyone was exhausted by the time the men were put back on a coast guard ship later the next day. They were grateful and shook hands with their rescuers, who went down to the shore to see them off.

The last one to leave said, "We won't soon forget Scatarie and the brave people who live here."

The Campbells especially deserved a good night's sleep, but lighthouses don't keep themselves. Hardy took the first shift and then crawled back to bed when Gerry relieved him. He put his arm over Mary Alice and the baby and was asleep in an instant, even though Mary Alice was snoring like a lumberjack.

When he did wake up, Mary Alice was nestled into her pillows beside him. That was one thing he hadn't known. Pregnant women seemed to need a pillow between their knees and under their belly, as well as their head. They took up most of the bed.

She was staring at him. "I'm so proud of you."

He gave her a sad smile. "I couldn't save them all."

"But you did the best you could."

He put his very sore arm under his head. "That doesn't mean anything, when men who are scared to death look at you as their only hope, and you can't help them."

She held the sheets up to her chin. "Am I being terribly selfish if I say I don't want you to be a lightkeeper anymore?"

"No. You sound exactly like my mother, who'd say the same thing every time my dad had a rescue. And then a month would go by, and a year, without anything happening, so she'd forget about it." He winced as he moved on the bed and held his hand to his ribs.

"You must be so sore. Let me look at you." Mary Alice took a peek under the old shirt he wore at night. "Good god! You're covered with purple bruises! Maybe your ribs are broken!"

"Don't be foolish," Hardy grumbled. "Everyone who was out there is covered in bruises. It comes with the territory. I'm not traipsing to the mainland to have the doctor tape me up. I can do that here if I have to. It's not that bad, so stop fussing."

She wasn't fussing, she was concerned. The father of her child risked life and limb for strangers, and if something happened to him, her life would be thrown into chaos. And then she thought about those young men and how it must have felt to see Hardy and the others rowing towards them. They were heroes.

After making everyone miserable with her complaints about how this baby was making her wait and why couldn't it just arrive already, Mary Alice went into labour on Easter Sunday morning, early. Mary had been with Rose for a week waiting for the blessed event.

She was still not bad in the afternoon, chatting with the ladies. Jane had brought two-month-old Louie over so he could be spoiled by two grandmothers. He was getting quite chunky. "Look at the rolls on those little legs," Mary tsked. "I can't imagine this baby will have rolls. Scrawny chicken legs, more like it."

"You'll have to love it anyway," Mary Alice told her before she felt a big contraction. All the women stopped talking when she rubbed her belly and put her head down to breathe. Suddenly she felt like a laboratory specimen. All they needed were charts and pens to write down their observations.

An hour later, Jane went home with Louie, kissing her friend before she left. “I can’t wait to hear.”

Hardy came in to check on her and she told him to go. “You’re making me nervous.” The poor man rushed out the door and went into his mother’s kitchen to grab a whole handful of molasses cookies to stuff in his mouth before heading back to the lighthouse.

Soon after that, Mary Alice’s mother, sister, and mother-in-law took her up to bed. They had everything they needed. Hot water, towels, scissors, extra sheets, water to drink. They were more than ready. The only one who wasn’t was the baby. Mary kept checking to see how dilated she was, and she seemed ready, but she wasn’t progressing.

Mary Alice was very stoic, but the longer it took the more painful it was. “Why is this taking so long? I’m frightened. Is something wrong with the baby?”

The three experts conferred at the end of the bed. Annie wrung her hands. “You don’t think the baby’s breech?”

Rose nixed that. “Her doctor would’ve picked up on that. She had an appointment a week ago.”

“Well, it’s not good to have her linger like this. I hope the umbilical cord isn’t wrapped around its neck.” Mary bit her lip. She wasn’t nearly as relaxed as she thought she’d be, because this was her child having a child. “I’m going to check things out with my finger.”

Mary told Mary Alice what she was going to do and said it was a standard procedure. Nothing to worry about. Annie took one hand and Rose the other, reassuring her, while Mary gently felt around the birth canal. The head was where it should’ve been and Mary was about to pull away when she felt a little hand grab her finger, so she gently pushed it back up and out of the way. The hand had been holding up the works.

Mary looked up at the other two. "I think I solved it."

The dam burst, and now when Mary Alice pushed Mary could see the head progress. Five more big pushes and Mary and Annie's granddaughter arrived, her screams exactly like her mother's had been. Mary Alice started to cry and they quickly went to work; cut the cord, cleaned up the baby and the afterbirth, all of them ecstatic.

When Mary Alice held her child, for once in her life she was speechless. She wasn't a scrawny chicken because she had her daddy in her, but the hair was Mary Alice's.

She heard Hardy run up the stairs. "Fred told me he heard a baby crying! Can I come in?"

His mother opened the door and beamed at him, but knew better than to get in his way. He sat on the bed and put his hands over his face. Mary Alice took one away.

"It's okay. It's real. She's here."

Imagine having a little one wave hello to you before she's even breathing air. This was a story that would be told endlessly, about how Annabelle Jane Campbell was in an all-fire hurry to introduce herself.

I was happy that Hardy had something to take his mind off the drowned sailors. One of them was found a few days later along the beach, but the other two were never seen again. All of their spirits left quickly. Only the man on the rock rescued by Hardy and the others lingered, as if to give thanks for their efforts on his behalf. He even acknowledged me, knowing I was connected to Hardy. And then he disappeared back to his home and his people.

This wreck affected Aisling dearly. She was so afraid for Hardy that she spent the entire time winging her way through the storm, letting it lash her about and shrieking her fury, demanding no misfortune ever find him.

She let me comfort her for the first time in a very long time and I felt like a bit of a mother too.

In the blink of an eye children grow up.

Annabelle and Louie were in their terrible twos and would spend most of their time hitting each other and yelling, "Mine!"

To Jane's way of thinking, Mary Alice was her sister and Annabelle, her niece. She couldn't imagine her life without them. And because she still wrote to Stuart from time to time, she considered him an uncle to Louie. Especially when a big red truck showed up in the mail with his congratulations on having a little boy. Sam thought that was a wonderful gesture and even wrote to thank Stuart himself, after Jane put the paper, envelope, and stamp on the table. She also walked it to the post office.

It was hard to believe that next year would be 1950. It wasn't possible that nine years ago her family had died. Almost a decade, and despite thinking she wouldn't last a day on this island, here she was three years later, still managing without a tub in the house.

Life was a little easier now that Sam would take her and Louie on a boat and drive it to Port Morien, where Uncle Howard and Aunt Muriel would pick them up so they could spend three days playing with Louie, and Jane spent that time lying around in the bath.

She was sitting on her whale stool, letting Louie play outside in a galvanized tub half full of water, on a beautiful July day, with her white wash blowing in the scented breeze. She looked out and could see Sam and Bob in the boat across the harbour, hauling lobster traps in the shimmering water. Now she understood why Sam had missed this place so much. On days like this it was paradise, with a bowl of wild strawberries to pop into Louie's mouth. He would point at them. "Pweese."

The calm was broken when Mary Alice and Annabelle came around the corner. The minute Annabelle saw the water, she wanted in, so her mother stripped her down and plunked her beside Louie.

"We'll change the water in a half an hour. It'll be full of pee by then."

Jane offered her a strawberry. "What are you up to this morning?"

Mary Alice ate it. "I've come to tell you I'm pregnant."

"Wow. I'm surprised it took that long. Every time Hardy looks at you, you know what he's thinking."

"Well, it wasn't for lack of trying. Did you hear the Buckleys and Halls are leaving? That's five more kids gone from the school. We're getting smaller all the time. It's so sad."

"But how can they afford to find another house?"

"Most people around here have relatives to stay with for a while until they get sorted and the men find new work. Look at my parents." Mary Alice looked over the water. "You know, this place was bustling once, especially in the summers when fishermen would come over and stay in huts by the beach. The fishermen's union started a cooperative store and factory in 1934. And I can remember a Credit Union set up for the fishermen here in the mid-thirties too."

Jane looked confused. "Do you mean an actual building? I can't imagine that."

"I think they started a building, but it wasn't finished. The residents were the officers. People could borrow or deposit money. And now we don't have anything like that anymore. It's like watching our lifeblood seep away. There were twenty families here during the war. I'm so glad I was born when I was. Sam, Hardy, and I had a wonderful childhood." She shook her head. "Poor Annabelle and Louie will have no one left by the time they go to school."

Jane smiled at them. "Thank goodness they have each other."

Annabelle hit Louie and he hit her back and they both began to cry and looked to their mothers for sympathy. Mary Alice clapped her hands at them. "Stop it! Or you're both getting out."

That kept them going for another fifteen minutes and then the fight resumed. Mary Alice picked up her naked daughter and slung her over her hip. Jane passed her the clothes. "I'll see ya later. This one should probably go down for a nap. She had a restless night."

"See ya."

Now that he was alone, Louie didn't want to be in the tub, so he gingerly stepped out and walked his dripping little bum through the kitchen door.

Sam was relishing this perfect day, even as they pulled traps out of the water, weighing and banding the lobsters' claws. They were getting good catches this year. All the fishermen said so. The two of them stopped for lunch and ate the sandwiches Jane made for them.

Bob was smoking even as he ate. "Your missus is getting better at this stuff. This isn't half bad."

Sam pointed at the house. "Say that loud enough for her to hear you and you'll be making your own lunches. Look, she's out there now, hanging up the sheets. Go on, tell her."

Bob squinted. "Might have to find myself a woman."

Sam choked on his food before he wheezed, "You?'

"Why not? I'm only thirty-two."

"Christ almighty, you look fifty-two. Maybe if you cut your hair once in a while and shaved that scraggly beard of yours."

Bob nodded. "I was at Mullins's the other day and who walked in but Ian. I didn't even know him. He looked like a banker."

"He's doing well for himself. He'll be the owner of that store before too long. At least one of us will be successful."

"Jesus b'y, go 'way with ya." Bob threw his butt in the water. "Just because he's wearing nice pants doesn't mean he's better than us. He used to fish too."

Sam put the last piece of bread in his mouth. "I always knew he never really liked it, not like us. I can't imagine any other life. You?"

"Nope. I'm happy to stay here forever."

"Me too. Although my wife might have something to say about that."

They came in mid-afternoon. They'd been out since five. Jane made Sam wash up before snuggling Louie. "Woman, this boy is going to be covered in fish guts before long. It's his fate."

"Nope." She laughed. "He's going to be a surgeon."

"A surgeon?"

"It just popped into my head."

"Great. He'll have human guts all over him. Is that any better?"

After dinner, Louie sat with his uncle Bob and played with his beard. Jane sipped her tea. "You have a nice way with little kids. You should have one of your own."

"Maybe. Gotta gets a woman first."

She nodded. "To get one of those, you have to go out and look for one. They're not going to show up on their own. Ask Jean if she knows anyone."

He jiggled Louie on his knee. "Nah, too much work."

Jane rolled her eyes at Sam. He shrugged.

A couple of days after that, Bob said he was going duck hunting, and asked Sam if he wanted to go. Sam hesitated.

"Lord tunderin', you always loved duck hunting. I'm getting tired of doing it on my own. No one's going to shoot you. You need to try, otherwise you'll never hunt again, and we could use some deer meat. You were always the better shot."

Sam remembered what Jane had said. That if he knew the sound was coming, it wouldn't be so startling.

She and Louie were over visiting Mary Alice, so he left a note on the table.

Gone duck hunting.

He'd forgotten how great it was to be in a small boat, rifle at his side, on the lookout for birds. He asked Bob to fire a shot to see how he reacted to it. And when he did, it wasn't anything like the gunfire overseas. Jane was right. Sam knew it was coming, and the sound reverberating over the water brought back memories of his childhood, shooting ducks with his dad, not of those awful years at war.

Why hadn't he tried this before now? He felt better about everything. The last piece was in place. He was himself again. What a lucky guy. A beautiful wife and son, great friends, a home he loved. Life was good.

He and Bob laughed and snorted at all the memories with their old man outside, hunting together, the campfires and the nonsense. "Remember when Curly O'Neill almost shot Da's head off? His eyes were as crooked as me arse. Da kept that hat with the hole through it even though Ma hated to look at it."

Sam chuckled. "Remember when Da's jacket caught fire roasting wieners and he had to roll around on the sand to put it out, and then after it was out Lauchie Timmons threw a bucket of water in his face and half drowned him?"

They had so much fun they almost forgot to shoot at the birds. Sam got one and they rowed over to get it. "Ya know, what we need is a dog to fetch it." They pulled it in and kept it at their feet. "Yes sirree. We should get a dog." Sam grew pensive. He paused to light another smoke and took a drag. "You know, I loved Buster. I swear that mutt kept me company on that endless march."

"What do you mean?" Bob asked.

"Maybe I'm nuts, but I felt him at my feet. I wasn't alone. And when that happened, I'd remember the times Hardy and Mary Alice and I were with him, and those memories would take me away from where I was. A couple hours would go by and I wasn't marching. He took me home."

Sam sighed and put the oar back in the water, cigarette dangling from his lips. "Yep, all little kids should have a dog. Louie would love it. That's just what I'm gonna do. Surprise him with a puppy."

Jane got back and saw the note on the table. She was happy for Sam. She knew it bothered him to not be able to hunt. This was how the people lived here. They needed meat and didn't always have money to buy it. To track a deer or point a gun in the sky as ducks and geese flew overhead was an everyday occurrence, as were a jig and fishing line with a mackerel at the end of it.

She gave Louie his supper and started on theirs. She had leftover chicken, so she made a chicken pie, since she was very good with crust now. Far better than Mary Alice, which she never let her friend forget.

It was done in no time and she took it out of the oven, wondering when the boys would be coming back. Eventually she ate hers, then got Louie ready for bed.

Louie was quick to fall asleep; he and Annabelle had run around the lighthouse all afternoon with Hardy chasing them. They played hide-and-seek, too, and neither one of them was great at it, thinking that if their heads were hidden, their bodies didn't matter. Mary Alice and Jane almost peed themselves laughing at those two.

Jane sat on the couch and listened to the radio while she tried to knit. Now that was something Mary Alice was good at, but Jane's efforts always looked like something a cat would throw up. She kept looking at the clock. She had no idea how long it took to hunt a duck, but she started to get uneasy when the sun went down. Surely they wouldn't shoot at night?

It was Hardy who saw a flashlight coming towards the house. "Were you expecting anybody?"

"No." Mary Alice was doing Annie's crossword puzzles. "What's another word for disaster? Seven letters."

"Tragedy."

The door opened and the blustering wind came in with it. Jane had her sleeping child in her arms.

Mary Alice stood up and Hardy went over to her. "What's wrong?"

"Sam and Bob went duck hunting. Shouldn't they be back by now?"

When Hardy and Mary Alice looked at each other, Jane knew the answer.

Forgive me. I can't speak about this just now.

CHAPTER TWENTY-ONE

Everyone on the island was searching, but it was Mrs. Wadden's husband who found the boat the next afternoon, broken up on the rocks. Hardy crouched down and wept, knowing he had to tell the girls. "What happened?!" he cried out. "What the hell happened?" The others on the beach didn't answer.

The wind had picked up later in the day, but if any two men could get out of that situation, it was Sam and Bob. It didn't make sense. Nothing made sense. As Hardy sat on the rocks, he saw Ian and Jean come running down the shore. Jean collapsed before she got there, and Ian had to hold her up.

"I don't understand." Ian looked pleadingly at Hardy. "How many times have they been out in a boat on the water? The weather wasn't even that bad. How is this possible?"

Hardy shook his head. Old Charlie Barnstable mumbled, "The sea has no favourites."

Jean's face was wet with tears. "Have you found them? Do we at least have their bodies?"

"Not yet."

She put her arms around Ian and sobbed. "We're the only ones left, Ian. The only ones left."

Now that they knew they were looking for bodies, the fishermen fanned out along the coast and some boats went out to search the water. They knew the currents and headed to the places their bodies might have drifted.

Hardy walked back with Ian and Jean and went into the Harris house. Both Jane and Mary Alice leapt up, but immediately knew it was over. The three women collapsed together on the couch and held each other. Hardy and Ian sat at the kitchen table and shook their heads in disbelief.

Ian looked over at the distraught trio and whispered, "Jean will never get over this, and Mary Alice? And what is Jane supposed to do? She can't live here alone."

Hardy said, "I don't know, Ian. I can't..." He put his head down and couldn't speak.

Ian rubbed his shoulder. "I know, buddy, I know. You were closer to him than I was. You were his chosen brother."

Mary Alice and Jean spent the night with Jane. Ian stayed with a friend on the island, and Hardy carried Louie over to Annie. He kissed the top of Louie's little head, vowing to be there for him throughout his life, because he knew that's what Sam would want.

They arranged a memorial once again at the Catholic church in Main-à-Dieu so the brothers' relatives could be there. Howard and Muriel, Fabian, Lucille, Danny, and Ruthanne. Danny was distraught. As they started singing the second hymn, *Sailor, speed thee o'er the sea, thy home and friends are far away,* he couldn't take anymore and walked out. There were many more Jane had never met. And because this was a tragic story, the church was completely packed, with people standing outside. Of course everyone wanted to see the English war bride. Widow.

Jane wasn't even aware they were there. She did what Mary Alice told her to, and if she felt she couldn't stand it anymore, Mary

Alice and Hardy said they would take her home. Hardy had his arm around her in the front pew as they listened to the service. It was nearly over when she looked up at him. "I need to see Louie."

They got up and left. Jane lifted her head and saw Howard and Muriel sitting in a pew by the aisle, so she quickly hugged both of them and said she would bring Louie over to see them, but she didn't wait to hear their reply.

Jean and Ian made an effort to be there talking to the relatives over tea and sweets, to take the pressure off Jane and those who were slightly scandalized that Sam's wife didn't stay for the whole service.

It was another sparkling day and the water was flat calm. For the first time Jane was glad to be on a small boat as the salty, refreshing wind hit her face and blew her hair about once she pulled her hat off. The sun bathed them in warmth and the cool spray felt good on her arms.

Both Hardy at the wheel and Jane on the bench beside her were lost in their own thoughts.

They were coming up to Eastern Harbour when Jane poked Hardy in the back and signalled him to turn off the motor. The boat slowed and rocked with the sudden stop. He turned around. "You all right?"

"I just need it to be quiet for a minute. I want to hear the gulls and the waves slapping on the boat." She put her hand over the side and pulled it back and forth through the bluish green water, not saying anything. She knew her friends would wait all day if they had to.

Jane didn't want to cry anymore. Not this minute, anyway. Sam told her not to. She heard him as if he were whispering in her ear.

And he was. He and Bob were with them the whole time. It's never easy to see one's family so distraught. But we stay close to try and comfort them.

They rocked in the water for quite some time.

And then Jane spoke. “It was around this spot that I last saw Sam and Bob in the boat fishing, a few days before they died. Remember, Mary Alice? The kids were in the tub.”

Mary Alice nodded and smiled.

“Is it awful to say that I’m glad we didn’t find their bodies? I don’t think they want us to find them. They’re exactly where they want to be. And they have each other, which makes this easier to bear.” She gazed out over the water and pointed. “Look. I can see our place from here. I wonder if they saw us that day.”

“Knowing old eagle eyes, he probably did,” Mary Alice said. “He couldn’t hear that well but he never missed a trick.”

Jane turned to Hardy. “Thank you. This is my memorial, not the one on the mainland. We are the three people Sam loved most in all the world, except for Louie. We’re all here. Let’s send them both a kiss from us.”

They kissed the tops of their fingers and held their hands over the water. The wind came and took their love away with it.

Do I know what it’s like to drown with a sibling? I never wanted this for Sam or Bob, but their lives were over in this world. I knew that, but it still broke my heart. Aisling disappeared with the island seals, Buster by her side. She might not come up for ages, but I knew they would take care of her.

I can tell you how it happened, and it’s so ridiculous that Sam and Bob don’t want me to tell you, but I know you are invested in this story and deserve to know. Yes, it was a little choppy, but nothing to worry two lifelong fishermen. They had six ducks and thought they’d head home, when Bob stood up to pee over the side. Sam made fun of him for how long it was taking, and Bob took a pretend swing at him just as the boat hit a larger wave, and because he was so close to the edge, he lost his balance and tumbled in to the water.

At first Sam laughed. "You're gonna get cold, buddy."

Bob said, "Piss off," as the waves hit him. That struck them both as funny and Bob swallowed some saltwater as he laughed.

Sam held out the oar. "Here, grab it." Bob reached for it, but it slipped out of his hand because he had a cramp in his leg that wouldn't let him straighten up. Another couple of waves took the boat farther away from him.

"Just a sec," Sam hollered and rowed back around to get closer. By the time he did, Bob's head was a little farther down in the water. "I'm coming. Do you hear me?"

It worried Sam that Bob didn't answer, and he didn't because Bob was trying to keep his mouth out of the waves, but he swallowed more seawater, which he knew wasn't good. His head went right under and he could see Sam in the boat and wanted to tell him to stay put, to not jump off the boat.

But when your brother or sister is drowning, common sense disappears.

Sam jumped off the boat to get Bob's head to the surface, but he was heavier, his clothes completely sodden with water. He managed for a moment, enough for Bob to cry, "Leave me. Get back in the boat."

"I've got ya, you bastard. Swim!" And as soon as Sam said it, he remembered that Bob was lousy at swimming. They used to joke about it.

When you're drowning, you do and you don't realize it. You think it can't possibly be happening, and yet your body knows it is. Bob knew he was, but Sam didn't believe it. Bob tried to take Sam's hands off him so his brother wouldn't sink along with him, but the more he struggled, the more Sam held on.

Sam forgot he had a wife and son. He only remembered the big brother who used to carry him on his shoulders when they were kids.

I know how that is. When you feel them slipping away from you, you can't let them go.

The absolute worst thing for Jane was when Louie would cry for his daddy and Bobo. Now she knew what hell was. It wasn't freezing outhouses and no running water. It was a little boy who would wait by the back door looking for his father and uncle to walk up the hill and wave at him at the end of the day.

He cried every night. And Jane would cry when her son finally fell asleep. She was in limbo. She didn't know what to do. She felt frozen. And one night Mary Alice asked one too many times what her plans were.

"Do you want me to go? This minute? Back to England?"

"Of course not."

"I don't have anyone there! It's not my home anymore, only a place with a lot of sad memories."

Mary Alice wrung her hands. "Okay. I'll stop asking. I just worry about you."

Jane dropped her head on the back of the couch. "I know that. I'm not angry with you. I'm angry at those two daft buggers who had to head out to shoot a stupid duck. How could they have been so careless? What did Sam think would happen to me and Louie if he drowned? Or did he even think of that? Is drowning so common here, no one gives it a second thought?"

"Kind of."

Jane put a flat pillow over her face. It was so old the fluffy had gone out of it years ago. She screamed into it. "I hate this place and I love this place. I have no idea who I am anymore now that Sam is gone."

"Well, you're Louie's mom."

"Thank god for that. I have a little piece of Sam alive with me. But how am I supposed to raise him?"

Mary Alice was floundering, trying to be helpful without breaking down. The fact that they were even having this conversation was so horrific she wanted to run out of the house, go down to the beach, and scream into the wind. Instead, she took a breath. "You'll have to move from here and get a job. You worked in a restaurant. You could move to Glace Bay and do that. I'll be bereft, of course, but this isn't about me."

Jane made a face. "Everything is about you, and you know it." She looked at the ceiling as if it had the answers. "Any road, who would look after him while I work? And don't say Howard and Muriel. They're delightful but too old to be running after a toddler."

"I could watch him. You could come home on weekends."

"What a load of tosh," Jane sighed.

Mary Alice snapped her fingers. "I've got it. Jean could look after him."

"What's she got now? About six kids. I can't keep up with her and her pregnancies."

Now Mary Alice pointed. "What about Ian and Judy?"

"She's pregnant. Ian told me at the memorial. Stop trying to give my kid away. Look, I have to stop talking. I've got a migraine."

Getting off the couch, she looked down at Jane. "If you need me..."

"...I'll ring you. Actually, I won't. We don't have a phone."

When the door shut behind her, Mary Alice didn't know what to do. She wished her mother was here, so she walked twenty steps and opened the door to the next best thing.

"Rose?"

Jeb turned around and put his finger on his lips. "She's putting the kids down. They're all in trouble."

"Oh no. What happened?"

"They cut each other's hair with the sheep shears."

She immediately thought of Annabelle's beautiful locks and cringed. "The little bastards, as Sam would say." She dropped into the familiar kitchen chair and hid her face. "I miss him so much."

"I have to say, the place isn't the same without him," Jeb said sadly. "Now Bob, you'd never know he was around, except when you needed help, but Sam would have you in stitches first thing in the morning as you were getting your gear ready to go out. I wonder what happened?"

Mary Alice raised her head and held her chin up with her fist, sighing. "They landed in the water and drowned. Flies do it all the time."

Jeb frowned. "You spend your whole life on a boat but you never think it's gonna happen to you. They were experienced seamen."

"It's simple, I think one of them somehow fell in and the other one tried to save him."

Jeb nodded. "It's the only sensible explanation. But what a senseless waste."

"And I know full well if that's what happened, it was Sam trying to save Bob. He was always too stubborn for his own good."

Rose came down the stairs and looked like she'd been crying. "Those bloody kids. They're all going to have to go to school in September looking like Alfalfa, even the girls."

Mary Alice crossed her arms. "In the scheme of things, it's not that important, is it? Not when Jane is crying every night trying to figure out what to do."

Now Rose crossed her arms. "I know that, obviously. What is she going to do?"

Mary Alice's only response was to shrug her shoulders. "Do you have any suggestions?"

"No. I hate to say it, but she's frigged, isn't she? Like every woman who doesn't have a job or husband, but has a child to feed. It's beyond sad. Especially when she doesn't have her own kin around her. She's very lucky she has you and Hardy, but at some point, even you guys won't be able to help."

As Mary Alice trudged home after that totally unsatisfactory visit with her now not-so-favourite sister, she looked up at the first stars visible in the twilight. "Sam, you better tell us what to do, because we're running out of ideas."

That night in bed, she snuggled next to Hardy. The best place in the whole world. "Okay, I've told you before, you have to promise not to die before I do."

"I already told you. I promise."

Placated, now she had to bring up something else and she wasn't sure how it would go over. Rubbing his arm, she said, "I think we should think seriously about leaving this place. I don't want you drowning trying to save someone else from drowning. There have to be better jobs. I mean, I love it here, and would stay if there was a machine shop you could work in, but I can see the pain Jane and Louie are in, and I don't want that for Annabelle and this little one."

Hardy took a deep breath and let it out slowly. "If we leave, this whole family leaves. We have to take my mother and brothers with us."

"Well, maybe not Fred. He seems to enjoy working on the light."

"So, you don't mind him drowning, is that it?"

She punched his shoulder and Toby looked up from the bottom of the bed and barked at her.

Little did she know that Hardy had been thinking the same thing. Losing Sam made living here not quite as wonderful as it once was. Everywhere he looked, everywhere he walked, a memory would pop up and make him miserable all over again. He was definitely at a crossroads himself, but he kept it close to his chest. He wanted to see how it played out with Jane. Who knew? He might be responsible for her and Louie as well.

He had always planned on being in their lives, but now they might actually be living their lives with him. And he didn't mind, but he needed Jane to figure it out for herself.

One night, while Louie walked around the kitchen with a tea towel on his head pretending to be Annabelle with her long hair, Jane giggled and turned her head to share the moment with Sam, when she remembered he wasn't there.

After Louie went to bed, she stood in the back doorway to look out over the water where she'd seen him last.

"Please tell me what to do, Sam."

Sam did the best he could. That night she had a dream about Louie's red truck, and it reminded her that in all the commotion she had never let Stuart know Sam had died. Louie wasn't even up when she sat at the kitchen table.

Dear Stuart,

I have some terrible news and I'm sorry I should have told you three weeks ago but I couldn't think straight. This is the first time I'm writing it down and now it seems real.

Sam is dead. He drowned with his brother Bob when they were duck hunting. Thank god for my friends Mary Alice and Hardy. I don't know what I would have done without them. I honestly don't know what to do. But I thought you should know. You and Sam were close at one point in time. I always think of you so fondly because you were there the day Sam and I got married. I'm sorry to be the bearer of such awful news.

Yours, Jane

P.S. Louie still loves that red truck.

She addressed it, and when Louie had his bowl of porridge, she took him and walked up to the post office and mailed it. On the way back she stopped at a place where she could look at the harbour from a different vantage point and remember the day Sam and Bob were on the boat. Louie sat in the grass and watched a little hole where minuscule ants were coming in and out, taking one grain of sand out at a time and dumping it before disappearing back down. It gave Jane a chance to think.

The letter to Stuart was the first time she'd written down *Sam is dead.*

The man who loved it when she put her hair up so he could kiss the back of her neck wasn't here anymore. Where had he gone? All the things he loved. And hated, like itchy wool socks and the runny white on a not-quite-boiled egg.

She tried to be truthful to herself and admit there were times when she didn't like some of his behaviour, like his temper and drinking too much and lapsing into bad grammar. When she found out he was only thirteen when he left school, she was shocked. Aunt Lou would have fainted dead away. There was no way she would have let her leave England if she'd known.

And yet, he was so smart with the things he did know. He knew everything about boats and fishing. He would take her around the island and show her plants and animals, and they'd lie out in the field some nights just to look at the stars, and he'd point out the North Star. "Da always said it was the most important one, because its position is constant and it makes navigation on the water easier."

Then she remembered soon after she'd arrived on the island, they went for a walk in the twilight, their arms around each other. The first stars appeared above in a sky that seemed endless looking out over the water. He had kissed her hand and said, "If you ever need help, look at the North Star and it will guide you home."

So that night, when she put Louie to bed, she got a blanket and stepped out by the clothesline, the back door open so she could hear if Louie cried out. She lay down and looked for the North Star. There were so many twinkling on this night that she thought she couldn't see it, and that upset her, but she took a deep breath and pretended Sam was next to her and eventually she was sure she had it. She remembered he told her to look for the Big Dipper and she had no idea what he meant. He explained as best he could and she realized he meant the Plough.

She looked for that and found it. It was brighter than the stars around it, but not the brightest. Something else he knew.

She was getting chilly now, so she wrapped her arms around herself and made a promise. "When I need help, I'll look for you. I know you're here. It's not possible that you aren't. Watch over us."

I can tell you that of course Sam was with me watching her. So was Bob. At first Sam was unsure of who I was, but when I told him I'd been with him all his life, he knew. He'd never seen me like

Mary Alice had, but he asked me if I was with him on his march and I told him I was. And Buster told him he was too, and Sam was delighted to know he was right. Buster was now dividing his time between Hardy and Sam and Aisling. Did I mention that we can be with everyone at the same time?

Bob was a shyer character and didn't say much but stayed close to his brother. Although he was the one who understood their wish had come true. They would always be here on Scatarie.

Sam was still wrapped up in his concern for Jane and Louie. I told him that would ease as the universe unfolded.

During the second week in September, they had the type of day that Hardy always called hit-and-miss showers, and on top of that a light fog decided to show up. It certainly didn't feel like summer.

Once again, Mary Alice was over with Annabelle so the kids could play together. Despite the weather, Jane sat on her whale stool peeling spuds. Mary Alice was keeping an eye on the little ones so they didn't wander off.

A boat came into the harbour, like the one Jane came home on with Louie, able to pull up on shore. A fisherman got out, and then someone Mary Alice didn't recognize. "God in heaven, I hope that's not a government man. You never know what those characters want."

Jane looked up then and had to squint her eyes to see through the fog. She immediately got to her feet and ran down the hill. The man held out his arms and she ran into them. They rocked back and forth, holding each other close.

"Holy mother," Mary Alice murmured.

Louie started after his mom, but Mary Alice picked him up by the seat of the pants, grabbed Annabelle by the hand, and hightailed it into the house. She had no idea what was going on, but she knew she'd know soon enough, so she made herself busy and brewed some tea. She gave the kids an apple each to shut them up.

She didn't have to wait long; the rain was now hitting more than missing, so the two friends came in the door. Jane looked like she'd been crying.

"Mary Alice, this is our friend Stuart Campbell from Halifax. He was the best man at our wedding."

Stuart came forward with a big smile on his face and shook her hand. "It's so nice to meet you. Jane has told me how much you and your husband have done for her. She's lucky to have such good friends."

Mary Alice smiled up at him, still astonished by their embrace on the shore. "You're a great friend too if you managed to get here from Halifax. Most people wouldn't know how." She pointed at the table. "Have some hot tea to warm your bones after that boat ride. It's not fit out today. And these are my mother-in-law's raisin tarts."

Jane lifted Louie up on her hip. "This is our son, Louie."

Stuart laughed. "Good old Aunt Lou comes back to life." He reached over to tousle his hair but Louie hid his face in his mother's dress. "Hello, young man. Gotta say, he looks like his dad."

Jane put him down. "Go get your red truck."

Louie went underneath the open stairs where he always parked it, and drove it over, with sound effects.

Stuart laughed. "You're going to be a construction worker."

Annabelle tried to grab it, but Louie was too quick, so miracle of miracles, she sat down on the floor and munched on her apple.

"This is Mary Alice's and Hardy's daughter, Annabelle. Louie's best friend."

"She's beautiful. And so well behaved."

Her mother shook her head. "She's a brat, but she's our brat. Come sit."

Once they sipped their tea and had a few mouthfuls, Mary Alice had to know. "When did you meet Sam?"

"In London, while we were waiting to be shipped home. We found out we were both from Nova Scotia and that was it. There's nothing like having someone from home to make you feel better when you're overseas. And who didn't like Sam? He was the life of the party in barracks. He'd tell more tales about this island. In the end we all wanted to come here." Stuart took another mouthful of tea. "And he spoke very fondly of his two pals, Mary Alice and Hardy. I remember thinking I wished I had friends I was that close to."

Mary Alice nodded and looked out the window, determined to keep composed, so she quickly asked, "And what do you do?"

"I'm studying to be a doctor. Trying to be like my old man. The war delayed my plans."

She suddenly realized she was monopolizing the conversation and sprang to her feet. "I hate to eat and run, but why don't I take the kids with me so you two can have a bit of quiet?"

Jane flashed her a smile. "Thanks."

Mary Alice put their jackets on.

"But it's raining out," Stuart said.

"Stuart, these are island children. Dry, wet, cold, hot. It matters not a whit." And out the door she went, the two little ones chatting behind her.

"You see? She's amazing. Like a sister."

Stuart put his hand over hers. "Tell me what happened."

They talked for two hours. It's always helpful to be able to speak about a lost loved one. It brings them back again. In the end, they were crying with laughter, remembering Sam and Aunt

Lou and the time he took the spoon out of the sugar bowl, licked it clean, and put it back.

They went over to the couch and Stuart looked around. “This is very...minimal, isn’t it?”

“That’s a nice word. I have to say I was in total shock when I arrived. It’s still shocking to think there’s no electricity or running water, but you can get used to anything if you are with someone you love.” She looked over at the kitchen window. “And now he’s not here. Everything is different.”

“You’re a strong woman, Jane. No wonder Sam loved you. But what will you do now that everything is different? Can you live here by yourself? In the winter?”

She rubbed the back of her neck to ease the constant pain. “My heart says yes but my head says no. I’m probably not going to be able to stay, as much as I want to, for Louie’s sake. That poor child is still crying for his daddy, and taking him away from Mary Alice and Annabelle will be like him losing even more family members. But I also want to stay for my sake. I can see Sam out the window every time I look. As much as I couldn’t imagine living here when I first arrived, now I can’t imagine leaving it. He was my husband.”

Stuart nodded. “But can I say one thing?”

“Sure.”

“Louie is two. As long as he still has his mother, he’ll be fine. And as for you, do you realize you only knew Sam for four years? That’s a very short time in a very long life. Of course you loved him and don’t want to leave your home, but when circumstances change, you have to change with them. You’ve already done that, so many times. Many more times than you should have had to. It’s a lot to ask, but it seems to me you’ve proven yourself to be resilient, like Aunt Lou. I’m ashamed to say that I couldn’t live like this. Having to take a boat whenever I want to go somewhere? Not having a shower or a telephone?"

Jane didn't say anything at first, and then got annoyed. She needed to stick up for her home. "It's not that primitive. I've kept my child alive."

He held his hands up, feeling slightly embarrassed. "I didn't come here to tell you what to do."

She looked at him. "Why did you come, then?"

"To give you my condolences, to offer support, and to let you know I'm always out there if you need a friend." He reached for her hand and held it in a comforting way. "If you do have to leave and return to England, please know you can always stay with my family for as long as you need, to get yourself sorted. You're not alone in this world. I know how difficult it will be to lose your friends here." He looked at his watch. "I better make tracks. That fisherman is coming back for me. I'm taking the train to Halifax in the morning. I have exams on Friday."

She was surprised. "Oh, this really is a flying visit. I was trying to think of where you'd stay tonight to keep the neighbours from talking."

He gave a half smile. "No need. I assumed we'd be able to hash it out over tea and I was right. Listen, Jane, whatever you decide, I'm in your corner. And Sam would want you to do whatever makes you happy, for your sake and for Louie. You're the one looking after his son."

He stood up and looked out the window. "That poor man has returned. I guess we'll both be soaked by the time I get back to that little village, Main something."

"Main-à-Dieu. Hand of God."

He smiled at her. "Do you believe in God?"

Jane looked out the window. "It was hard to when my family was taken from me so brutally, and now Sam...but when I look at our child, I do."

He gave her a big hug. "Wish me luck on my pediatric exam. I'll be studying on the train."

"Thank you for coming all this way. I'll never forget it."

Stuart opened the door and made a dash for it, holding his overcoat above his head. Jane watched him until he got in the boat and waved back at her. She raised her hand and shut the door, bewildered at the effort he'd made just to have a conversation.

Sam, Aunt Lou, and I agreed that Stuart was a very nice man. And he'd make a great doctor.

CHAPTER TWENTY-TWO

Jane kept her word and took Louie over to visit Howard and Muriel. They met her on the wharf in Main-à-Dieu, thanks to a neighbour, Buddy Dan, who was going over anyway. They drove them to Mike's Lunch in Glace Bay, to give Louie his first taste of restaurant food. He was excited about everything—the boat ride, the car ride, and now his hamburger and fries.

Naturally, the first thing Jane did was get in the tub. Muriel had put new towels and bubble bath where she could find them. Laying in the soapy, fragrant hot water, she felt her muscles release. She'd been walking around stiff as a stick, trying to hold everything together. And once her body relaxed, her heart loosened and the tears came, oozing down her cheeks.

It took three straight days of soaking in that tub for Jane to realize what she needed to do. Not for anyone else, just her.

Back they went to the wharf and after lots of thank yous, kisses, and hugs, she and Louie got on Jeb's boat and made their way to the island.

They dropped their bags off, then walked straight to the lighthouse. Hardy saw them coming and Louie ran to him, which made Jane doubt her decision for a moment, but there were going to be massive regrets no matter which way she moved forward. As Stuart said, she had a long life ahead of her.

As they sat around Annie's happy table, Louie told Annabelle that he went to a "resront" and had ice cream. Annabelle folded her arms exactly like her mother and pouted.

Fred and James took the kids into the parlour to play horsey.

Hardy cut himself a piece of pie. "Mary Alice told me what a nice guy Stuart is. Imagine coming all this way just for a couple of hours."

"True." Jane nodded. She didn't really want to talk about him. "I've decided what I'm going to do, and no, it was nothing Stuart said. He doesn't know my plans."

The other three at the table stopped eating.

Jane took a deep breath. "I'm going to have to go. As much as I don't want to. What you don't know is that when my Aunt Lou died, she left me her estate. Not a great deal money wise, but she gave me her home, which was my grandfather's house. I've been renting it out in the meantime, so I'm earning some money from that."

Hardy breathed a little easier. She wasn't completely destitute. "Did Sam know this?"

"No. I'm not sure why I didn't tell him. I wanted to keep it to myself. It was about my family, and everything else we did or had was about his."

"You're going to move back to England?" Mary Alice looked shell-shocked. "But you said you had no family there."

"Not living. But I need to go back to straighten out my affairs, and decide if I'm going to sell the house or keep it. I want to see my parents' and brother's graves, and Aunt Lou's. I need to be near them. Just seeing my grandfather's house again might help me decide what to do. England is Louie's heritage too, remember. Not just this island and boats and fishing. Does that make sense?"

"Perfect sense," said Hardy.

Mary Alice hit him on the shoulder.

Jane put her hand on Mary Alice's arm. "Don't be mad at me. I can't bear to leave you either. I can't bear not having Annabelle be with Louie. I can't bear not being here when your baby comes. But I'm not going to *never* see you again. They have planes now, you know. People do fly in them and visit other countries."

Mary Alice held a napkin to her face and muttered, "It's not like we can afford to hop on a plane. We can only go to Sydney once a month if we're lucky. We'll be stuck here forever."

"But you love it here."

The napkin came down. "Do I? Maybe I don't. Not anymore. Sam's not here. You're not going to be here. My little boy Louie will be gone. My parents have left. Who am I going to hang around with? Flossie? If I want to take a trip to England, Hardy has to stop being a lighthouse keeper and get a job that actually makes enough money for us to do things like that." Mary Alice got up from the table. "I know I'm acting like my daughter, but I can't be here right now."

She went out the kitchen door and banged it behind her.

The other three looked down at the table, Jane with her hands scrunched over her eyes. Hardy pushed his plate away and his mother started sniffing.

"That wasn't a very nice thing to say. My Len was a lighthouse keeper all his life, and he always provided for this family, didn't he?"

Hardy closed his eyes before turning to his mother. "She wasn't taking a potshot at Dad. She's upset that Jane is leaving. And she's right, quite frankly. A lot of the people we love aren't here anymore. Maybe it's time for a change."

Annie stood up, her mouth hanging open. "And leave my home and my wonderful oven? Over my dead body." She burst into tears and ran up the stairs.

James showed up at the door. "What's going on?"

"I'll tell you later," Hardy said. "Keep the kids occupied."

He sat back in his chair until the front legs were off the floor, Toby watching every move he made. "For what it's worth, despite this fiasco, I think you're doing the right thing."

Jane looked up, her eyes red. "Really?"

"And Sam would think so too. Mary Alice will calm down, and whatever happens with this family, we'll sort it. You're not responsible for that. It's honestly been something I've been thinking about. Not just Mary Alice."

Jane gave a great sigh of relief. "Thanks, Hardy. Having you think I'm doing the right thing confirms it for me. You've always been our North Star. Our one true constant."

"And my wife has always been our fickle firecracker. Sometimes she wears me out."

Jane smiled. "Not a chance."

He and Toby walked her and Louie home. On his way back, Hardy sat on the flat rock where he and Sam used to talk. "Christ, I miss you. And if we do leave it'll break my heart, but I'll always come back here to visit with you. You're never far away, buddy."

He went in the house, told James and Fred what everyone's meltdown was about, and then picked up his daughter, went out one door on the porch, and walked in the other. He washed Annabelle's face and hands and put her pyjamas on. She refused to wear a diaper and had basically toilet trained herself. Louie was miles behind her, even though he was two months older.

She had a small crib in the next room, and Toby would stay by it until she was asleep before he'd hop on their bed. Hardy sat on the floor and read *The Pokey Little Puppy*, her favourite. He thought it was too advanced for her, but Mary Alice disagreed, and it turned out she was right. She'd stick her hand out of the bars and twist his hair while she sucked her thumb. "No desserts ever unless puppies never dig holes under this fence again."

He'd close the book and she'd grin. "More." He'd start and only get to page three before she was out.

He got undressed and climbed into bed. Mary Alice was facing the wall but she turned over and cuddled under his arm. "I'm so sad. And as you know, it's all about me."

"I know."

"What am I going to do?"

"You're going to go over there in the morning and tell her that she's doing the right thing for herself and her son. That wherever she lives, you'll always be her best friend. That you'll miss her but you'll be the world's best pen pal."

"Okay."

Jane had to make a lot of arrangements and wait to hear from her solicitor, Mr. Hampton. She wanted to know whether she could move into the house right away or if the renters were locked into a yearly agreement. He wrote back to say no, he'd made sure it was on a monthly basis, in the event she ever changed her mind. Jane wrote immediately to say he was brilliant and couldn't wait to meet him. She also asked him to apologize to the tenants for such short notice.

Then she wrote to Stuart and asked him if he could make arrangements to secure a ticket on a passenger ship from Halifax to Southampton, tourist class, in mid-October. He replied that he was on it. She was able to do it because Mr. Hampton released more money from Aunt Lou's savings. Stuart booked passage on the Cunard Line RMS *Aquitania*. It was $124 one way, as Louie would sleep in the bunk with her.

She knew she might be seasick again, but was counting on her boat experience to mitigate that. She also didn't think she'd be able to take a whale vertebrae and kettle on a plane. Lastly, even though Louie was little, it would be nice for him to watch the waves on the ocean his father loved so much.

She was only taking their clothes and a few belongings. Everything in the house was Jean and Ian's. She had no idea what they would do with it, but that was their problem. Jane spent what little time she had left with Mary Alice, Annabelle, and Hardy when he was off duty.

Mary Alice suggested they go for a hike to take a last look at some of the views. They got the children ready and took a picnic. It was a typical fall day, no wind to speak of. The kids wanted to pat the horses in the field. The mothers put the kibosh on the sheep, pigs, and cows.

They ate molasses sandwiches, everyone's favourite.

"I want you to have the jars of jam your mother taught me how to make," Jane said. "Whenever I see a bakeapple I'll think of that day you told me I was pregnant."

"Do they have bakeapples in England?"

"Probably not. I'm going to take a few jars for myself. Just pack them really well. And I want you to have the bassinet for the new baby—"

"No! You love that bassinet!"

"And I love you. This way I can give baby a cuddle every night. Don't argue with me."

The two of them were running out of things to say to each other. The pending departure was too awful to talk about you. Mary Alice started to pack up. "We should head back. Annie said something about warm chocolate chip cookies."

When they walked in the door, Mary Alice turned around and shouted, "Surprise!" scaring Jane and the little ones. Everyone poured into the kitchen. Annie, Hardy, Fred, James, and Dorothy, with her husband, Lyle. Tom and Mary, Rose and Jeb. All of Sam's relatives. Louie ran to Muriel and Howard. Ian and Judy, Jean and Terry, Fabian and Lucille, Danny and Ruthanne, and other familiar faces. Even Flossie was there.

Mary Alice clapped and clapped. "That's why I took you for a walk to the other side. Everyone had to get off the boats and get up here without you seeing them."

Jane hugged her friend and whispered, "Thank you."

They had a bang-up time. There were so many people talking and laughing at once that no one could hear themselves. They ate the lunch that Annie and the other ladies prepared, plates and plates of sandwiches and sweets, and washed it down with gallons of tea. Some of the men grumbled there was no liquor.

"My lighthouse, my rules!" Hardy shouted.

When they all had a glass in their hand, Mary Alice clinked the side of hers and waited for quiet.

"Now, we all remember when Sam said he was bringing home a war bride. We couldn't believe it. Some more than others." Those in the know laughed, especially Flossie. "But he didn't end up bringing home just a bride who changed his life and his family's forever. He brought me my first female best friend. Hardy and Sam were always teased because I was in their company and wouldn't play with girls, but I stand by that decision."

Mary Alice cleared her throat. "She also brought Sam's son into the world. And he is like a son to us in this household, and now a grandson to Howard and Muriel. All you have to do is look at Louie and his father stares back. We're going to miss those eyes."

She refused to get maudlin so she stood up straight. "But all of us on Scatarie and beyond are glad that we met you, Jane. Got to know you and love you. The rest of your journey will be across the sea, for now. Maybe you'll miss your outhouse so much you'll come running back!"

The crowd laughed again, and Mary Alice thought she could continue, but her voice cracked and she raised her glass instead. "To Jane and Louie. And Sam and Bob."

They all repeated the toast and Jane hid her face in Mary Alice's shoulder. No words were needed.

For a moment the guests wondered if Jane would respond and she did. She was composed and calm.

"This is a wonderful surprise, and I'm so glad you're all here in one place, because I have been practicing what I've wanted to say to all of you, every night when I can't sleep."

She made a sheepish face. "All of you know I cried for the first month I lived here. And many, many more times after that. I heard through the grapevine that I was a wet blanket and needed to haul up my rubber boots and get on with things. And eventually I did. To a point."

She glanced down and then back up. "And the only reason I did was thanks to the women here." She looked at each of them when she said their names. "Mary Alice, Mary, Jean, Rose, Annie, Dorothy, Muriel, and my neighbours, especially poor Theresa at the post office. I've bothered you day and night and you always had a smile on your face."

Now she licked her lips to make sure she could keep going. "When I left England, I had one relative, my Aunt Lou. Sam had plenty of friends here, and he often talked about his two pals who died on the beach in front of him. And then he met Stuart Campbell, who became a friend to both of us. That was all I had, though. Aunt Lou, Sam, and Stuart. No one else. And when Sam and Stuart headed back to Nova Scotia, I realized how lonely I'd been since my family was killed in 1941. Their lives were over, but so was mine."

She held out her hands. "And now look at this. Look at all the people here I can call a friend. Sam told me there weren't many families on Scatarie, but this entire room is full, and I had nobody in one of the most populated cities in the world."

Everyone was getting teary, and she knew that. "And now my life is over again. My Sam is gone. At first, I didn't think I'd live through it, but then I remembered I've done this before. You and your caring, kind ways put me on my feet again, and it gives me the courage to keep going. Sam was right. This island is the best place in the world. I'll miss you."

Well, I don't know about you, but the spirits who love her here were very proud. She reminded me of the great Irish woman warrior Gráinne Ní Mháille, Grace O'Malley to you. The Pirate Queen, born three hundred years before my time.

Sam was doing a jig. Any excuse for a party.

It was the last day. Jane and Louie walked out the door and she didn't look back. Everyone helped put her belongings on the Cape Islander. Ian was at the helm. It was his now, for the time being. Mary Alice and Hardy were going with her to Sydney. Howard left his car on the wharf for them to use, and went back on the S&L train to Glace Bay. He'd return in the morning the same way to retrieve it.

Annie had Annabelle at the shore when she suddenly started waving and Hardy had to go back in the skiff to see what she wanted. "She has to go, Mom, to catch her train."

"I forgot to give her this." She pulled out a small notepad. "All my recipes."

Hardy nodded. "I want a copy of that."

The hardest part for Jane was watching Annabelle get smaller and smaller, still waving and telling Louie to come back. And then the spot in the harbour that would always be Sam and Bob's in her mind.

Hardy held Louie up to point out the round heads of the grey seals popping out of the water. They always did when they heard an engine. Very nosy. Sam used to say, "Like Aunt Muriel and her cronies." Then they looked at the gulls and an eagle and an osprey who came to say goodbye.

Mary Alice and Jane held hands on the back of the boat, not saying a word. The motor was their excuse. Ian pulled up to the wharf and Danny was there to help them unload the baggage into the car. Ian would stay with him until Hardy and Mary Alice came back to the wharf, so he could take them home.

Jane hugged the cousins but didn't say anything. It seemed like if she did, Danny might explode. The four of them got in the car and left, aware that Fabien, Lucille, and Ruthanne were standing outside their house.

It ended up that the only one who said anything on the drive into Sydney was Louie. He pointed at every car that went by. The other three were too dejected.

Now another hauling of luggage out of the car. Jane got their tickets and Hardy carried her possessions right into the train and put half of them on the rack above and a few on the floor by where she'd be sitting. Jane and Mary Alice held their cold cheeks together. "Write to me all the time." Jane kissed her. "Especially when the baby is born. I want pictures!"

Hardy got down off the steps and Jane couldn't do it anymore. She just held out her hand and he gave it a squeeze. Then she and her son got on the train.

The two of them stood outside, with Hardy's arm around Mary Alice, rubbing her arm with his hand every so often. Jane wished they would just leave. She waved at them and mouthed, "Go!" They didn't, until Louie realized they were out there and wanted to be with them. When he put his little hands on the window and shouted at them, Mary Alice turned around and hurried to the car, Hardy in tears behind her.

They sat there until the train left. And then drove back to the wharf, neither one of them speaking. Only when Hardy put the car in park did she say, "We have to get an automobile."

Thank heavens there was an older woman going to Halifax; she was delighted with Louie and kept him entertained the entire time with things from her purse. Jane leaned her head on the window and said goodbye to Cape Breton. Crossing the train bridge was the highlight of Louie's trip but that was her last look.

The woman could see Jane was upset, and reached out. "Just close your eyes. I'll watch him. He's sleepy anyway."

Jane wasn't aware of how weary she was, but suddenly they were pulling into the Halifax station. She blinked and looked around wondering where she was, and then instantly panicked. "Louie!?"

He was sitting on his guardian angel's lap eating a cookie while she read him the train schedule.

"I'm so sorry..."

The woman put her hand up. "Don't be. I remember. I'm glad I could help."

It took quite a while to get her son to cooperate once his babysitter disappeared. The conductor helped with Jane's bags and she held her boy's hand as she stepped onto the platform. If Stuart wasn't—

"Hi!"

Of course, her tall saviour was here. He was like Hardy.

Constant.

Once again it was dealing with suitcases in a car. Then it was out again when Stuart told her that his mother insisted she stay with them for the three days until her ship sailed.

Jane decided to be honest with him. "Look, Louie is still acting up, taking his diaper off and peeing in corners when he gets the chance, crying for Sam, and hitting me. I don't want your mother putting up with that. I told you to tell her not to invite me. I'll be perfectly okay in a hotel room."

Stuart nodded. "You'll be perfectly okay by yourself in a hotel room for three days and then another five or six days on a ship? Firstly, I think you should take the company while you can get it. Secondly, you never say no to my mother, and thirdly, my youngest sister is a great babysitter. Oh yeah. And we have a glorious tub. Not some rinky-dink hotel model."

That sealed the deal.

Stuart was right. Jane needed these few days to get her head straight. So much had happened in a short amount of time, and dealing with Louie being upset had drained her.

Jane felt like a new woman under the Campells' care. Stuart was in class the entire time, but while his sister Deborah played with her new favourite kid, his mother, Annette, had a lot of practical advice for a new widow.

"Don't move for twelve months."

"I just did."

"Right." She washed the beans they were having for dinner. "Don't befriend a man. You're like candy to a baby at this stage."

"Does that include your son?"

She burst out laughing. "Stuart? He doesn't even know what a girl looks like. His head is never out of his books, so you're safe. And what was the other thing? Don't listen to other people."

"Okay."

Jane spent most of her tub time crying quietly. She missed Sam. His smile, his cowlick, the things he'd whisper in her ear before kissing her. "Just be with me."

Her life was going to be lonely. She didn't want to be with another man.

She thanked the Campbells for their incredible generosity, and Stuart drove her and Louie to the docks. Pier 21. It never entered her head; she'd been in such a muddle since Sam's death. The minute they arrived she burst into tears, hanging on to Louie with one hand and Stuart's neck with the other.

"I can't go! Don't leave me! You were here with me last time, and Sam was alive. I never knew what was coming. I can't do this. What am I doing?"

He put his arm around her and patted her back gently. "You *can* do this. You *need* to do this. And if you find things don't work out, you can always come back to me."

She looked at him. "To you?"

He hesitated. "I mean...to me and my family. And Hardy and Mary Alice. You won't be alone, and best of all you'll have a phone, so you can call me."

She calmed down a little. Poor Louie's fingers were almost blue between her squeezing his hand and him pulling against her. She let Stuart go and collected herself. "I'm sorry, I panicked. Being here is like walking into my past." She took a deep breath. "Okay, where do I go?"

They figured it out and her baggage was tended to by someone from the ship and they stood in the lineup with hundreds of others. Louie kept shrieking, "Ship, Mama. Ship!"

Jane held on to Stuart's arm as long as she could, and he put his hand over hers.

"Remember. I'm only a phone call away."

"That means so much to me. You have no idea."

"I think I do."

She realized that she and Louie had to get on the gangplank so she reached up to kiss Stuart goodbye on the cheek and he reached down to kiss her cheek too. But with the jostling crowd, their lips ended up connecting, and neither one of them pulled away until she was forced to move because Louie was scrambling away from her. "I'm sorry," she called out.

"I'm not," he said quietly, his whole body humming with an electric charge that started at his lips. He held up his hand and stayed where she could see him.

When they got to the top, Jane gave the purser their tickets. And then she picked Louie up and held him tightly against her so she could stand by the rail and try and see Stuart.

There he was. Taller than those around him. Sam had always been jealous of his height. She waved at him and he waved back, so he'd seen her. And she was grateful he wouldn't leave until the ship sailed away. A small piece of her broken heart had started to beat faster when he said she could come back to him.

It confused her, but she held it under her pillow for courage.

Meanwhile, Stuart watched her sail away out of Halifax Harbour and realized he'd made a mistake.

The *Aquitania* was called by its passengers the Ship Beautiful. And little did Jane know that she was on one of its last voyages. It was a completely different experience from when she'd arrived with the war brides and their children. She wasn't sick, Louie kept her entertained, and she met a lot of people, thanks to the friendliness of her son.

They spent a lot of time on deck because they were used to being outside in all weather, and Louie did want to watch the waves. One day he even fell asleep on her lap in a deck chair. Jane found her worried thoughts were blown out to sea. She needed this time to reflect. If she had flown over to Britain, it would have been too much of a shock. Worlds colliding and all that.

By the time they could see Southampton in the distance, Jane was ready for it to be over. Louie had a meltdown at dinner and she could see the disapproving glances of the older passengers. She wanted to tell them to sod off and leave her alone. She was doing the best she could. A younger woman held the door open for her as she and her flailing child went back to their cabin. She said, "Don't mind those old buzzards. They probably beat their kids into good behaviour."

Jane was grateful she had a comrade.

It was stressful getting off the ship, so many people wanting to debark first, and Jane was worried she'd lose Louie in all the confusion, so she waited until the worst of it was over before she walked down the gangplank and stepped onto her native land.

This was the part that had her anxious. Getting Louis and the bags from the ship to the train, for the two-hour ride to Dorking. This was her reality now. No Sam, no Hardy, no Stuart. But did she need a man?

Yes. To do the heavy lifting.

And as if by magic, one appeared. He was so non-descript and grey she would have missed him if he hadn't been holding a sign with her name on it. "Mrs. Harris? I'm Herbert Hampton."

She grabbed him and gave him a hug, which completely threw him for a loop. "Oh, thank you! What are you doing here?"

"You told me which ship you were on and I surmised with a small child and luggage you would need help."

"You surmised correctly. I can't thank you enough."

"We'll go, shall we?"

She soon learned that Herbert was practical and serious. He nodded at Louie but made no attempt to engage with him. Everything he said was to the point. No fussy conversation.

When they were settled in his Morris Minor, off they went. He was a stranger, but Jane felt like he was a friend. "I feel I know you, Mr. Hampton. After so many letters over the years, and so much good advice."

"It's my job to give good advice. That's why your aunt hired me."

"And that's why it made things easier for me to keep my family property after she died. I never would have managed it myself from where I was living. I didn't even have phone."

"I can't imagine."

Louie was on her lap and kept trying to touch the gearshift. She repeatedly took his hand away before remembering she had a lolly in her purse, so she gave him that.

"Were the tenants terribly upset?"

"Yes. But that is not your problem. This house belongs to you. And while you are here, we must go to the bank and straighten out the accounts. Going forward, they will be in your name. I will relinquish those duties. If you end up selling the house, I will help you with that process."

"You're an angel, Mr. Hampton. I'm so grateful to you."

He loosened up slightly. "Call me Herbert."

"And I'm Jane. This is Louie. Do you have children, Herbert?"

"Me? Heavens no."

She didn't ask him any more personal questions.

When they rounded the corner, drove up the street, and she saw Aunt Lou's house, her first thought was that she'd have to fix up her front garden. No one had bothered with it and it looked untidy, which would've driven Aunt Lou crazy.

"Look, Louie. This is your great-grandfather's house. His name was James Sinclair, just like my dad and just like you."

Jane wasn't sad. Too many happy childhood memories came flooding in. All the times her family had celebrated Christmas here. She could see everyone in her mind. She'd missed them. It was nice to be close to them.

She didn't know how close we were. Her whole family surrounded her and her son, everyone proud of her bravery. Her father was deeply grateful that his little grandson was going to spend time in the house where he'd grown up. And Aunt Lou was thrilled when Jane mentioned fixing up the garden.

Herbert took the key and opened it for her before he went back to the car to gather her things. She remembered how nervous Sam had been standing outside this door. When she went inside it smelled different. And it wasn't that clean. Aunt Lou's things were still about, but not in the right order. The tenants hadn't bothered to straighten up, probably too miffed about the situation, and Jane was dismayed by the state of the fridge and cooker.

Still, there were no holes in the walls or big divots in the hardwood floor, so it wasn't anything a lot of elbow grease couldn't fix. She and Louie climbed the stairs and he went around the two rooms and bounced on the beds. Jane peeked in the bathroom. There was the ancient claw-foot tub she remembered. Not pristine like Aunt Lou always kept it, but she would remedy that in a big fat hurry. She wanted to be in it tonight.

They went back downstairs and Herbert was waiting by the door to hand her the keys. “This is wonderful,” she said.

Herbert passed her his card. “As you can see, my office is on the high street, and that’s my phone number. If you need anything, call me. No need to write.”

She grinned. His idea of a joke.

“Again, you’re a lifesaver, Herbert. Could I put you out for one more favour?”

He scowled slightly. “Yes.”

“Would you take me to the shops on your way home? I won’t get a lot, just cleaning supplies and something for tea, and breakfast tomorrow. I’ll take the bus back.”

He thought about it. “The day is shot anyway. I’ll take you, wait in the car, and drive you home. Buy as many groceries as you can, while you have a car.”

“You’re a saint. Oh! I don’t have any British money, only Canadian. I never even thought of it.”

“I will lend you some and you can pay me back when we go to the bank.”

“I think I love you, Herbert.”

He put his fedora back on his head. “Many have tried. None have succeeded.”

CHAPTER TWENTY-THREE

Mary Alice and Hardy's baby boy, Sam, was born in February 1950. As promised, Mary Alice sent a picture with her weekly letter to Jane, and Jane sent one back saying she was beyond touched that Sam had a namesake. This baby had brown hair and eyes like his dad. Annabelle adored him but was quite sooky that her mama was so busy. Annie to the rescue.

The Campbells were in a state of flux. Hardy had decided to seek another job off island. He had made inquiries and found out there was currently a residential construction boom happening in rural communities. While he wasn't a trained carpenter, he could fix anything. He took a day off and went to talk to a job foreman in Glace Bay. When the man found out Hardy had been a lighthouse keeper all his working life, he took off his ballcap and scratched his head. "Jeez, b'y, you friggers are experts at everything. Trustworthy, dependable. I'll take a lightkeeper any day of the week."

He went home and told Mary Alice. Her hormones were all over the place. At first, she cheered, and then she cried. "I don't know! I'll do whatever you say."

Hardy discussed it with his family. As next in line, Gerry was ready to take over top spot, with Fred as his assistant. He needed some paperwork filed, but Fred had proven his worth.

Hardy confessed to them, "When I first thought of this, for some reason I thought you'd all come with us. But with Fred on the light, and James now the official teacher, and Mom never leaving her stove, I guess I was wrong."

"Ya got that right," Annie sniffed.

"I don't have the money to get our own place, so I'm going to have to work for a year at least to save up for a down payment on maybe a company house. Mary Alice and the kids will have to stay here. I can visit on weekends. Do you think your cousin in Table Head would let me sleep on a couch?"

"Ducky?" Annie waved her hand. "She practically runs a boarding house for her mob's friends. She'll never notice ya."

"So should I send in my resignation once I'm officially hired in town? I know it's a big step but it feels right for us."

They gave Hardy their blessing and he went over next door. Annabelle was asleep and Sam was nursing in his mother's arms. He sat on the bed. "It's done. I've made a decision."

He set out the plan and at first, Mary Alice was dismayed that he'd be living away but quickly elected not to make a stink. She had a grandmother living on the premises, the best thing since sliced bread. She'd miss him, but it wasn't forever.

It had only been sixteen months since Jane left Scatarie, but it seemed like forever. She had cleaned the house a thousand times just for something to do. She said hi to the neighbours and talked to other mothers in the playground, so Louie would have some company, but she made no fast friends. Her heart wasn't in it.

She'd taken Louie on a trip to Camden Town to bring flowers to her parents' grave and show him off. They'd been to Aunt Lou's burial site several times and made sure it was nice and tidy.

Her trips to mail letters at the post office were frequent, and it always gave her a lift to hear the letterbox clink. Louie would run to the front door first and grab an envelope from Mary Alice, Annie, Aunt Muriel, or Stuart. Jane would read them out loud and ask him if he remembered them. Depending on the day, it was yes or no.

In late March 1952, she heard from Mary Alice.

Well, we did it. We've moved into our little house on Fifth Street in Glace Bay. It's traumatizing to watch cars go by! We have to keep Toby tied up and he's not happy about it. But oh my, how did I ever live without a bathroom?! And to flip on a light switch is almost as good as Hardy kissing me! He loves his job, and doesn't miss the constant shift work. Although he does miss Gerry and his brothers, and his mom's cooking. As you know, I never was her best student. Golly, I miss you though. I wish you could see Sam. He's a year old and still doesn't walk. Talk about rolls on his pudgy legs! My mother delights in them, says she can't believe he came from me! Annabelle is her usual saucy self, but God, I love her. She's so interesting. Five is a perfect age most of the time. How's Louie? Pinch those cheeks for me. I love you, kiddo, and hope you are doing well. I thought you sounded a little down in your last letter. I'm sending you a kiss to feel better. All my love, MA xoxo

Jane sighed and folded the letter back up. She was happy for her friend. To be in her own house with her husband and children. Mary Alice deserved every bit of it.

"What shall we do today, little man?"

"Drawing."

She loved it when her son said that. He was quiet and not running around. Sometimes she got so tired of always making sure he was where he was supposed to be.

The next morning there was a pretty bad storm. Not the kind of snow that Scatarie got, but enough for this part of the world. Naturally, Louie wanted to go outside, so Jane dressed them both up and headed out. When they first arrived, one of her neighbours, the miserable harpy, told her she was crazy for going out on days like this.

"It reminds me of home," Jane would say.

"Where ya from, Siberia?"

They ran around trying to catch snowflakes and build a snowman, but it wasn't the right kind of snow. Louie rolled over and over and made snow angels, and when he sat up, his hat nearly off, his nose running, and his cheeks a crimson red, Jane broke inside.

That was it. She needed to get home. She'd sell this house that belonged in her past and take the money and create a life somewhere else. Probably Glace Bay, so she'd be close to Mary Alice, Hardy, Muriel, and Howard. Just thinking about it made her happy, so she knew it was the right thing to do. Louie would have to leave his primary class, but he hated it anyway, so got upset every time she left him. His teacher said he was too clingy and Jane needed to be more disciplined with him. And Jane would think, *My husband would wipe the floor with you.*

They went inside and piled their wet clothes by the front door. She would dry them later by the gas heater. While she made Louie lunch, he sat at the kitchen table and stared at his best friend. A small clock on the wall shaped like a fat frog with bulbous eyes that looked left and right on time with the second hand. It had always been in this house. Jane had loved it as a kid and it was coming with them.

As they finished up their dippy eggs and soldiers, the letterbox clanked. Louie rushed over and got the envelope. "Who's it from?" he asked.

"Stuart." She smiled and proceeded to read it.

Dear Jane,

You can address me as Dr. Stuart Campell, GP extraordinaire! It feels mighty good to finally be able to say it. Now that that's done, I just have to figure out the rest of my life. But I wanted you to be one of the first to know. Mom is baking a cake and inviting friends and neighbours around. As one never says no to her, I shall bear it with clenched teeth. I hope you and Louie are okay. You sounded a little down in your last letter. Remember, you can always call me.

Bye for now,

Stuart

That's right! She ran upstairs to get her purse. The paper with his address and phone number, worn around the edges, was still stuck in a small pocket. She'd never thrown it away. Jane had to tell him her news.

After getting directory assistance involved, since she'd never called overseas, Jane heard the phone ringing. She hoped it wouldn't be Mrs. Campbell. She'd talk her ear off and Jane wouldn't be able to say, "No, please get off this phone and give me your son."

Someone up there heard her. "Hello?"

"Stuart! It's me, Jane!"

"Jane! How wonderful to hear your voice. Did you get my letter?"

"Yes, I did, Dr. Campbell. Congratulations. Sam would have been very pleased."

"Sam would have said, 'Ya smart bastard!'"

They laughed together. "I have my own news. I'm coming home."

There was silence on the other end.

"Stuart?"

When Stuart could catch his breath, he finally blurted, "That's... that's incredible. What home? Where? Why did you change your mind?" He was bombarding her with questions.

"I miss you...and everyone. I miss Nova Scotia. Mary Alice and Hardy live in Glace Bay now, so I could live near them. I'll have money when I sell this house to see me through until I can find a job."

"Have you told them yet?"

She cradled the phone against her ear and peeled the orange Louie was sticking in her face. "No. You're the first to know. I'll tell them once I have a better idea of when I can come. I have to get in touch with Herbert."

"Your man Jeeves?"

"He's quite a character, but has always done right by me."

"Will you let me know your plans? I'll be there to pick you up when you and Louie come back."

"It seems I can't go or leave anywhere without you."

"Remember that."

The idea had taken hold and Jane was impatient to get it done. She called Herbert right away. Basically, he said her wish was his command.

"Will you be my pen pal, Herbert?"

"No."

"I'm going to miss you."

It turned out the previous tenants wanted to buy Aunt Lou's house, so that made things incredibly easy. She called Stuart again to tell him she'd be leaving in a week or so, but would give him the exact date soon.

Jane and Louie were having their lunch three days later when they remembered they had to take Froggie off the wall. That's when the letterbox clinked. Louie skipped over to get the envelope and brought it back to her.

"Oh nice," she smiled. "It's from Stuart."

She ripped the envelope open.

Dear Jane,

I'm outside.

Love Stuart

Her heart did that rumbly thing before she ran to the door and flung it open. He was standing there with three plane tickets in his hand.

"It seems you can't go or leave anywhere without me."

EPILOGUE

Don't you just love a happy beginning?

It was Sam himself who made Annette Campbell's hot tin of banana muffins fall on the floor to make sure she was occupied while Stuart answered Jane's phone call.

He was getting better at that. It's a learning curve, as I believe I've told you before.

I was delighted that my favourite people from this island were now living their lives as they should.

But I knew what was coming. There were fewer and fewer families here. They had to move away because it was no longer sensible to stay. Almost all of them were bereft as they crossed the tittle to Main-à-Dieu and beyond.

By the late fifties, the only people left were the lighthouse keepers. Mrs. Eliza Campbell on the western end, and Gerry and Fred on the other.

Dear Annie is now with us, and her beloved Len, and you can rest assured these two souls are going nowhere. They will always be by the lighthouse.

Aisling and I are having to adjust. For two hundred years we've had so many people to spend time with, whether they knew it or not. And now it's lonely. Not that we can't be with our family, as we call them, whenever we want and at the same time, but our roots are here and everyone needs a place to call home.

Eventually even the lightkeepers became redundant and automated lights were installed. I'm sure they are efficient, but not nearly as romantic as the old days, when men had to battle their way through the storms and stay at the top of the lighthouse all night, the whole structure shaking, to keep the lamp going and guide ships from a terrible fate.

Our home is now empty of human life, but other creatures are here. And a few of the former residents have a cabin for hunting or camping. Such is the pull to this place the relatives of the original residents have an annual pilgrimage here, a mass the first Sunday in August to remember. Boatloads of people come from Main-à-Dieu for a picnic, and games and races for their children.

And plenty arrive on their own, especially in the summer. Families will pull into Northwest Cove to make a small fire on the beach with dry driftwood, cook hot dogs, eat bags of homemade goodies, and have a swim. That makes Aisling especially happy. She likes to swirl around their toes and make them say, "What was that?"

One group in particular began to arrive every August to camp for a week. The Campbells and the Campbells. Annabelle and Louie took their younger siblings, Sam, Alice, and Maude to their favourite haunts to play and swim all day. Their parents, Hardy, Mary Alice, Jane, and Stuart, would sit in their lawn chairs by the tents near the water and laugh at old memories. Then they'd tell ghost stories to the kids around the campfire while they ate their s'mores.

They stayed in each other's lives, because when they were together Sam was with them. After Stuart and Jane were married (his mother arranged everything), he didn't hesitate to move to Cape Breton. They bought a roomy house with a wraparound porch on South Street, five minutes from the Glace Bay General Hospital. Jane was always grateful when she turned on a tap or a light switch.

And soaked daily in her claw-foot tub. Stuart had a busy medical practice and Jane was perfectly content to stay at home with her children. She was known for her wonderful baking, thanks to Annie's notebook of recipes.

Hardy and Mary Alice stayed in Glace Bay. Mary Alice said it would take an excavator to haul her ass out of there. They lived in a smaller house on Blackett Street, two minutes from Jane and Stuart. Nothing spectacular, but it suited them. Hardy was hired on as a Fisheries officer for the federal government. Seems he missed the water. Mary Alice got her teacher's license and was around more kids than her mother and sisters combined.

In 2005, a boat drove through the water and anchored off Eastern Harbour. I knew who it was. Mary Alice's family were bringing her home to scatter her ashes. Hardy had a bit of a time getting off the boat, but his two strong grandsons made sure he made it.

He held his wife's urn as tenderly as he'd always held her. "Goodbye, my girl. I kept my promise."

Her ashes swirled away over the beach and water. She and Sam had a joyful reunion. And quickly, she sensed me.

"Hello, Cara. My very first female friend."

"Hello, Mary Alice. It's wonderful to meet you properly. This is Aisling. She's been on pins and needles for eighty-three years waiting for you to come."

"The little girl in the water! Hello, child. You look like your sister."

Together we watched her family walk the shore, Annabelle, Sam, her four grandchildren, and three great-grandchildren. The youngest was three, and Mary Alice kept her eyes on her. "Do you always yearn for them?" she asked Cara.

"Always. But you'll see her grown up. You won't miss anything."

"Thank god."

Hardy stood where her house was, and insisted on walking to the lighthouse, but he sat on the flat rock first, again needing a bit of help to get down and back up. He continued walking with his cane to stand next to the lighthouse where he'd spent so much of his life. He put his hand on the shingles and patted it. It would be the last time he'd see it from a living point of view.

"The stubborn old bastard," Sam said. "Can't wait for him to get here."

"You know Hardy." His best friend smiled. "He was born late, and he'll die late because I asked him to."

My favourite thing in all the world is when the coastal wind blows the grass on the barrens close to the shore of Northwest Cove on Scatarie. But it's heaven when your kindred spirits are with you.

I remember the Bible verse read at Sam's funeral a long time ago. It perfectly describes what I've attempted to tell you with this tale of mine.

But I would not have you lose courage, even now;
there is no loss of life among you, only the ship.

ACKNOWLEDGEMENTS

When I put a post on my Facebook page about my intention to write a book set on Scatarie Island, I was inundated with people willing to help. I met some in their kitchens and living rooms, over the phone, and at Tim Horton's, and others when I had a meeting at the Coastal Discovery Centre in Main-à-Dieu in April of 2024. On that occasion people came from Halifax, Baddeck, Sydney, Louisbourg, and Main-à-Dieu with their pictures and stories, magazines, and articles. Other information I gathered from the helpful staff at the James McConnell Memorial Library in Sydney and Cape Breton University's Beaton Institute and a kind gentleman, Gerard White, who let me read his thesis, "Modernization and the Small Fishing Community," from fifty years ago.

Thank you to Rose Matheson, Helen Parpoulas, Eileen Trimm Burke, Fabian Trimm, Edgar Wadden, Lise Wadden, Jack and Evelyn Steele's family, Frances Steele, Vanessa Wadden, Bill Bellfontaine, Patsy Baldwin, Pat Bates, Janette Wadden, Patricia Bray, Elizabeth McDougall, Carol Ann Bates, Amanda McDougall, Beatrice Walker, Eileen Carroll, Pat Bates, Bob Campbell, Jim Mullins, Herman Wadden, John Langley, and Margo Patrick. To anyone I've forgotten while adding frantically to my list of names that day, I apologize.

My biggest thank you goes to Lionel and Georgina Wadden and family for taking me to Scatarie one gorgeous afternoon, August 11, 2024, on Keith Campbell's Cape Islander, *Christie A1*. It was a day I will never forget and led me down the path I needed, to try and do justice to the many stories that unfolded and were lived on this isolated and unforgettable island.

I'd also like to thank and acknowledge Jim Parks, George Couture, and Bill Wilson, three Canadian soldiers who recounted their war experiences on D-Day and the aftermath in videos for the CBC. We owe everything to these young men. What they lived through was unimaginable. We can't ever forget them.

Also by Lesley Crewe

Death & Other Inconveniences

Recipe for a Good Life

Nosy Parker

The Spoon Stealer

Beholden

Mary, Mary

Amazing Grace

Chloe Sparrow

Kin

Her Mother's Daughter

Hit and Mrs.

Ava Comes Home

Shoot Me

Relative Happiness

Non-fiction

I Kid You Not!

Are You Kidding Me?!